DANNI TO PIECES

Book One: Forced

L. T. Varner

ISBN: 0692620958
ISBN 13: 9780692620953

Editors:
Rachel Guerin / Bridge Town Editing
Editing by Jared Carew
Cover Art by: The Book Cover Designer

Disclaimer: This work is purely fiction and not in reference to any person or event. This is a dark story and may be sensitive for some readers. If sexual situations, profanity, substance abuse, and physical violence offends you, this book may not be for you.

TABLE OF CONTENTS

PROLOGUE
BOO

I kept telling myself that I wouldn't yell at anybody tonight even though my perfect weekend was ruined. It was my first day off in four months, and I planned on taking off on my motorcycle and just getting lost for three days. As I got out of my truck and started walking to my office, I could already hear the thumping of the music, making my angry mood even worse. Dumping my stuff on my overflowing desk, I jumped when I heard a voice say, "What's with the bad mood?"

Instantly I knew who it was, and I had to smile.

Mike's my best friend and business partner. My dad hired his mom, Rosa, to be my nanny when I was six years old. We have been inseparable since. We tried dating in high school before Mike admitted he was gay, but I had already known. A lot of people say that high school is the best time in your life, well, not in our case. It was hell for us!

We both had weight issues and were incessantly bullied. Mike was extremely skinny no matter what he ate, and I hated him for it. I, on the other hand, was the fat, smart girl who no one talked to unless they needed help with their homework.

As soon as we graduated high school, we left Austin. College was the best time of my life! Mike and I had our apartment because neither one of us wanted weird roommates or curfews. Halfway through our freshman year after watching him try to hide his sexuality and listening to me complain about my weight. We made a deal with each other that we still follow. I promised to take better care of myself if he lived openly. Mike's goal was to make me over from head to toe. Until then, I hadn't worn make-up, I had never done anything with my wild, curly brown hair besides wearing it in a ponytail, and I was about fifty pounds' overweight.

We started running religiously every day. Five miles a day no matter what the weather was like. He introduced me to makeup and taught me how to manage my wild hair. By the end of our sophomore year, I had lost about sixty pounds and felt like an entirely different person. He was dating regularly and openly talking about his feelings.

The rest of college was a little crazier. We were going to parties, staying out all night, and enjoying having lots of friends for the first time in our lives. Both of us had a busy dating life, but nothing that seemed to last very long. I always attracted the wrong type of guy; the guy who's popular and just wants you to look beautiful and be quiet, or the guy who knows my dad is a famous musician and sees dollar signs when he looks at you. My personal favorite has always been the bad boy, the guy who asks you for money or a place to stay even though you know you're not the only girl he's dating. For some reason, he's a little harder to talk yourself out of.

After college, Mike wanted to go to South Dakota to run his uncle's restaurant and see where that took him. This was the first time Mike and I were apart since we were six years old, and it scared both of us. My dad decided my fate, enlisting me to work with him on his tour.

Now, three years later, here we are with not only a restaurant but also a bar. Damn Mike and his ideas! We went through six months of renovations after purchasing the empty store next to the restaurant, but it's turning into a huge success. It's a blessing and a curse that we're always busy, and that's why I never get a weekend off to ride. Since moving here Mike and I started riding motorcycles, and it is the best stress reliever I've ever experienced. We've developed a group of friends who are more like family.

This brings me back to the moment as Mike tells me about the staff and what's going on tonight. He had called an extra bartender to help me out. I loved concocting different drinks, but being behind the bar was not where I wanted to be anymore. Shortly after we opened, we put together a house band, and I realized the stage was the only place I loved. Since I have been playing guitar since I was six years old, it was only fitting that I get that job. It's quite a powerful thing to be on stage watching the reaction from the crowd. Although it has been fun, it can be a pain in the ass at the same time. Being onstage elicits stupid behavior from horny drunks that I try my best to ignore.

Luckily for the band, this weekend Mike hired a local DJ so we could all have a break, except I still had to oversee the bar. The night started out simple with almost everyone ordering a beer and nothing fancy. My favorite and equally irritating waitress, Jackie, was working. She walked out with the most tips every night she worked. I liked her because she was reliable and very blunt with people. Jackie was always quick to handle any situation that would come up and easily talked people out of fighting. I dislike how she would step on anyone to get her way. In a way, she reminded me of Mike; they both know what they want in life and how to go about getting it. Mike was just more honest in the way he succeeded. By 10:30, the bar was packed, and we had to start turning them away at the door.

"Mike I'm fine. Just go on your date and I will lock up and see you tomorrow," I yelled over the music.

"Are you sure?" he asked me, looking way too happy.

"Just go before I kick your ass," I shouted back.

For the past week, all I had heard was Mike talking about his upcoming date with a nurse from the hospital. I was frankly tired of hearing about it. I had tried to distract him by going to a bonfire party a couple of nights ago but only ended up hung over as hell the last two days.

"Here do one shot with me," Mike said, handing me a shot of whiskey.

"Did you pay for that, Sir?" I asked, mocking him. Mike was in charge of watching employees, so they didn't drink all of our profits, although at the moment he didn't seem like the best person for this task.

He laughed and said, "No. That guy over there bought it for you. He asked about you if you're interested."

I looked through the crowd to where he pointed and quickly gave Mike a look of "hell no" upon seeing a dirty older man who looked like he just crawled out from under a car hood.

Mike winked at me and said, "I didn't think so. He smelled awful and is drunk as hell." We clinked glasses and drank them down.

Finally, it was last call, and all the customers started making their way out of the bar except, of course, for the ones who didn't want to leave. Creepy Guy, who bought my shot of whiskey earlier, set another shot in front of me. Ten minutes and one shot later, we escorted them all out, Creepy Guy included, so we could close. I noticed he just kept walking back and forth on the sidewalk in front of the bar.

Jackie leaned into me and said, "He's been asking about you all night."

"What did you tell him?" I asked.

"I told him that you have a boyfriend and aren't interested."

Something just seemed off about this man. He was excited and nervous at the same time and appeared to be talking to himself. Eventually, he took off down the street and we all decided to call it a night. I locked the door and went to my office to start on the night's paperwork. But, after ten minutes of looking at staff reports and my computer, I started feeling lightheaded and exhausted, so I decided to take it all home.

I gathered up my laptop and put the money in the safe for the night. I was anxious to go home, get in a nice hot shower, and sleep. After throwing my stuff in my truck, I noticed the three bags of garbage still waiting to go out.

"Seriously, Jackie . . . you couldn't take out the fucking trash?" I grumbled to myself as I hit the button to open the overhead door.

Directly behind the bar was the alley and beyond that was a field of corn about seven feet high waiting to be harvested. I stopped walking halfway to the dumpster as a wall of dizziness hit me. I realized something wasn't right.

"Danni, you're tired and hungry, so hurry up," I said this out loud to myself in hopes that it would get me mentally and physically going again.

Taking a couple of deep breaths, I picked up the bags I had dropped. Before I could take two steps, I fell to my knees as my legs completely gave out on me. I caught myself with my hands as beer bottles shattered on the cement around me. It felt like slow motion as everything became fuzzy and I couldn't feel my hands still holding me up. I could see them touching the ground, but I couldn't make them move as I fell forward on my face. Complete panic set in as I saw the outline of a shadow on the cement next to me.

"Need some help?" asked a deep husky voice before everything went dark.

It felt like an awful dream as I heard voices around me. I realized I wasn't dreaming, and I started trying to push someone off of me, then I felt cold metal against my throat.

"Do you want to die?" a winded voice asked close to my ear.

Feeling a sharp pinch to my throat, I instantly held still, realizing that this man was going to kill me.

Everything faded in and out. I noticed different smells that didn't make sense to me. Grease, smoke, and strong cologne registered at various times. Never one distinct smell, it kept changing.

That deep voice said, in-between his vicious thrusts into my body, "The minute I saw you, I knew you would be perfect."

It had felt like hours before he was done raping me. I rolled onto my side and could feel the cold October air against my naked body. I was on the verge of throwing up. I kept praying he would just leave.

"Shut her up before someone hears her," a breathless voice said directly over me.

It had not registered to me at this point that I was screaming and sobbing. That's when I felt a swift kick to my back. Suddenly the air left my lungs, and I couldn't breathe. He just kept kicking me all over as I tried to move away from it. I felt a knife pierce my chest as I started gasping for air. Everything went dark again after a kick to the side of my head.

I came around again and felt if I moved I would fall into a thousand pieces. I couldn't catch my breath, and that's when the panic came back. I started looking around to see if he was still there, but there was nothing except a red flashing light in the distance. I wondered how long I had been out, seeing the sun starting to rise over the cornstalks. I felt frozen to the ground as my body shook violently in the dirt. I was so sleepy and fell unconscious again.

I woke up later to what sounded like someone calling my name, and I tried to lift my head to look around. My lungs burned if I moved and I couldn't get a full breath. I tried to answer back, but nothing would come out. I started to wonder if I was going to die naked in the middle of a cornfield.

I just hoped if someone were calling my name, they would find me as I dozed off again.

"Danni, please don't die, please. God, I beg you, please," Mike sobbed as he tried to hold down my arms trying to hit him.

"Please stop fighting me, Danni. Just keep breathing, some-one help us!" He screamed.

I finally saw his face above mine with tears rolling down his cheeks.

"I got you, Danni. It's me. Please stop moving you're hurt. Let me help you."

Mike had found me, and that's when I stopped moving, only hearing the screams tearing from my throat before falling un-conscious again.

CHAPTER 1
EVENING NEWS

I was sure I would be in that cornfield again if I opened my eyes. Then I felt someone squeeze my hand, and I quickly tried to pull it away to protect myself. My eyes flew open, and I saw Mike was the one holding my hand. Wrapping our arms around each other, we both started sobbing while he repeated the same sentence over and over again:

"I am so sorry, Danni. This is my fault."

I knew it wasn't his fault, but at that moment, I was not strong enough to tell him otherwise.

The nurses and doctors came to my room to check on me now that I was awake. They kept asking if I remembered what had happened. How could I forget what had just happened to me? I thought it was stupid of them to even ask. That's when all the pain set in. I felt every part of my body throbbing, and I was extremely exhausted.

Dammit, I was angry and wanted everyone just to leave me the hell alone. I couldn't control myself as I screamed and thrashed around in the narrow hospital bed. I was frantically trying to pull tubes out of me when a cold tingly sensation started up my arm. Calmness washed over me as I stilled and lay back. Closing my eyes felt so good and soon sleep claimed me.

Mike and my dad wouldn't leave me alone for the next week. Day after miserable day, I had to be sedated for "violent outbursts," as the doctors referred to them. I was glad when the doctor asked if he could speak to me in private so they all would have to give me some peace for at least a couple minutes.

The doctor told me that I had two broken ribs, a broken arm, and five stab wounds with two in my chest and three in my lower abdomen. He kept telling me, "You are very lucky you didn't bleed to death." That would have been better than how I felt at the moment, I thought, rolling my eyes and looking away from him. He cleared his throat and told me that the police were outside my door wanting to speak with me.

"Great, I get to re-live it all over again," I mumbled while looking everywhere but into his eyes.

The detectives came in the room and started telling me how sorry they were that this happened. How could they be sorry when they weren't there and had nothing to do with it? The detectives asked me if I remembered what had happened.

I asked in an annoyed tone, "If this happened to you, could you forget?"

As they both examined the floor, I asked, "How did you find me?"

One of the detectives looked at me and said, "Your friend Seth was out walking his dog before work and saw the garage door open, so he stopped. That's when he noticed that your truck's door was open, and your bag was still on the passenger seat. Being a cop, he knew that something was wrong after he couldn't find you in the bar."

So far, they had questioned all of the employees who worked that night. Jackie mentioned the creepy guy who had been asking about me. Still, it seemed no one knew his identity or had noticed him before. It felt like hours going over all the details with the detectives. They just kept asking more and more questions that I didn't have the answers to. Then they completely stumped me when they asked about my clothes. Apparently they still hadn't been able to recover them from the scene.

I told them four times, "I have no idea."

I was exhausted from talking about it. I just wanted to be left alone. They said that they would contact me when they had more information, but I knew that wouldn't happen anytime soon.

I was too scared to look down at myself and see the damage that was inflicted upon me. I just kept the covers tucked in around me and put the thought out of my head. The nurse came in to check on me after they left. This was my first hospital experience, and it was like being a child again. The nurse told me that the sooner I got up and moved around, the sooner I could go home. That was all it took for me to get out of bed.

The thought of going home and being alone was all I could focus on. Before she left my room, the nurse asked if I wanted my family to come back in. For the first time in my life, I didn't want to see them. I longed to be around strangers who didn't know anything about me. I asked the nurse to lie and tell them that I had fallen asleep. She stepped into the hall as they stood right outside my door and was very gracious when she explained that I needed my rest and they both left without a fight. I think this was the first time I had seen Mike do something he didn't want to do without a fight.

I studied the flowers and balloons people had brought me as I slowly walked around the room. Of all the flowers in the room, the lilies were the ones I couldn't bring myself to touch or smell. The nurse took them away after I "accidentally" knocked over the vase and it crashed to pieces on the tile floor.

Later that night, I caught the evening news, and that's when I saw it: what happened to me was the top story on all the channels. Both local and Hollywood gossip had a lot of the details already. I retched when I saw my picture next to the taped-off alleyway behind the bar on the television.

⟞⊹ ⊹⟝

The next morning, Mike and my dad showed up bright and early with breakfast, hoping not to wake me. I didn't have it in me to tell them that every time I closed my eyes, I re-lived the whole event. Mike still had that look of guilt and sadness in his eyes. My dad didn't know what to say, so he didn't talk much. Feelings weren't something he or I addressed well, so we both just ignored them.

After two long weeks of being in the hospital, I was told I could go home to rest. Finally, I could be alone! The doctor came in to sign my release papers and again he asked if he could have a moment alone with me. After everyone had left the room, he informed me that I would need to come back in the next couple weeks to do a pregnancy test.

"What the hell are you talking about?" I yelled at the doctor.

He explained that when I was first brought to the hospital and examined, the doctors had determined that a condom had not been used. I could potentially be pregnant, but it was too early to tell. It was at that moment when I felt I had been pushed over the edge. The only thought that kept going through my head was that I just wanted to go home and kill myself.

I signed all the necessary paperwork and got the hell out of there. When we left the hospital, a blizzard was raging around us. I wondered what else I wasn't noticing as dad helped me settle into the back of his SUV.

I tried to ask Mike about the bar and the day-to-day operations. He kept telling me not to worry about it right now and just to focus on recovering. It would all be there when I got better, he said. I felt like a small child. Everybody was watching what they said and how they acted around me, and it was getting old, really quick.

Once we got to my house, I went straight to my bathroom. Turning on the shower, I caught a glimpse of myself naked in the mirror for the first time in two weeks. I was speechless. Yellow and purple bruises covered my body, and scars were forming around the stitches they used to close the stab wounds. I pulled my hair back and saw the cut running down my forehead. I had no memory of how that injury even happened. I leaned over the toilet just in time as I lost what little lunch I had managed to eat earlier.

I started feeling numb, inside and out. I wondered where the person who did this to me was right now. Was he sitting in a bar bragging about his conquest, or in another country by now? Would the detectives ever be able to catch him? Probably not, I guessed.

I realized I was over-thinking again, so I decided just to get in the shower and do my best to forget about it as much as possible by making the water as hot as I could. I had taken numerous showers in the hospital, but I never felt like I could get rid of his scent. He smelled like grease, strong cologne, and smoke and just the thought made my stomach turn.

I was in the shower for a while when I heard Mike ask if I was okay. I yelled at him to "get out." Instead, he opened the door, and I watched him look at my damaged body. His hands flew to his mouth, and he lost it. Tears streamed down his face as he fell to his knees. It tore out my heart to see how badly this was affecting him, as well. I held my arms out to him, and he pulled me down into his lap as the water sprayed us both. We stayed there crying, just holding onto each other. As he held me, I had an epiphany. Even though Mike hadn't been assaulted, he was feeling everything I was, too.

After a silence that seemed to last forever, he said, "The water is probably warm again if you want to finish your shower."

"I'm done," I told him in a tone that only Mike could instantly recognize when I didn't want to talk anymore.

He helped me without hesitation. My favorite sweatpants and t-shirt were on the bed. After pulling off the plastic around my cast, he quietly went back to the bathroom to get my glasses and my hairbrush. I got dressed and tried not to pay attention to the bruises or the aches and pains.

I just concentrated on Mike. All the things he was doing were giving me a hint of what *I* should be doing. Normal things I guess.

After I had put on the clothes he had set out for me, Mike pulled the blue comforter back and urged me to get into bed. He crawled in behind me, pulled me into his arms, and held me tight against him. I could feel him crying. It broke my heart to see him in that much pain.

I had no idea what to do to make him feel better. I couldn't even make myself feel better. We just lay there in silence, both of us crying. I soundly fell asleep without medication for the first time in two weeks.

After that night, Mike and I seemed to be on the same page without speaking. He would quickly get visitors out of the house soon after they arrived, so I didn't have to deal with their questions or their pity.

Dad soon realized too that I just wanted to handle this silently. After another week, he decided to go back to Austin to work with Uncle Tony. He told Mike a handful of times that if anything changed, he had better be the first person called at which point he would come back right away.

Mike made me go with him to take Dad to the airport. I hadn't left the house since I had been released from the hospital and he said I needed some fresh air. He decided "we" would run some errands while we were in Rapid City. I wasn't looking forward to the forty-five-minute drive alone with them both.

As soon as I stepped outside, I wanted to go back in. I complained about it being cold outside. Mike curtly said, "Well, yeah, it is almost Christmas. It's going to be cold."

After dropping my dad off at the airport, we went to a movie, then to the grocery store before we headed back home. I felt I was being watched the whole time we walked through the grocery store as Mike loaded the cart. I just wanted to get away from people.

On the way home, Mike could sense my mood and asked if I wanted to talk.

I glanced at him and said, "That is the first time you have asked."

"Just waiting till you are ready."

"How do you know I am ready?" I replied, playing with the zipper of my black leather jacket.

"I could tell when you *actually* left the house." He took his eyes off the road and glanced at me.

"How did you find me?" I asked quietly while still focusing on my zipper.

"I heard your voice in my head telling me to look there."

I just looked at him in complete astonishment and asked, "Are you serious?"

"Very!"

Mike explained that it was something he had never experienced before, and will never forget. He talked about finding me just lying there in the dirt, covered in blood, and how he thought I was dead. After hearing me wheezing for air, he knew I was alive, so he started screaming for help. By the time he got to the hospital, I was already in the trauma room. He was covered in blood, shirtless, and yelling for me, so the police questioned him. As we sat, he continued talking about the questions they asked and everyone else who showed up and were sent away. He had never before felt so helpless.

It seemed like he needed to talk more than I did, so I just let him.

He promised me that he would always be there for me, and he guaranteed that nothing would ever happen to me again.

"Mike, you can't protect me from every bad thing that will ever happen to me. I am going to fall along the way. I just need you to help pick me up and keep moving forward."

"I promise you, Danni, I will always help you get up and keep going. I love you so much," he said, holding the back of my hand up to his lips before he kissed it.

The next morning, we went for a very slow walk, and I told him I wanted to go to the bar to catch up on paperwork. He started hyperventilating, saying I wasn't ready to be there yet. He had only left my side over the last month for a couple of hours at a time. I wondered if he had a hard time seeing the cornfield now. As if reading my mind, he started yelling, "The cornfield is gone, Danni. They harvested it about a week after the attack. We are in negotiations to buy the land and make it a parking lot."

"What the fuck, Mike? How could you go ahead with this without even telling me?" I yelled back at him, immediately regretting it as I felt a deep ache in my ribs.

That's when it dawned on both of us that we were raising our voices at each other. This was a milestone for us, We hadn't said unpleasant things out loud since the attack. Mike grabbed my hand to stop me and began to speak softly "Get ready, and we can go to the bar and catch up on some work, *but*, if too many people start bothering you, we're coming home."

I grabbed the closest pair of jeans I could find and just pulled a shirt off the hanger without even looking to see what it was. I quickly dressed, threw on a pair of shoes, and headed to the door.

Sitting in the passenger seat on the way to town, I looked out the window and noticed all the Christmas lights. I wondered what it was about pretty lights that made people feel more festive. I had never been overly excited about the holidays. I usually spent Christmas with Dad, Mike, and Rosa. We would laugh and make fun of each other until someone became mad and the fighting began. Rosa would tell us to act our age and to be thankful we had a family. The thought of Rosa standing in front of us in her Santa robe yelling at us made me laugh out loud. Mike asked what was funny and after explaining it through my tears of laughter, he started laughing too.

"What do you want for Christmas, Mike?" I asked wiping my eyes.

"I would love to catch the man who did this to you and kill him," he answered without looking at me.

The rest of the way to the bar, neither one of us spoke. Quietly, we looked out of our opposite windows.

"Oh, *crap*, there's the bar," I thought, as my heartbeat picked up. It looked busy, and I started feeling like I might see my lunch again at the thought of going in. Mike could see the panic on my face, and he kept driving. He didn't pull into the alley where we have always parked. Instead, he parked a block away, and neither one of us said anything about it.

All I could do was take a deep breath and get out of the truck. Mike was standing there, with the door open, and his hand out for me. It took me a minute to put my hand in his before getting out of the truck.

"Danni, you don't have to do this. It's too soon. Maybe more time wouldn't hurt."

"No, Mike. I have to do this. I have to live my life."

All I could do now was go inside and try to blend in. Mike pulled the door open and motioned me forward. I wondered if I could make it to my office without being noticed. The bar fell quiet, and I could feel all eyes on me, I froze, clutching onto Mike.

I noticed Chuck, walking toward me while he was moving people out of his way. He had been with us since we opened the bar and was one of our best friends. He put his large hand on the small of my back and pushed me to my office.

He had been in Colorado at his sister's wedding when the attack happened. Mike had told me that he had not taken the whole thing very well.

As we entered the office, Chuck gave me a big hug, and I could tell he was trying not to cry. I hugged him back when Mike said something about my ribs and Chuck slowly let go of me.

"I am glad you're back, Boss. I am so sor—"

Putting his hand over his face, he quickly walked out of the office, accidentally slamming the door on his way out. He was upset, and I had no idea what to say to make him feel any better. Tears blurred my vision, and Mike went to talk to him and see if he could help. I hated how this was affecting all of us.

As I looked around the office at my collection of autographed guitars hanging on the wall, I realized that this was the longest I had ever gone without playing. Music made me feel alive, but right now I couldn't bring myself to even touch one.

I heard Mike come in the door behind me. "He will be okay. Just give him a couple of minutes."

Then it was an endless line of people coming in the office, hugging me, and giving a bit of encouragement. Others wanted to know if there was anything I needed, and in my regular Danni fashion, I kept telling everyone I was fine and didn't need anything.

I put on a happy face and started joking around. I made people smile, and it mostly came at Mike's expense. He was such a good sport and, at one point he gave it right back to me. It was wonderful.

CHAPTER 2
FIRES

Two days later, after a long, scalding shower, I walked into my room and saw that my bed had been made, and my room was neat and orderly. Like always, I knew that Rosa had been here. For the first time, I noticed how quietly and quickly she had always taken care of me.

I got dressed and went downstairs to find some coffee, immediately noticing that Mike wasn't around. This was odd because lately it felt like he was attached to my hip.

I took advantage of the moment, grabbed a cup of coffee, and headed to my office to check my email. Logging onto my computer, I cringed seeing the local news: "Rapist Still At Large" and "Local Business Owner Recovering After Attack."

I did some maintenance on the bar's website just to put the headlines out of my mind. An hour later, Mike came walking in with a huge smile on his face.

"Where have you been?" I asked, genuinely smiling for the first time in a long time.

"Out," he said, leaning over my desk to see what I was doing.

"And where exactly is 'out'?" I asked, studying his expression.

"I will be ready in ten minutes so we can leave." He leaned down and kissed me on the cheek. With a huge grin on his face, he went upstairs to get ready to go to Rapid City. He definitely had my attention.

An hour later we were finally walking out of the house. I stopped short as soon as I saw my truck. The man who assaulted me would know this truck. Panic filled me, and I instantly knew I had to get rid of it. My dad had given me my truck two years ago for my birthday and at the time I loved it. Now it was part of a nightmare I was trying to wake up from.

On the way to town, I looked through every compartment, gathering up all my stuff and trying to clean it up the best I could. I blurted my plan to Mike and, surprisingly, he thought it was a great idea, that is, *after* my appointment. Mike didn't press it further, and I was thankful.

Today was my follow-up doctor's appointment. I had tried to get out of it, but Mike wasn't going to let that happen. I blocked it from my mind after I had blood drawn last week and decided not to think about what the results could mean.

I quickly made my way to a chair in the corner of the exam room, but the doctor solemnly pointed to the exam table. I gave him a dirty look and climbed up as he opened my chart. He ran through the results and declared that everything was clean. *Thank, God!* That was a huge load off my mind until he reminded me I needed to do another pregnancy test next week.

After instructing me to remove my shirt, the doctor looked over my scars from the stab wounds. He studied them for a bit before indicating that everything was healing quite well. Seemingly satisfied with my recovery, he scribbled some names onto a piece of paper and handed it to me. I stared blankly at him as he encouraged me once again to see a therapist for the emotional effects he was concerned I was suffering from. Mike didn't help considering he was the one who brought up the idea when I was still in the hospital. I put my shirt back on, knowing I had no plans of touching that piece of paper.

It felt like the last day of school, waiting for the bell to ring so you could get the hell out of there. I didn't want to hear anything else from the doctor. It was a huge relief to know that, physically, everything was fine with me, but I was convinced that if I stuck around any longer, the doctor was going to change his mind.

Mike asked if I was okay as I stepped back into the waiting area, and I told him that I just needed food.

After lunch, we decided to do some shopping and just make a day of it in the city. We walked around the mall, picking up some things for ourselves, along with last-minute Christmas presents. After three hours, we decided it was time to look at vehicles.

After driving through four car lots, I finally found exactly what I wanted. Now it was time to deal. Mike loved to watch me get the best deal I could. It would be a long process, so he knew to sit back and watch.

Later that night, Mike made dinner as he did every night, and we talked like we used to. You know the kind of conversations that you take nothing away from, a conversation filled with gossip and poking fun at others. It was great to feel finally normal again, the two of us never ran out of things to talk about.

As I went outside to check on the steaks on the grill, I noticed it was snowing. It was beautiful seeing everything covered in a blanket of snow. It gave me a minute to think with absolute silence.

As I lifted the lid to the grill, I heard the phone ring and hoped it wasn't my dad. He had been calling more than ever, and it was driving me nuts.

Mike popped his head out and said Chuck and a few of his friends were coming over to have a couple drinks down by the fire pit. After he went back inside, I just stood there, admiring how beautiful the snow was. I wished that my life was that quiet and beautiful.

Chuck showed up with about five of his friends, and lots of beer. Dinner was fantastic. Chuck pointed out that if I didn't have Mike, I would probably starve to death. Cooking had never been my favorite pastime, it takes too long, and creates too much of a mess. I am the one who cleans up after Mike, who seems to use every pot, pan, and dish in the house every time he cooks. I wondered if he did this so that I would have to clean it all up.

Chuck asked about the new SUV sitting in the garage, and Mike told him it was his, just to take the focus off the absence of my truck. He always knew when to speak for me.

The fire pit had become pretty popular around our house. Lots of our friends would go down there, just to sit around and have a couple of beers.

About half an hour in, we had a roaring fire and not a moment too soon, as I was starting to lose feeling in my feet and hands.

I noticed that the number of people had multiplied. There was only one person I wasn't familiar with. From the way he kept watching me with concern, I had an idea who he was and how much he knew.

Mike quickly introduced me to his friend Mark, with a huge smile on his face.

"Danni, this is Mark. Mark, this is Danni."

That is when my brain put it together why Mike had been out all night, and why he had had that ridiculous grin on his face when he returned home this morning. Mark was not the typical guy Mike usually brought home. He was about the same height as Mike, and had a very athletic build to him, sandy blonde short hair, pale blue eyes, with a sweet look to him.

I smiled and said, "Nice to meet you, Mark."

"Nice to finally meet you, too, Danni. Mike talks about you all the time, mostly good things."

The look on Mike's face was hilarious. He looked like he had just put Mark in front of a firing squad, looking around at everyone's face for approval. I smiled at him and quietly told him to sit by his boyfriend. He just couldn't quit grinning. It was nice to see him happy.

We sat around the fire, and everyone told stories about the holidays.

The beer seemed to be endless, and I wondered how much our guests had brought with them. I was on my sixth beer and hoped there was a lot more. I knew I was going to feel horrible tomorrow, but I liked the numbness finding me and how it seemed to make it harder to remember things. I asked Mike to pass me another beer and he quietly snapped at me.

"I think you have had enough, Danni."

"I'm still conscious, so probably not," I said, glaring at him.

He gave me a dirty look when Chuck handed me another anyway.

Chuck asked me if I was going to the New Year's Eve party at the bar this weekend. I had been told nothing about it. Normally, I was the one who planned the events at the bar. Mike piped up and explained that he hadn't told me about it yet because he didn't want me to worry. I could tell he didn't plan on telling me, and that he wanted me nowhere near the bar.

At this point, it was getting pretty late, and the party seemed to be winding down. I looked at my watch and saw that it was 1:30 in the morning, but I wasn't ready to give up the party just yet.

I pulled out my cell and started texting Amber, one of the waitresses from the restaurant who always knew where the party was. She replied that she was just leaving the bar to meet some people, and asked if I wanted to be picked up. I quickly text-messaged her back.

Me: Give me half an hour to get rid of my company. I would love to go☺

Amber: Awesome!! Be there shortly!

Chuck picked up the shovel, then got a scoop of snow and put it on the fire. It quickly went dark.

I walked back up to the house, clutching Mike's arm in the darkness.

"Mark and I are going back to his place to watch a movie. You want to come with us?" Mike asked as I noticed Mark slip his hand into Mike's.

"Really Danni, you should come. It is supposed to be a great movie," Mark said smiling at me.

"No guys, you go ahead. I am super tired. Maybe some other time," I responded.

Knowing Mike, he would freak out if he knew who I was going out with. He knew all about Amber's reputation as well as I did, but I knew what would make me feel better.

As the last of my guests pulled out of the driveway, Amber pulled in. I was starting to sober up. I hated all those thoughts and feelings creeping back in.

"I've asked you a hundred times to party with me, but you always tell me 'no.' What changed your mind?" she asked as I slid into the passenger seat of her old Camaro.

"I need some excitement in my life."

"I will provide that for you," she declared as she pulled a joint out of her purse.

The truth was, Amber hung around with a group of people that made me a bit uneasy. They always came to the bar late, and it never failed that they would start a fight with a patron or bother the staff. Nobody liked waiting on them. They were always willing to spend their money quickly to make sure they had a good time. I was grateful that I was the boss and could, therefore, escape their attention.

I noticed a sweet scent swirling in the car. Somehow I knew that smell, but I couldn't place it. Amber pulled a deep, long drag off the joint and held her breath for a few seconds before slowly exhaling.

"You want some?" she asked with a cough, holding the joint out to me.

I had never taken part in the drug scene before. My dad threatened me within an inch of my life when I was younger if he ever caught me doing drugs.

"What the hell, let me try," I said, as I took the joint from her and simply did what she did.

Amber asked, "Have you ever been high before?"

"No," I answered, and she gasped.

"I figured with your dad being who he is that you would be into this."

By the time we got to the party, my mind was blank, and my body was numb. I didn't have a care in the world. We pulled up to a little white house in the middle of nowhere. It was intimidating with the tall trees, high fences, and what looked like cameras all around the property. People were coming and going through a gate, where two guys stopped them on their way in.

I turned to Amber and asked, "Is the party over?"

"No," she said with a wink.

After parking in a barn, she had a garage door opener for, we walked to the house. People recognized and greeted me in passing with perplexed looks on their faces, and I could tell they were all wondering why I was there.

In the house, the music was loud, and I couldn't hear her as she kept talking. I just followed behind her, heading to the back of the house. Once again, I smelled the strong, sweet scent that I smelled in the car. Amber pointed toward the keg, and I nodded. She must have known from the look on my face that I was interested in more.

"See that guy on the couch?" she asked, leaning into me. I nodded.

"He will take good care of you. I am going to find my boyfriend, be right back."

"Danni, sit by me." I heard a voice coming from the couch and realized it was James, from the gas station.

I hadn't seen him in a while, but I knew him well. I went to sit by him, knowing he was harmless.

"What's a good girl like you doing in a place like this?" he asked with a wicked smile.

"Probably the same reason you're here," I responded, crossing my legs as I settled in next to him.

He laughed and said, "I doubt that very much, beautiful."

He lit a joint, took a long drag, and held it out to me. *Not a moment too soon,* I thought. "I can share with you if you don't mind staying right here with me." Without a second thought, I took it and sat back, once again finding my numb place.

I wasn't dumb. I knew he was aware of my assault, and I took advantage of his pity and stayed put, smoking the joint with him until it was gone. Immediately, I began to feel its effects.

I looked around the living room and was surprised by how many people I recognized, people I never thought would be doing drugs. I saw Bobbi, a local hair stylist, Trudy, from the bank, Tyler, from the car dealership, and Kelley, from the hospital gift shop. It was awkward how everyone didn't want to talk much, but I was appreciative of it. It seemed that we were all in our way trying to become numb to something.

I sat there, watching people, making meaningless talk with others off and on. I was enjoying feeling nothing and was exactly where I wanted to be.

Amber walked in and motioned me to come with her. I got up and followed her.

Stepping into the backyard, I noticed the bonfire and the continued high fence theme around the yard.

"Danni, this is my boyfriend, Ron," she said holding onto his arm.

He was tall and well-built, not the most attractive guy, but he appeared to be in control of everything around him. He gave me a dangerous grin as he looked me over from head to toe.

"This is quite the surprise. Amber told me she was bringing a friend to the party, but I would never have guessed it was you," he said.

"Nice to meet you, Ron. Hope you don't mind me tagging along."

He laughed and said, "I hope you tag along more often. I have a feeling you will be an excellent customer."

It didn't register what he meant for a few minutes, but then I thought to myself, *this will not become a regular thing for me.*

"Ron, you have a friendly customer!" yelled someone from the house.

He got up and walked inside. I wanted to ask Amber what that was about, but I kept my mouth shut as she passed me a bottle of whiskey. Suddenly, my pocket was vibrating. I pulled out my phone, saw it was Mike calling, and quickly tapped the ignore button. I knew he would be furious if he knew where I was, so I decided I would send a text.

Me: I am at Chuck's watching a movie. You home?

I hoped he would buy it.

Mike: At 3:45 in the morning?

Wow, time had slipped away from me.

Me: Yes, I'm just going to spend the night.

Mike: I am staying with Mark. I will see you later. Love You ;).

Amber asked me if I wanted to go home and I told her "no"; she looked relieved with my answer. I hadn't felt so numb in my life, and I wanted to relish every moment of it. We were laughing at stupid little things and everyone around us chimed in with their comments.

One of my favorite newer rock bands, Dark Pieces, came on over the speakers and Amber, and I got up and started dancing, and then others joined in with us. It was easy to close my eyes and just move to the music, getting lost in my world.

After a while, I saw Ron and Amber were dancing slowly. He was starting to take off her clothes, and she seemed completely fine with it. Then, I noticed a lot more people were doing the same thing. *Maybe it's time to go home,* I thought. I couldn't ask Amber for a ride home, apparently. I looked at the door and saw

James walking toward me. He looked angry and on a mission as he jogged the final distance to me. He grabbed my arm and said, "We're leaving right now."

Suddenly lots of people were leaving at the same time, too. I poked James in the ribs to try and get his attention, but he kept walking with his hand firmly around my good wrist. He appeared to be in a hurry to get us both out of there.

We made our way out to James' old, single-cab truck. He opened the driver-side door and motioned to me to get in. It was very crowded as three other guys squeezed in through the passenger side.

"That shit was getting intense," one of the guys stated, looking irritated as James started his truck and we headed back to town.

"It always does when Ron is involved," another one mumbled, annoyed.

I fell asleep on the ride home and was awakened by James shaking my shoulder.

"Hey, beautiful, you're home."

I let him help me out of the truck and to my front door. I was so drowsy and just wanted to go back to sleep.

"Can you make it the rest of the way? If you need me to, I can help you to bed." He said, grinning at me.

"Thanks, James, but I'm all right," I replied, putting my key in the lock and opening the door.

He had a worried look on his face, so I had to change what was on his mind.

"You were going to explain why everyone was leaving the party so quickly," I said, praying for the distraction, but also curious.

"You're tired; maybe we could go to lunch or something, and I could explain everything then?" He ran his fingers lightly over the scar forming on my forehead.

He was a good-looking man: very tall, with long, messy brown hair that hung over his eyes, which he would often run his hand through, pushing it all back, while showing all the beautiful colorful tattoos over his arms and hands. Looking into his blue eyes that appeared to be filled with pain, I leaned into his hand now touching my cheek.

"Sweet dreams, beautiful girl," he whispered while he pressed a kiss to my forehead before he turned around and left.

I looked at my clock when I entered my room and was surprised when I saw it was seven a.m. I didn't even bother taking off my shoes as I fell on my bed and went to sleep.

CHAPTER 3
NUMB & JAMES

Over the next couple of days, Mike repeatedly called to check on me. I assured him I was fine, and he decided to stay at Mark's again. It was nice not to feel like he was watching my every move to see when I was going to fall apart. After a week of not leaving my house, I thought I would go to the bar and try to get some work done, or maybe try to find James. Thinking back to the numb feeling I had experienced that night at the party, I had an urge to feel that good again.

As I walked into the bar, it appeared that everyone was back to normal. Nobody gave me a second look as I walked to my office. My desk looked like a tornado had gone through it: there were pieces of mail, timecards, and invoices scattered haphazardly all over my desk. I had a feeling I would be there a while as I began to regret my decision to come to work after all.

After I had got everything put in the appropriate place, I started working on payroll. Jackie had been working a lot of overtime, which irritated me, so I went to find her and ask what was going on. Mike and I had agreed early in our business venture that we would run a very tight ship, but it seemed to be quickly sinking. Jackie was waiting on a table, and I told one of the bartenders to send her to my office when she was done.

My mood was changing quickly, and I was pissed that I was suddenly being left out of the bar's decisions. *Who the hell did she think she was? Trying to run my damn bar?!* As I walked back toward my office, I continued past it and headed to the storage room. I grabbed a bottle of whiskey and thought to myself, *being sober is overrated.* I returned to my office and mixed it into a cup of pop I had brought with me, before quickly hiding the whiskey under my desk. Halfway through my drink, the alcohol had warmed my body and taken the edge off. Jackie finally walked in.

"Shut the door and sit down," I barked at her.

The look on her face was complete panic. I never asked anyone to close the door unless I was firing someone.

"Why are you working sixty hours a week? Who gave you permission?"

"Mike approved my hours. I was just trying to help out so you could rest," she said with tears filling her eyes.

Sarcastically, I thought, *well, isn't that nice?* I hadn't even been at the bar for an hour, and I was mad as hell!

"You will go back to your forty hours a week and nothing more. Do you understand me?"

"I was just trying to help you out, Danni. I know you have been through a lot."

Suddenly I was yelling at her. "I don't need your fucking help. I don't need anyone's help. This is my bar, and I will call the shots. If you don't like it, you can leave."

"Does Mike know you're here?" she asked as the tears began to roll down her cheeks.

I yelled louder, standing up from my desk, "Get the fuck out of my bar. You're done now!"

"You can't be serious, Danni. I love this place. I work hard, and I know you're just hurting right now."

"GET THE FUCK OUT NOW!" I screamed at her as rage began to pour out of me.

She left my office crying, and I shuddered in disgust. I have never been comfortable with that kind of emotion. I knew as soon as she left, she would be on the phone with Mike. I thought this might be a good time to call James and get the hell out of there.

Dammit, it went straight to his voicemail. I wondered if he was at Ron's house. I gathered up all my stuff so I could finish my work from home. On the way out, I told one of the bartenders that Jackie was no longer allowed in the bar. I headed for the door, but not before grabbing the whiskey that was under my desk.

My phone rang just as I started my truck and prayed it wouldn't be Mike. Sure enough, it was. I hit the ignore button.

I wondered if I could find Ron's place by myself although I didn't even know the address. I was trying to decide if I should go home or just drive around in the country when my phone rang again. This time, it was James; I breathed a sigh of relief. We made small talk for a couple of minutes; I didn't want him to think I just wanted something from him. I told him my dilemma, not wanting to go home and not wanting to go back to the bar. He asked me to come pick him up, and I agreed.

I found his address in a nice neighborhood. Pulling into the driveway, I was surprised when he walked to the driver's side.

"Slide over and let me drive. I know the way to Ron's better than you do."

I couldn't argue with that as I climbed over to the passenger seat. He launched into twenty questions.

"Why haven't you called me?"

I fired right back, "Why haven't *you* called *me?*"

"I didn't think I was your type."

"Oh," I said hoping he wasn't getting the wrong idea.

I wondered if this was going to become a problem. He seemed to read my thoughts.

"Relax. We can stick with the friend thing."

I immediately felt better. I liked him a little more than I thought, wondering where the hell that came from. Mike kept calling me, but I figured that at this point he was beyond pissed at me, so I turned off my phone and just put it in the center console.

"What are you drinking?" he asked as he picked up my cup.

"Soda."

"I don't believe you." He took a swig and then gave me his sexy smile.

As he drove us to Ron's, we made small talk, and I told him about Jackie. He was quick to mention that I had grown harsher than I used to be, but, he said he understood.

"How are you doing with what happened?" he asked, before pulling over to make another drink. He had, apparently, noticed the whiskey bottle behind my seat.

"The whiskey is helping right now."

"Sometimes you just need some help forgetting," he said, handing the cup back to me.

We made small talk about life in general as we passed the cup back and forth. He told me about his parents and the gas station. His dad had Alzheimer's, and his mom had asked him to help the family. He went on to say that when she called, he had been at a low point and thought it would be an ideal time to do right by them. When moved here with them, he bought the gas station so his dad could still work and lead a normal life. It went fine for about a year until suddenly his mom died of a heart attack and he needed to take care of his dad full-time. I asked if his father was still alive and he mentioned he was in a nursing home, saying they took better care of him than he could. He visited every day, he said, even though his father couldn't recognize him anymore.

"Your turn to tell me about your family."

I just laughed at him before reluctantly replying, "Mike and my dad are my family."

He added, "I know exactly who your dad is, and I am a big fan. More people in town know more about you two than you think."

"My dad and I have a dysfunctional relationship. Neither one of us asks or tells each other details. Feelings aren't brought up much," I said looking out my window.

"Ok, what about your mom?"

"You know as much as I do: nothing."

Changing the subject, I asked, "So, why was everyone leaving the other night so suddenly?"

I waited for a reply. He was silent for a moment.

"It's complicated and something you don't want to know."

"I want to know," I fired back at him, taking the whiskey bottle from his hand.

"Ok, fine," he said. "You probably already guessed anyways. Ron is the local drug dealer in town and, if you value your life, you don't cross him. His group of friends is very tight knit; it's better to keep a little distance from them."

"You're not answering my question."

"I was getting to that. Are you sure you want to know?"

I nodded my head, and he explained that I would be surprised what people will do for drugs when they don't have any money. Sometimes the party turns into a sex party, and it was better not to get involved. He explained that when the party starts changing, you have to get out quickly because if Ron asks you to stay, you do. I asked if he had ever stayed and he said no. In the past, he and Ron had some differences when it came to Amber. James continued telling me that he and Amber were dating when Ron moved to town, and he quickly went after Amber. She liked drugs, so it was no problem for her to become Ron's girlfriend. Now she did exactly what she was told and never asked questions. Amber did stand up for James and told Ron to leave him alone; they developed a kind of tolerance for each other mostly because Ron liked James' money and James wanted the drugs, too. He stressed the point of staying a safe distance from both Amber and Ron for my safety. I told him that I would only go out there with him. He squeezed my hand and said that was a good idea.

As we pulled up to the house, I saw lots of cars. We stopped at the gate, and a huge guy with a shaved head and braided beard asked if we were lost. Then he recognized James and told him to go ahead. I was hoping it would be like last time when no one paid much attention to me. James grabbed my hand and told me to stay with him as we went inside.

Funny, it hadn't seemed dangerous the last time I was here, but now it appeared to be a little scary. As he led me through the house, James stopped at the couch, telling me to stay put and that he would be right back. I hate people telling me what to do, but I sat down and did as I was directed. I recognized a lot of the same faces with a few new ones as people made small talk with me. I did my best to blend in as James came into the room and sat down by me.

"Where did you go?"

"To get something to help you forget," he said, pulling a joint from his shirt pocket.

He lit it and passed it to me. The numbness started to settle in, and I felt better than the last time. I mentioned it to him, and he said he was sure the whiskey had something to do with that.

We sat there just watching people come and go, when someone yelled, "Ron, you have a friendly customer."

"What is a friendly customer?" I whispered in James' ear.

"Give it a second and you will find out."

Ron came into the house as a girl came forward. She was not attractive, very thin, sores all over her face, and missing a lot of teeth. He pointed her toward a room, and they both went in while one of his friends stood in front of the door. It made me even more curious about what was going on.

James whispered in my ear, "A friendly customer is someone who trades a sexual favor for drugs."

I had no idea that really happened. James passed the joint back to me and put his arm around me. I felt safer nestled by his side, so that is where I stayed.

After about twenty minutes, Ron and the girl came out of the room. She quickly left, and I wondered if she wanted to get high or if she was humiliated.

Ron started talking to different people, and I hoped he wouldn't notice me and would just go back outside. Then he looked right at me, smiled, and started walking toward me. *Dammit*, I thought, feeling James pull me closer to his side.

"I wondered if we would ever see you again," Ron said, noticing James holding onto me.

"We just stopped by for a minute," I mumbled.

"You want to come outside and have a beer?"

James answered quickly, "It's time for us to leave."

"Sorry, I didn't realize that you two were together."

"Well, now you do," James said, standing up in front of Ron.

"I hope to see you again real soon, Danni, and I'll let Amber know that you stopped by."

Ron smiled at me, then turned and left the room. Everyone stared at me for a moment before they went back to their business.

We quickly left. James didn't let go of my hand until he opened the passenger-side door for me. I got in, and he shut the door behind me. I sat there alone, locked in my SUV, waiting for him while he went back inside.

I thought about getting my phone out and turning it on. I knew Mike was just going to yell at me, so why bother? I was starting to miss him. I hadn't seen him in what seemed like a month even though it had only been five days. He was only looking out for my best interests, although I was making that difficult for him these days.

James opened the driver-side door and scared the crap out of me.

"Where did you go to?" I asked.

"I got our party to go," he said and patted his shirt pocket.

We didn't say much on the way back to town. I looked at the clock and noticed it was only 11 p.m. I didn't want to go home yet.

"James, would it be okay if we went to your place to hang out?"

"I hoped you would say that."

He was careful to take back streets, so we didn't drive by the bar, avoiding Mike. At his house, he pulled in the driveway, hopped out, and went inside. The garage door opened, and he jumped back into the driver's seat, before pulling into the garage.

"It will be a little harder for Mike to find you if your car isn't in plain sight."

I felt myself a little hesitant to get out of the car. I hadn't been alone with a guy since the whole assault thing. I started to panic, and he sensed my anxiety.

"We can just stay here and talk if you want. I would never make you do anything you didn't want to do," he said while holding my hand to his chest.

Well, I thought, *I don't want my SUV to smell like weed either.* I took a deep breath and climbed out. Inside his house, I was surprised that it looked so cozy and clean. I made fun of him a bit, asking if he was a decorator. He laughed and rolled his eyes.

"Take off your jacket and get comfortable, please."

I shrugged out of my coat and laid it on the dark brown leather sofa as he made us another drink. Sitting down on the couch, he reached into his pocket and pulled out four pills in a small plastic bag.

"Do you want something to go with our drinks?"

"Most definitely," I said, perhaps a little too quickly.

I thought maybe I was a bit too sober, and I needed to fix that. It was easy talking to James. He didn't make me feel like it was anything more than just hanging out. He now sensed my relaxation and started to make fun of me.

"You know, when you moved to town you were the topic of conversation for single guys."

"Did you take part in that conversation?" I asked him with a smile.

"No, you came across like a stuck-up princess. I don't like that."

We just sat there, talking for what felt like hours about nothing important. Eventually, we both started getting quiet. I could tell he was just as tired as I was.

"Do you mind if I sleep on your couch?" I asked, knowing I was in no shape to drive.

"No, but you can stay in my room, and I'll sleep on the couch."

He showed me to his room, and again I was surprised by how clean it was. He grabbed a pillow off his bed and pointed toward the door.

"There is a lock on the door if that makes you feel better. You're welcome to use it."

"No need, James, but thank you for being so kind to me."

He nodded and pulled the door shut after him. I took off my shoes and jeans and crawled into his bed. I fell asleep right away, despite being in a strange place.

I woke up to the smell of bacon and coffee. I had started making a habit of staying up late and sleeping most of the day. I got dressed and tried to make myself presentable.

James greeted me saying, "There is coffee, breakfast will be ready shortly."

"Wow, you cook, too. I am impressed," I said.

"Be quiet and drink your coffee," he said, mocking me.

After breakfast, on our way out the door, I said, "Thank you, James. It was a great night."

"I hope it's the first of many."

I secretly hoped for more as well. After saying he would call me later to see how much trouble I was in, I headed for home. I stopped for coffee on the way home, delaying the wrath of Mike. As soon as I turned into my driveway, I saw his truck sitting in the usual spot. I thought about leaving, but I knew eventually he would find me.

I pulled into the garage, got out, and went to the passenger-side to get my laptop and paperwork from the bar. As I walked into the kitchen, it appeared that nobody was around, and for a moment I thought he might not be home.

"Where the hell have you been and what the hell did you think when you fired Jackie?" he angrily greeted me from out of nowhere.

"Well, hello to you, too," I said. He was not amused.

I started walking toward my office, trying to avoid him. He was right behind me, and I knew this conversation was not going just to go away. I put my stuff on my desk and turned and looked at him.

"Mike, you know I love you, but you have to stop treating me like an injured child. I am appreciative that you are concerned, but you are smothering me."

He looked at the floor and said, "I know that I am a little over-protective, but that's my job. I'm worried about you. You don't seem to be making the best choices right now. I'm just looking out for you. Please, Danni, I wish you would see a therapist and work on getting better."

"What the hell is wrong with me that you think I need to fix?"

He just went off yelling, "You have never addressed the rape. You avoid it at all costs, and you are becoming *so* angry. This isn't who you are."

"I know I am angry. I'm handling it," I grumbled, sitting down in my chair.

"I know all about the firing of people. Plus, you're drinking, and getting high." He threw his hands up in the air.

Apparently, word of my recent addictions, attitude, and actions had somehow been spread to him.

I opened my mouth to reply, but he cut me off and yelled, "Oh, don't fucking lie to me. You're a horrible liar."

I wanted the conversation to end now. "Fine, Mike, I will make an appointment with a therapist."

"Are you *really* going to make an appointment, or are you just telling me this so I'll feel better?" he asked.

"Yes! I will make an appointment, Mike."

I stood up and put my hand in his as he hugged me and said, "Thank you, Danni. That is all I ask."

"We need to address the Jackie issue," I said, pulling my face away from his chest.

"I already handled it and told her she wasn't fired. She knows we are having a hard time right now," he whispered.

"Wow, do you make all the decisions now or what?" I asked, mocking him.

"She's trying to help us and is just concerned about you."

I wish everyone would quit worrying about me, I thought. Mike continued ranting about it being a good idea if I just took care of the business end from home right now. He and Jackie would handle the rest, he said. I agreed so that we could change the subject.

I asked him about Mark, and he immediately started telling me how great he was, how much fun they had together, and blah blah blah. After a few minutes, I started tuning him out. I didn't want to hear about anyone's love life at the moment, but at least the focus of the conversation wasn't on me.

We started going through the work stuff I had brought home, and between the two of us, we finished it rather quickly. About two hours later, he left to go clean up and take a shower for work.

The doorbell rang, and I hoped Mike would get it, but when it rang again, I went to the door. I was surprised to see a huge bouquet of white roses.

The teenage delivery girl with blue hair asked, "Is there, like, a Danni here or, like, a Denny or something?"

Wow, her education was paying off.

"That's me, and for your information, it's Danni," I said before she shoved her little clipboard in my face and asked for a signature.

I signed and took the flowers inside, wondering who would be sending me flowers. Opening the card, I saw they were from James. It said simply:

Hi, beautiful. Something to help you forget.

—James

Looking in the envelope, I saw that there were two joints. Well, my evening had taken a turn for the better.

CHAPTER 4
LIAR'S BLOCK

Over the next couple of months, my life became an endless cycle of sleeping till noon, staying out all night, and getting high. I was able to work from home with a lot more free time now that I wasn't going to the bar to work every day.

James and I had grown closer. We were just friends with nothing else attached to it. I wasn't dumb and knew from the way he sometimes looked at me that he hoped something more would come out of our friendship. I hated to break his heart, but the whole idea of a sexual relationship with anyone just made me sick. I couldn't deal with my feelings right now let alone someone else's feelings.

While James and I grew close, Mike and I became distant. I wasn't sure who was to blame. Maybe both of us. I was continually ignoring him so I wouldn't get lectured about my behavior and he was disregarding me because he was in love. He and Mark were around each other every moment they could be together. I knew it was serious between them, and I couldn't help but be a little jealous of what they had, in addition to missing my time with Mike. But, on the other hand, not having to hear about how *in love* they were was great, too.

Mike and I lived together so we could catch each other for work-related issues, but for now, I wanted nothing more than to live alone. Apparently everyone in town informed him about my every move. He made sure to tell me that he knew what I was up to every day, hoping I would fix my life before I did something stupid.

Mike had also pulled James aside at the bar one night, telling him what he thought of the situation between us. It led to a very heated argument between the two, ending with Chuck kicking James out and telling him he was no longer welcome in the bar. I knew that what James and I were doing would probably not end well, but I didn't care. I enjoyed James and everything he supplied me with, and that was what mattered most to me.

Sitting on my bed one afternoon after sleeping till noon, I stared at my phone. I was dreading the phone call that I needed to make. It was the end of March and every year at this time my dad and I would take a trip somewhere for a little quality time together. I was trying to find a way out of it. Being with my dad for a solid month sober was just something I couldn't do right now. Mike had mentioned yesterday that my dad was excited about our trip, but I wasn't thrilled at all. They had always been very close. I knew that Mike told my dad everything I was up to and the company I kept, although my father hadn't said a word about it to me. He had taken it upon himself to plan our trip without me this year. The worst part was that he had invited Mike and Mark to go with us. The thought of the four of us together for a month was something out of a horror novel. I needed an excuse fast, and I couldn't come up with anything.

Just then, my phone lit up with a text.

James: What are you doing?

Me: I have liar's block!

We had already talked about this trip and what I should do. He suggested that the two of us just go to Vegas instead. The idea was tempting, but I had no desire to go anywhere with anyone right now. I only wanted to stay here and have a supply on hand at all times.

James: Do you want to go out to Ron's tonight? We are out of our supply right now.

Typically he just ran out there, wanting me to stay away from them. My answer involved little thought.

Me: Yes, I will pick you up. What time?

James: Pick me up in an hour from the gas station.

That gave me enough time to run to the bar and drop off the bills and payroll. Twenty minutes later, my phone call to dad was long-forgotten. I pulled up to the bar and noticed that Mike and Mark were both there. I was sure to hear about the trip. Maybe I could give everything to Jackie and make my way out without running into either of them.

Walking in the door, I saw that the regular 5 o'clock crowd was gathered. Quickly looking around for Jackie, I realized she was, of course, in the office with both of them. *Crap. I'll just make it as short as possible.* Walking into the office with the usual hello's and such, I gave Jackie the payroll to hand out. Mike had taken the rest before he started gathering up the current invoices. I knew he wanted to talk to me, so I tried to avoid him. I walked to the back to pick up the new bills, and I could tell he was following me.

"Danni, you can't ignore me forever," he said.

"I am not trying to ignore you. I just have things I need to do."

"Like, getting high?!"

"Worry about yourself and your little happy-go-lucky fucking relationship, Mike."

Knowing it was time to leave, I tried to step out. That is when he decided to stand in the doorway and not let me through.

"You're going to listen to what I have to say because you know I'm only saying it because I love you and miss you. I need my best friend back."

I didn't say a word; the things he said were hurtful and, although I knew they were true, I wasn't going to admit any of it. I was on the verge of tears when my phone went off. Mike grabbed it out of my hand and hit the ignore button after looking at the name. I hadn't seen him this angry in years.

"Am I free to go or what, Mike?" I snapped, trying to grab my phone back.

"Where are you going?" he asked.

For once I told him the truth and said, "I am going to get *high* with James. You shouldn't wait up."

"Baby, let her go. It's her choice what she does," Mark whispered, as he moved in front of Mike to try and calm him down.

Mike uncurled his fist and held my phone out to me, but as I went to grab it, he threw it against the wall, smashing it into about ten pieces.

Stepping aside, he yelled: "I am so tired of your crap, Danni. Just get the hell out."

A part of me wanted to argue with him, but instead, I gathered up my stuff and left. People stared as I walked out of the bar: It was obvious everyone had heard us arguing.

I got into my SUV and went to pick up James. On my way there, I was reminiscing on my attack. When I left the hospital, all I wanted to do was go home and end my life. I wondered what stopped me because now it felt like it would have been a good idea.

The ride out to Ron's was silent. Mike's words kept racing through my thoughts. *Screw Mike*, I thought, *who does he think he is?*

James finally broke the silence.

"Do you still have liar's block?"

"I don't think I will have to lie after all."

I told him about Mike and the whole argument.

"I think maybe we need to kick up our party a bit."

"How is that?" I asked.

"I know what will make you feel better, trust me."

We arrived at the house, and I immediately noticed not too many people were there. Ten people at the most. Amber came up and told us to come out back to talk alone. Once outside, she explained that Ron and his friends had run into some trouble. They didn't think they would be back until tomorrow. James asked what she had, and she rattled off a few terms I apparently didn't know. He told her what he wanted, and she explained that she would have to call Ron to get a price. A couple of minutes later she came back with it and the price per Ron. James nodded in agreement and took what she offered after giving her a few hundreds. I was confused about what was happening.

Amber waved as we were leaving and I stopped dead in my tracks, suddenly finding myself a little mad at James.

"What the hell is going on?" I asked.

He calmly said, "Just get in the car and I will explain later."

"No, I want to know now!" I was starting to act like a spoiled child.

"Just get in the car!"

The urgency in his voice made the decision for me as I climbed into the passenger seat. On the way back to town, he explained that usually when Ron ran into trouble, that meant he was in jail or thought he was being watched. Either way, James explained, it was a good idea for us not to be there. We didn't take the usual way back to town, and he mentioned that he wanted to show me something.

We pulled up to a run-down little cabin in the middle of nowhere. He looks at me and explains, "It doesn't look like much now, but give me six months, and it will be different."

Walking into the cabin, I smelled fresh-cut wood and dust. I could tell that James had already started remodeling it. He went into detail about all the things he was going to do to it, explaining that, hopefully, it would be his full-time home soon.

It was dark, and he said he would make a fire if I wanted to look around. I went to the kitchen and was surprised when I opened the fridge and saw it was full. He had everything planned out in detail. It was amazing how quiet it was with no television, radio, or internet. I was not interested in having a nice dinner or talking, for that matter. Mike's words were still burning in my ears, and all I wanted to do was tune them all out.

I asked James what he had gotten from Amber, and he said, "Just some pills because that was all she had to sell." He handed me a beer and asked if I was ready to kick up the party a little. Of course, I was more than ready.

After taking the pills and starting on my second beer, we sat on the couch in front of the fire. Our conversation segued from one subject to the next when, suddenly, we were talking about sex. He was going on about how long it had been since he had had sex. I was surprised when he said it was only two months ago.

"I don't remember you dating anyone," I said.

"I haven't dated anyone. Amber and I just ran into each other at the bar one night, and it went from there."

Surprisingly, I felt a rush of jealousy and asked, "Why didn't you mention it to me?"

"Sorry, I didn't think that was something you wanted to hear about."

Changing the subject, I found myself telling him about my last attempt at dating.

"It happened a couple of weeks before I was…never mind."

At that moment, I couldn't believe what I had just said. I was horrified! I couldn't even look at him, but I could feel James staring at me. I wanted to crawl under the couch and hide.

"Do you by chance have any more pills? I don't think I took enough," I said.

"I feel the same way," he answered, looking more mad than upset.

We each took a couple more and just sat there waiting for them to kick in.

Out of the blue, he asked, "When was the last time someone kissed you the way you should be kissed?"

I had no answer for him. I just stared at the fire. I couldn't remember the last time I had shared a passionate kiss with anyone. I got up and walked to the kitchen to get the whiskey. Obviously, the pills weren't doing anything.

As I closed the fridge, James was standing uncomfortably close to me, and neither one of us said a word. He put his hands on my face, leaned forward, and kissed me.

At that moment, I forgot who I was and how to move all at the same time. His lips were warm on mine, and I felt something, a need that I had all but forgotten about. The more I let myself feel, the more passionate our kissing became. His hand slipped inside my shirt and without being aware of my actions, I was taking off his shirt, trying to get closer to him. Sensing my response to everything happening, he pulled my shirt off, too. I started tugging at his belt, and he guided me toward the couch. Unbuttoning my pants at the same time, he sat down on the sofa, pulling me down to straddle his lap. He was trying to take off my bra, but suddenly I felt like I was going to be sick.

I took off running to the bathroom, and as soon as I shut the door, I was throwing up and shaking uncontrollably. I could feel the knife against my neck, the smell of grease and oil in my nose; I felt myself pushing against his chest to try and get him off of me, and that stupid cornfield.

The first time since the attack I was sobbing hysterically and feeling every emotion that I had pushed as far down as I could.

The door flew open behind me, and James fell to the floor with me, pulling me into his arms.

"It's okay to cry, beautiful," he said, holding me tight against his chest.

And I did. I cried and cried, and all the while, James never let go of me. At some point during my crying, James carried me to the bedroom and told me to try and sleep it off; we could talk more in the morning.

I woke up from the best night of sleep I had in six months, feeling fantastic. I didn't have that typical headache I always seemed to have.

I could hear James talking in the living room, and I was wondering who he was on the phone with, especially since I thought I heard my name a time or two. I just lay there listening, trying to understand the conversation. I started to sit up, quickly realizing that all I had on was my underwear and bra.

James must have heard me moving around, and he knocked on the door.

"Can I come in?" he asked, slowly pushing the door open a little.

I grabbed the sheet, wrapped it around me, and said, "Yes, James, come in."

He sat on the bed beside me and asked, "You okay?"

"Did we . . . ?" I mumbled, motioning between us.

"No, calm down. I will explain the last couple days to you."

"The last *couple* days? We just got here last night." I must have looked utterly confused as he covered my mouth with his hand to stop me from rambling.

"That was two nights ago. You cried for hours. I picked you up off the bathroom floor and put you in bed. You slept for thirty six hours straight, and you were talking and crying in your sleep."

"Mike is probably worried sick about me," I mumbled.

"I called him against my better judgment. Of course, he wanted to know where we were so he could come get you. I told him that maybe it was better just to let you sleep. We can call him now if you want, or I can take you home myself."

"I'm not sure what I want to do," I said.

For the first time in months, I felt calm, relaxed, and less angry. Sleeping more than a couple hours probably had made the most difference.

"Danni, I don't want to tell you how to live your life, but I think you might need to talk about the assault. I would gladly listen and help any way I can."

That was a turning point for me: for once, the proposition didn't make me mad. Maybe I just didn't feel judged by James. Sensing I wasn't going to speak up quite yet, he got up and went to get my clothes for me.

While getting dressed, I thought about my fight with Mike. I wondered how he was feeling about this mess. I was dragging everybody I cared about into my pain. I just hoped it wasn't too late to apologize.

When I pulled into my driveway, I noticed the extra car and wondered who was at my house. Of course, Mike and Mark were there, but I had hoped that Mark had gone home for once.

When I walked in, I heard a familiar voice and almost had to pick myself off the floor; it was my dad. I was instantly frozen. Do I walk in casually like nothing had ever happened? Do I just hug him like normal? I chose to walk in casually and just see what would happen.

They all stopped talking as soon as the door shut behind me. I marched forward to whatever was coming to me. As soon as my dad looked at me, I could see tears building up in his eyes. This was new to me, and I just watched him until he walked over and hugged me tight.

"Baby girl, I am so sorry for not being here for you when you needed me. It won't ever happen again."

Am I in the right house? My dad, this big rock star guy, who never showed feelings in his life, suddenly had his arms around me, apologizing for what he hadn't done. I thought I was the one who needed to apologize. I didn't know what to say, so I just hugged him back.

My dad whispered in my ear, "Someone else wants to apologize for his behavior, as well."

He let go of me and looked at Mike. The look on his face was priceless: it was as if he were being scolded by the principal, and he didn't like it one bit. Mike walked toward me and motioned me to come with him. I followed him into our home office. I knew this was going to be interesting.

"Danni, I am sorry for trying to control your life and telling you how to live it. We have always been able to talk to each other about everything, but now you just shut down and push me away."

I stopped him and asked, "Mike, what would you do?"

He hung his head and said, "I have no idea."

For once, I had a voice and started telling him exactly what I thought and how I felt.

"The one time I needed you most, you chose your love life over me, and that hurt."

That struck a nerve. Now we were both crying. *Finally, everything was out in the open.* After about an hour of us pouring our hearts out to each other, Mike had only one thing to ask of me.

"Please give Mark a chance?"

I admit my behavior toward Mark was not the best, but he came into our lives at an awful time, and he had taken Mike from me.

"I will start over with him and give him a chance, as long as you still make time for me."

"I promise you, Danni, you are a priority to me. I love you very much."

"I love you, too, Mike."

We went back out to the kitchen, and I recognized a familiar smell. It was the smell of my dad making fried chicken. That was something he had done a lot when we were kids. It was a way for me to know that he was home from the road for a while. It turned out to be one of my better nights with Dad, Mike, and Mark. We talked about life in general, and I got to know Mark a little better.

After I had stepped into my hot shower that night, I wondered what my next step was going to be. Do I see a therapist? Do I go away to one of those rehabs that seem more like a spa than somewhere you go to get help? I shrugged the thought off quickly, knowing all too well I wasn't about to talk to a stranger about what had happened. I liked where all the feelings and emotions were already stored, deep down so I could continue ignoring them.

We all decided the best therapy for me was to escape South Dakota for a while and go on the road with my dad.

CHAPTER 5
HOLY HOT HOT HOT

A few months flew by, and I remembered why I loved traveling with Dad so much. Watching him perform helped me remember why I loved music. It was an adrenaline high to get on stage and play the music that fires you up, even when you were watching someone else do it.

I met a lot of new artists: some were nice, and some were jerks. You never know what you're going to encounter on the road. It was always fun watching women try to get my dad's attention and I was surprised by the way he thought it was amusing to me that he was not interested in them in the least bit. He mentioned that once you have a daughter, you see things differently.

I laughed, "When did you become so wise?"

"As soon as you grew up and started testing my patience."

We were starting to become comfortable talking to each other, and no topic was off limits. One-night sitting on the bus while we were writing a song together, he put his guitar down and looked carefully at me for a minute, almost as though he were putting a thought together.

"You can ask me about your mom, you know? I'll tell you anything you want to know about her."

No questions came to mind. I didn't respond, knowing he pretty much summed it up for me when I was a kid.

"You make rash decisions the way she used to, and you look a lot like her. I sometimes wish she would have stayed," he said, looking more at his guitar than at me.

I was confused, "I thought you said she took the money you offered and left?"

"The truth is, she desperately tried to take you with her, but the thought of losing you was more than I could handle. I offered her the money to leave without you. She knew she couldn't take care of you by herself; she couldn't even take care of herself. I think deep down she knew I could take better care of you than she could. I know it broke her heart when she left."

"So, why has she never tried to see me at all?" I asked, sounding irritated.

He shook his head and said, "I don't know. I've sent her invitations to birthdays, graduations, and holiday parties, but I never get a response. At this point, I have no idea if she is even alive."

Nothing was said for a little bit, and we both just picked up our guitars and went back to writing. The mood had changed.

An hour later, he said he needed to get some sleep and kissed the top of my head as he went to the back of the tour bus.

My mind was spinning. I was lost in thought wondering if my mother was alive, if she had another family, or if she had even thought about me.

I felt my phone vibrating next to me and saw it was Mike. We talked for two hours about my conversation with my dad and life in general. His only question was if I wanted to try to find her and, at this moment, the answer was no. I was finally getting the relationship with my dad that I had always wanted, which made me content for now.

It was the end of May and already hot and dry outside. Thankfully, we were at the last festival before we headed back, and I was ready to go home and sleep in my bed.

We had just wrapped up our sound check and Dad was out finishing some interviews. I relaxed on the couch and started to close my eyes. Suddenly the door opened. Frank, the bus driver, came up, looking like the heat wasn't agreeing with him either.

"Hi, Danni, Billy told these two gentlemen they could cool down here while the air conditioning on their bus gets fixed."

Super, I thought, and stood to leave.

"You don't need to leave on our account, baby," one of them said in a sarcastic tone.

Great, I thought, *another rock star with a massive ego.* I wanted nothing to do with it. They looked me up and down, and all I could think about was why they were trying so hard to look like bad boys in their ripped jeans, tight T-shirts, and cocky attitudes.

"Hi, I am Collin, and this is Rick," the other one said, holding his hand out to me. I ignored it and just stood there, staring at his face.

Wow, Collin was holy hot hot hot. He was a head taller than me, very broad shouldered, with the body of a man that must work out often. With the latest short spiky haircut, his dark brown hair made his blue eyes stand out. I realized I was staring at his pouty lips and strong jaw line when I forced myself to look at the other one. Rick was not as good looking. Shorter and not very athletic, he smiled at me; "creepy" came to mind quickly.

"I have to go," I stated, feeling a little panicked being alone with them.

"Aw, baby, don't leave. We're enjoying the view," Creepy Rick said.

I wanted to get as far away from them as possible.

After I had stormed off the bus without a word, I was halfway to the media tent when I realized I had left my phone on the bus. I needed to go back and get it. Maybe Frank will get it for me, I thought.

No such luck, he was asleep in the driver's seat as I approached our bus. *These spoiled little rock stars are not going to get the best of me.* I walked back on the bus defiantly.

"You come back to strip for us, baby?" the creepy one asked.

I rolled my eyes, grabbing my phone off the couch before walking out. Who needs people like that? My phone went off, and it was the stage manager texting that I was up for the last run-through. Immersing my mind in work seemed to be exactly what I needed to forget the two idiots on the bus.

The run-through went well as I was putting Dad's guitars back the way he had always liked them arranged. Walking off the stage, I noticed that the two idiots from the bus were standing on the bridge watching me. I thought it would be safer to go back to the bus and hide.

The sun was setting, and Dad was talking about the interviews and how they always seem to ask the same questions and maybe he was starting to get too old for this business. I laughed, knowing retirement was something he could never do.

The first band started as the lights came up and Dad said he was going to get ready. I went to make sure everything was ready for him.

When I rounded the corner by the stage, I was overwhelmed by that sweet smell and had to stop for a minute. Staying out of the drug scene was hard since it was everywhere on the road. The thought of turning everything off for a little bit seemed pretty appealing at that moment. So far, I had been able to keep my head down and stay away from it, but this time, everything in my body screamed for the drug. I stood there for a little bit just enjoying the smell, contemplating what to do next.

Loud arguing answered my question for me. It was Collin, and he seemed to have his hands full with a fired-up bottle-blond. Something about a "wandering eye."

Hours later, after forcing myself to behave and watch the show, I figured I had better get back to the bus. Dad always wanted to go as soon as they were done, and he knew I was ready to head back home. I had been away for two months now, and I think we were both ready for a little downtime.

I knew he was worried about me going home and falling back into the old pattern I had started in the last six months. I had been text messaging James off and on the whole time. He constantly told me to come home, saying he would take care of me. He didn't bring up the night in the cabin and my famous meltdown. It was one of those subjects I couldn't bring myself to talk about, and yet it was always on the tip of my tongue. Honestly, I was nervous to face James. I didn't know exactly how I felt about him. He was sweet, charming, and good looking. But, for some reason, I was just unable to get past the whole "feelings" thing. I wasn't ready to have a relationship. Being gone for two months had put that into perspective for me.

I knocked on the bus door after discovering it was locked. Frank let me in, smiling. Walking on the bus, I saw my dad talking to the two idiots from earlier. I wanted to turn around and run, but it was too late. My dad started introducing me to them.

"Baby girl, let me introduce you to Collin and Rick. They are in the band Dark Pieces. Boys, this is my daughter, Danni."

REALLY?!! Collin Tabert was the lead singer and Rick was the bass player from none other than one of my favorite bands. Well, now *that* was ruined for me. Mike and I had seen them in concert four different times. They put on a great show. Collin had long hair until he recently cut it off and perhaps that is why I had not recognized him.

My dad introduced me as his daughter, and the look on their faces was priceless. I played along, pretending I hadn't met them earlier and just let it be. Funny, with my dad around, they were complete gentlemen. I tried to pull my hand away from Collin's handshake, but he kept it and said, "I heard you earlier during run-through, and I am impressed. You obviously know your way around a guitar."

Yanking my hand back, I said, "Thanks. It was nice to meet the both of you."

"Baby girl, let us finish up some business and we will head home."

I nodded at Dad, went to the back of the bus, and shut the door. My heart was hammering in my chest, and my hands were all sweaty. God, Collin was so damn sexy and those eyes, *WOW!*

About an hour later, the lights went down, and the bus started moving finally. Dad came to the back and thanked me for being polite to Collin and Rick, even though Frank had already informed him how they had treated me. He said they had approached him about working together on a couple of projects, and he was interested. Also, after I excused myself, Collin had questioned him about me. He thought they seemed a little scared of me. He had told me, ever since I was young, people were scared of me. For some reason, I was often told I was a very intimidating person. I never understood why people thought that, and still don't. Mike had tried to explain my behavior to me a few times, but I still didn't understand.

Truth-be-told, I had had a crush on Collin for the last couple years. I didn't know if it was because he was a rock star or a little bit of a bad boy. I never thought I would meet him, and now I wish I never had.

My dad told me a little bit about the work they wanted to do together and that he had invited them to his ranch in Texas.

"You're going back home?" I asked, surprising myself at the sadness in my voice.

He looked at me, a bit startled.

"I thought you needed some space."

"I just like having you around, Dad."

"I could move to South Dakota, all you would have to do is ask," he said, with a huge grin on his face.

I didn't even say the words and he knew my answer.

I wasn't home long before I realized Mark had pretty much moved in with us. I wasn't sure how I felt about that. Mike just kept saying that they weren't living together. Mark was only staying over occasionally; he assured me. I knew better. I was used to living with Mike and having him around, but Mark always seemed to be where you didn't want him. I had never owned a robe, but now I needed one. I still was unsure of what I thought of Mark: he seemed nice with good intentions, but there was something about him that I just wasn't sure about. My dad had mentioned that he thought I was a little jealous of him with all the attention he got from Mike. Maybe I did just need to give him a chance, but it was easier just to ignore him. Mike and I had gotten into an argument one night about how I treated Mark, and we both agreed that I could be nicer to him and that he could perhaps not stay at our house every night.

After two weeks of being home with them, I told Mike that they needed to stay at Mark's for a while because I was ready to kill one of them. So, Mike decided they would go to Hawaii for a romantic getaway. This was music to my ears. I assured him that I could take care of the bar and that it was a very good idea for them to go. I even volunteered to drive them to the airport.

Sitting in the office one day working with Jackie, after I apologized to her for my past behavior I asked if she had heard anything new about the assault. She doubted if the cops would ever figure anything out and I knew she was right. By now, I thought it was just a mystery to them; it had been months since I had heard from any of them. Besides, it was easier not thinking about it. Whenever they were around asking questions, I always learned some painful detail I was unaware of, which would trigger me to make a wrong decision and end up doing something I shouldn't.

Jackie asked, "Have you talked to James lately?"

"We text each other occasionally, but we haven't seen each other since I left with my dad."

"Oh, have you heard what he's up to now?"

I shook my head, and she explained in detail that Amber's boyfriend, Ron, had been put in jail for assault for sixty days. *Well, that makes sense,* I thought. When James had dropped me off after my meltdown, he kept saying he had something to do, and now I realized it had been Amber. The way James had talked about her, I knew he liked her more than friends. It didn't bother me considering we were just friends. Jackie went on to inform me that Ron was getting out of jail the following week. Amber would be right back at his side because she loved everything he supplied her with.

"What about James?" I asked.

"You will probably hear from him again. Are you aware that James is in love with both Amber and you?"

I laughed at her and said, "We are just friends."

"Only because he didn't want to push you into something you're not ready for."

"No, Jackie, it's not that way between us. You've got it all wrong."

The last night in the cabin popped into my head, how he kissed me and I liked it. That is until it started becoming more than kissing.

She brought me back to earth asking, "You realize how much James and Mike hate each other right?"

Mike had a way of stepping in to try and protect me, and James was something he thought was bad for me.

"James was a friend when I needed someone to talk to, plus he is easy to be around and not feel judged."

She explained Mike's jealousy. How he was trying to be that person for me and I just pushed him away. How much it had hurt him. I knew I was horrible to him after the assault. They had talked about it, and she mentioned that he had even cried because he didn't know how to help me. Mike was jealous of James, also trying to protect me from him at the same time. He had known exactly why I liked to be with James, and that I was messed up in the drug scene. Mike had even reached out to my dad for help and was told that I would come around, but I needed to do it on my terms. I realized then that my father did know me better than I thought. We talked more about the bar, all the gossip I had missed, and everything else in between.

We finished all the work just in time for the crowd to start rolling in. I stood behind the bar and realized how much I missed it at times. It was fun to serve drinks and watch people change after getting a little alcohol in them. The night flew by and soon it was closing time. I thought about the last time I closed up, instantly getting the chills. I decided it wasn't going to get to me this time. Jackie seemed more anxious to make sure I got out safely than anything else. I assured her I was fine and went home to a nice quiet house for a change.

I was trying to get my dad off the phone so I could head to the airport to pick up the love birds, but he just kept talking. He wanted me to look at homes with a realtor for him. With all these demands he had, I didn't know if we could find anything for him. I agreed that tomorrow I would make Mike go with me and look. He told me that he was going to make it to the street dance to see me back on stage with the band and that he just needed to clear up some work stuff.

Finally, heading to the airport, a thunderstorm was raging, and it made seeing the road difficult. Somehow I made it to the airport just in time to watch their plane land. Mike and Mark got off the plane, both very tan and seemingly more in love than ever.

All the way home they talked about the trip and how great it had been to get away and lounge on the beach all day. I had been to Hawaii a couple of times, and I never found it that great, but I had never been there in love either.

I cringed, hearing the radio play my former favorite band, Dark Pieces.

Mike laughed, asking how much I liked them now. I thought about that day on the bus with the two idiots, thankful they were easy to get out of my head. I ignored his joke.

"By the way, Mike, tomorrow you're going with me to look at houses for Dad."

"Can Mark come?"

Out of the backseat, Mark replied, "I have stuff I need to do tomorrow, so you two go without me."

He winked at me in the rearview mirror. I shot a smile back to him, thinking that maybe he finally understood I needed Mike's time, as well.

We got home, and they started to unpack but were talking more about the trip and everything they had done. Mark had somehow managed to get Mike in the ocean even though it had been something he had been afraid of his whole life. Of course, they had plenty of pictures and little mementos they brought back with them.

Lying in bed that night, I thought about texting James, wondering if he was with Amber. I could hear Jackie's words in my head about how James was in love with both of us. I started to think about him that way, wondering if I did have feelings for him. I could not come up with an answer.

CHAPTER 6

DEFECTIVE

A week later, Mike and I finally went house hunting for Dad. When we walked into the ninth place, I realized Mike knew my father's taste better than I did.

It was an old two-story country school in the middle of no-where, nestled in among lots of trees. The house needed a lot of renovation to be even livable, having been abandoned for the last five years. You could tell that people had used it as a party house at some point with graffiti on the walls and holes in the floor. There was a total of four buildings that went with it. In what was once the main schoolhouse, there were twenty rooms including a full-size gym with a stage. It was awesome, to say the least. As we stepped from room to room, I started talking with-out thinking about it, planning what each space could be and all the things that could be done. I stopped, realizing Mike was staring at me with his mouth open.

"What?" I asked, not knowing if I had said something wrong.

"You like it more for yourself than for your dad," he accused, smiling at me.

He was right: I did like it a lot.

"What do you think of me buying a home and us not living together?" I blurted out.

"Danni, we can't live together forever. Besides, my hot boyfriend annoys you," he said, laughing.

I had put in an offer before we left. The place was a steal, as the county still had ownership and just wanted to get rid of it. The look on the realtor's face was priceless; he looked as though he had just won the lottery. Now I just had to wait to see if they took the offer.

We got back into town just in time for lunch, so we headed to the diner. While we ate, we talked more about me moving out and making way for Mark. I could tell it was something the two of them had discussed before. Mike confirmed my suspicions by saying he was scared to talk to me about it because we had always lived together and it would be weird for us to live apart.

Finally, it was the night of the street dance, and the weather could not have been better.

The house band was performing for the first time in almost ten months. Rehearsals were tough since we'd added new songs and new members. My ten-month absence was noticeable. We worked hard for the last couple weeks getting our sound just right and, so far, I liked it more than our previous lineup. Kendrick, our lead singer, had kept me up-to-date on our band. He was our local attorney and town playboy. Even though Kendrick was ten years older than me, I found him magnificent looking. Unfortunately, mix that with his heavy flirting and he could gain the attention of any willing woman. He and I were the only two original members left in the band.

In the past, I had put a lot of effort into my appearance when we played, but now I didn't give a damn. I threw on a pair of faded jeans, a bar shirt, and sneakers. A baseball cap with my wild, dark brown hair tucked in the back rounded out the look. Mike had noticed how much I wore hats lately and, surprisingly, said that he liked the look. He may have liked it, but all I cared about was the shadows it afforded me. I just didn't want people to look at me now that I was that woman they whispered about, 'the one who was raped.'

After going through the last sound check, the gates opened, and it quickly got crowded and loud. Lots of people were glad we were playing again. Backstage, I quickly shut people down when they tried to console me or give me some encouragement. I was not about to talk to anyone about what happened. Why couldn't they just let it go?

Standing behind a speaker, I saw my dad sitting in the sound tent with his guests. I was still mad that he had brought those two idiots along, as well as the other two from their band. I avoided Collin and his goons the whole day since they had arrived. The funny thing was, nobody seemed to realize who they were. All of them were able to blend in without being noticed. Mike was excited to meet them but was too busy getting the bar and staff ready for the street dance.

Finally, it was time. I was a little nervous and excited. I nodded toward Kendrick as he started talking to the crowd, walked out onto the stage, and just went for it. The first song we played had heavy guitar riffs, lots of hooks and was a bar favorite. The looks on Collin and Rick's faces were of total shock as I played and sang backup. My father smiled the whole time, giving me his "I am proud of you" look. I forgot about them and concentrated on the music, letting myself simply get lost in it.

After an hour of playing full-speed, it was time for a break, and I needed it. As I jumped down, Mike was standing there with a beer for me, saying we sounded great. He had been walking around with the camcorder so we could post some footage on the website tomorrow. He made his way around the crowd, and I headed in the direction of my dad.

"You guys were amazing. I think you sound better than ever!" he said, putting his arms around me.

"Well, I did learn from the best!" I said as I grinned. He laughed and pulled me closer to his side, gestured toward the idiots.

"You remember Collin and Rick. This is Daniel and Jake, the other members of their band."

"It's good to see you again," I said with just enough sarcasm laced in my tone.

Dad immediately shot me a look. Mike walked up, and Dad introduced him as well.

"It's very cool to meet you guys. We are big fans and have seen you live four times!" Mike excitedly said, sounding like a teenage fan meeting the latest Pop artist. I didn't know if I should laugh or feel embarrassed for him.

Collin smiled devilishly at me and said, "You *do* like us. I thought so."

I rolled my eyes at him and called Mike a dumbass in Spanish. That was one of the benefits of Rosa raising us: we learned Spanish together. It came in handy several times when we needed to have a private conversation in a group of people.

In true Mike style, he said, "Él es caliente." He is hot, as he pointed at Collin while looking at me. I walked away to the beer tent, and I knew Mike was laughing at me.

I avoided them until it was time to get back on stage.

During the second set, we played lots of southern rock, which was my personal favorite. I looked at the playlist to see the next song and instantly wanted to skip it, but I knew we couldn't, it was very popular right now. It was Dark Pieces' new song and the thought of Collin watching me play it made me very uncomfortable. To make matters worse, I was taking lead vocals because Kendrick mentioned I "sang angry" better than he did. I wanted to throw up as I felt sweat all over my body. To sing their song to them was something I never thought I would do. Taking a deep breath, I chanted to myself, "I do this with my dad's music all the time: I can do this. I can do this!"

As soon as we started playing, I watched their reaction and realized I had both Collin and Rick's undivided attention. It wasn't easy to sing to them as they watched, but for the first time in months, I felt like I was on fire and we nailed it. I tried not to look at them too much. Instead, I just concentrated on the crowd. They were all entirely unaware that the actual band was sitting right behind them.

Out of the corner of my eye, I saw James leaning on the gate, watching me. I found myself smiling at him. He made me feel more comfortable with myself. It was funny how he had that effect on me.

When the song ended, Jackie jumped on stage as we had rehearsed and started introducing us. She had come up with something to say about each of us, one by one. When it came time for her to say something about me, I tried to be a good sport even though I was nervous. Being on stage didn't bother me at all; in fact, I love being on stage, but having someone talk about me in front of a crowd gave me that "butterflies in the stomach" feeling. Jackie stood right next to me and put her arm around my shoulders.

"This is our boss, Danni Brisco. She is an equal-opportunity lover and one hell of a guitar player." I smiled and waved, although deep down, I wanted to kill her.

A huge roar from the crowd started as people stood up clapping and yelling. Dad was even standing and cheering for me. A wave of panic hit me as I felt so many eyes on me. Mike was instantly next to me, knowing I was crumbling. He quickly took the mic from Jackie.

"Give a big round of applause for our house band. Please look on our website to see when they will be playing again. Also, if you buy a bar shirt like the one Danni is wearing, they will sign it for you."

Keeping his arm around me, he pulled me over to the side, careful not to step on any cords. I turned to him when we stopped and buried my face in his chest while he hugged me. This was new to me. I had never felt panic on stage, but now I could hardly breathe with so many eyes on me.

"It's okay, Danni," Mike said, running his hand up and down my back. "It's your first night back; it will get more comfortable. I promise."

I looked up at him and felt myself relax. "Mike, I don't understand any of this. People have never freaked me out and now . . ."

"You are trying not to be the girl that was assaulted, aren't you?" he asked, placing his hands on my cheeks, not letting me hide my face from him. "Honey, I am sorry to say this, but *you are that girl.*"

Tears slid down my cheeks as he continued. "You have to deal with it, so this doesn't bother you. You used to be so alive on stage and tonight you haven't moved more than a foot from your mic. You used to show off and fire up the crowd and now, well . . . You look terrified. Please, Danni, I will go with you to talk to someone. You're self-destructing the way you are trying to handle it. Let me help you."

I felt sick hearing all of that out loud. The word "assault" pierced my heart the way the knife had pierced my skin repeatedly that night. Anger quickly consumed me, and I pushed Mike away. He held his hands up in surrender. I walked back out on stage doing what I do best: just burying all that bullshit. Talk to someone? *Well, fuck that.* I can deal with it, with James' help, my way.

An hour later we wrapped up our set. It was a good show after ten long and miserable months of not playing. I knew Mike was right when we ended our set, and I saw that I hadn't moved from my mark on the stage.

Kendrick encouraged me to go inside the bar to enjoy some air conditioning and have a drink with him. I knew it wouldn't be long before Dad and his new friends found us.

Inside the bar we did our traditional shot of after-show whiskey, sitting at our usual booth, and talking about the performance. I confessed to Kendrick that the band Dark Pieces was here and that they had indeed heard our cover of their song. I don't think he believed me until they walked up to us and asked if they could join us at our table. Then introductions began as Kendrick instantly pounced on Collin.

"I couldn't be prouder of you," Dad said, and it felt more like parental encouragement than a compliment as he hugged me.

Collin was standing behind him now and said, "I need a hug, or I am going to sue you for covering our song without permission."

I half hugged him, too. Feeling his hot breath on my neck and his arms pulling me close against him, he whispered in my ear, "You are wickedly talented and very cute."

I moved away from him as panic was threatening to overtake me. The feeling of his hands on me ignited the emotions that I had been trying to bury all night. I wasn't willing to feel them yet. Or possibly ever again. I moved away from him, choosing to ignore him altogether. He probably thought I was a bitch. I was getting good at playing that role.

The other members gave their opinions, and it went over really well. I sat down again, and Collin nudged me to move over so he could sit beside me. Dad and Rick went to get pitchers of beer for the ever-growing crowd at our table. I was practically sitting on Collin's lap when I decided I would rather stand than be that close to him.

While he stood up to let me out, he asked, "Is it something I said?" I just shook my head.

He gave me a sly grin and said, "Then I am not going to let you out. I want to get to know you a little more."

"Maybe you should let her out now," Kendrick replied, looking directly at him.

Collin moved aside and held his hands up. I don't think my dad had told him about my issues, and I was okay with that.

Mike walked up at that moment complimenting us on how great we had played. Apparently, I had a look on my face that said everything to him as he leaned into me and quietly asked, "You okay?"

Everyone was staring at me, and I was instantly pissed that *once again* I was put in that position.

"I am completely fricking perfect," I mumbled before I walked off.

I wanted to find James and get the hell out of there. I wondered if I was going to fall back into the same pattern if I found him. I walked outside and saw him still leaning up against the fence, talking to someone. He gave me his complete attention as I moved to his side.

"Are you okay, beautiful?" he asked, as he put his arm around me. I nodded and said I was fine.

We saw Mike peek his head through the door, and I instantly ducked behind James' shoulder. Grabbing my hand, he led me in through the back door of the bar, right to the middle of a packed dance floor. The lights were low, and the DJ had the music pumping loud.

As he pulled me against him, he said, "We can hide here."

It was a slow song playing as we both hid our faces in each other's necks, blocking out the world. The way he held my waist and his breath on my skin was starting to make me feel things again. I think I answered my question from earlier regarding my feelings for him at that moment, and the answer was a screaming "YES!" I wasn't sure whether they were sexual or genuine feelings of love. James must have felt my response in the way I pulled him closer to me.

"I missed you, and it feels like you missed me, as well," he whispered. I didn't deny it.

I calmed down and relaxed, wondering if I overreacted a little to Collin. The song changed to a club mix, and we loosened our grip on each other. It never failed, James had me laughing, and all was great again. We danced to a couple more songs.

James pulled me close and said, "Your babysitter is making his way towards us, and I think I should go."

He slipped something in my back pocket and kissed me on the neck in front of Mike, winking before he made his retreat. A slower song came on, and Mike held his arms open for me to dance with him. The look on his face wasn't anger. It was worry. I walked into his arms, and we danced and said nothing for a little bit.

"Danni, I am not going to tell how to live your life, but if you ran to James because you were uncomfortable with how Collin made you feel, then that wasn't fair to James. I think he cares about you, and it would be unfair to lead him on if you don't feel the same about him."

I was more confused now than ever about how I felt toward anyone, including myself.

CHAPTER 7
NICE HAIR

The next morning, I thought it would be best to let all the drama from the street dance die down. So, Mike and I took the opportunity to hide in the basement and watch movies: we had no intentions of leaving the comfort of home. I didn't even shower, just got up and found my favorite pair of sweats along with an old football shirt. Mike followed suit and donned the same thing. Owning the bar never allowed us time to stay home and watch movies like this, and it was much needed, to say the least.

As we started the third movie, I glanced at my phone and saw a few text messages from a number I didn't recognize. I didn't even bother to read them because I figured it was a wrong number.

Grabbing a blanket, I settled into my little nest on our red sectional couch. Ten minutes into the movie, I started getting sleepy. Looking at the clock, I saw that it was only eight p.m., but it felt more like it should be two or three in the morning. Closing my eyes for a little bit felt good, as the movie was more Mike's taste than mine. I fell asleep quickly.

I woke up to the sounds of people talking around me. I lay there a little bit longer with my eyes closed, hearing Mike tell someone that I fell asleep a little bit ago. I recognized who it was and silently prayed he wasn't staying long. It was Collin and Daniel, and I wondered how they knew where we lived and why they were here.

Hoping to hide from them, I pulled my blanket over my head and curled into a small ball. Mike realized I was awake and said, "You're missing a great movie, Danni. And by the way, we have company."

My blanket was being slowly pulled away, so it no longer hid my face. I knew I looked like a train wreck as I saw Collin sitting by my feet.

"What are you guys doing here?" I asked with a little bit of condescension in my tone.

Collin was quick to answer, "If you had answered your text messages, you would know why."

"Oh, that was *you* texting me? How did you get my number?"

Giving me a huge grin, Collin replied, "Your dad gave it to me. I think, unlike his baby girl, *he* likes me."

"Remind me to thank Dad," I said, eyeing Mike, who had a huge smile on his face.

Collin said, "I've been trying to get a hold of you guys to see if you wanted to go to a movie or something because we're bored."

Mike said, "I saw your phone light up when you were asleep, so I answered it and told them to come over."

I am going to get him back for this later, I told myself. Of course, Collin's bandmate Daniel chimed in with a goofy grin on his face and said, "Nice hair."

They all laughed, except me. Mike shifted the conversation by asking what everyone was in the mood to watch. He and Daniel went to the computer to look up the options. That left just Collin and me sitting on the couch, it felt incredibly awkward. Looking into his dark blue eyes, I felt butterflies in my stomach. Just the way his mouth curved up into a sexy smile made my skin tingle. No one had made me feel that way in a long time. I chalked it up to the fact that I was just embarrassed from the other night.

Collin looked at me more seriously and quietly said, "I called to apologize to you. I didn't mean to make you feel uncomfortable, and I'm very sorry."

"Don't worry about it. Lately, everyone's been telling me I have issues, so it was probably just me," I said, frustrated as I sat up straighter.

"Is everything okay?" he asked, looking concerned.

"It is way too early to tell," I said, feeling a little bit of panic that yet another person wanted to hear my sad story.

"I'm a really good listener if you need someone to talk to," he said as he reached out and touched my hand.

"Thank you, but talking just makes it worse," I quickly pulled my hand away from his.

Changing the direction of the conversation, we made small talk.

"I am impressed with your house band. You are quite good. Your dad did a good job teaching you to play."

"Thanks. It's our thing. You're pretty good yourself. Congrats on the Music Up and Coming Award nomination," I said as a huge smile grew across his face.

"Thank you. I hope to catch up with your award count."

Now I was the one smiling and said, "Well, you only need three to catch up." I could feel my face turning red. I didn't talk about my awards for writing and producing. It wasn't why I did it. It was simply for the music.

"Are you coming to the awards show with your dad in a couple of weeks?" he asked shyly.

I looked at my hands twisting in my lap and quietly answered, "No. People aren't my thing lately."

"I noticed that at the street dance." I looked up at him, and he continued. "I have seen videos of you performing, and you are usually very determined with your performance. The other night you looked like you wanted to hide behind the speaker."

I closed my eyes and sighed. *So, it was noticeable.*

"I can't wait to get you on stage with me," he said as I looked at him and he winked at me. I relaxed and gave him a doubtful look.

Mike and Daniel sat back down, announcing the movie as it started. I pulled my feet back to give Collin more room on the couch. He grabbed them and wrapped the blanket around them and placed them on his lap without even looking at me or saying anything. Emotionally, it felt awkward, but oddly enough, it felt comfortable in a physical way as he kept his hands on my feet.

Halfway through the movie, I found myself looking more at Collin than at the movie. *Cut it the hell out, Danni!* I mentally yelled at myself. I knew why I had a crush on him during his concerts: he was gorgeous. With his stylish dark-brown hair, his muscular body that is a foot taller than me, but the most dominant feature was his sly smile, you know that smile that could get a woman into trouble real fast. That, along with the way he moved and carried himself, made me want to look at him and never stop. I wondered if he was married and tried to see his left hand, but he had it around my feet so I couldn't tell. I figured he probably was. In the music business, it would be easy for him to find a wife.

Mike paused the movie saying it was intermission time, and that he needed to call Mark. I thought it would be a good opportunity to go to the bathroom as well and try to put myself together a little bit. As Mike and I walked upstairs together, he quietly sang, "Collin and Danni sitting in a tree, k-i-s-s-i-n-g, first comes love and then comes the baby in the baby carriage."

I couldn't help but laugh hearing his childish mocking as I tackled him on the stairs. He laughed too, trying to get away from me. We heard someone clear their throat and looked back and saw Collin and Daniel watching us as they smiled, too.

Looking in the mirror, I saw what a mess I was and wondered if I had time for a shower. Instead, I combed my hair and brushed my teeth. This was as good as it was going to get right now. I surprised myself when I realized that I was lusting after Collin. The butterflies in my stomach weren't just from nerves, deep down I think I liked him. *That can't be it. I am not ready for this yet.* Then I began to wonder who made up the time limit I had placed on myself. *I am thinking too much about this.* I inhaled a deep breath and decided just to watch the movie.

Collin was sitting in my place as I motioned for him to move. He laughed and said, "Just sit your ass down right there." He was pointing at where he had been sitting.

I heard Daniel let out a quick laugh, and I had no choice but to sit at the end of the couch. Now he would be able to watch me. I was regretting not taking a quick shower after all. Grabbing the blanket, I sat down with my back to him.

The movie was good, considering I was lost after not paying very good attention to the first half. I looked at the clock, and it was almost one in the morning.

"Well, we better go. Your dad will be pissed if we aren't at the studio first thing in the morning," Collin said as he stood up and stretched.

L. T. Varner

I walked them out while Mike stayed in the kitchen. I assumed it was so he could hear us. Daniel went outside, and Collin stopped and looked at me.

"I am sorry if I made you uncomfortable the other night. It was not my intention. Remember, I'm a good listener if you need someone to talk to."

"Thanks, but I am fine."

"What are you up to this afternoon?" he asked, taking a step closer to me.

"Just hanging out here, I guess."

"If you get bored, I wouldn't mind getting a tour of this town and then maybe we could get dinner or something."

"Yeah, okay," I stumbled over my words as he stepped forward again and I stepped back.

I wasn't sure if he was asking me on a date or simply looking for a tour guide. Then he hugged me, and I couldn't help but get a little caught up in the way he felt. His embrace was warm and strong, but it was too much for me. I moved away from him as though he were electrocuting me. He dropped his arms, not looking offended at all.

"I hope I see you later, Danni," he said before he turned and left.

I walked back toward the kitchen and knew Mike had listened to the whole thing. He was smiling and said, "I am confused. Did he ask you out or does he just want to *hang out?*" He asked as he made air quotes.

"I'm asking myself the same question, trust me."

We sat at the table and talked a little more about the evening, and I told him about the conversation I had with myself while I was in the bathroom.

"I've wondered how you felt about the whole dating thing, as well." Very bluntly he asked, "Have you and James slept together?"

"God, no!" I fired back at him with nervousness. After taking a deep breath, I calmly said, "Okay, we may have kissed a little. But I got sick before it went any further. I know it's stupid, but every time I think or feel anything sexual, I just freak out. I am such a mess."

He put his hand on my arm. "Honey, you aren't a mess! *The situation is a mess.* How do you feel about James? I mean, is he someone you *want* to love?"

"I have no idea," I grumbled, looking down at my hands as they played with the salt shaker on the kitchen counter.

He repeated what Jackie had told him about James liking both Amber and me, and then said, "Jackie said if Amber is available, she is usually his first choice."

That comment stung a little bit, but I knew he was right.

"Is Ron out of jail yet?" I asked, looking at Mike's hands as he pushed around the pepper shaker.

"Why do you want to know?" He was suddenly more serious. I shrugged my shoulders as he continued. "Jackie informed me that James will probably start coming around again when Ron is out of jail."

I headed for the stairs to go to my room feeling the pain that even James preferred someone that wasn't as defective as me.

Mike continued, and I stopped on the third stair but didn't turn around.

"Danni, I won't lie to you. I think James is nothing but trouble. And we know about the drugs he has access to that you *think* make you feel better. I can't stop you from seeing him, but I pray that you come to your senses and stay away from him before you end up in jail or dead from an overdose. We all love you very much, but Danni, please, start helping yourself and talk to someone. I can't lose my best friend."

I knew he was right about the whole situation. I kept my back to him and slowly nodded that I heard him. But still I craved the numbness James was able to give me.

"Goodnight, Mike," I said quietly before walking up the stairs to my room.

CHAPTER 8

DOOR JAMB

I put in extra time getting ready the next morning. After half an hour of looking for my favorite pair of jeans, I found them in the "donate" pile I had started last week out of boredom. Pulling them on, I looked in my closet and decided on a black button-up shirt. I usually wore my shirts unbuttoned enough so one could see my bra underneath if I even bothered to put one on. That was the only benefit of being an A-cup, I suppose. I usually chose to forgo bras altogether for comfort's sake. Now that I thought about it, maybe I *did* dress to get a little attention without even realizing it. I sat on the bed feeling slightly sick as I again heard that menacing voice in my head:

"You wanted this to happen. I am happy to give you what you want."

So far I hadn't told the investigators or anyone else the little pieces that were coming back to me about that night. The taunting voices and sudden visions in my head were what my nightmares were made of lately.

Was it true? Did I want it to happen? Was it my fault after all? I quickly threw the black shirt in the trash, feeling all my anger surfacing once again. I was instantly pissed off at myself and wanted nothing more than to make all the feelings stop. At that exact moment, I remembered that James had put something in my back pocket the night of the street dance. I had an idea of what it was and frantically started tearing my closet apart. I found the jeans I had on that night at the bottom of my laundry basket but stopped myself before going any further. Maybe I should check and see if I had the house to myself first. If Mike were home, he would freak out knowing what I was holding in my hand.

I checked the house and was alone. I found myself locking the doors and closing the blinds. It was mid-morning, and I was already considering getting high. This couldn't be a good thing. It would lead me down the same path I had been on a couple of months ago, but I started planning how to get out of my obligations that day anyway.

Whatever drugs James had given me wouldn't last long enough, and I had to get more. It had been so long since I had taken any of the painkillers from the attack, but right now, they were all I could think about.

I had to find out if Ron was out of jail yet. If he was, I was sure I could talk James into getting me more. All I had to do was text James and wait. After thirty minutes with no response to my "hi" message, I knew he was probably with Amber.

Feeling desperate, I sent Amber a text, and sure enough, she responded almost instantly.

Amber: James and I are just getting up. We could meet you later at Ron's if that works?

Not wanting anything to do with the two of them together, I threw on a red shirt with my black leather jacket. I pulled my hair up in a bun in the back of my red baseball cap. I didn't care how I looked at this point. I just needed to get numb and be alone. On the way out of the house, I grabbed the bottle of whiskey that was almost empty, using it to wash down my three painkillers. I knew I needed to stop at the bar and at least drop-off payroll so they wouldn't bug me all day about it. I could grab a bottle of whiskey while I was there, as well.

When I got to the bar, the painkillers were slowly taking effect, and I could feel myself getting more and more relaxed. Mike was there, so I put on my "happy face" and tried to act like everything was great. After giving Jackie payroll to hand out, I walked into my office. Turning my cell off, I placed it in the top drawer of my desk. I knew Mike had installed a tracking app on my phone, and I wasn't going to let him ruin what I had planned for today, the less he knew, the better. I decided to wait and grab some whiskey at the liquor store so he wouldn't see me with it. On the way out, he stopped me by the door.

"You excited to see Collin later?" he asked, a little too eager.

I had forgotten about that but decided to play along. I nodded.

"Why are you wearing the baseball cap then?" he asked, trying to reach for the hat as I pulled back from him.

"I'm just having a bad hair day," I said, reaching out to block his hand from my hat.

He laughed and said, "I don't think you could have a bad hair day if you tried. Besides, even if you did, I think you're still pretty."

The compliment at that moment meant nothing to me, but I smiled big and fake, and said, "I have some errands to run so that I can catch up with you later."

He smiled and said, "I can't wait. You do remember that Mark will be joining us for dinner, right?"

I was already out the door when I heard that and, quite frankly, didn't care. I just wanted to punish myself for what I had caused.

After leaving the bar, I headed straight to the liquor store. Grabbing the expensive bottle of whiskey, I quickly snatched up a bottle of pop to give the cashier the illusion I wasn't a drunk or something. Walking out, I found myself going numb and hazy. It was a very welcome feeling I needed to make last. I threw the pop in a nearby dumpster, then jumped into the driver's seat and opened the bottle. Taking a long chug, I instantly felt the burn down my throat and closed my eyes.

I drove by James' house out of curiosity. Amber's car was in his driveway. I thought to myself, *at least he put* my *car in the garage, maybe I had one up on her. But, why do I care?* I turned down a dirt road to get out of town before anyone saw me. Not paying much attention to the road, I found the Dark Pieces CD in my center console. Mike must have put it in there. I pushed the button to lower the window and threw out the CD, rolling my eyes at the thought of listening to Collin. I drove around for a while drinking, as the numbness began taking over, to the point where I didn't even care if Collin or James liked me. At this stage, nothing mattered, except staying numb.

The sun was setting, and I needed something more to make everything go away completely. Looking around, the scenery started becoming familiar. If I were right, around the corner I would find Ron's house. Seeing the tall fence surrounding his place, I thought to myself; *this is perfect.* It was only eight o'clock, and there were already ten cars there. Ron must be out of jail, so where was Amber's car? I found myself with absolutely no fear as I parked and walked right up to the house. Usually, we just walked in, this time, the door was locked. I rang the bell and some guy I had never seen answered the door.

"What the hell do you want?" he asked, not opening the door more than an inch.

"I want to see Ron, you little fucker," I snapped at him with all kinds of new bravery.

He laughed, "You're Danni, right?" I nodded, and he shut the door in my face.

What the hell? I thought, wondering if I should ring the bell again. The allure of more painkillers kept me standing on that porch for five more minutes until the door finally opened and the guy said, "Come in. Ron is in the backyard waiting for you."

Walking to the back, I noticed a lot of people there. I wasn't dumb. I knew what they were there for, and I bet it was the same thing I was after. I stepped out into the backyard.

Ron was standing there as though he had been waiting for me: "I'm glad to see you, Danni."

"Hey, Ron, I hope you're out of trouble," I said, keeping a little distance between the two of us.

"Have you seen James lately?" he asked, studying me carefully.

"It isn't my day to watch him."

He laughed even though I was clearly not joking.

"You talk to Amber lately?" he asked, a little more serious this time.

"Yes, she said she would meet me here, but I don't see her."

"Just wait, she'll be back, and you'll get your little James back, too."

We both seemed to be angry at them, but for two entirely different reasons.

"Why are ya here, Danni?" he asked, looking me up and down.

"You probably know why already."

"What do you want?" he asked, leaning against the wall.

"I need something to take the edge off for a while."

He motioned me to follow him, and I didn't hesitate. I trailed him into the room he usually reserved for his "friendly customers" and he shut the door behind us.

"You want what James usually gets?" he asked as he opened a cabinet.

"No, I need something stronger this time."

He smiled and said, "I thought James was holding you back."

I was so not in the mood to talk, and he was starting to catch on at that point. I looked at what he was pointing at, wondering what the hell I was doing. It was a bag of little white pills.

"Is that painkillers?" I asked. He stepped closer to me and shook his head, more annoyed by my questioning.

"Once you try it, the name won't matter, but a couple of pills go a long way, remember that. And, just for you, I will let you have it for a couple hundred."

Crap, I hadn't planned this very well, I thought, realizing I didn't have any cash on me. At the same time, Ron seemed to realize my dilemma.

"I know you are more than good for it, but I don't extend credit to many people, so don't fuck me over . . . or you could pay another way," he said, looking me up and down.

He could tell by the look on my face that I would pay him later. He opened the door and said, "One week, Danni. It is always a pleasure to see you."

I tucked the bag of whatever into my pocket and nodded as I started to walk out the door. Turning the corner, I almost walked right into James. My anger hit a new high as I saw Amber standing right behind him while they held hands. I tried to push past him as he reached out his free hand to stop me.

"I just want to talk for a minute. Please, Danni, don't do anything stupid. What did he give you?" he asked quietly as I felt Ron move closer behind me.

I yelled in front of everybody as I glared at him and Amber:

"You seem to have everything you need at the moment; so don't worry about what I do!" I shoved him away.

He just looked at me, dumbfounded, all the while keeping hold of Amber's hand. As I turned to walk out, I tripped over his foot. I fell forward, hitting my face on the door jamb before I could right myself. It took a moment to register what had happened before I felt the pain starting to throb around my eye. I continued forward and walked out.

I got into my SUV, wanting to get the hell out of there before anyone stopped me. I turned down the opposite road I came in on and took off, wheels spinning. Grabbing the bottle of whiskey from the passenger seat, I took a long drink to help calm my nerves.

After driving and drinking for a half an hour, I found a little turn-off that seemed to go nowhere, and I pulled in there. Shutting the engine off, I decided it was time to get serious and pulled the bag from my pocket. I set it on the console and looked down after feeling something run down my face. Blood dripped onto my jeans, and I realized I must have cut my forehead when I fell. *Great*, I thought, *what else could go wrong?* I remembered James standing there holding hands with Amber and quickly put the image out of my head, only for it to be replaced by the voice of my rapist saying, "You want it." It was all I could take. I snapped at that very moment, grabbed the bag and whiskey, and got out of the car.

After climbing on my hood, I took two pills and washed it down with the whiskey. I knew I had done it right within ten minutes, as the calming feeling began spreading throughout my body. I felt a new level of numbness as I fell back against the windshield.

I sat there looking at the stars and resolved this was the perfect way to go. Just looking at the stars and feeling numb, I decided it couldn't get any better than this. It became hard to pinpoint any one thought as I drifted along in numbness. With the bottle of whiskey between my legs and the pills on the hood, I decided it was a perfect evening. It was unbelievable how calm I felt. Nobody around to yell at me for the decisions I was making or not making. I knew at some point I would have to return to reality, but for now, being numb from head to toe, sitting on the hood of my SUV in the middle of nowhere, and staring at the stars. It seemed like the best idea I had ever had.

I jerked awake feeling myself falling. I landed with a thud on the cold ground and was instantly fully awake. *Damn, that hurt,* I moaned, fully feeling that the numbness had worn off. The sun was already overhead, and I felt the heat radiating on me. I pulled myself up and climbed into the driver's seat. I hid my leftover drugs in a locked compartment in the center console so no one would find it, then I threw out the whiskey bottle and re-alized I had consumed the whole bottle in a little less than a day. It probably wasn't a good idea, but I didn't care.

I pulled the rearview mirror down so I could see how bad I looked and if I could try to make myself presentable. I gasped at my reflection, realizing I was in worse shape than I thought. I had a nasty black eye that was very swollen, along with a gash above my eyebrow that probably needed stitches, it was still bleeding a little bit. I sat there deciding if a bandage would be enough to stop the bleeding, basically trying to figure a way out of going to the hospital. It became apparent that I had to go and get stitched up as the gash oozed more.

I drove to town trying to come up with a plausible lie for what happened. I decided to go with the "I don't know" approach and leave it at that. I knew Mark would be off work by now, so I wouldn't have to see him either. I circled the hospital parking lot just to make sure his car wasn't there before I parked.

I knew I had to quit doing crap like this and start owning my problems, but I also knew it was out of my reach right now. Walking into the emergency room, I kept my baseball cap pulled low and put my sunglasses on, hoping I could lay low and not be noticed.

The receptionist gave me a steely nod before she asked the obvious question: "What do you need to be seen for today?"

"I need a couple of stitches in my forehead, I think." I glared right back at her under my sunglasses. I couldn't help it; I am a bitch when I'm uncomfortable. Mike and Dad had told me that millions of times.

She took my information without another snippy comment and told me to have a seat and wait to be called. There were plenty of people who looked in far worse shape than me, so I sat down among them and waited an hour before my name was called.

"Good thing I didn't bleed to death," I snapped in a very sarcastic tone as I walked past a nurse holding the door open.

The nurse smiled and pointed down the hall to a room labeled, *Procedure Room.* I went into the very sterile white room before the strong odor hit my nose and I coughed.

"Sit on the bed and take off your hat and sunglasses, then lie back so I can have a look," she said, a little too cheerfully.

I placed my stuff down and lay back on the exam table.

"WOW, what happened to you?"

I casually responded, "I'm not exactly sure."

I knew she could hear the sarcasm in my voice. She looked at my forehead before mentioning it would take around six stitches. She then started cleaning out the cut.

The doctor walked in the room twenty minutes later. If you could call him a doctor. He looked like a teenager. I groaned, *this could be interesting.* He looked at my eye and the cut, and before he asked what happened, I gave him the same answer I had given the nurse. She was catching on now and knew I wasn't going to tell them anything.

The doctor starting numbing around the cut with tiny pokes of the needle he held in his latex-covered hands. The effects of last night had not entirely worn off. I was still relaxed and not in pain. He let it set for a couple of minutes before he put seven stitches in and directed me to come back in ten days to have them removed.

"You are going to be uncomfortable for a couple of days. Do you need something for the pain?" he asked, pulling off his gloves.

"That would be great," I said, a little too quickly. "—you know, something to help with the pain."

I took the script he held out and hastily left. The look on his face was skepticism. I was sure they both knew *I* was an idiot who had a drug problem.

As I sat in the pharmacy parking lot waiting for the medicine, I downed a bottle of water, knowing I had probably just made it to the top of Mike's hit list. I wondered how bad he was probably freaking out at that moment.

"Oh, crap," I said, as I slid down in my seat seeing Mark pull into the parking lot. He parked a few cars down and then casually walked inside, still in his work clothes. I wondered how I was going to pull this off. I decided to go to the drive-thru and see if it was ready yet so I could escape.

Pulling up to the window, the clerk smiled and thankfully said it was ready. I slid my debit card in the drawer for her and hoped she would hurry. *Oh, no, that would be too helpful.* I was trying to lean back in my seat after I saw Mark standing at the counter paying for something.

"Thanks, Danni. Have a good day," the flirty clerk said, sliding the drawer back to me.

Mark looked right at me with a glare. Then it turned into a game of, "how do I get out of here without him catching me?" I saw him grab his stuff and start running to the front of the store. I snatched up my crap and took off as fast as I could. I was out of the parking lot before Mark had even made it to his car.

A couple of blocks down the road, I turned into a parking garage. I found a spot and sat there for a good half an hour. I had time to kill, so I knew it was the right time to try out those painkillers.

CHAPTER 9

YOUR FACE

After a long nap and a hot shower, it was dark when I left the house. I was cutting it close as our band was playing in fifteen minutes. Since I was late, I hoped I could avoid talking to as many people as possible. I decided to park a couple of blocks away so it would be easier to leave later.

Having a couple of extra minutes, I turned my phone back on. It had been lying on the kitchen counter when I got home, so I knew Mike had found it hidden in my desk. I scrolled through my dozens of missed text messages: some from Mike stating he was worried about me, but he wasn't mad. Some from my dad, someone had apparently asked if he knew where I was. A few from Collin asking if I was avoiding him. I nodded yes, as though he could see me. The last was from James, he was apologizing, and quite frankly, I didn't care. The only real message I got was from my realtor. The offer I had made on the old school had been accepted. *Finally,* I can live alone.

I knew I should get inside and decided to go in through the back door. I saw Mike's truck and, next to his, my dad's. *Great. What the hell was I thinking wanting him to move here anyway?* I pulled my hat down and put my sunglasses on, walking straight to my office.

Kendrick noticed and came in. "Hurry up, Danni. People are waiting for us," he stated, looking annoyed before he walked back out.

I trailed behind him, heading to the stage for a quick sound check. I wasn't noticed as I put in my inner-ear monitors and hopped on stage just in time for Kendrick to announce us.

"The boss is finally here. Now we can start this party."

Thanks, Kendrick, I thought to myself. I looked down at the playlist taped to the floor. The first song in, I sang backup vocals as I played my guitar. I looked out at the crowd and saw my dad, Collin, and the other band members sitting at the big booth in the corner. I could tell by the look on Dad's face; I was in a little hot water with him. I noticed Mike behind the bar working diligently and hoped no one thought much about not seeing me yesterday. *Could I be that lucky?*

It was close to the end of the first set when the next song to come up was Collin's. I felt big-time relief that I wasn't doing vocals. Before we started the song, Kendrick went through the band introductions and held up shots to toast the audience. The crowd roared back before everyone downed them. The whiskey helped take the edge off for now.

At the end of the set, I needed a break. Handing my guitar to the latest sound crew newbie, I decided to walk out to my SUV so I could take a little something to help me get through the night. As soon as I hopped off stage, my dad was standing there waiting.

"Where were you yesterday, baby girl, and what happened to your face?"

"I am a big girl, Dad. You don't need to worry about me," I said, as he continued blocking my path.

He could always tell by my tone when I wasn't messing around. He decided not to question me any further and then stepped forward and kissed me on the cheek.

"You can always talk to me, baby girl. No judgments." He turned around and walked back to his table.

I tried to make my way to the front door, but people kept stopping me wanting to chat. I heard Mike call my name as he motioned for me to come to the bar. I was nervous about what he was going to say. I was a little more hesitant when I saw Collin standing up at the bar ordering drinks.

I walked behind the bar trying to put on a brave face. He was putting a couple of drinks in front of Collin as I approached him.

"What do you need?" I practically yelled so we could hear each other.

He must have noticed my face just as I saw the anger in his eyes.

"Where were you yesterday?" He gripped my upper arm and moved me under the lights before he yanked off my sunglasses and examined me.

I started pulling away from him when he yelled in front of everyone at the bar, "Just walk away, Danni, because that is the only thing you are good at these days."

I yelled right back, "Perhaps you should mind your own fucking business."

Tempers escalated quickly between us, and I shoved him as he tried to take my hat, too. Chuck was suddenly between us, telling us to relax and just get back to work.

"Go to hell," we both yelled at each other in unison.

Someone was pulling me backward, and all I wanted to do was hit Mike for once. He was just as mad at me, giving me a nasty glare.

"Let go of me!" I yelled, not realizing that two people had a hold of me.

I turned and found Collin and Daniel pulling me back. I screamed a few choice words before I finally regained my composure and walked out the front door. The two of them followed me.

"What are you looking at?!" I yelled at Collin as he kept up with me.

"Nothing I haven't seen before."

I starting walking toward my car when Collin asked, "Where are you going?"

"You're nosey as hell, aren't you?" I snapped back at him.

Daniel chimed in with a smirk on his face asking, "Are you going to get anything *special* out of your car?"

I stopped dead in my tracks and looked at both of them.

"We already found what you're looking for. It's not there anymore," Daniel said in a mocking voice.

"What are you talking about?" I asked, glaring at him.

Collin said, "We've already taken your stash. Perhaps you don't need it as much as you think you do."

"How dare you get into my fucking car?" I yelled.

Daniel stopped me and said, "Technically, we had a key, so we could, and we did."

I instantly knew who gave them the key, Mike. At this point, there wasn't a lot I could do, and I knew it. I played calm and took a deep breath, so I didn't kill both of them.

"If you two idiots will excuse me, I'm going back inside to play the second set unless you have an objection to that."

They both shook their heads. We walked back inside, and Collin moved his hand to the small of my back. I shrugged him off and walked back toward the stage, stopping a waitress on the way to ask for some whiskey.

We played out the last set of the night and everyone, including myself, calmed down. I think the whiskey had something to do with that.

I was putting my guitar away and remembered that I had put a painkiller in my pocket before I left the house. I needed it more than ever as I dug it out and took it with a shot of whiskey. The stage was dark, and I didn't realize someone was behind me until after I swallowed it. *Well, that can't be good.* I turned around, and it was Mike, not looking quite so mad. Mike put his hands up in a surrender position.

"I just want to apologize for earlier and make sure you're okay."

I still had on my sunglasses and said, "I'm sorry, too. Yesterday was just a bad day, and I wanted to be alone."

"Danni, maybe if you would tell me that, I wouldn't have been so worried about you."

"Don't worry about me, Mike. The damage is already done."

"I *do* worry about you. I love you and couldn't live without you," he said as he put his hands on my shoulders, looking at me with pity on his face.

I knew he had good intentions and said, "right now I don't want to talk about any of it."

"Okay, I won't push the issue," he said as he pulled me into his arms for a hug. I couldn't help but hug him back.

"Why did Collin and Daniel go through my car?" I asked with my face buried in his chest.

"Because we care about your well-being and I know you. I wasn't surprised by what they found. I know you hurt, Danni, but it would hurt less if you just talked to me."

I didn't have a response for him and he seemed satisfied with the conversation before he motioned that he needed to get back to the bar.

Over his shoulder, he said, "You need to apologize to Mark."

Ugh, he was the last of my worries. The waitress appeared one more time with some more whiskey. I quickly downed two of them before deciding it was time to get the hell out of there.

Walking toward my SUV, my heart started to hammer in my chest when I saw someone was leaning against it waiting for me. I took a deep breath and calmed down. I had a feeling I knew who it was as I approached. I looked across the street and saw James' old truck.

"What do you want, James?" I asked, stopping in front of him.

"Look, I'm sorry for what happened last night. I didn't think you cared if I was with Amber or not," he said, folding his arms over his chest. "How is your eye?"

"I told you, I am not your business."

"Ok, Danni, I deserve that, but you know I care about you more than just a friend."

"Where is your girlfriend?" I asked sarcastically.

"I don't have one," he snapped back this time.

"Sure didn't look that way last night!"

He calmly asked, "Danni are you okay? How is your eye?"

I took off my sunglasses, slowly showing him as he looked more upset. He put his hand on my cheek and stepped closer to me.

"I'm sorry, and I feel horrible about the way things turned out last night. I miss you. Can we start over please?"

I melted into him feeling his warmth and caring. He leaned close to my face as his arms went around my waist before he whispered in my ear, "You okay?"

"I am working on it," I quietly replied as I put my arms around his neck.

"You want to go back to my place?" he asked as he placed soft kisses along my jaw.

I put my hand on his chest and explained that my babysitters are everywhere right now, and perhaps I should just lay low. He agreed with a sigh and a nod. He pulled me closer against him, and I didn't object. I wasn't sure if it was the warmth of him or the way he smelled—I couldn't help myself. I kissed him, and he kissed me back, eagerly. After a minute or so he pulled away from me, giving me a couple of smaller kisses before he turned and walked toward his truck, smiling at me as he left. I found myself unsure what to do as I climbed into my SUV.

I sat there for a couple of minutes thinking about the kiss before coming back to reality. Did Collin and Daniel really take my stash? I unlocked the console and, sure enough, there was nothing there but a note from the two idiots.

It is bad for you.

I could hear Daniel's sarcasm implied in the note. I just decided that I wasn't going to fight anymore tonight and headed home.

CHAPTER 10

WE ALL FALL DOWN

I spent the next two days on my couch sick as hell. At first, I thought it was the effects of my extracurricular activities, but it was now the second evening of feeling horrible, and I decided I probably had the flu. I was bored as I lay on the couch flipping through channel after channel for hours.

James had been true to his word and had called a couple of times wanting me to come over. Dad called every couple hours with a few other friends texting and calling in between, hoping I felt better soon. Before he left for work, Mike had set up a nice camp for me on the couch in the basement with everything I could need. He had been home a couple of times to check on me so far. I didn't know if this was so he could see if I was still alive or to make sure I hadn't taken off again, and I couldn't blame him for that at all. I totally appreciated that, until he let my dad know what they found in my SUV, which was not at all appreciated.

I hadn't taken any more painkillers either, considering I was throwing everything up at this point. I was completely aware of how horrible I felt inside and out. *Was I being punished or something?*

I felt worse when I would move around, so I lay there feeling sorry for myself and hoping it would end soon.

My phone beeped, but I didn't answer because it seemed like a lot of work at the time. A couple of minutes later I managed to look to see who it was: Collin *again*. After two days of me ignoring him, he still hadn't given up. I knew if I didn't answer soon he would show up and I didn't want that right now, so I answered the latest call and gave up the fight.

"What do you want?" I moaned, trying to move as little as possible.

"I want you to open your door, for starters," he said, sounding too cheerful.

"Collin, I feel awful, and the door is *sooo* far away!" I whined, closing my eyes, feeling lightheaded.

"I'm here to take care of you, so just tell me the code to the garage door then."

"You should go away, so you don't get sick."

"That's a chance I am willing to take. Now, what's the code?"

I knew he wasn't going away, so I told him the code. I didn't even have the energy to think about how I looked when I heard him call my name from upstairs. *Am I hearing things or did I just hear my microwave door close? Maybe I am sicker than I thought.* I wondered what the hell he was doing after ten minutes. Finally, he came downstairs holding a tray of food and supplies. He set the tray in front of me, and the smell instantly made my stomach start turning, so I closed my eyes. I took a deep breath, not wanting to throw up in front of him. After I had settled back down, I opened my eyes to see him standing over me.

"You should try to eat something. You'll feel better," he said, smiling his sly smile at me.

Damn, even sick, I couldn't help but notice how gorgeous he was in his tight blue jeans and blue shirt. Don't even get me started on his eyes.

"Why are you here?" I groaned, pulling the blanket over my face.

"I want to make you feel better," he said, sitting down by me.

"Can I help you sit up?" he asked, pulling my blanket away.

I explained how much worse I felt when I moved, and he laughed, pulling me up anyway. Giving up, I put my hands on his forearms as he gently put a pillow behind me and told me to just take a couple of deep breaths and relax. *Okay*, I thought, *not so bad sitting up*. The chicken soup made my mouth water every time I breathed in.

"Your eye still hurt?" he asked, as he set up the tray over my lap.

I shook my head slowly, giving him the "I don't want to talk about it" look. He laughed and said "It looks likes it hurts. How did it happen?"

"Later," I mumbled, picking up the soup spoon. He nodded.

I had to admit it was pretty nice of him to come over and help me out. I thanked him, and he smiled again as he picked up the remote and sat down.

"What the hell are you watching?" he asked before he started channel surfing and landed on some music channel.

I ate the soup and was trying to put the bowl back on the tray when he stood up and took it from me. It was then that I noticed a card and a rose also lying on the tray. I read the goofy card and smelled the red rose.

"Please don't tell me you're one of those guys who likes to talk about feelings and unicorns?" I asked, trying not to laugh.

Laughing, he replied, "Yes, some of us guys *do* like to talk about our feelings and unicorns."

He reached over and put his hand on my forehead and indicated that I still had a fever. I didn't know if it was a fever or my reaction to his touch.

We watched TV and made small talk about little things in our lives, and I started to fall asleep.

I woke up and glanced over at him, he had fallen asleep as well. I sat up and realized the room had stopped spinning, and my stomach had settled down. I had sweat running down me. My shirt was soaking wet, and my hair was matted down. Collin woke up and glanced over at me.

"I bet your fever broke. You want to go upstairs and take a shower or change clothes?" he asked, moving closer to me.

I nodded. That was exactly what I wanted to do. He put his arm around me for support as I slowly stood up and helped me up the stairs.

"I've never been in your room before," he chuckled.

I told him it wouldn't be my room much longer and explained about the old schoolhouse I had just bought. He congratulated me and said he couldn't wait to see it.

I sat down on my bed to catch my breath after the two sets of stairs we had just climbed. I was tired and felt weak. He held up his finger indicating for me to stay put for a minute as he went into my bathroom. I heard the water running in the shower and wondered, *is he really starting my shower for me?* No guy had ever done something like that for me before, except Mike and he didn't count. I wished it was under different circumstances.

"I could help you shower if you want," he said, smirking at me as he dried off his hands.

I grinned and said, "I'm pretty sure I got it from here."

"Just offering, sexy," he said quietly as his eyes trailed up and down my body.

I realized he wasn't making me uncomfortable, oddly enough. I stood up and weakly pushed him out of my room after I assured him I could handle it. If he had stayed longer, I might have let him in the shower with me.

After a hot shower, I got dressed and brushed my teeth. I was starting to feel much better. I left my dark brown curly hair hanging down my back. I caught sight of my black eye in the mirror: *that was probably the dumbest thing I have ever done,* I thought. I was embarrassed by my behavior.

I went back downstairs feeling nervous. Mike and Collin were in the kitchen talking. Mike said he was glad I was feeling better after he gave me a quick hug and kiss on the cheek. I questioned why he was home so early, and he explained it was slow at the bar. He decided he was going to town to have a late dinner with Mark since Collin was here taking care of me. I knew he loved Collin taking an interest in my care.

I started looking around for something to eat when Collin gave me a look as he started pushing me toward the stairs.

"I'll make you something to eat. Just go downstairs and wait for me," he said, as I was trying to grab a bag of candy off the counter that he blocked.

He came back with more soup and some crackers. I groaned and gave him my sad puppy dog face. He explained it was a good idea so I wouldn't get sick again and I had to agree with him. I noticed my mess from the last couple days had been cleaned up. A fresh pillow and blanket were out for me.

I had to ask, "Do you take care of everyone this way?"

With a big smile on his face, he sat next to me and said, "Just the special ones."

I didn't know what to say to him. I started eating the crackers, and he went back to flipping channels.

"I tripped and fell into a door jamb in a fit of anger the other night when I was making a horribly bad decision," I said, suddenly finding myself wanting to confess everything to Collin.

He turned the volume down and looked at me with no judgment on his face.

"We all make those decisions once in a while."

I couldn't help myself, I told him about wanting to be alone and making myself numb from the world. He sat there in silence just listening to me. I kept going on about being angry and how I felt I was always upsetting everyone around me. I didn't know why or how to explain my anger to anyone, so I didn't.

"No one is pissed at you, Danni. No one knows how to help you, or how to make you feel better. You haven't dealt with it yet."

"What?" I asked, "What exactly do you know about my issues?"

"Don't get mad, but your dad has talked to me. I think he's looking for someone to talk to you and—you know I've said it before—I'm a great listener," he stated giving me a slow, sly grin.

Hearing that, I couldn't be mad at anyone, considering I was the one causing the train wreck in my life.

He asked, "Do you know that once a week, your dad calls the investigators to see if they've found out anything yet?"

"What do you know about that?" I asked, feeling horrified.

"Pretty much everything your dad knows. If I were in your situation, I would probably be falling into door jambs, too. Mike has come to me, as well. I was the one who told him to back off and let you do what you needed to do the other night. He was ready to send out a search party for you."

"Thanks for that. He is starting to really get on my nerves," I said, looking at my empty bowl of soup.

"I noticed that the other night when we took you outside to cool off," he said, as he cleared away my dishes and handed me a blanket.

"You will get through this, Danni, but it won't be easy. You should be prepared to trip and fall into many door jambs, but you can call me, and I will help you out."

We ended up sitting there on the couch talking for three hours before we finally both fell asleep. Weight had been lifted off my shoulders. I said things I hadn't spoken out loud to anyone about that night. I told him everything—like why I acted out the other night, the memories that were slowly coming back to me, and not wanting to see pity in people's faces anymore.

He stayed with me until the next evening when he mentioned he had to catch a flight home. I didn't want him to leave, and I couldn't explain it. We talked about so many different things, and I wanted it to continue. It was easy just to talk for the first time in months about pleasant things and very unpleasant things, too.

I found out how much fun he was to be around until he told me about his fiancée back home. That broke my heart, but I congratulated him anyways. I knew we would never be anything more than friends, and I decided that would be okay. There was something about him that made me feel safe. He had a way of making me want to talk to him and tell him about my messed up life.

A couple of days later Daniel let me know after they got home that Collin was in bed with the flu. When I found that out, all I could do was laugh.

CHAPTER 11
DISTURBING THE PEACE

I finally closed on my new house and got the keys the following day. My dad, the contractor, and I was all surprised by how well the building had been preserved. On the first floor, the blue lockers stretched from one end to the other. I knew that was a cool detail I would have to keep. I took pictures of all the features we kept finding and sent them to Collin and Mike.

I wanted to restore the gym and stage to the original state and fix up the old locker room. Dad agreed we should put a studio on the first floor that would take up two of the standing classrooms. It was going to be amazing.

I got up to the second floor where Dad and the contractor were talking. Dad was quick to point out how long this was going to take to fix up. I asked if he knew how cool it was going to be and he smiled, knowing I had a point. The contractor explained that it would take eight months to a year before everything would be done. Even though I was itching to live on my own, I knew it would be well worth the wait. The contractor left with many notes and instructions that both Dad and I gave him.

"I have something I want to talk to you about, baby girl," Dad said, sitting down on the cement steps outside.

I thought to myself, *what was I in trouble for now?* The look on my face must have told him that, too.

He laughed and said, "You're not in trouble this time if that's what you're thinking." I couldn't help but laugh as I sat down next to him.

"How do you feel about sharing the land with your old man?"

"I'm confused," I said. He explained he hadn't found anything that he wanted to buy in town.

"What do you think about me building my house over there?" he asked, pointing to the open field next to the old bus barn.

"I'm okay with that, Dad," I said as he smiled.

"I hoped you would be because I'm having blueprints drawn up as we speak."

I wouldn't have expected anything less from my dad. We talked for an hour about all the ideas we both had before he finally got in his truck and drove back to my house.

Before I headed to work, I called Collin to tell him all about the schoolhouse. I rambled on for ten minutes about how excited I was before I noticed he wasn't in a great mood.

"You okay, Collin?" I asked.

"Yeah. Steph and I were fighting. I'm just tired from touring and need a break."

I asked, "Is there anything I can do to cheer you up?"

"All the pictures and texts help a lot. I like talking to you, Danni. It calms me in a weird way."

Hearing him say that brought butterflies to my stomach, and I had to stop my mind from creating more than there was between us. He touched on the subject of his fiancée more, saying some days he wondered if she was with him just for the money. He went on to explain how she hates traveling with him. It didn't add up to me, but I knew he loved her. Honestly, I was the last person who should give out any advice on relationships. We said our goodbyes and he told me to keep the pictures coming.

Driving to work, I found myself daydreaming about Collin and how much I liked him. I was still having a hard time putting my finger on exactly what it was about him that drew me in so much. I was starting to really dislike the fiancée after all the things he had told me about her over the last couple months. I questioned if he liked her, as well.

I had managed to stay sober since Collin helped me when I was sick. Surprisingly, after talking to him, I wanted to do better. I paid my debt back to Ron and had stayed clear of him and his goons. Staying away from James was also easy. Rumor has it, he and Amber worked things out, and they were now living together. He would text me once in a while, but I kept my responses to a minimum if I even replied at all.

Mike had always said that James was trouble, and nothing good could come of being around him. I was starting to see

Mike's point on that subject, but there was still something about James I craved.

I bartended after someone called in sick so that Mike could have a night off. It was slow, so I was able to work on other things behind the bar at the same time. Jackie walked up with another order—I quickly noticed that she wasn't acting like her usual self.

"What is up with you?" I asked as I poured shots of tequila.

She looked at me carefully before asking, "Do you realize it's been a year since the assault?"

It was the last thing on my mind these days, and I just shrugged my shoulders and gave her the drinks. She knew I didn't like talking about it; *why did she think she needed to remind me of the worst night of my life?*

"Can I get a drink?"

I looked down the bar at the sound of the voice and saw James pulling out a stool. He looked like he had seen better days. I smiled a little and was genuinely happy to see him even though I probably shouldn't have been.

I slid a beer in front of him and said, "You look horrible. Need a friend?"

He studied his beer label for a couple of minutes and then nodded slowly. There weren't any other patrons, so I stood there waiting for him to start.

"My dad died a couple of days ago," he said quietly as he kept looking at the beer label.

I instantly felt sorry for him. I knew they were close.

"James, I am so sorry. Anything I can do to help?" I asked as I put my hand on his.

"I'm dealing with it. Thank you for asking, though."

I asked without thinking, "Is Amber helping you out?"

He responded with a simple, "No."

James told me all about their fighting, how she was always running back and forth between him and Ron, and how he had finally had enough. Talking to James had always been easy even though we had a way of not talking about important things. He stayed until closing, and I let him stay inside after I locked the doors.

He wasn't in a good state to drive himself home, and I wasn't about to let him. After I had taken his keys, he mumbled that this would probably be best anyway. We walked to the back garage, and he mentioned that he was surprised I was parking back there again. I just shrugged off the comment.

I pulled in front of his house, parked, and didn't take off my seatbelt. I had no intention of staying.

"Can you make it inside by yourself?" I asked, hoping he wouldn't make this more than what it was.

He replied with a simple "yes", and we sat there in silence for a couple of minutes.

"Do you know that I miss you so much? I miss us." he said as I closed my eyes at the words finally spoken out loud.

I had no idea what to say. I didn't want to feel any of those emotions. The only things we had in common right now were drugs. Since I decided to leave them behind, I was able to see it was merely just a friendship of convenience. I just sat there in silence. My mind was blank.

I felt him turn and look at me as he said, "I know you feel something for me, too. After what you've been through, I can't imagine this is easy for you, but I wanted you to know what I feel."

After several minutes of me looking at my hands, he finally broke the silence and said, "Just being friends is okay, Danni. Just know, I do love you, and I know that anything romantic can't be easy for you, so friends it is."

He pulled me toward him into a warm hug, and I couldn't help but sink into him at that moment. We hugged for what felt like forever before he let go of me, keeping his face close to mine. We lingered there before he leaned in and kissed me.

My heart was beating out of my chest as panic raced throughout my body. I opened my eyes as he pulled back a little, sensing my reluctance. I didn't know if I felt sorry for him as I pulled him back and kissed him. I knew I was taking advantage of the situation because I was never going to admit my feelings for him.

In the back of my mind, I knew this was a dangerous emotion, but it felt too good to stop. Even though I was the one being touched and kissed in such an intense and passionate way, oddly enough, that made the panic subside. I felt light-headed, almost like I was in a dream, but the kind of dream where you are in complete control. The way he kissed my lips and neck all made me want more. Our breathing was loud and labored.

Soon, I was crawling over the console on top of him. Everything was happening so fast, but I was the one leading the charge. He pushed off my jacket and slid his hands up my shirt. I was touching him in places I knew were going to get me into a lot of trouble as he moaned. He pulled off my shirt, and I was undressing him at the same time. I realized I had intentions of going all the way. Neither of us had a shirt on at this point. I had skipped the bra tonight, which made it even more intense as we pressed against each other. We attempted to take off each other's pants, as fingers fumbled with belts and buttons. All of a sudden there was a sharp tap on the window. Looking up, we saw two police officers standing there with smiles on their faces. *Shit*, I thought, seeing my friend Seth starting to laugh.

That was a definite mood killer. Officer Taylor—according to his name tag—told us to put our clothes back on and get out of the car. I wanted to die from complete embarrassment as I crawled back into my seat and found my shirt. I looked over at James, and he was laughing. That did help lighten the mood a little bit. We got dressed and stepped out of the car as we both started chuckling at this point. Even the officers were smiling and trying to contain their laughter.

Each cop took one of us aside, requested identification, and asked what we had been doing. Seth was the local deputy I had known since I moved to town. We also rode bikes together in the summer. He was the one who had seen my truck and knew something was wrong the night I was assaulted.

"Seth, I think you have an idea of what we were doing," I smirked, handing over my license.

He really started laughing and stopped writing my ticket, bending over and holding his side. I looked over at James, and his officer was laughing, too.

After about ten minutes, Seth stopped making small talk with me and finished writing me a ticket for disturbing the peace.

"Normally, Danni, I wouldn't give you a ticket for something this minor, but the gentleman who called us was complaining that he has kids, and it can't be tolerated."

"Yeah, Seth, I totally get it. Sorry, it just got out of hand," I said, taking the ticket he held out for me to sign.

"Perhaps you should find something better to do, but I'm not going to lie, Danni, it's nice to see you moving forward, perhaps, not in public next time," he said, as laughter began getting the better of him again. I agreed, rolling my eyes.

James finished with his officer at the same time. We stood on James' front porch as the officers left and reminded us to keep our clothes on in public.

"You want to come inside and finish what we started?" James asked, pulling me into his arms and kissing my neck.

"Uh, I think that was pretty much a mood killer for me. Maybe it would be best if I went home instead," I said, stepping back.

He mumbled, "I can't argue with that. Can I see you again?"

"How about we just see what happens between us naturally?" I said as we both started to laugh again.

He agreed and gave me a quick kiss on the lips before we said goodnight and I walked back to my car. All the way home, I wanted to die of embarrassment and hoped no one would find out about this night. It was somewhat of a small town, and people love to gossip, so it was more than likely going to get out.

—⚔ ⚔—

The following morning, I was in bed contemplating getting up when Mike burst in my door laughing hysterically.

"I'm having your ticket framed for the bar. You should go to court and fight it," he said with complete sarcasm in his voice.

"Get the hell out, douchebag!" I yelled, throwing a pillow at him.

Of course, he said *no*, wanting me to get up so we could go for a run. Something I had promised him, we would do yesterday. I knew he wasn't going to leave unless he got his way.

Sure enough, while running, he pulled all the details out of me. He was surprised I was ready for that, and I explained I hadn't known what I was doing, and I had just gone with it at the moment.

"You gonna tell Collin about it?" he asked, looking more serious as we slowed to a walk.

"I don't plan on it. He'll just make fun of me."

"Maybe not make fun of you, per se, but it might not be a bad idea for him not to know about it," he said, with an expression of concern that I didn't understand.

Over the next couple of days, all my friends teased me. Everyone knew about the incident in the car, which made it much worse, especially when Dad asked me about it at dinner one night with Mike and Mark. I just couldn't wait for all the hype to go away already. I hadn't talked to Collin in a couple of days, so I had no idea if he knew or if he had worked everything out with the fiancée.

I was lying in bed playing with my phone when I got a text from Collin.

Collin: Sorry I haven't talked to you in a while, we have been super busy. How are things?

I decided to forgo the humiliation and not tell him the story as we texted each other for a little bit, catching up on each other's lives. He was in Canada touring, and things had gotten a bit better. He mentioned he was counting down the days until his next chance to come back and hang out with us. I told him I was looking forward to that as well, more than I wanted to admit to myself.

The next couple of days flew by, and I hardly had a chance to get back to Collin before the weekend came. *Wow,* I thought, walking in the front door of the bar, it was packed.

Mike yelled, "This is crazy!" as I stepped behind the bar to hear him better.

It was fall break at the local colleges, and it had been just as packed the last couple nights. I mumbled, "Super, a bunch of drunken college kids," as I rolled my eyes. I knew this crowd usually brought trouble with them, not to mention what crappy tippers they were. I went to my office and put my things down, noticing that my dad's regular table was blocked off. I didn't remember him saying he would be here, in fact I thought he was going back to Texas to take care of some business. Who had reserved the table? The new sound guy was motioning he was ready to do my sound check, so I let it go and went to the stage.

Mike walked up when I was done and asked, "You want something to drink?"

I said, "Water. Who reserved Dad's table?"

"I'm not sure. Someone called earlier and booked it with Jackie. Hey, can we go for breakfast later?"

I couldn't help but smile and said, "I would like that. Just like old times."

He hugged me and said, "Just like old times. You and me against the world."

The house band members were ready to go and even though we had a good half an hour before we were scheduled to go on, we decided to go ahead. The crowd was starting to get restless, and that was never a good thing.

I wasn't looking forward to doing lead vocals on some songs again. Kendrick was better at it than I was, but he insisted, arguing that he liked my voice better on certain songs. He was one of the biggest pains in the ass if he didn't get his way, so I had agreed to do it. Luckily, he offered to help with guitar while I was singing. I would rather hide behind a guitar than sing. Being in the spotlight made me feel uncomfortable over the past year, and I was sure it had something to do with that night.

I noticed that the reserved table had filled up, but I couldn't tell who it was with the lights shining on us. I was singing a slower rock song about sex, pulling my baseball cap down a little further to try and block out the lights as well as the crowd. As I sang, I had a quick flashback to the night in my car with James and I was able to put a little more passion into the song. I still couldn't help but wonder why I hadn't heard from him since that night.

I opened my eyes and messed up my words seeing Collin dancing with some blonde, fervently making out with each other on the dance floor. *What the hell?* Kendrick took over singing as I glared at them, feeling myself turn red.

It was Collin's band that had reserved the table. Apparently they had all brought their girlfriends and wives, as I saw they were all paired up. The next song was faster as Kendrick kept singing and I found myself again watching Collin. He couldn't keep his hands off the blonde he had with him, as they were practically dry humping on the dance floor. I was pissed at him, and I didn't exactly know why. I forced myself to concentrate on my guitar and planned to ignore him and get out of here as soon as we were done.

We made it to the first break, and I hopped off stage to talk to the sound guy about my mic and the reverb in some of the vocals. I talked to him for a while, trying to distract myself. I even helped him fix the problem before I headed over to the bar to speak to Mike.

I leaned over the bar and asked, "Did you know Collin was coming?"

"No, he never mentioned it to me," he said, handing me a shot of whiskey.

"Who is the blonde he is practically fucking on my dance floor?" I couldn't help but be bitchy about it.

"Daniel said that's Steph, the famous fiancée. You want an introduction?" he asked, smirking at me.

"I would rather face a firing squad," I mumbled before I threw my shot back.

Mike started laughing and said, "Your dad informed them about your ticket, so you should plan on being made fun of tonight."

Well, that just made me more pissed off. I decided it would be best just to avoid all of them instead.

We went back on for our final set. It was my favorite because this was when we always played the harder rock. It would be easier to block everything out except the music.

Of course, I had to watch Collin and his fiancée make out some more on the dance floor. *Do they ever get enough?* I glared as they kissed and he had his hands up her shirt for everyone to see. This was getting more annoying by the minute. I liked Collin. He was a good friend, and I kept telling myself that, maybe hoping I would convince myself. I was just mad because he seemed so in love with a woman who was just using him for money, but it wasn't my battle to fight.

The set finally ended. I was tired and just wanted to go home. I noticed that Jackie was clearing Collin's table. They all must have left. I was glad that I didn't have to talk to any of them now.

Mike and I went to breakfast, and we talked about old times. He stopped laughing when this look of complete amazement came over his face, and he suddenly looked right at me.

Practically shouting at me in the restaurant, "You know what we haven't done since college?"

I was horrified to ask at this point but knew that whatever it was, it was going to happen.

"Clubbing, baby!" he yelled, throwing his hands up. After that, all I wanted to do was crawl under the table and hide.

CHAPTER 12

YOU GET IT YET?

As Mike planned our evening, it was like watching a little kid in a candy store. We decided to stay in town at Mark's apartment since he was included in this, as well. It was a blizzard outside, and I thought we should just go home, but Mike was determined. We were going clubbing.

It was something we would do in college usually very mild. It entailed us going to a bar (usually a gay bar), dancing all night, and getting so drunk that we would be hungover for at least a day or two. It was fun when we were younger, but now I was a little more hesitant. But, it was a gay bar after all, so chances are I had nothing to worry about.

Because of the weather, it took us an hour to get to town when it usually only took twenty minutes. Snow had always been one of my favorite things probably because it gave me a great reason to stay home. Whatever the reason, I loved it and welcomed it.

After almost two hours getting ready and two small meltdowns from me I gave up and let Mike have his way. I planned on just wearing jeans and a T-shirt, but the look on his face said, "I don't think so."

He had chosen an outfit for me while we were still at home: black shorts, a red sparkly off-the-shoulder shirt, and my least favorite thing in my closet, black strappy heels. I looked at Mike and complained that it was too cold outside, but he just responded by saying we were going to be inside. I knew it was a battle I couldn't win, so I gave up and let him dress me. Making matters worse, he did my makeup and hair because apparently I wasn't good at it.

I grabbed my long black dress coat as we were leaving and caught myself in the mirror. I looked like someone I didn't know, but damn, she looked good. The outfit was snug on my trim figure, my hair was straight hanging down the middle of my back, and my make-up was dark around my blue eyes. I felt sexy for the first time in a year.

Checking our coats at the club, the music was blaring loud. I followed the love birds in front of me as we walked up one flight of stairs to a private booth. We had the perfect view overlooking the dance floor. We ordered drinks and were working on the third round, and I was finally relaxed as I leaned against the railing enjoying the view of Mike and Mark on the dance floor.

"You come here often sexy stranger? I can totally play the naughty stranger if you want." I turned to look and saw it was Daniel giving me a devilish grin.

I burst out laughing at his lame pick up attempt before I jumped in his arms and hugged him.

"What are you doing here?" I asked when we pulled back and smiled at each other.

"Our flight got canceled, so we are stuck here," Daniel said, stepping back. "Wow, you look awesome. Those legs just go on and on and don't get me started on the shoes. Mmmmm, baby."

I laughed and shoved him away, loving his sense of humor. He was always calling me or texting me, and eventually I starting doing it back to him just to be annoying. It didn't work, and we became friends, instead, but he was a complete goofball. We sat down and started talking.

"Where is the rest of your group?" I asked, hoping he said they made it home.

"Getting drinks. They'll be up soon unless Rick finds someone to bang in the bathroom. I mean if he makes it that far."

Daniel must have seen the look of panic on my face, and he told me to relax, explaining that the girls had left early this morning to get back home for a wedding instead of catching up on the tour with them. I was greatly relieved.

Mike and Mark walked up about that time. Mike looked at Daniel and said, "Hey, glad you guys could make it."

Mark looked at me and just pointed at Mike behind his back, mouthing "All him."

I need another drink, I thought and tried to get up. Daniel motioned I was not going anywhere as he held my arm. Our private booth consisted of two long black leather couches put together in an L shape with a cocktail table in the middle. I was trapped in the corner, and Daniel knew I was stuck until he moved.

Collin and the rest of them walked up asking if they could join the party. I wanted to say no, but Daniel pinched my leg. Collin had done a double-take before he realized it was me. *Wow, maybe I need to start putting more effort into my appearance.* He nodded, smiled at me, and sat at the other end of the couch. I snatched up a shot of something blue in front of me and downed it.

I grabbed Daniel's hand and said, "You're dancing with me. Now."

He looked at me and said, "I will gladly dance with you, but so that you know. *I* will be the one everyone is watching." He winked at me, and I had to laugh.

I felt Collin and Rick look me up and down as we walked away, and I couldn't help but feel a little good about myself. Daniel followed me to the dance floor. I was starting to get the impression that Daniel took very little seriously as we screwed around more than we danced. We sang along to the music, and I had to keep removing his hands from my ass. I had a pretty good buzz going, and I found it easy to let loose. At the end of the third song, Daniel said he needed a break. Grabbing my hand, he started leading me back upstairs, and I told him I was going to stay downstairs.

He quickly pulled me into his arms and whispered in my ear, "You can't ignore him forever, ya know,"

"Fine, you spoilsport."

Collin was sitting in the same spot, enjoying himself and talking with everyone. I sat down with Mike on the other couch and he handed me another drink, something red with beads around the bottom of the glass. It was some fancy drink I usually wouldn't touch. I was more of a beer or whiskey girl, but at the moment, this was working quite well.

A favorite drinking song came on as Daniel encouraged everyone to join in. It was pretty obvious that everyone was getting sloshed. We all danced more, losing our inhibitions. A slower song came on as Mike and Mark left to dance. I noticed Daniel elbow Collin in the ribs and exchange a look with him. *I am not watching this*, I thought to myself. I headed to the dance floor to escape the awkward situation.

About halfway down the stairs, I realized Collin was following me, and I hoped he was getting another drink or something. When I walked out on the dance floor, I felt his hands around my waist turning me around to face him. He pulled me close, and neither one of us said a word, I couldn't think with his hands on me. I was mesmerized looking up at him, his dark blue eyes piercing into mine as I felt a tingle run down my spine. I put my arms around his neck as he pulled my hips closer to his. I knew I was mad at him, but I couldn't exactly remember why at that moment.

That smell of musky cologne and leather, his arms around me, and the way his eyes watched me left me utterly intoxicated. I didn't know what it was about him, but I always felt a fire deep down when I was with him. It confused me.

He whispered in my ear as his hands moved further down my back, "You look beautiful."

I could tell something was off in his voice, an emotion I couldn't quite place.

I whispered back, "I'm glad you're here."

He pulled me even closer, grinding our hips together as the song ended and another one came on that was still slow, but a little hotter. I figured we would stop, but he didn't loosen his grip on me and, quite frankly, I was enjoying it probably more than I should have. His breathing was speeding up as he put his hand around the back of my neck. This brought his face closer to mine, and I slipped my hands inside his jacket around his waist. As the song was coming to an end, I noticed everyone at our booth was watching us.

"We have an audience," I whispered close to his ear. I could feel goose bumps on his neck.

He put his hand on my hip and pushed back a little bit. *Ok,* I thought, *I wish I knew what was going on with him.* He simply seemed to switch off.

Mike was suddenly beside us asking if he could dance with me, so Collin stepped back without a word and walked away.

Mike leaned in as we danced together and asked, "You get it yet?"

"Get what?" I asked, with a look of confusion on my face.

He looked at me and said, "You know I love you, but sometimes you have a hard time seeing things right in front of you."

"Thanks," I mumbled, not liking the unintentional insult.

He smiled and said, "You'll get it eventually, but until then, I'm going to let you figure it out for yourself."

I looked at him and said, "You know I love you, but sometimes you can be a little annoying."

He laughed, knowing I was mocking him, as well.

I walked back upstairs and sat down in time to ask the waitress for a shot of whiskey. I sat next to Daniel again, so I was as far away from Collin as possible. He sat in the corner with an angry scowl on his beautiful face.

"When did you start drinking whiskey sexy stranger?" Daniel asked as he smiled at me.

"When she is trying to forget things or avoid them altogether. Get drunk, Danni. That always helps, doesn't it?" Collin snapped as he stood up and then walked away looking pissed off.

"What is with him?" I said.

Daniel mumbled, "Long story."

It was closing time as we gathered our stuff to leave. I realized that Mike and Mark were having trouble keeping their hands off each other, and I was not looking forward to sharing an apartment with them tonight.

I quickly asked Daniel, "Where are you staying tonight?"

"What? You want to miss that?" he asked as he pointed to Mike and Mark practically undressing each other. "You can stay with me, but no hanky panky. You're not my type." he said, giving me a fake disgusted look. I couldn't help but start laughing at him.

I was pretty drunk and just wanted to sleep. Mike and Mark were completely fine with having the apartment to themselves. I got into a town car with Daniel, Rick, and some girl that Rick must have picked up. I noticed he didn't have a wedding ring on anymore, even though last night I could have sworn I saw one.

No sooner did we get in the elevator at their hotel than Rick and this girl were all over each other. Even Daniel looked creeped out with them. Daniel pushed me into the corner and tried to block me so I wouldn't have to see the whole mess, and I liked him more for that. We got off on the fifth floor and not a moment too soon. It was like really bad porn; the kind you couldn't help but watch.

Daniel grabbed my coat and said, "We're going this way, drunkpants." He yanked me to the right, down the hallway.

We kept laughing and messing with each other; I think we were both pretty drunk.

"Sing to me, sexy stranger," I said, before jumping in his arms while he held me up around his waist.

"I just play drums and look good. I leave the singing to Collin. Now be quiet. People are sleeping." That just made me laugh more.

At the end of the hall, he leaned me up against the wall, pointed in my face, and only said, "Stay" like I was a dog.

He opened the door and pushed me inside. I walked in giggling and said, "You're bossy. Maybe that's why you don't have a girlfriend."

He laughed and said, "Probably."

I took off my coat and laid it on the chair before falling back on the bed.

He asked, "You want some water or coffee?"

"Just something to sleep in, Daniel, my sweet boy," I said as I yawned.

He grabbed a shirt out of his bag and threw it at me when there was a knock on the door. Looking at me, he said, "Be quiet," before he went to answer the door.

He only opened the door a little, so I thought I could change my shirt quick. I pulled off my shirt and all of a sudden I heard Collin yelling.

"What the hell is she doing in your room?"

Making matters much worse, I was standing there with my back to them without a shirt or bra on. Collin pushed his way in and got in Daniel's face. I could tell he was angry as I quickly pulled on Daniel's shirt so I could help stop the fight.

I pried them both apart and stood between them, one hand on each of their chests.

"Both of you calm down and Collin, stop yelling before some-one calls the cops."

Daniel was laughing and looked at me. "You get it, yet?"

Throwing my hands up, I left them to kill each other and went and sat on the bed.

"Why does everyone keep asking me that tonight?" I mumbled more to myself than to them.

Daniel just looked at me with a huge smile on his face. I looked at Collin, and he was clearly glowing mad at this point.

"What the hell is your problem, Collin?" I asked as he stepped back, his eyes traveling up and down my body.

"What are you doing with Daniel?" he asked, looking like he was fighting an internal battle, attempting to restrain himself from beating the crap out of poor Daniel.

I explained the situation with Mike and Mark, and it finally dawned on me what he probably thought.

"Do you think I'm here to have sex with Daniel?" I asked, with a shocked look on my face.

He asked Daniel if he could see him alone in the hall for a moment and they both walked out of the room, pulling the door shut behind them.

Well, this will sober someone up real quick. After another ten minutes, Daniel walked back into the room carrying a light blue T-shirt and threw it at me.

"I need my shirt back?" he said, trying to contain his laughter.

I asked, "Why exactly?"

"When you finally get it, it will make sense."

"Whose shirt is this then?"

He said, "Collin's, and by the way, it's his favorite shirt. He wears it all the damn time."

"I don't understand anything going on," I grumbled as I changed into Collin's shirt.

Daniel just laughed and lay on the bed, turning on the flatscreen. I crawled into the other bed, curled up, and was asleep before I knew what hit me.

CHAPTER 13

I GET IT

During the next couple of weeks, the schoolhouse demanded my constant attention. From cabinets, tile, paint color, to wood floors, molding, and fixtures. I couldn't get away from it. My contractor was constantly asking me things I had never thought of before. Trying to find things to restore the school as close to its original form as possible became a full-time job. Mike and Dad helped as much as they could.

Dad was in the process of building his house and going back and forth to Texas to work at his ranch. Mike and Mark were planning on going to Mark's family cabin in Colorado to spend Thanksgiving with his family. They would be gone a week, which meant that I had to work at the bar every night. It was going to be the first week in a long time I was going to be alone, and I was okay with it.

Finally, Mike, Mark, and Dad all left town on their trips and I was excited that after work I could go home and be alone. I just had to make it through work first. That would be easy enough if I closed early.

Since we had gone clubbing, Daniel and I had been in constant contact. He had come to be more like a naughty little brother to me, and he knew I would tell him what I thought about some of the things he did, usually him being a jackass to some poor girl. He hadn't brought up Collin once since that night, and neither did I. I hadn't received one call or text from Collin, and I hadn't sent him anything either. I didn't know what to say to him now.

Time went by quickly at the bar, considering I felt like all I did was text Daniel and Mike most of the night. Finally, at 8:30, I kicked out my last two customers. We had the bar cleaned up by nine, and the new waitress left. I decided to finish my paperwork so I wouldn't have to take it home. I turned on the stereo, thinking it would keep me motivated, and it did.

An hour later it was snowing when I looked outside, putting on my coat and eager to get home. I had parked out front earlier since snow drifts in the back of the garage had prevented me from getting in. After reading a quick text from Daniel telling me to call him when I got home, I texted him back saying I was just leaving the bar and would be home in twenty minutes. He wanted to tell me about his video ideas for their next song. I shook my head, knowing Daniel, he will have naked women mud wrestling in it, or something ridiculous like that. I gathered my stuff and headed outside noticing how quiet it was with all the snow.

The streets were empty, and my SUV was the only one left as I started it with the remote. I walked carefully across the road, my headlights shining on me as I crossed the icy street. Stepping onto the sidewalk, through the snow drift left by the snow plow, one of my headlights darkened. Complete panic set in as I felt a presence. With the keys in my hand, I started walking when I noticed too many footsteps around me. I froze, as my purse, laptop, and bank bag crashed onto the snowy sidewalk. Feeling a warm hand grasp my throat, I stayed still, praying it wasn't what I thought.

It was. He spoke very slowly and calmly, as I heard the familiar voice from my nightmares behind me.

"Did you miss me?"

I tried to turn around to see the monster's face as he shoved me up against my car, my head hitting the back door window. The sound of shattering glass that rang in my ears was incredibly loud against the insulation of the snow. I was trying to think what to do when he yanked me backward by my hair. My mind woke up, shouting at me not to let this happen. *I won't let it.* He opened the driver's door and started trying to push me inside. I was not about to get in a small space with him. I started grabbing ahold of anything that I could get a grip on. He shoved me up against the seat trying to hold onto me. My back was to his front when he pressed up against me.

"Stop fighting or I'll kill you this time," he said close to my ear, as the smell of alcohol and grease reached my nose.

I kept fighting back, knowing the worst he could do was kill me. As both of us kept fighting for control, I remembered my keys in my hand. With fumbling fingers, I started hitting all the buttons until I found the panic button. The horn started going off, and the lights were flashing.

"Now, why couldn't you just play nice with me? Like we did last time? It was so much fun," he said through his heavy breathing with a bit of excitement in his voice.

He grabbed my hair, yanked back, and said, "Too bad, maybe next time."

Something sharp crashed into the back of my head before everything went dark.

⊨ ⊨

I woke up with a freight train running through my head. Judging from the commotion around me, I had a feeling I was in the hospital. Opening my eyes, I saw I was right. An older woman in pink scrubs was standing over me. I couldn't tell what hurt worse, the front or back of my head.

"What happened?" I moaned, hoping I had just had a new nightmare.

She replied after she hit a button on a flashing machine, "Honey, I think you were robbed."

I hope that's all they think. Maybe keeping as much to myself as possible was a smarter way to play this. I was so light-headed and suddenly felt like I was going to get sick, so I sucked in a deep breath. I was furious. Mostly mad at myself for not killing him when I had the chance. I stayed still trying to catch my breath; I didn't want to do anything stupid.

After ten minutes my temper got the best of me. *To hell with this. I'm leaving.* I was in a hospital gown and that made me angrier as the nurse came back with a tray of unpleasant looking instruments.

"I want my fucking clothes back now!" I shouted at her. It didn't seem to faze her at all.

"You need to calm down and just relax," she said with nothing but calmness in her tone.

I roared back, "Get my clothes now."

I felt blood running down my face, and realized that this can't be a good sign. The very calm nurse was putting something in my IV, and before I even had a chance to pull it out of my arm, the darkness found me once again.

I woke a couple of hours later and tried to get up, but quickly understood that I couldn't move my hands. *Really? I'm the one that is assaulted, but I am the one restrained. How ironic,* I mumbled to myself seeing the restraints that attached my wrists to the bed rails.

A different nurse came around this time looking more serious than the last one. He was trying to be funny and charming at the same time. It wasn't working. He joked that they would remove the restraints if I would behave this time. I assured him it wouldn't be a problem. After freeing me, he asked me to try to sit up and drink some water. I thought back to what the nurse had told me last time I was in the hospital. The sooner I got up and walked around, the sooner I could go home. He helped me sit up. I didn't feel so light-headed this time, which I knew was a good sign.

The bandages covered half my eye as I questioned the nurse endlessly if they were necessary. He assured me they were, much to my dismay. They had just finished stitching up my forehead and the back of my head, mentioning I would probably have a headache for a couple of days.

I asked, "Are the cops here?"

"Yes, they're outside waiting to talk to you," he said, moving the bed into a more comfortable upright position.

Casually trying to do what I seem to do best, I played it down, "What exactly happened?"

"They think you were robbed. Is that what you remember?"

I decided at that moment that that was all they needed to know. I was going to leave out the fact it had been the same man who had assaulted me. It was a moot point, and I wasn't going to touch on it anymore for anyone.

Oh, goody. The same two detectives from my first assault stood by my bed asking endless questions. I only answered vaguely, telling them he had just wanted money. Next, they asked me if I had had a purse or anything with me. I replied that I had my purse, laptop, and bank deposit bag with me. They hadn't found any of it, I wasn't surprised. I remembered that I had put my phone in my coat pocket.

"Wait, do you have my phone?" I asked, hopeful that they did.

"Yes, that is the only thing we found in your coat. Also, we haven't been able to locate your keys, any ideas?" The older detective asked.

"I had them in my hand. That's how I was able to hit the panic button. Can I have my phone back?" I snapped at them, calling them idiots in my head.

They knew I wasn't telling them everything, judging by the looks on their faces.

"We called the last number that contacted you, a gentleman named Daniel answered. We explained that you had been robbed and were being taken care of here at the hospital," he said, handing me back my phone and yet another one of their cards before they finally left.

I had a collection of their cards from all of their previous drop-ins to see if I had remembered anything more yet. I remembered lots of things, but nothing I was sharing with anyone.

Wow, I thought, looking at my phone. Twenty-four missed calls, tons of text messages, and I had no desire to look through any of them. I called the only person I could think of at the time.

"Hello," he said in a sleepy voice.

"Can you come get me, James? I need a ride home," I said, trying not to choke the nurse still pestering me that I should stay another day.

"Danni, why do you need a ride home at six in the morning? Are you okay?" he asked, sounding more awake now.

"I'm at the hospital. They don't think I'm fit to drive. They took my ride as well, so can you help me out?" I mumbled as the nurse gave up and left.

"I will be right there."

Twenty minutes later the nurse came in with all the discharge papers and an irritated look on his face. He explained I had an appointment in two days for a follow-up. He also ran down all the instructions they said I needed to follow. A concussion seems to have a lot of directions, and I had no idea how they thought I could remember all of them.

I saw James running down the hall towards me, and I couldn't help but climb out of my wheelchair. He put his arms around me, and I told him I wanted to go home.

"Are you okay?" he asked in a very shaky voice. I nodded.

We walked inside my quiet home, and I collapsed on the couch feeling overwhelmed with dizziness. We sat there for a while as James had his arms around me whispering that it would be okay.

Opening my eyes, I saw the way-too-bright sunlight filling the room and sat up, wondering if it had all been a dream. Major head rush. The room started spinning, and I closed my eyes and took a deep breath. After a couple of minutes of deep breaths, I slowly stood up. Black spots filled my vision, and I started to fall forward as my head became fuzzy. I suddenly found myself a little steadier on my feet. Not crashing into the coffee table, I realized I had two people holding me up, one on each side. I sat back down mumbling that I was sleepy.

I woke up a little later with lots of body heat under me as I was sweating. *I must be lying on someone's chest.* I slowly opened my eyes hoping the dizziness was done.

The first thing I saw was Daniel sitting across from me in the chair, grinning at me.

"Good afternoon, sleepy head. How are you feeling?" he asked as I felt movement below me.

Whose chest am I lying on? I started pulling myself up and saw it was Collin.

"What are you two doing here?" I asked in an exhausted voice.

Daniel looked at me and said, "You didn't call me back. I want to tell you my idea for the video." His voice was full of sarcasm, but he had a look of concern on his face.

Collin sat up with me and tried to hold onto me so I wouldn't fall over. I just looked at him and could tell that he was very worried. I was too tired to ask any questions as I gripped his upper arms. We sat there and looked at each other as if nothing else in the world mattered. He cupped my cheek gently with his hand and sighed when I leaned into his palm. Tears streamed down my face, and I whispered, "It was him."

I watched his eyes water before a tear ran down his cheek and he nodded at me before pulling me in for a tight hug.

Later that evening they both helped me upstairs as the room wouldn't quit spinning. Daniel left and shut the door behind him, leaving me alone with Collin. Neither of us had anything to say. He sat down on the bed with me as I leaned into him, feeling his warmth.

"I'll start a hot shower for you. Danni, promise me you're okay?" He breathed close to my ear as I noticed his hands shaking.

I nodded, pulling his shaking hand to my mouth as I gently kissed it, fighting my urge to cry. After twenty more minutes of trying to console each other, I finally managed to get in the shower as he stayed right outside the door, saying he wasn't going to leave me alone in case I fell or something.

As I was pulling my wet curly hair up in a bun, he stepped back into the bathroom after I kicked him out so I could get dressed. I stood there in my bra and underwear as he looked at me in the mirror and, as he came to stand behind me, our eyes found each others. Neither of us spoke.

Gently he touched the scars on my chest and stomach from the first assault. This was the first time I let anyone other than a doctor touch them. He looked at me, and I nodded that he could touch. As his fingertips ran over the two pink scars on my chest, then to the three on my stomach, I didn't feel panic. I felt alive and beautiful after a year of hiding them from the world. His face looked more than concerned; lust and passion are what I saw. What this man did to me was unlike anything I had ever felt before.

"You take my breath away. You are so beautiful, Danni," he whispered before he planted a sensual kiss on my shoulder. He stepped back and left the room quietly.

My heart was pounding; the way he made me feel was everything I was trying not to feel. But, he was not giving me a choice when he touched me or looked at me with lust all over his face. I was sure my face showed him I felt it as much as he did.

I grabbed a T-shirt and a pair of sweats, got dressed, and went back into the bedroom when there was a knock on my bedroom door.

"Come in," I said as I pulled on socks.

"You up for some dinner?" Collin asked as he sat on my bed next to me.

"That would be great. I'm starving."

I looked at him and asked, "You alright?"

He gave me a half-smile and said, "I just have a lot of things on my mind. Just need some time to work through them. Don't worry about me."

Being the smartass I am, I replied, "Well, if you need to talk, I am a pretty good listener."

Wearing his sly smile, he asked, "Where is my shirt that I gave you to wear?"

I played dumb saying, "What shirt? Oh, that shirt. It's on the dresser. I was just waiting to see you to give it back." I knew he wasn't buying it.

The truth was, it had become my favorite night shirt, and I had no intentions of giving it back. He found it on the dresser and threw it at me to put on instead of the one I had on, and I did.

When we got to the kitchen, I was completely ready to order dinner. I was shocked when the table was set, and they had made hamburgers. It was a great meal. They even did the dishes while I watched from the table. Collin asked when they would get to see the schoolhouse. A subject I loved to talk about. I told them it would hopefully be done in the spring and then described everything I was trying to do to restore some of the old traits of the school. I told them that we had tried a couple of times to save the scoreboard in the gym, but it was too run-down and couldn't be saved. So far I had had no luck finding another. We talked about the schoolhouse for a while when it dawned on me that James had brought me home, but was gone when I woke up.

I asked, "What happened to James?"

They looked at each other and said, "Rock, paper, scissors," and then played and Daniel lost. He came and sat down at the table with me while Collin loaded the dishwasher and kept his back to me.

Daniel explained, "When we got here, James was here. It got a little heated between the three of us because a certain someone," he pointed to Collin, "wanted him to leave. There may have been a little standoff over who was staying. I'm sure you can guess who won."

I was confused why there would be any bad feelings between them. They had never even met before. I remained quiet on the subject and thought maybe I could find out more details from James later. My phone started ringing at that moment, breaking the silence between the three of us.

Mike was surprised I answered the phone. He seemed quite eager to talk about his trip and the fun they were having. I caught on that no one had called him about the robbery. I wondered if anyone had called my dad either. I was okay with that. It put off the drama for a different time. I let him tell me all about what they had been doing. I said things were fine here, and I was enjoying some quiet time. Daniel kicked me under the table, hinting for me to tell him, so I quickly said goodbye.

I just stood up and looked at Collin and Daniel, returning their dirty looks as I went into my office. I sat down and started looking for my phone charger, moving things on my desk around and opening drawers. I saw the painkillers from the last time I had stitches and just stared at them. My mind reminded me of the peace they brought. I closed the drawer when they both came in and sat down.

"How long do you plan on staying?" I asked, hearing the spiteful tone in my voice.

Daniel was quick to say, "A day or two."

I had such a strong need to feel numb, but yet the idea of hanging out with them was great, too. I told them that I had to work tomorrow.

Collin looked at me and asked, "Do you need to work? I think you should take it easy for a couple of days."

Collin just watched me as I noticed his eyes go between me and the drawer handle I was still holding. I knew he wasn't as easily fooled like everybody else.

Daniel went downstairs to get a head start on picking out a movie, and I went to the kitchen to get a bottle of water, hopefully, to down a few painkillers. Collin grabbed my arm as I tried to leave the kitchen to go back to my office.

"What are you looking for, Danni?" Collin asked very close to me.

"I have a headache."

He placed two ibuprofen on the counter and said, "This will do. This is the strongest thing in the house, *now.*"

Instantly I knew he had found the painkillers and more than likely got rid of them. His phone started ringing. He looked at it and sighed as he walked toward my office, shutting the door behind him.

I went downstairs after taking the Tylenol, and Daniel asked, "Where is Collin?"

"He got a call and took it in my office," I answered, sitting down by him.

"Great," Daniel said in an annoyed voice.

"Everything okay?"

"Just don't be surprised if he's in a bad mood the rest of the night."

"Why?" I asked.

Daniel just said, "Because apparently that is what a fiancée does to you."

I hated being reminded that he had a fiancée. I would have been happy never having learned that detail.

Ten minutes later, sure enough, Collin came downstairs and looked pissed off, sitting on the opposite end of the couch. I grabbed a blanket, cuddled up, and didn't even bother to ask what we were watching. I was more interested in what the phone call was about.

Daniel had picked a romantic movie. I thought he was more suspense or sports guy. I wasn't watching the movie anyway. I hated romance flicks. They never appeared real to me, so I fell asleep.

All of a sudden I was sitting up yelling, "Don't touch me again!"

As I realized what the hell was happening, Collin and Daniel were watching me. *Stupid damn nightmares. Just once let me sleep without hearing their stupid voices or the mental pictures—just once.*

It was too real. I was going to be sick, and I ran upstairs to my bathroom and slammed the door behind me. Barely making it to the toilet in time, I lost my dinner. I lay down on the cold wood floor hoping that would cool me off. I stayed there a while before I heard a knock on the door.

Collin asked, "Can I come in?"

I was about to say no when he came in anyway. I just lay there on the floor as he sat on the edge of the tub.

"I am not going to ask if you are okay, it's clear that you are not," he said, reaching out to grab my hands to pull me up.

I took a minute to brush my teeth and put myself back together before entering my room, where he was already lying on the bed. I lay down facing him.

"What the hell is wrong with me?"

"Nothing is wrong with you. Just a crappy situation you're in," he said, pulling me closer to him, so I was right up against his body with my head buried in his neck.

We lay there just holding onto each other for many quiet moments. My arm started to fall asleep as I turned over. He cuddled up next to me with his arms still around me and kissed me on the shoulder.

"You want to talk about what really happened?"

I said no, but found myself telling him every detail anyway. He just lay there listening to me.

After an extended period of silence, he said, "Turn over and face me. I want to tell you something."

I turned, and he just stared at me with a look of confusion on his face. He moved closer to me, propping himself up on his elbow. He looked at me for what felt like forever and then he put his hand on my cheek. Slowly he leaned closer to me and kissed me. A tingling sensation ran through every part of my body. I had never felt a kiss like this before. I couldn't stop myself from kissing him back, and I put my arms around him, pulling him closer to me. I wanted every part of him, every second of his attention for the rest of my life.

He moved so he was lying on top of me, and I wrapped my legs around him. He was pulling my shirt off as I started pulling his off. Suddenly he pulled back and was standing at the foot of the bed with his hands on his head.

"We can't do this," he stood there breathless for a beat, before quickly leaving the room and slamming the door behind him.

I sat up wondering what had just happened. *I don't have those kinds of feelings for Collin. He's just a friend.* Then I had a moment of clarity.

"Well, hell, I finally get it," I mumbled, realizing I had been lying to myself all along. *No, he can't possibly feel that way about me. He is getting married for Christ's sake. I don't do serious, never have. I don't want any of this—ever.* I stayed in the room, deciding that would probably be a good idea for the night.

The next morning there was a knock on my bedroom door. Hoping to hear Collin's voice, I instead heard Daniel saying he was coming in. He came in and sat on the bed, and I knew he had already figured it all out.

"We have to get back home. Will you be okay alone?"

"Daniel, I'll be just fine. Thank you for coming to help me out. I appreciate it, sweet boy," I said, holding his hand.

"I'll call when we get home. You better text me back this time, or I will be back again, I swear," he said, laughing as he always did.

"Daniel," I said, as he was walking out the door, "I get it now."

He came back and hugged me and said, "I knew you would eventually."

CHAPTER 14

FINAL CARD?

I had gotten pretty lucky over the next month with the assault not going much further than the local news. Mike was mad at me for a couple of days because I hadn't called him when it happened. Business was busy at the bar, and our band played every weekend. I was okay with that because it gave me less time to think about the whole Collin thing. A month had gone by, and Daniel and I talked almost every day, but nothing was brought up about Collin. The schoolhouse was on track to being finished in May, and I couldn't wait. Mark had officially moved in with us, and the house became tiny.

I told Mike of the incident with Collin and how I finally "got it." We talked about it incessantly, the good and the bad. In the end, I decided it was best just to let it go considering Collin was getting married this summer. I caught a couple of the band's appearances on television. Collin was saying he was excited to get married, and he was lucky to have such a great woman in his life, which made me want to throw up.

One afternoon, while I was at the schoolhouse talking to the contractor, my dad showed up. I gave him a tour of everything that was getting completed, and I saved the gym for last. He was impressed. We had also talked about a few details about Collin. He mentioned he could tell there was some tension between us.

"What's up, Dad?" I asked, wondering why he seemed to be looking everywhere but at me after his comment about Collin.

"I was wondering if we could use the gym to shoot the new music video."

I answered quickly, "You know you can. You don't have to ask me."

He looked at me for a minute finally saying, "It isn't that easy, baby girl. It's the music video for the song we've been working on with Collin's band. They're going to be in it as well. Is that a problem for you?"

I looked at the floor as my heart dropped into my stomach and I grumbled, "No, Dad, it won't be a problem."

"Good. We're going to do it in two weeks. They'll be here for four days at the most. I'll have them just park here at the bus barn. We have power out there now, so they can stay there."

I thought maybe a nice trip to Hawaii during their visit would be a good idea for me, but unfortunately, I remembered I had to play that weekend, so I had no choice but to try to avoid them at all costs.

⚰ ⚰

Over the next couple days, Mike convinced me to do some shopping for clothes, which was never something I enjoyed. I couldn't remember the last time I had bought anything other than T-shirts, jeans, or sneakers. I was starting to think he was more concerned about how I looked than I was. He was picking out bras and underwear for me, too, this was new. Typically, he stayed out of this store saying that, in this department, I was on my own.

"Why are you doing all this?" I asked, watching in shock at the lingerie he was choosing for me.

"Just because you and Collin didn't work out is no reason not to make him see what he's missing," he said, giving me a big cheesy grin.

I found myself completely on board with his plan, and I started picking out more racy underwear.

A week later I lay in bed waking up, trying to answer Daniel's text:

Daniel: I am excited to hang out with you, boobless.
I hope we can have dinner or something.
I need to ask you a question.

I was eager to see him, as well, even though his new little nickname for me irritated the hell out of me.

Me: I'm glad we get to hang out.
Yes, dinner can be arranged.
Stop calling me boobless, you little shit!

Mike jumped in the middle of my bed, taking my phone as he started reading the messages, too.

"I have bad news for you, Boobless. They'll be here tonight and Rick's wife, and Steph are with them. Sorry, Daniel told me earlier."

"Stop calling me that! It's mean and could really affect my self-esteem," I said, trying to contain my laughter as I pried my phone out of Mike's hand. He burst out laughing.

I thought about just staying at home, but in the end, I decided I wanted to see Daniel. My dad is purposely scheduling them to do the video at night. It would keep them away from the bar, and I had thanked him a couple of times for that.

After deciding to make the best of it, I got dressed in the new clothes Mike had picked out for me. Deciding on the red button-up shirt with bar logos all over it, I made sure to leave it undone enough to see the top of my lacey black bra. I put much more effort into my hair and make-up than I had all year. When I left for the bar, I felt as good about myself as I did the night when we had gone clubbing.

We had just started our second set of the night when I noticed all of them walk in. I was instantly furious that Dad hadn't kept them away. I worked hard to concentrate on the music, but seeing Collin with his arms around his fiancée made me want to disappear.

Leave it up to Daniel: he started yelling, "Danni, you rock," as he waved at me. I couldn't help but laugh at him since he was messing up my backup vocals.

The next song was the one I always liked to show off with whenever we played. It went over so well, just as it had many times in the past. Screaming guitars and sex innuendos had the crowd's attention. I was doing everything not to look at Collin and his group. I noticed Mike standing by the stage watching me; by the look on his face, I could tell something wasn't right. After a song had ended, I moved over to the side of the stage as he climbed up.

"You're needed in the office," he said, as he leaned into my ear.

"Okay, let me finish first and I will go in there. Why? What's up?" I asked, not at all comfortable with the way he was shaking.

"Danni, please just meet me in the office after this set, okay?"

I nodded at him as we both went our separate ways. Everything was flowing perfectly with the house band tonight. We had never sounded better when we ended the second encore. As Kendrick and I were laughing at some drunk guy trying to ask me out, I heard Mike whistle from the bar.

I walked behind the bar as he said, "Those two gentlemen are here to talk to you." He was pointing over by my dad.

I saw the two detectives in suits and instantly recognized them. After all, I had a collection of their cards. *Why the fuck are they here now?* I made my way over to the reserved table where Dad sat with Collin and his group. The only way to talk to the detectives was to stand in front of Collin as he watched carefully. The music was loud so it wouldn't be easy for them to hear us anyway as I waved at Daniel as I walked up, as well.

The older detective said, "Hi, Danni. Can we have a few words with you?" He handed me yet another one of their business cards.

"I told you I would call if I remembered anything new. Why are you here when I'm working?" I asked, as my anger was starting to surface. I felt a hand wrap around my arm, and I knew it was Mike trying to calm me.

"Is there somewhere we could go and talk privately for a moment?"

I motioned that my office was down the hallway. I laid the card down on the table and slid it toward my dad. He got up to follow as Collin picked up the card. I think the look on my face must have said everything because the mood changed completely around the table.

I followed them into my office and shut the door. They took a seat where Mike pointed to the couch, and I sat in my chair behind my desk. It was hard to breathe as everything was moving in slow motion and the office became so small. Dad gripped my shoulder as he stood to my right and I leaned into him. Mike pulled up a chair on my left and grasped my hand.

The older detective said, "We are here to talk to you about both of your assault cases."

I was paralyzed, unable to breathe, realizing they must have put together what happened last month.

"We caught a break and possibly have the man in custody. We found your clothes from the night of the sexual assault. Also, we found your purse, laptop, and the bank bag."

I tried to move toward the door, but Dad and Mike held me in my seat.

"Do you know this man?" The younger detective asked as he put a mugshot on my desk and slid it toward me.

It took me a minute for my eyes to focus as I gripped both Mike and Dad's hands. I didn't have a face to go with the voice before, and I wasn't sure I wanted to put one with it now. I didn't want it in my nightmares. I finally looked at his picture and let out a gasp: I *did* recognize the guy.

Quietly I said, "He's one of our regular customers. He was one of the two men I kicked out early on Thanksgiving."

I sat back in my chair and started hyperventilating. *I knew him. I've waited on him so many times. He was always nice to me; why would he want to hurt me?* The dirty mechanic's shirt he always wore had his name stitched on the left breast pocket: Thom. I sat forward in my chair and put my head between my legs in an attempt to calm down and breathe. No one said anything for a couple of minutes.

Finally, the detectives talked more to Mike since he recognized him, too. I don't think I heard anything more they said. Dad was squatting in front of me moving his hands up and down my arms as he told me to take deep breaths.

"We need both of you to come to the station tomorrow, and sign statements stating this is, in fact, him. Danni, we need you to accurately identify him as the man that sexually assaulted you, but you have to be certain," the older detective said as Mike leaped out of his seat, losing his temper as the chair hit the wall.

"We will be there, and I'm sure she is certain who raped her!"

"Mike, sit down now! They are just doing their job," Dad yelled loud enough to get the attention of some people outside the office.

After Dad walked out with the detectives, Mike and I just sat there in silence, unsure what to do next. Finally, it just became too much. I had no choice. I had to find my numb. I walked out of the office and headed to the storage room to find a bottle of whiskey to crawl into. Mike didn't move, and I wondered if he was in shock.

Dad grabbed my arm and asked, "Baby girl, what are you doing?"

I pulled my arm back and yelled, "Who gives a shit what I do? I can't do this. I won't do this!"

I had gone from feeling pretty good about myself to being destroyed in a matter of twenty minutes. It was like my mind couldn't get the words of the detectives out of my head, and they were stuck on repeat. Dad let me go as I entered the storage room and locked the door behind me. With my back to the door, I slid down to the floor, feeling like I was breaking into a million little pieces. *I won't do this again; I won't.* I pulled my phone from my pocket and sent a text to the one person who could make it all stop.

Me: I need you. I need it to stop!

James: On my way.

Twenty minutes later, as I walked into my office with my bottle of opened whiskey, I glanced over to my dad's table. I saw them all still sitting there, and it pissed me off even more.

"I'm here. I will make it all go away, beautiful," James said as he slid up behind me and put his arms around my waist.

I smiled and raised the bottle toward James. He gladly took it. *Perfect*, I thought. *My night was about to get a lot better.* I also noticed that my dad, Collin, Mike, and Daniel were watching me. They all looked mad seeing James with me. He took my hand and pulled me to the middle of the dance floor, making it harder to be watched.

Pulling me close to him, he said, "I was glad to hear from you. I missed you."

I quickly asked, "Why didn't you call me?"

"I was under the impression that that guy over there," he pointed to Collin, "is your new man."

"Oh, hell no, that is not at all the case," I said as I wrapped my arms around his neck and he put his hands on my lower back, pulling me closer to him.

"Where is Amber?"

He laughed and simply said, "With Ron. Why are you concerned with her, anyway?"

"I was hoping you were single?"

He jokingly said, "Sorry, I'm saving myself for someone," as he winked at me.

He made me laugh and feel more relaxed, but I knew we were being watched.

"James, maybe we should take our party somewhere else," I said as I leaned into his neck with my fingers in his hair.

"I would rather put on a little show for Collin. He pissed me off at Thanksgiving when he kicked me out," he said as he started kissing my neck.

"Collin doesn't care what I do. That's his fiancée sitting with him."

He smiled down at me and said, "Even better."

Ironically, that's when one of Collin's steamier songs came on over the speakers. James and I began grinding on each other.

He whispered in my ear, "I was hoping that we could pick up where we left off before the cops stopped us."

I looked at him with my naughty smile and said, "Definitely. Can we go back to your place?"

"How about we start the party here?" He pulled something out of his shirt pocket.

I had to ask, "Is that the party?"

He smiled and said, "Let's get started."

Right there, in front of everyone on the dance floor, he kissed me. Not a simple, quick kiss either. It was a make-you-forget-your-name kind of kiss, and it felt so good. I kissed him back, and I suddenly wasn't concerned about who was watching or where I was. I was very turned on, just wanting to go to his place so I could undress him. He was kissing my neck at this point while running his hands over all the right places as mine made their way inside his shirt.

"I want to go now," I mumbled through our heavy breathing.

He came back to my lips, and, in between kisses, he said, "Think of this as foreplay."

He had popped a pill before he resumed our kissing. He passed me the pill with his tongue, and I swallowed it as I felt a tap on my shoulder. I turned to see Daniel.

"Dance with me," he stated, without looking away from my eyes.

James said, "I needed to use the bathroom, then we can go."

After watching James walk toward the bathroom, Daniel grabbed me by the waist and started dancing with me.

"What the hell are you doing, Danni?" he asked, and it wasn't in his usual upbeat way.

"Nothing, Daniel. I'm all right."

"Liar. This wouldn't make you feel any better. You know everyone is concerned that you are about to make a huge mistake right now."

Perhaps it was the whiskey or James, but I didn't care. I was just finding numbness.

"I don't care what any of you think. Get Collin and his stupid fiancée the hell out of my bar."

Daniel chuckled and replied, "You don't mean that. You're just angry, and you have every right to be, but don't do something you'll regret tomorrow."

James walked back up to us, and Daniel put his hands up in a surrendering move before he turned around and walked away. James didn't ask what happened or what was said. He just started kissing me again. He consumed me. I couldn't help but want more of him. He pushed me off the dance floor until we were up against a wall in a darker corner. We were getting very carried away with hands, lips, and rubbing. I needed him now before I let the voices from my nightmares tear me down again.

I said, "Wait for me out front while I grab my coat." He gave me a quick kiss on the lips before heading for the door.

Back in the office, I started pulling on my coat when I heard someone behind me as the door shut.

"Are you numbing yourself with that fucking loser?" I instantly knew it was Collin, and he sounded mad.

"I'm trying."

"Where are you going?"

I didn't know if I was jealous of his fiancée or just didn't care; I told him the truth. "I'm going with James to have mind-blowing sex."

"NO! That is just stupid. You can't," he yelled as his hand came down on the desk, hard.

Very bluntly, I fired back, "Why not? I'm sure you're going to fuck your fiancée tonight. I don't want you to do that." This moment of honesty seemed to surprise both of us.

He just stood there looking at me for a minute, and then said in a more concerned tone, "Because I don't want you to either, Danni. Please, just talk to me."

I bumped into him as I stormed out of my office. I was done with this conversation. He followed me, grabbing me by the arm and spinning me around. "Please. I'm asking you not to do this."

I pulled my arm back and just looked at him more frustrated than before. I turned away and headed for the door.

CHAPTER 15
COFFEE ANYONE

James dropped me off at the bar, so I could get my SUV from the garage after more kissing and touching goodbye for the day. My head was pounding from a major hangover. After we had left the bar the night before, we drove around in the country finishing the whiskey and remaining pills. I realized what I had done when I woke up naked next to him. I knew we had had sex, just by how sore I was in a particular region of my body. I was glad I didn't remember most of it. In my head, it was the perfect way to get the first time since the assault out of the way.

Dammit, I thought, seeing a huge line in the drive-thru at the diner. Deciding just to go inside, I wish I would have realized what a mistake I was going to be making. Wearing the same clothes from last night and looking like I had been up all night, I froze, seeing my dad, Collin, and all the band members sitting there eating breakfast.

Wow, this is awkward. I pushed my sunglasses up when I was asked for my order. I hoped they would all ignore me or maybe not realize it was me. There was a tap on my shoulder after I placed my order. I turned, and Daniel, with a smile on his face, knew my humiliation.

"Can I buy you breakfast?" he asked, handing the cashier money for my coffee.

"No thanks, sweet Daniel. I was just getting a cup of coffee to go," I said, stuffing my debit card back inside my wallet.

He had a huge smile on his face and said, "Come on, you must be starving and you know greasy food helps a hangover."

I couldn't help but smile back at him. He could read my moods and body language better than Mike could, and it made me nervous. The clerk sat my cup of coffee in a to-go cup on the counter, and Daniel picked it up.

"You want this? You have to come get it." He headed back to his table with my coffee.

The clerk asked, "You want a new cup?"

I smiled and said, "I'm pretty sure I can get it back, but he is an evil little man."

I was going to kill Daniel for this as he sat there taunting me with my coffee. I sat down with Dad. Collin was sitting on the opposite side of the table with Daniel. I decided to keep my sunglasses on and try not to make eye contact with anyone. My dad said good morning and asked if he could talk to me later; I nodded. I knew he would be upset. Hell, even I hated that I had done that to myself.

Collin had not yet looked up at me, and I knew he was angry. I thought *he can't be mad at me for anything. I don't belong to him, or to anyone, for that matter.*

After I hit Daniel in the arm, he finally gave me my coffee and asked, "You sure you don't want something to eat?"

"I have a few things I need to do," I mumbled, adjusting my sunglasses again. But, going to the police station wasn't one of them.

Without even looking up from his plate, Collin muttered, "Like fuck James."

I rolled my eyes and Dad must have kicked Collin under the table since he flinched. I said goodbye and headed for the door. I got in my car when a text from Daniel chimed:

Daniel: Sorry!! He is such an asshole! It was uncalled for. Can we have dinner tonight?

Me: Sounds great. I'll call you later with where and when.

Daniel: Super! I have something to ask you, boobless ;)

Mike was in the office working when I arrived home. I sat on the couch as he looked up at me.

"What are you doing?" I asked as I noticed he was very chipper this morning.

"I'm waiting to talk to you," he said as a huge grin came over his face.

I said, "You don't seem mad at me. Why is that exactly?"

"Why would I be? You're an adult. I may not agree with everything you do, but they are your choices. The only person that seemed mad last night was Collin, and he had no reason to be," he stated as he sat by me on the couch.

We talked for a while, and somehow I gave up the details of last night with James. Mike was glad I was starting to get back out there again, and I seemed happy considering the detectives' visit last night. I told him the truth: part of me did it out of my newly-admitted jealousy toward Collin and Steph. Of course, Mike had already put that together. I told him how I felt about James and that I wasn't sure I had the same feelings for him that he seemed to have for me. I joked that I should keep testing the water to find out, and Mike burst out laughing.

"You are completely back to your old normal self," Mike said after his fit of laughter. I rolled my eyes and changed the subject.

We talked about bar business a little bit before I asked, "Where is Mark?"

The look on his face wasn't quite right as his smile disappeared.

"We decided to take a break for a while. Mark has been pushing the marriage issue, and I don't know if that is something I want to do yet," he said, looking out the window.

I replied, "I'm surprised. I thought you always wanted the family thing."

"I am taking a page from your book by not being sure of what I want."

I had to laugh at him. "It sucks, doesn't it?"

We made plans to go to a bonfire party at Jackie's place later tonight. I mentioned that I didn't know anything about it, and he said she had sent him an email that morning and was hoping we would come.

After a very long nap and careful planning, I got everything worked out. I could have dinner with Daniel, go to the party with Mike, and spend the night with James. He had text messaged me once saying he couldn't wait to see me, but that he had to work until ten.

I met Daniel at the pizza place. He was sitting in a booth drinking a beer when I arrived. We talked about last night's events and he again apologized and mentioned that everyone eating breakfast with us thought that what Collin had said was cruel. I asked how long they were staying, and he said two more days. He told me Dad walked them around the schoolhouse and that he loved it, joking that he had even found the perfect room for when he comes to stay with me, and I laughed knowing he was serious. We ate pizza and talked some more, and I asked how he liked having all the girlfriends hanging around. He hated it. It wasn't because Daniel didn't have a girlfriend; it was because Rick and his wife fought the whole time and Collin changed when he was around his fiancée. He said that she was bossy and always got her way, and even mocked her with a whiny voice and hand movements. I couldn't help but laugh. He thought Steph liked Collin's money more than Collin himself.

Daniel's tone changed as he said, "I have something to ask you, and you can't laugh. I'm serious."

I laughed and said, "No, Daniel. I've told you before; I won't be your fuck buddy."

He put his beer down and placed his hand on his chest dramatically. "I'm hurt. I told you, 'friends that fuck,' not 'fuck buddies!' That is just mean."

I rolled my eyes at his ability to make everything dirty.

"Danni, would you please be my plus one for Collin's wedding?"

I started choking on my pizza when I realized he was serious. He sat there watching my reaction while he gave me his best puppy-dog face.

"Are you crazy? I absolutely have no desire to go whatsoever. I would rather be dragged over hot coals than go!"

Then, all sweet, he asked, "Would you please do it for me? I would be honored if you were my date."

"When is it?" I asked, hating myself for so quickly caving into him.

"July 29th.," he said as I snorted with laughter, pointing at him like he was making this shit up.

"Why is that funny, Danni?" he asked, looking confused as hell.

"Oh, sweet Daniel, that's my birthday, you know that!" I answered when he started laughing hysterically, too. "I'll think about it and get back to you."

"I will take that as a yes and RSVP. Would you like steak or lobster?" he asked, pretending to write it down.

I just shook my head knowing it was a losing battle with Daniel. It was only February, so I knew I had plenty of time to get out of it. We talked some more about our plans for the night, and I told him about the bonfire party. He was much more interested in it and stated he would find us after the video shoot. I chuckled as I asked if he got the half-naked girls he wanted and he joked that that was always the first thing they got rid of. He also told me that the wives and girlfriends had left that morning to go home. I was relieved not to have to witness any more of Collin and his fiancée all over each other. Daniel mentioned he got tired of watching it himself. Walking out of the restaurant, he said if they got done early, he would find me. I told him it was out in the middle of nowhere, and he wouldn't be able to find it. He just laughed and joked that he could always find me.

I stopped by the house and picked up Mike. Holding a bottle of whiskey, he climbed into the SUV. He punched the address into the navigation system and away we went. He asked about James and I told him he had to work until ten, and we would just catch up with each other later. I said that Daniel had asked me to be his date to Collin's wedding, and then he chuckled when I added that it was on my birthday. He ended up in tears because he was laughing so hard.

We shared the bottle of whiskey while we drove out to Jackie's and talked more about the Mark and Collin situations. Neither one of us knew what to do or if we even wanted to do anything. I had forgotten how much fun Mike and I always had together about the time he said it out loud.

We finally found Jackie's place and were shocked at how many cars were there already. I asked Mike how many people she had invited, and from what he had heard, it was pretty much everyone in town. After parking, we walked out to the middle of the field where the fire was going. Jackie came and hugged me and stated she was glad I was there. She started explaining where the beer was before stopping. "Never mind, what you two want is over there," as she pointed to the table with the hard liquor on it. We smiled and headed in that direction. We got a drink and found a table where we could watch the fire and stay warm. As I was sitting down, I heard a voice that I had hoped not to hear again.

"Hey, Danni, I haven't seen you for a while," Ron said, walking by me toward the beer table. *This can't be good.*

"Hi, Ron, how are you?" I asked, hoping to keep talk to a minimum.

Mike looked at me and asked quietly, "Who is that?"

I casually looked away and said, "Ron, or more commonly known as my dealer."

By the look on his face, he knew exactly who Ron was and didn't seem eager to talk to him either Jackie walked by asking if we had found a drink and I nodded at her. She walked over and sat on Ron's lap. I couldn't look away. He put his arm around her and his free hand on her thigh. Mike and I were sitting on a bench and practically fell off when we saw them, appearing very much together.

Mike looked at me and knew exactly what that meant. If Jackie was with Ron, that meant Amber was with James again. Mike put his arm around me and asked if I wanted to leave, but I shook my head no.

I pulled out my phone when it vibrated. Speak of the devil: James. I casually stood up and walked away from the crowd.

Trying to sound happy, I said, "Hey, what's up?"

"Sorry. I won't be able to make it tonight. Something has come up," he said, sounding as casual as ever.

I laughed and said, "James, I'm not dumb, so don't play games with me."

"What the fuck do you mean by that?"

"James, I'm not stupid. Ron is at this party with Jackie hanging on him. I know that means Amber is with you. Am I correct in that assumption?" I asked, hoping he would say no.

After a couple of moments of silence, he said, "You know how I feel about you. Nothing has changed between us."

I laughed and sarcastically responded, "So, is that why you're with someone who runs back to Ron every five minutes?" He said nothing.

After a few seconds, he let out a long sigh. "Listen, Danni, you are fun to play with, and we have a lot of things in common. You also know I am not interested in one woman. That hasn't changed. Now listen to me carefully. Please do your thing and I will do mine as we always have. Have fun at your party, and if you want, you can stop by later."

"Why the hell would I stop by with Amber there?" I yelled into the phone since I couldn't believe that he would even say that to me.

"Not just Amber, her friend Anne is also here. You are welcome to join. I would prefer if you did, but I realize Amber is not your favorite person. Just have fun at the party, okay?"

Mike had walked up and stood by me as I was talking to James. I hit the end button on the phone when he reached over and grabbed for it. I was close to stomping on it, and he knew I broke a lot of phones. He put his hand on my back and said how sorry he was, and we stood there for a little bit so I could compose myself. Apparently now I was a crier, which pissed me off even further. I hate when others cry around me. I have walked away from it many times. Not that I didn't have sympathy for people, just don't ask me to make you feel better when I'm far from fine myself.

Mike grabbed the drink out of my hand, downed the last of it, and then threw the cup on the ground angrily. Grabbing my hand, he said he knew what would make me feel better, and I didn't have it in me to argue. We stopped at my car, and he took the keys and motioned me to get in.

As I put my seat belt on, I asked, "Where are we going?"

He smiled as he started my SUV and said, "We're going to do something we haven't done in years, and I'm sure it will make both of us feel better."

I had a hunch he felt as emotionally screwed up as I was at that point.

We got back to town and it was only nine, so we headed for the bar. After pulling into the back garage, he told me to follow him. The bar was closed, considering it was Sunday night, so we had the place all to ourselves. When I saw him pulling all the blinds closed, I knew exactly what we were going to do. When we first started the bar and we didn't know many people in town, we would hang out here and try to invent the weirdest drinks we could come up with. Oh, how I had missed that.

He was a full-time bartender now, and I was only part-time, so this would not end well for me. To make it more fun, we started applying rules: namely, you can't touch the shot glass with your hands or ask what was in it. If you forgot these rules, you had to drink one of the bad shots from the old bottles of liquor no one ever ordered from. They were lined up on the back counter, and Mike had even lit one on fire and dared me to drink it. We decided that would be the loser's glass.

After a bathroom break, I came back to Mike, who was talking to someone on my phone. When I got closer, he hung up quickly and tried to act like nothing happened.

"Who was that?" I asked, and he smiled while turning on the stereo, drowning my question out.

Mike sang along as he put a shot of something black in color in front of me and told me to try it. I heard my phone go off then, and Mike pulled it from his pocket. He listened to someone and mumbled quietly before hanging up. He took off jogging toward the back garage, and I realized he was letting someone in. I wondered if it was Mark, but then realized that he wouldn't call my phone. Then I saw all of them walking in Daniel, Collin, and Rick. I was not thrilled, to say the least.

Standing behind the bar, I leaned over the shot and used my mouth to pick it up, quickly swallowing it in one gulp. It burned all the way down and my tongue felt like it was on fire as I quickly grabbed my water.

They sat up at the bar across from us, as Mike filled them in on the rules and how to play.

Daniel smiled ready to play our drinking game and said, "I knew there was a reason I liked the two of you!"

So far Collin and I hadn't looked at each other, and I hoped it stayed that way. My turn came up to make a shot, and now I had to make four of them. I wanted to make it as putrid as possible. I used the mint liquor and the cinnamon that no one ever asked for, knowing it was a horrible combination. I put one in front of each of them and told them to enjoy. When I handed Collin his shot, he made eye contact with me; instead of looking mad, he looked dejected, and I felt a little sorry for him.

Rick asked, "What are those?" as he pointed to the back counter where the one shot still burned. Mike pointed out that he had just broken a rule and had to drink one.

Rick laughed and said, "They can't be that bad."

Mike handed him one and said, "Good luck."

They all mimicked what they saw me do minutes ago, quickly drinking down their shots without using their hands.

Daniel was quick to say, "That was the worst shot I have ever had!"

I laughed and said, "This is also the first time you've played with us."

My phone rang at that point, and I looked to see who it was, already having an idea. James' name flashed across the screen, and I lost my temper. I threw the phone across the bar where it hit the brick wall and fell to pieces. Everyone looked at me with confused faces except Mike, who probably expected it.

Daniel asked, "What the hell was that for?"

I didn't say a word when Mike said, "A bad idea," before he looked at me for my turn in our game.

I asked, "When did it become the four of you against me?"

Mike laughed and said, "You could easily out-drink all of us."

I smiled knowing he was a lightweight when Collin quickly responded, "I think we can give you a run for your money."

"How much money are you talking?" I asked, very curious.

"How does one-hundred bucks each sound?" He didn't break eye contact with me, and my brain screamed that this was a bad idea.

We all put a one-hundred-dollar bill on the bar and agreed that the person who took the last shot would win. Mike put a shot in front of me that was pee-yellow, and I picked it up to look at it. Instantly I knew I shouldn't have done that when Daniel called me on it. Mike put another in front of me that was clear, and I hoped it was water. The first one tasted like beef jerky, and I quickly wondered what could taste that horrid. I used the second shot to wash it down, and that one was good, it tasted like whipped cream, so I knew it was flavored vodka. This went on for a while before I finally convinced Daniel to come to my side. With the music playing, we danced and just had fun screwing around.

The look on Collin's face was hilarious when Daniel asked if he could make the next round for them and I agreed. Collin shook his head at me and mouthed "no" and I just laughed as Daniel got to work, knowing this wouldn't be good for them.

Apparently, Daniel makes worse drinks than I do. Collin and Rick both looked like they were going to throw up after they took theirs. After a short rest period, Collin decided he needed to make our next shot. I was a little nervous about what he could come up with now.

While Collin carefully put a shot in my cleavage, he said "I have a new rule. You have to do the shots off someone."

I had worn a low-cut shirt with a push-up bra for tonight for other reasons, but it came in handy now. Collin smiled at me and went back to his side of the bar. Daniel didn't hesitate as I felt his hot breath on my chest and his hands on my hips. He took the shot quickly before he moved away and glanced at Collin. Daniel complained that Collin didn't know how to make drinks at all. I was scared of what was in store for me.

Daniel looked at me smiling and said, "Where do you want me to put it?" I was completely blank when he said, "Here, I'll help you."

As he put the glass between his stomach and his belt buckle, I quickly felt my cheeks turn red. I was not about to lose to Collin, though. I just went for it and took the shot, avoiding touching Daniel as much as possible. Daniel was right: the drink was awful. It tasted like cotton candy and tomatoes.

It was Collin's turn considering Mike was passed out on the couch in my office, and Rick had his head down on the bar, mumbling about surrender. I grabbed the hottest cinnamon I could find and decided not to water it down. Daniel grabbed the shot and shoved it in my cleavage, looked at Collin, and said: "your turn" as he started walking away.

"Where are you going?" I asked as Collin started laughing.

"To throw up."

Collin quickly asked, "You admitting defeat?"

"Yes!" Daniel said, starting to run to the bathroom.

Collin got up and walked over to me and said, "You know I'm going to win, right?"

I assured him that I could hold my own. He put his hands on my hips and slowly took the shot and drank it. He instantly grabbed his water and drank all of it.

"Fuck! What the hell was that?" he asked, reaching in the cooler for more water.

I couldn't help but double over in laughter at how red his face was turning.

"I can come up with something much worse, little girl," he stated as I sat up at the bar to watch him.

After searching through all the bottles, he settled on one and turned his back to me. I didn't see what he grabbed until he walked toward me with something green. Stopping incredibly close to me, he grinned, and I leaned away slightly. As I sat on the bar, he put the shot in between my thighs then placed his hands on my thighs. He was so close I could feel his breath on my neck, using my brain didn't seem to be working at this point.

"Danni, how about we make this much more interesting?" he said, running his finger down my neck.

"How could we do that?" I asked while trying to calm my racing heart.

"I see that you have a stripper pole over there."

"Oh, hell no, Collin!" I said as my brain started working again.

He went back to thinking and smiled at me and said, "If I win, you have to make an appearance in the video we're shooting."

I thought to myself, *how bad could that be?* I agreed and countered that if I won, they would play free one night at the bar. He agreed. I could feel the sexual tension between us and tried to get back to the game, ignoring the fact that I wanted to kiss and undress him. I told myself to stop and come back to reality.

He moved the shot so I could hop down off the bar. I fell sideways when gravity took over, and he grabbed me, so I didn't face plant on the floor. He pulled me close to him, and that didn't help at all considering I had other ideas of what I wanted to do with him. I stepped back, and he let go of me just in time for Daniel to sit down at the bar, asking what he had missed. Collin told him how we made the bet more interesting. I knew I couldn't lose and still keep my dignity intact.

"Let me help you out, Danni," Collin said as he picked up the shot and placed it between his stomach and jeans.

I looked down at the shot as he held up his shirt and I could see his hard, tanned stomach. *Dammit, why did he have to be so sexy? No wonder he was on magazine covers all the time.* I took the plunge, leaned over the shot, my fingers lingered on the flesh at his waistband. I heard his sharp intake of breath as my lips brushed against his skin before I pulled the shot free and drank it.

I stood there for a minute when it hit me: I was going to be sick. I took off running for the bathroom.

After ten minutes of putting myself back together, I walked back to the bar. Collin and Daniel were sitting there drinking water, and Rick was still face down on the bar, out cold. I grabbed water and a bottle of pain reliever, hoping not to be sick anymore.

"How does it feel to lose?" Collin asked, grinning.

I knew when I threw up that I had lost and slowly turned to face them. They both had huge smiles on their faces. I started walking toward the employee lounge.

"Where are you going?" Daniel asked.
"I'm going to sleep on one of the couches in the lounge. Goodnight, boys."

They both got up and followed me. Daniel plopped down on one couch and made sure there was no room for anyone else. I grabbed a blanket and collapsed, just wanting to sleep.

"Move over so I can lie down, too," Collin said, lowering himself behind me on the narrow couch.

Considering how much sexual tension there was between us, I wondered if that would be a good idea. He left me no choice as he made himself comfortable and smashed me up against the back of the couch. I had my back to him, and he swung his arm over me and pulled me close to him. I was too tired to care at this point and the comfort I felt in his arms made me stay still as we both fell asleep.

A couple of hours later I got up and went to the bathroom to get sick again. When I went back to the couch, I noticed Collin was sitting up waiting for me.

I whispered to him, "Go back to sleep."

He got up to go to the bathroom, looking pretty much like I felt. I crawled back on the couch and got comfortable just in time for him to come back and make it not so comfortable. He crawled in behind me like he had earlier and this time he didn't put his arm around me. I was relieved just to go back to sleep.

"Turn around and face me, Danni," he whispered while running his hand down my arm.

I whispered back, "I don't think that's a very good idea."

"Why? Does it have anything to do with fucking James last night?" he stated in an annoyed whisper.

That instantly pissed me off, and I tried to get up. He grabbed me, turned me on my back, and held my hands down. This set off all my panic buttons. I was confused, crying and screaming hysterically at him.

"Please don't kill me! Please don't kill me!" I kept screaming without even thinking about my choice of words as I fought back.

Daniel yanked him off of me, and I was shaking uncontrollably. He was yelling at Collin as all these pictures popped in my head: a cornfield, a knife, and the moon above me.

"Danni, it's me, Mike. Take a breath for me. You're okay. I got you. You're safe. Look at me, Danni," Mike rambled as I focused on him above me.

"That's it, Danni, just keep looking at me, deep breaths for me," he continued as he put his palm against my cheek.

I stopped screaming and grabbed onto him as the cloud in my mind started to clear. I realized where I was and what triggered my response with tears running down my face.

"There is my girl. You okay now?" Mike asked when I realized my hands had a death grip on his forearms.

I relaxed and let go of him, nodding.

"Come on. I think we should go home now," he said as I heard Daniel screaming.

"What were you thinking to do that to her? Don't you ever do that again or I will kill you. Mike warned you what sets her off and you couldn't even fucking listen to him."

Collin didn't say anything. He just looked at me with concern in his eyes. I knew he didn't mean to scare me, but I also knew he was an ass when he mentioned James. Mike was right. I needed to go home. Daniel's words sunk in and I wondered what he meant by "what sets me off."

CHAPTER 16
FEELINGS SUCK

It was three in the afternoon when I finally crawled out of bed feeling like I had been hit by a bus. I was hungover big time. It took me two attempts to take a shower: I needed to sit for a minute in between to make the room stop spinning.

I got dressed and put my sunglasses on before going downstairs. Someone had made coffee. Normally it smelled wonderful, but right now it made me gag. I saw Mike sitting at the table, and he looked worse than I did. I had to laugh a little at our situation. I sat down at the table with him, and we compared how horrible we each felt, both remembering why we had quit playing that game.

"I heard you lost a bet last night?" he said, looking over his coffee cup.

"Yeah, but it was only a hundred bucks. No big deal," I said.

"I heard it was more than that."

I shot him a nasty look, and he changed the subject by mentioning he put my phone back together, and it seemed to be fine. He pointed to the counter where it was charging, and I walked over and grabbed it. Seventeen text messages and twenty-two missed calls.

"Wow," I said out loud, shocked at the number of messages.

Mike winked at me and said, "Only one of them is from your dad. The rest are from Collin."

I asked, "What does Dad want?"

"He needs you to come out to the schoolhouse and sign some papers for something."

I vaguely remembered he had mentioned that a couple of days ago. I texted Dad that I would be out in a little bit. Afterward, I deleted all of Collin's texts and calls. It was over and done, and I hoped never again to bring up what had happened.

An hour later Mike and I headed out to the schoolhouse. He mentioned on the way out that he and Daniel talked to Collin about last night. Mike explained that he didn't think Collin meant to scare me. I agreed with him, it had just freaked me out a little.

"You know, Mike, it wasn't him grabbing me like that, it was the comment he made about me sleeping with James that pissed me off," I said as we turned down the dirt road.

"I hadn't heard that part. I think you should hear him out and let him apologize before you hate his guts forever," he said casually, trying to defuse the situation.

We turned into the schoolhouse driveway, and I couldn't help rolling my eyes when I saw the tour buses still there.

"I thought they were leaving this morning, dammit," I mumbled more to myself before Mike changed the subject mentioning that he thought Dad's house would be done before ours. I laughed and said, "Ours?"

He responded, "It looks like you have plenty of room to spare. So, I should just stick with you."

I laughed and said, "I like the idea, Mike, but I don't think you should give up on Mark quite yet." He rolled his eyes at me as we got out of the SUV.

We walked into the schoolhouse and were surprised by how much it had changed. The main floor looked like a school until you looked inside what was once the classrooms. The area was now a huge recording studio and the other side had turned into an apartment for overnight guests. I planned that part with Daniel in mind. We walked upstairs into the kitchen, and it looked impressive. The cherry cabinets had been put in, and the hardwood floors were finished. They were working on the wiring and the fireplaces today.

I walked past the kitchen dragging Mike to the first extra bedroom. He asked if it was too late for him to pick the paint color. Then I took him into what was going to be my room. I explained to him that I wanted to restore most of it the best I could, leaving the old original red brick walls. Next, I showed him what was going to be the closet and the bathroom. He laughed at me when he saw there was a fireplace in the bathroom as well as in the bedroom. We heard the music stop, and he seemed eager for us to go down to see the band shoot their scenes.

I was surprised at how many people were working when we walked into the gym. An incredible amount of equipment was lined up around the sides of the space. Mike and I climbed up on the bleachers on the opposite side. I waved at my dad, and he waved back, grinning at me. It was then that I noticed Collin looking at me, as well. I gave him a small wave, and instantly his face lit up. Daniel yelled hello to us before he beat on his drums.

They started playing at the director's cue. It was downright exhilarating to watch them in action, and, once again, I was reminded of why I thought Collin was so sexy: his deep, scratchy voice and the way he moved when he played. Holy hell, I wanted to jump on him and take his clothes off right there. Instantly I scolded myself for how easy I could get lost in him with all my dirty thoughts. I didn't want to be physically or emotionally attached to anyone other than my family members. End of story...or, so I thought as I hopped down and walked out of the gym.

Mike came to me and asked, "Danni, what's wrong?" He had to yell so I could hear him over the music.

I yelled back as I pointed down the hall toward the stage, "What the hell is it about him that consumes me? I find myself wanting to kiss him among other things, and it drives me nuts!"

I realized the music had stopped, and I was still yelling. *How perfect*, I thought and started heading for the front door.

Mike was instantly by my side "Do you want an answer to that question or not?"

"Sure, why not," I snapped as we both stopped and looked at each other.

He put his hands on my shoulders and very calmly said, "You are so good at ignoring unpleasant things that sometimes you ignore the good moments, as well."

I looked at him and asked, "What are you talking about?" I hated riddles, and he knew this.

"Danni, you're in love with him," he said before he stepped back to let me absorb that.

"What? No. NO! Are you crazy?" I scoffed at him, and he just looked at me smiling.

I stood there for a minute trying to process what he had just said. *No way. I am not capable of being in love. Not me.* I was internally arguing with myself, and Mike knew it as he watched me.

"Collin is getting married, *remember?*" I said, running my hands through my hair.

"Why do you think Collin struggles to be around you, as well? He is in love with you, too. He's trying to deny it as much as you are."

I leaned against the wall replaying things in my head. In a roundabout way, it made sense. I hated admitting that to myself.

Mike said, "Daniel and I have known this for the past ten months, and we thought you both realized it, too."

About that time Daniel came down the hall and asked, "Hey, why did you run off?"

Mike quickly caught him up and he laughed and said, "Finally, we can talk about it now. Man, you are slow, Danni."

I tried to hit him, but Mike blocked my clear shot. Daniel looked at me and said, "If you think Collin isn't aware of how he feels for you, you're wrong. He's well aware of who he wants to be with. It's not that easy, though."

"Then why is he getting married?" I asked, frustrated.

Mike answered, "That is a question none of us can answer right now."

Collin turned the corner pulling his ear pieces out as we all stopped talking.

"What's going on? Danni, are you okay?" Collin asked, stopping directly in front of me.

I nodded as Mike quickly changed the subject. I felt weird around him suddenly as I just stood there saying nothing. Collin stepped closer not caring who was around as he put his hands on my cheeks. His dark blue eyes stared into mine as I inhaled a quick breath and tried not to touch him back.

Oh, thank God, I thought, hearing Dad call my name. I yelled back and started walking toward the gym.

Collin grabbed my hand and asked, "Can I talk to you alone for a minute?"

Mike and Daniel quickly made their way to the gym, looking back at me and smiling. I leaned against the wall again and tried to control all the new information in my head.

Collin asked again, "Are you okay?"

"Collin, I am fine. I just reacted a little quickly. I'm sorry. I'm working on it."

"Danni, I feel horrible. I should never have touched you that way or tried to provoke you. I was a complete dick, and I'm sorry. Please forgive me."

I nodded at him, unable to look him in the eye without wanting to kiss him.

"Come on, you can watch us do the last take," he said, grabbing my hand and lacing his fingers in mine as we walked back to the gym.

"By the way," he said, glancing at me, "I think this place is the coolest home I have ever seen."

He took off to the stage as we entered the gym and I walked over to my dad. He was standing with a gentleman I didn't recognize who was wearing a suit.

"Hey, Dad, what do you need me to sign?" I asked as he pointed to a contract sitting on a table between them. "What is it?" I asked, picking it up.

"A present, baby girl. Read it and we can answer any questions you have," he replied, signaling between him and whoever the guy was standing by us.

I quickly scanned the contract. It was the record company's offer to pay me for letting them use the school for the video. I had to grab my dad's arm for support when I saw how much. *No freaking way. Just to let them use my unfinished home?*

I told him it was too much, and he assured me it was what the going rate was.

"Sign the contract and take the money or I will tell Collin you love him," he joked, holding a pen out to me.

I looked at him asked, "What are you talking about?"

"You know exactly what I am talking about."

"Fine," I said and signed the papers before handing them back to him.

As I tried to walk off, he said, "Baby girl, I have one more thing for you to sign."

The man in the suit put a large envelope in front of me. It had a different attorney's name embossed on the outside. I took the papers from the envelope and saw it was a barrister in Canada. Obviously, this must be the man in front of me.

"Hi, Danni, my name is Dave Slage. I represent Carter Sanchez, or 'Shorty,' as most people called him."

I shook his hand and asked, "What is all of this?"

"Take a moment and read it and then I will answer any questions you have."

I started reading the papers talking about inheritance. Some guy named Shorty named me as one of two of his beneficiaries. I didn't even know this person. He was leaving me a significant amount of money and property in Vancouver, BC.

"Dad, I think they have the wrong person," I said, dumbfounded.

"No, Baby Girl. You're the right person. Shorty was your grandfather on your mom's side. He recently passed away and listed you as a beneficiary."

"What about Mom?" I asked, realizing how weird it was to say that word.

"I don't know anything about that. I asked Dave, and he can't answer any questions unrelated to your grandfather's wishes."

I signed the papers and gave them back to the lawyer, mostly because of frustration of not being comfortable enough to talk about anything related to my mom.

After signing a dozen times and getting Dave to leave already, Mike and I watched the band finish up the video.

"Are you Danni?" I turned to a tall redheaded woman tapping me on the shoulder.

"Yes. Why?" I asked a little snippy, not in the mood to deal with anyone else today.

"We need to get you ready. Will you please come with me?" she asked, seeming a little afraid of me.

I looked at her with complete confusion on my face and said, "Look, chick, I have no idea what you're talking about. I probably don't want to know either, so run along."

"Danni, be nice!" Mike snapped at me with a mean look on his face.

Collin and Daniel hopped off the stage and came toward us. Both of them had huge smiles on their faces. Instantly I had an idea of what the redhead was talking about.

I looked at Mike and said, "Oh, hell no. Not gonna happen."

Collin sat down beside me and said, "You remember that bet?" As his sly smile that always seemed to get the best of me appeared on his face, I decided to play dumb and shook my head, and Collin started laughing. Dad had walked over at that point smiling, as well.

"I'm leaving now because I don't think me being here will make you two comfortable. Collin, I expect you to treat my baby girl with nothing but respect. Do you understand me?" Dad asked, focusing his protective look toward Collin.

"Yes, Billy. I will take excellent care of your baby girl," Collin said, trying to keep a straight face with Daniel already laughing.

Mike stood up about that time, and I grabbed his arm and quickly said, "You are not leaving!"

He looked back at me and said, "I wouldn't miss this for the world. I'm going to get my camera from the car."

He gave me the smile he always used when he couldn't wait to watch me make an ass of myself. At this point, I was giving up on the idea that I might get out of this.

I finally asked, "What exactly do I have to do?"

Daniel kept laughing and took off after Mike to avoid the conversation. Collin put his arm around my shoulders.

"I will lead, and all you have to do is follow me. I'm sure you will catch on quickly."

Well, that confused me even more. The redhead was back, and Collin urged me to follow her, which I reluctantly did. I followed the woman to the locker room trying to remember if there was an exit in there. A sign greeted me indicating that this was the costume, hair, and make-up room. I felt sick to my stomach just thinking about anyone touching me, even if it was just to make me look camera-ready.

It had been years since I went with my dad to his video's shoots. I remembered being a kid and Mike and me running around getting yelled at the whole time. Dad would always end up calling Rosa to tell her to get us because we could never behave. It made me smile thinking back to all the trouble Mike, and I could get into.

The redhead led me to a chair and told me to have a seat. Another older woman was waiting for us as I sat down. The redhead explained what I was here for. The first question she asked me was when the last time was that I had waxed or shaved. After I heard that question, I started to panic. *What had I gotten myself into?* I told her it had been a while, and she sighed and started pulling all kinds of beauty products out of a box. The truth was I hadn't been waxed or even been to a salon since the assault. I hated what I looked like naked and had no desire for anyone else to see my scars. They still broke me a little emotionally when I saw them.

I spent two hours getting waxed, spray tanned, and made-up, before she did my hair and makeup, and finally took me to a room and told me I needed to get dressed. I stepped into the one-person shower stall, pulled the red drape back, and saw my outfit draped over the chair. It was a very tiny pair of black lacy boy shorts, which I was okay with considering that is usually what I wore. The problem was that there was no top. I laughed hysterically and walked back out to find the grumpy lady.

Finding Grumpy, I said, "Excuse me but there is no top. I need a top."

She rolled her eyes and said, "I am aware that there is no top. Please finish getting ready."

"Nope!" I said popping the "p" sound and giving her back some attitude, "I need a top. No top, no video!"

She left the dressing room looking like she was ready to kill me. A couple of minutes later I heard Collin asking if everything was okay outside my makeshift dressing room.

"I need a top," I said from behind the curtain, hoping he couldn't hear the panic in my voice. This was making me super uncomfortable. It was a known fact by most who knew me that my discomfort meant I was going to show my extremely bitchy side. Mike could control it, but this took years of practice.

Collin came in as I stood there in the underwear and robe. He looked at me and said, "Wow, Danni, you are stunning."

"I wouldn't put too much appreciation into what can easily be wiped off," I said, pulling my robe snug around me.

He put his hands on my shoulders, which instantly made me think of other things I shouldn't have been thinking of.

"Come on. I promise you I won't let anyone see anything they shouldn't," he said, pulling me along behind him.

I wondered perhaps if I tried not to touch him maybe that would help me remember he's getting married. That seemed to be a good theory. Also, not looking at his ass when he walked in front of me would probably be a good idea, too. I completely failed at that part. *Damn, the way his dark jeans hugged him in all the right spots was not helping.*

We made our way to the gym and the director told me exactly what the scene was and what I needed to do. *It was official: this was the worst bet I had ever made.*

I walked up onto the stage, and the only thing I could see was a bed in the middle of the platform. It was covered with a black satin sheet with candles strategically placed all around it. I couldn't tell if anyone was watching since the only soft lights directed toward the bed. I hoped they all had left to save me further embarrassment.

I asked the redhead, "Are there going to be a lot of people watching?"

"No, honey, Collin asked for it to be a closed set."

Oh, thank holy heaven on Earth, I praised, feeling much better until she told me to take off my robe and lie on the bed. Nausea rolled over me. *I don't have the guts to do this.* My body reminded me what the director said I was supposed to do, and I found myself a little excited. I grabbed the top sheet off the bed before I took off my robe and covered my chest so no one would get a good look. I lay down on the bed quickly.

I heard a couple of whistles and knew that Mike and Daniel were being removed from the gym. I pulled the sheet over my head. Feeling someone else lie down on the bed, I jerked away automatically.

"Why are you covering your face, pretty girl?" Collin asked in a playful voice.

"I want to die," I said, trying to keep a hold of the sheet he was pulling away.

He laughed and said, "Relax. It's just you and me and maybe three camera people. They are professionals just doing their jobs. I will direct you with movements. Just play along with what I do first."

I groaned in complete frustration trying to disappear in the sheet.

He laughed managing to pull the sheet away as I moved onto my stomach to hide my boobs. We made eye contact and looked at each other with lust all over our faces. *This was not good.* It just forced me to want more of what I couldn't have.

"You look beautiful," he said in a whisper as he ran his fingertips down my back and I shivered.

I noticed he wasn't wearing a shirt either. I wanted to reach out and run my fingers down his chest and stomach.

"Danni, why are you looking at me like that? I can't think when you do that," he whispered, moving closer as I rolled onto my side and he pulled me against his chest.

Earlier the director told me we were supposed to roll around basically in bed very passionately, and now that felt exactly right. The music came on full blast and scared me out of my daydream. Collin must have felt me jump, and he pulled me toward him, so our fronts were touching. I moaned low, feeling our skin touching. He leaned further over me, moving my hair away from my neck.

I was half-naked and knew getting up meant being naked in front of everyone and that was not an option. The music was slow as he rolled on top of me. My whole body instantly felt like I was on fire and I couldn't help but gasp for air. Lying there with both of us shirtless, I started letting myself feel his touch. He radiated heat off his tan, muscular chest. I ran my fingers over his cheeks and into his disheveled hair.

"Put your arms around me," he said, leaning into my neck as I felt his hand slide down my side.

He rolled me over, so I was on top of him, making me bring my legs up to straddle his hips. I closed my eyes, feeling his hands run down my back and over my ass. I tried to listen to the music, so I wouldn't do anything embarrassing. He slowly started kissing my neck. His hands ran down my sides, and I put my hands on his shoulders and then on his neck.

"Open your eyes and look at me," he said, planting kisses along my jaw and ear.

When I did look at him, I realized Mike and Daniel, and everyone for that matter was right. I was madly in love with this man and wanted every part of him. I leaned in and planted my lips on his, hoping the director wouldn't stop me. Instead, he pulled me closer and started kissing me back with more force. The music kept playing with no one yelling "stop." I forgot about everyone around us, and I let myself get lost in him. Collin's tongue ran along my lips when I opened my mouth more, giving into anything he wanted to do.

I noticed the song had started over, and the lighting was a little different, and we rolled over so he was on top of me. He was kissing my neck and chest like a man losing control. I arched my back and moaned as he came back up to my neck and pulled my hands over my head.

"Keep them there, baby," Collin said as he slowly pulled his hands back down to my chest and I felt him touching me. I couldn't help myself as I arched my back again and let out a louder moan. He must have liked it because he started kissing me even more passionately after that. I pushed him back over, so I was on top of him. I did what he had done and pulled his hands over his head while I started kissing his neck and chest. I let myself perhaps go a little too low as I kissed his stomach near his jeans. I couldn't stop myself as I popped open the top button and licked his lower stomach. I felt his hand fist my hair as he propped himself up on an elbow to watch me. The music stopped, and the director yelled that that was a wrap.

No, it can't be over. I needed so much more of Collin and judging from his impressive erection, he wanted more, too. I had to take a moment before I could move. Otherwise, I might do something I couldn't stop. I was so close to ecstasy.

"You okay, baby?" Collin asked, breathing heavily as I glanced up at him and shook my head.

"Shut up and don't move," I quietly said letting my body win as pleasure clouded my mind.

He lay back and started laughing silently. I felt like an idiot. After a couple of minutes, I saw my robe lying on the bed. I grabbed it and started back to the dressing room.

Instead of being embarrassed, I was pissed off. I knew exactly why I was mad, and it had everything to do with him getting married. *I wanted him, and she didn't deserve him.* I got dressed and walked out when I heard Mike and Daniel make catcalls. I flipped them off and could tell that they both knew I was upset.

I got in my car and left, not even thinking that Mike had rode out with me. I had no idea where I was going. I just knew I needed to make all these feelings and thoughts stop.

CHAPTER 17

KISS ME

After half an hour of driving around in the country, with my phone off, I found Ron's house.

The door was open this time, and I walked right in. As always, there were a lot of people crowded in the little room. I looked down, trying to keep a low profile as I heard a couple of people say "hi." I nodded back, realizing I still had on all the stupid make-up and crap from the video. I saw a guy I recognized and knew he was the one to help me find Ron. I walked over to him, not knowing what to say; he grabbed my elbow and led me to the bedroom. He motioned for me to sit on a chair in the corner before leaving me in the room by myself. The room seemed darker than the last time I had been here. I wondered if that had to do with Amber being gone.

Ron walked through the door and said, "Well, hello stranger. I was wondering when I would see you again." He got right in my face and eyed me up and down, saying, "You look like a stripper. Want to give me a private show?"

I rolled my eyes and said, "That isn't why I'm here, Ron, I'm sure you know that."

"I had to ask. I know why you're here. But I can always hope for more," he said, looking more at my chest than at my face. "Have you heard from Amber or James?"

"Not since the last time I saw you. You and Jackie a thing now?" I asked, mocking him.

Ron laughed and said, "For now." He slid his arms around my waist and continued. "What exactly are you trying to forget?"

"Everything. Can you help me with that?" I said, pushing his arms away from me.

"You like what I gave you last time?"

I nodded at him before thinking maybe I shouldn't be doing this. I had turned my life back around after everything that had happened. But rolling around on that stupid bed with Collin came back to the front of my mind.

Ron opened a closet after getting keys out of his pocket and said, "I have exactly what you need. Open your hand."

I walked over to him and was taken back seeing what I assumed was tons of illegal drugs. I held out my hand as he turned toward me and dropped three little white pills into my palm.

"What is it?" I asked, wondering if that was enough.

"Does it matter, Danni? It will take care of you. I don't have what you got last time, so this will have to do. I can let you know when I get the other stuff," he said as he locked the closet door.

I took the pills, leaving one for later as I shoved it in my back pocket. "How much do I owe you?"

He suddenly became all business, talking prices, quality, and value. He appeared very proud of himself. I pulled a couple of hundred-dollar bills from my pocket and held them out to him.

He smiled and said, "You know we could make another arrangement if you want." He put his arms around me and tried to kiss me.

I pulled back and seethed, "Let go of me. I have no intentions of any sexual favors. Ever!"

He didn't let go of me. Instead, he backed me into a corner and said, "Come on, Danni. I'll make it quick."

I shoved him away successfully as he had started unbuttoning my shirt. I didn't have a bra on and had no intention of showing him anything. He finally gave up and smiled at me, whispering, "maybe next time." He took the money out of my hand, and I quickly headed for the door. I climbed back in my car and got the hell out of there as fast as I could. I knew it wasn't a good idea to ever come back.

I didn't have any idea where to go or what to do. I was in the mood to party and decided to go to town and see what I could find. *Wow*, I thought, *I feel great*. I was completely relaxed and easily forgot about Collin and all that crap. I had found a half-full bottle of whiskey that Mike had left in the car. *Even better.*

As I got into town, I drove by the sleazy strip bar that I had never stopped at before. Lots of motorcycles were sitting out front. *What the hell? I'm here, and I wouldn't mind seeing a naked woman.* Sure, we women could be catty and jealous, but I still appreciated a beautiful body, male or female. I liked both and wasn't ashamed of it. I pulled into the parking lot and went in to have a drink, stumbling a little bit before I made it to the door. *Perhaps I had had enough . . . Nope, I'm still conscious.*

I opened the door and quickly realized that it was one of those bars where you walked in, and everyone turned and stared at you. I was no exception. I ignored them, sat at the bar, and ordered a whiskey.

An older man placed the whiskey in front of me and said, "Drinks are free if you want to get up on stage and show us that sexy little body of yours, sweetie."

I slid a twenty across the bar. He could tell by the look on my face the answer was "no."

An hour later I was on my third drink and barely functioning when I saw Jackie on the stage taking off her clothes. I thought to myself, *do I see this right?* She made eye contact with me, looking just as surprised to see me. She smiled at me and continued dancing. I was impressed. She was beautiful naked. *The things I could do to her . . .*

After the song had ended, Jackie got her clothes on and came and sat by me. I could tell she did not approve of my current condition.

"Danni, what are you doing here? You're drunk and practically falling off the bar stool. Can I call Mike to get you?" she asked, leaning against me.

"Better question. What are *you* doing here?" I slurred, looking more at her boobs than at her face.

She said, "That's not important. You've had enough to drink." She started taking my glass away, and I grabbed it back from her.

"I could never have too much to drink, Jackie," I yelled at her before pushing her back.

I noticed she was looking at someone behind me, and suddenly there was a hand on my shoulder.

"Is there a problem here, lady?"

"No. Quit fucking touching me or I will beat your ass, buddy," I yelled at him while removing his hand.

He smiled at me and said, "Hey now, Tiger, maybe we could party alone."

I have no idea what caused me to lose all my self-control at that moment, and I punched him as hard as I could, right in the face. Blood started spraying out of his nose as Jackie jumped up.

She yelled at me, "Danni, you need to get some help. You are out of control."

"Shut the fuck up!" I yelled before I turned my back to them and sat down again at the bar. I went back to my drink as she helped the guy.

About ten minutes later another tap on my shoulder. *Seriously, people, just leave me alone.*

While turning around, I asked, "What the hell do you want now?"

I was horrified when I saw two state troopers standing in front of me. *Ok, maybe I had gone too far this time.*

"Ma'am, can we have a word with you outside?" the taller one asked as I watched Jackie walk up to us.

"Okay," I said, attempting to stand up. Both the troopers grabbed me before I fell.

"That is exactly what we thought," the trooper said as they both helped me outside.

"How much you had to drink tonight, Danni?" the younger trooper asked.

"I wasn't counting, so why don't you tell me?"

Apparently you don't joke with the troopers. They didn't seem to share in my humor at all.

"Okay, tough crowd. If you two idiots will excuse me, I am going to go now. I will catch up with you later," I said as I tried to turn around and walk away.

They shoved me face-first into the wall and wasted no time putting handcuffs on me.

"It would be best if you went with us instead. You are under arrest for public intoxication and assault...*so far.* Let's not add to those charges, okay?" The troopers then walked me to the patrol car and put me in the back seat.

I had never been arrested before. I had never even had a speeding ticket before. I realized I still had a pill in my jean pocket and thought, *this could be interesting. Maybe I should get rid of it?*

It was hard to get to it without letting on to what I was doing, having handcuffs on made it even more challenging. I finally got the pill out of my pocket and tucked it into the seat.

Twenty minutes later, after taking statements, they took me to the police station. They did all the usual stuff: fingerprints, mug shots, and a full body search. A guard asked if I wanted to call someone. I asked if I had to and they said no. The funny part of this whole mess was that the police station was only about four blocks from the bar. They took me to an empty cell, took off the handcuffs, and told me to sleep it off.

I lay down on the bunk and tried to close my eyes. The room spun around me when all of the memories of rolling around with Collin came flooding back to me. I couldn't help but replay the way he felt, the way he kissed me, and the way he touched me. I just wanted him, and I hated both of us for that. I wanted to be the one he was marrying, the one he went home to. *This is not me! What was so special about him anyway? Ugh* . . . I wished I had never met him.

The sun was filtering into the cell as a guard was yelling at me to wake up because I was being released. I groaned, opening my eyes as I slowly sat up and tried to compose myself. The room wouldn't stop spinning. I felt like hell and probably looked like hell, too. I started to wonder to myself if I was getting too old for this crap.

I was not anxious to see who had bailed me out as the guard walked me to the counter and started taking off the handcuffs. I heard two people laughing hysterically and had a feeling who it was. I didn't even turn around to look at them.

The guard gave me my shoes, coat, and a plastic bag with what had been in my pockets when they arrested me. I flinched when he took the handcuffs off. My right hand was throbbing. Looking down, I noticed it was black and blue with dried blood all over my fingers and knuckles. *Ah, yes.* I suddenly remembered punching that guy. *That was dumb.*

As I put my shoes and coat on, the guard told me to sign the papers stating when my court date was and told me I was free to go. Finally, I turned and headed for the door.

I knew that Mike and Daniel were still laughing at me while they followed me out. I would have probably hit them if my hand hadn't hurt so much. I stopped on the top step when I saw my SUV sitting at the curb. Jackie must have called Mike. I started walking toward it when Mike and Daniel both grabbed me around my arms.

Mike said, "I think you have someone and something to deal with."

They walked me to my SUV and Daniel opened the passenger door to help me in. They shut the door, and I looked over and saw Collin in the driver's seat. I could tell he was mad and maybe a little more furious than I think I had ever seen him.

"I don't want to hear anything you have to say. Just take me home," I said. He kept his eyes straight ahead.

From the direction he drove us I knew home is not where he intended to take me. We sat in silence for a little bit when he turned into the schoolhouse driveway.

All the vehicles and people from earlier were gone, no one was there but Collin and me. He parked in front of the incomplete new steps leading up to the door and got out. He then walked over to my side and opened the door, grabbing my arm and pulling me out of the SUV. He dragged me with him into the schoolhouse as I yelled at him to let go because he was hurting me. He ignored me and led me into the school. We were standing in the gym before he finally let go of me.

He just stood there with his back to me with his hands on his head. After ten minutes of the silent treatment, I mumbled, "Whatever," and started walking down the hall toward the front door. He grabbed my arm, spun me around, and started kissing me. I tried to push him away, but he put his arms around me and held me tighter. I finally gave up and kissed him back.

A very passionate make-out session later, he pulled away with his face still close to mine and his hands on my cheeks. Neither one of us said anything. I finally looked up at him and could tell that he was as confused as I was. This made me feel like the worst person on the planet.

I said the only thing that I could right then, "Collin, I am in love with you."

I leaned toward him and tried to kiss him again, and he just held me back with his grip on my hair. I stood there looking at him, thinking, *you just kissed me, and now you're stopping me?* He turned and started walking back toward the gym. *Do I let him go or what?*

I yelled, "What the hell do you want from me?"

He immediately stopped without turning around.

I started walking toward him shouting, "I don't know what I'm supposed to do about you! You are all I think about. I want every part of you. I want to be the one you marry!"

There it was. My true feelings on the table, scaring the hell out of him and me both. I had finally said exactly what I had wanted to say to him, and now he wouldn't even look at me. He just stood there with his back to me for the longest time. I heard the front doors open and saw Daniel and Mike walking toward us. I wiped the tears from my face before they could see them. When they noticed Collin at the other end of the hall, Daniel put his hands up.

"What is going on here?" Daniel asked in a more serious tone than was normal for him.

"Nothing is happening. Mike, please take me home. I have officially had enough of all this crap," I muttered, trying to contain the lump in my throat.

Mike said, "Sure, let's go."

I gave Daniel a quick hug before he took off down the hall toward Collin.

As soon as we got in the car, I started crying.

Sniffling I said, "I don't know what to do."

Mike squeezed my hand and, trying to lighten the mood, said, "Well, maybe not getting arrested would be a step in the right direction."

CHAPTER 18
LOWER THAN I THOUGHT

The next couple days were quiet. I went to the doctor regarding my hand, and he assured me that nothing was broken. Mike and I had talked in great detail about what had happened that night. He and Daniel hadn't even stayed to watch the video shoot because they had a feeling it was a bad idea. It was something Collin had come up with all on his own. Daniel was mad about it because Collin had always told him "no" to having girls in their videos before. I guess I was the exception. I told Mike that I did feel better after I finally expressed all my feelings out loud to Collin.

All the work pertaining to my dad and Collin's collaboration were done. Maybe I wouldn't have to see him ever again. Of course, I wanted to see Daniel, although I didn't even have a chance to say goodbye to him. I had told him over the phone that I was mad about the way he had left town. He apologized and promised he would see me soon.

Things were slow at the bar. The schoolhouse would be ready in a couple of months and, for the moment, things were once again normal.

I had managed to quit crying and obsessing over Collin. Mike and I got to the point where we were trying not to bring him up anymore.

My court date finally came. With Dad's expensive lawyer, I managed to get time served with six months' probation. Dad had told him just to make it go away, hoping the papers hadn't caught any of my latest troubles. I swore to my dad I would never do it again. He only laughed at the idea of me staying out of trouble. The one thing that did suck, the guy I punched knew who my dad was. He ended up suing me for damages and medical expenses and the lawyers quickly settled that, as well. I agreed because it was my fault and I did feel sorry for hitting the guy.

After all, that was settled, Mike and I decided we needed a vacation. It had been three years since we had taken one together. We decided to go to Mexico and sit on the beach for two weeks, soaking up the sun and relaxing.

It was beautiful when we landed in Cancún and even better to be around strangers. Mike and I both spoke Spanish, so it was easy to talk to the locals and get around.

Of course, we kept sending Daniel pictures teasing him that we were having more fun than he was. They had gone back out on tour, and he didn't seem to have time for anything other than work, so we tried to make him jealous. He would text me back right away and one time told me to "quit it with the pictures" or he was going to leave the band and come to us. We knew he was joking, but it was fun to mess with him. I also noticed Mike was on his phone a lot and had even made comments about it.

He finally admitted that he and Mark were going to try to work things out and give it another shot. I was happy for him and told him that one of us deserved some happiness. Yes, and maybe I *was* feeling a little lonely myself.

One night, while sitting on the beach leaning against each other, watching the waves crash against the shore with drinks in hand Mike said, "If we make it to forty with no kids, we should have them together."

That thought totally took me by surprise. We had never mentioned kids in either of our lives before.

"I thought you didn't like kids," I said, leaning back to look at him as he watched the ocean.

"No, *you're* the one that doesn't like kids," he said, looking back at me.

"I don't mind kids. But no one wants kids with me. If *you* do, then that's good enough for me. You have a deal. If we make it to forty with no children, we will have them together," I said, leaning over and kissing him on the lips, both of us smiling like idiots.

I knew people walking by us assumed we were a couple kissing and touching each other, but this was normal for us. We didn't make out with each other, but a quick kiss on the lips was what we had always done, and it was comfortable to us.

Our vacation was over as we were sitting in the airport waiting for our flight home when I got out my laptop. I started checking my email when I saw that Daniel had sent me something.

Probably another video of him drumming during one of their shows. He sent them all the time.

To: Danni B.
From: Danielbeatsdrums
Subject: You naked

I thought you would want to see this before it is released. You might want to watch it alone because it is hot☺ dirty girl!

Mike leaned over and asked, "What are you looking at?"

"I'm not sure. Something Daniel sent, so it is probably dirty or him playing his drums. *Hopefully, not together,*" I said, laughing before handing Mike my laptop.

"What the hell is he talking about?" he asked, reading the message.

"I don't know. It's hard to tell with sweet, dirty Daniel. I'm going to go to the bathroom before the flight."

I took my time in the stall, as though I were trying to delay the flight by sitting in a steel tube and praying we wouldn't crash to the ground. I went back to Mike and noticed he had put the laptop away.

"They called our flight for boarding, so let's go, you royal pain in my ass," Mike said, handing my carry-on to me while shaking his head.

Walking to the plane, I asked, "Mike, what video was it?"

"Just something dumb that only Daniel would send. Don't worry about it."

I let it go and got on the plane to head home.

━┿ ┿━

I wasn't surprised to see Mark at the airport waiting for us. They appeared very happy to see each other, throwing their arms around each other and kissing. Mike decided to go with Mark instead of coming home, and I had no problem with that.

I spent the next three days alone, buried in paperwork for the bar as Mike hadn't come home yet to help. Our St. Patrick's Day party needed planning, and I was starting to get a little mad at him when he finally got home.

As I watched him sitting on the couch with a huge smile on his face, I knew it was another life-changing moment for us. It always was with that smile.

"I have huge news!" he said, spreading his arms out in the air: he was way too happy for my comfort zone. "You need to sit down, Danni, this is big!"

"Uh, Mike, I am sitting down, dumbass," I said, looking at him like he was losing his mind or something as he started laughing.

He was perhaps a little *too* happy and I had an idea of what he was going to say.

He blurted out very loudly, "I am getting married!"

He grabbed me out of my leather office chair and hugged me while he jumped up and down.

"Wow. Congratulations, Mike," I said, trying to act surprised even though I knew they would eventually get married.

⟞⟝ ⟞⟝

It was finally St. Patrick's Day and the bar was getting loud and packed with our regulars and lots of faces I had never seen before. The house band was playing that night. We were one bartender short, so I had the task of doing two jobs that night. I wondered if I could even pull it off.

I had talked to Daniel about all the festivities at the bar and Mike and Mark's wedding plans. Daniel claimed that he wouldn't be my date because I wouldn't be his date to Collin's. I knew he was joking and even told him I put him down as my plus-one anyway.

Neither one of us brought up Collin anymore, nor did I care to think about him.

About that time, Mike was yelling at me, threatening to take my phone away if I didn't stop texting Daniel and help him behind the bar. I stuck my tongue out at him and started taking orders.

It was crazy! The bar was packed, and all of our servers seemed to be struggling to keep up. Kendrick started yelling at me that it was time to get the band on stage. I was frustrated when Mark walked up to me, shot me a smile, and said, "I can try my hand at bartending. The worst thing that can happen is Mike will get bossy, and that turns me on a little."

Laughing, I handed him the drink cheat sheet and said, "Okay, lover boy, just try to help the guys. They usually order a beer and that's easy."

He nodded, playfully slapping me on the ass when I stepped by him. I laughed and gave him a look. Mark was getting more on my good side.

I almost ran into one of the girls we had hired to dance for us and had to wait for her to do whatever move she was doing on the pole so I could get by her, not that I was complaining about seeing a hot, half-naked woman spinning around. I smiled at her, and she winked at me as she let me pass.

I finally made it to the stage as Kendrick was already getting the crowd stirred up. Starting, I felt great just to get lost in the music without having a reason to want to get lost. Somehow I had been nominated to do more of the singing for the heavy rock songs. Kendrick mentioned that he thought I was better at them than he was. I didn't mind. In fact, it was fun to put my spin on the songs. The only bad thing was that I always lost my voice for a day or two after each show, but it was so worth it.

Looking out at the crowd, I thought I saw Daniel and decided it was a sign that it had been too long since we had seen each other. I knew he was in Denver at his show tonight.

Finally, the last song of the set started playing, and everyone was wound up. I had no problem getting the crowd to sing with me. The girls we hired to dance also had kept things pretty lively as well. We made it through and signed off for a break. I knew I couldn't rest and went back to the bar.

I was picking up empty bottles on tables as Kendrick was engaging the crowd in contests. I was wearing torn jeans, a white t-shirt with a red bra underneath, and of course, my baseball cap. As I turned toward the bar with an armful of empty beer bottles, one of the guys we hired to manage the wet T-shirt contest threw a pitcher of water at me. The bottles went crashing to the ground, and I was soaking wet.

I calmly asked whoever was listening, "How do you instantly piss someone off? Oh, I know, throw water at them."

I lost control and went charging after the jerk as he started backing away from me. I felt an arm around my waist pulling me backward.

"Remember, you are on probation, dirty girl," a low, playful voice said close to my ear as he now had his chest pressed against my back to try and contain me. I said a few more choice words to the jerk before I calmed down and regained control of myself. Whoever it was, he was starting to get on my last nerve when I heard his voice again, "You look good wet."

I turned around, realizing it was Daniel, and instantly I jumped into his arms and hugged him, getting him just as wet as I was.

"Sweet Daniel, I am so happy to see you," I said, messing up his hair.

He put me down and said with a little dose of sarcasm, "Hey, you got me all wet."

"It is so great to see you. I thought you were playing in Denver tonight," I said, finally stepping back so we could see each other.

He shook his head at me in frustration and said, "You don't listen to me, do you? I told you that *last* night we played in Denver, and we were making a pit stop here for tonight so that I could see you."

"Oh," I said.

He leaned closer to me and said, "The answer is, yes, that includes my whole band. But, don't worry, I warned him to stay as far away from you as possible."

I nodded as I absorbed this uncomfortable information and Daniel helped me pick up the bottles. I heard Kendrick on the mic asking for his fearless leader. I wanted to stay and talk to Daniel, but he started pushing me toward the stage, saying I had work to do.

I didn't even have time to change my shirt before we began again. I was going to sing this entire set because Kendrick and I decided to try something different. "Different" was his way of telling me I could get the crowd worked up faster than he could. It was a little weird not to have a guitar in my hands as I stepped up to the mic. We got through the first song and knowing we were covering Collin's song, I found myself getting nervous.

We started up, and I saw Daniel front and center recording us on his phone. I knew I had him on my side as I held nothing back and neither did anyone else in the band. Everyone was fired up as we sang his lyrics about playing a dangerous game. It was probably the loudest I had ever heard the bar before. That was awesome, even better when I saw Collin on the side of the stage glaring at me with a dirty look on his face.

The next song started, and I still felt on top of the world, until I realized I was about to sing a song about wanting someone you couldn't have. Collin had disappeared by now, and I hoped it remained that way for the rest of their stopover.

We finally came to the end of the set, and I didn't know if my shirt was still wet or I was just sweating that much, I decided to change. I unlocked my office door and went to the box in the corner with all the new bar shirts in it.

I heard Daniel behind me asking, "Can I have a shirt too? You got me dirty."

Without looking up from the box I was digging in, I asked, "What size, dirty boy?"

"Large. Large all over, if you wanted to know that." I couldn't help but laugh.

"You got another large T-shirt I could have?" Collin asked, I hadn't even realized he was in the room.

Super, I thought as I kept digging through the box trying not to let the butterflies in my stomach make me sick. *Why did his stupid voice affect me this much? So annoying.* I found the size I needed and stood up. I tore off my wet shirt with my back to them and then my bra because it was wet, too. I pulled on a red bar shirt and turned around to throw two shirts at Daniel, all while trying not to make eye contact with Collin.

I looked at Daniel and said, "Let's have a drink." They followed me towards the back.

In the garage, where it was a lot quieter, they leaned up against my SUV as I grabbed beers out of the cooler. I handed two to Daniel, determined not to talk to Collin. I think he got my point then because he headed back inside.

"So, what did you think?" Daniel asked with a mischievous smile on his face.

"About what?" I asked before taking a drink of my beer.

"The finished video I sent you," he said, before drinking his beer.

"What video?"

"The music video you are in that I emailed to you."

He knew by the look on my face that I hadn't seen it yet. As it dawned on me what video he was talking about, we both started hurrying for my office at the same time. We kept trying to stop each other, and when I finally got to the door, we both realized it was locked. Staring at each other, we calmly put our beers down. Then we started running for the back door while trying to stop each other as we made it outside.

I could tell he wasn't a runner as I quickly jogged around the bar ahead of him. I got to the door first and started to make my way through the crowd when Daniel grabbed the back of my pants. Pulling me back, he was now in front of me and people were noticing that we were both trying to get somewhere first. I grabbed Jackie's arm and put her in his way because he likes cute girls and of course he stopped. I got ahead of him, and he quickly looked at Jackie and told her he would be right back. I was trying to push through when again he grabbed the back of my pants and pulled me back.

"You want to play dirty? I can play dirty," Daniel said as he shoved me right into Collin's arms. I looked up at him after I crashed into his chest, noticing the way he didn't hesitate to put his arms around me.

"Sorry, Collin," I said as he was laughing.

"What are you two doing?" Collin asked, leaning closer to my face.

I saw Chuck standing by my office door, and I yelled over the crowd, "Grab him!"

Chuck pointed at Daniel and I nodded as he yanked Daniel to a stop by his shirt. I backed away from Collin, and he started following me, not letting go of my belt loop that he had managed to get his finger through. I got to the office door and was getting the key from my pocket when I realized Collin was telling Chuck we were playing a game and he was helping me cheat. He let Daniel go as he laughed at us before walking away.

Daniel and I started fighting over the keys, trying to unlock the door first. Collin was there pushing up behind me, trying to help Daniel. Collin's arms had gone around my waist before he lifted me off the ground. I couldn't move as Daniel got the door open and went to my computer. Collin put me down, and I ran in and tried to knock Daniel out of my chair. Then it became a fight over the chair as we noticed that Collin and Mike were sitting down on the couch across from my desk laughing at us. We fell out of the chair, and I landed on top of Daniel.

"Oh, baby, just like that," Daniel said through his laughter as he tried to pull me away from my desk.

He managed to roll me over and sit on my stomach while holding my arms down. He started typing on my computer as Mike told him my email password.

Daniel calmly asked, "Are you ready to act like an adult yet? Or, do you need to stay in time-out a little longer?"

I couldn't help laughing hysterically at Daniel as he started poking me in the chest. Collin and Mike were still laughing at us, so I gave up and nodded yes.

Before he would let me up, he asked, "What did you learn?"

I rolled my eyes, and he said, "I'm pretty sure rolling your eyes wasn't it, so I ask again, what did you learn? The correct answer is: Daniel is the king, and he is sexy as hell."

I thought to myself; *you have got to be kidding.* I heard Collin say, "Wait," to Daniel as he got out his phone and started recording us. Daniel started over by asking what I had learned.

I quietly said, "Daniel is the king and is sexy as hell." Of course, he said he couldn't hear me and made me repeat it until I was practically yelling it.

"Good. Now you have to play nice. You're on probation, and I am not above calling the police and having you arrested so I can see you handcuffed again. That was hot."

Daniel sat in my chair and pulled me onto his lap, asking if I was ready. I wasn't sure but just nodded my head yes anyway. Mike and Collin moved behind us to see the video, too. My dad came up first thing with his guitar, and I thought *wow, he looks great*. I realized Daniel had grabbed my hand because apparently I was tapping it nervously.

At first, it wasn't too bad, and then I gasped in sheer panic. I saw Collin and me on the bed rolling around together. I couldn't remove my hand from my mouth. I was so embarrassed.

Mike said, "You guys look great. This is great."

I was horrified seeing what little clothing I had on and Collin's hands all over my ass on the screen. They had cut out the parts of us kissing, but had left in the part when I arched my back as he kissed my chest. I thought, w*ell this can't get any more humiliating*. That is until I saw that they had left in the part of me kissing Collin's stomach and how low I had got-ten, much lower than I thought I had. I wanted to die when it ended.

I asked, "Has my dad seen this yet? Please tell me no."

Daniel laughed and said, "Yes and he loved it."

"Well, that is just great," I said, my voice dripping with frustra-tion as I stood up.

Mike asked, "Anyone want to have breakfast?"

Thank God for Mike, always trying to help me get through an awkward situation. I adore him for that.

CHAPTER 19
ACT LIKE ADULTS

C ollin sat across from me at breakfast at our full table of his road crew members and some people from the bar as well. He watched me the whole time with a look of anger and frustration on his face. I was probably as confused as he was. We made small talk with each other about neutral subjects. He asked about the bar and I, in turn, asked about his tour. Nothing was mentioned of his last visit that Daniel conveniently started calling "The Strip Club Beat Down." Leave it to Daniel to make it stick when others mentioned it, as well.

Breakfast was great, but I was ready for bed. It had been a long day. The waitress put the check down beside me and walked away after giving Collin a desperately longing glance. He shrugged and ignored her. I'm sure it was nothing new to him. I grabbed the check and headed up to the counter to pay. As I laid the check on the counter hoping to get the attention of a cashier, Collin grabbed it.

"I will gladly take care of this baby," he said, giving me a sly smile that stopped me from arguing with him.

Walk away now or jump on him, I thought to myself. The right side of my brain won out, and I walked back to the table. As we exited the diner, Daniel put his arms around me from behind, almost making me fall forward as he picked me up off the ground.

"Dirty girl, I was wondering what your plans are next week?" He held me up, attempting to walk while glued to my back.

I laughed and said, "Recovering from my humiliation of that awful video."

"You need some excitement in your life, and I know exactly how to give it to you," he said against my ear, trying to unzip my jacket playfully.

"Again, Daniel, I am not sleeping with you or showing you my boobs. We've talked about this in depth, remember?" I joked as I removed his hand from my jacket.

"Sorry, I forget the 'no' part," he said jokingly as he carried me to the SUV.

Daniel was determined not to let go of me as we both kept laughing at each other; Mike helped catch us before we both fell face-first onto the cement.

"Danni, give me a week of your time. I promise it will be fun, and I will *try* to keep my hands off your nonexistent boobs."

"Ok, Sweet Daniel, what the hell are you talking about?"

He laughed and said, "Wow, and they say *I'm* slow. You are the slow one."

I hit him in the ribs jokingly and said, "Last week you asked me how to spell 'nonexistent' so you could mock me in a text and now you're calling *me* slow?"

He put his hands up in surrender and said, "Guilty as charged, but I'm serious. Please go with me for a week on the bus and keep me company."

Hanging out with Daniel for a week sounded great, but close quarters was probably not the best thing for Collin and me.

Daniel leaned in close and whispered, "Collin has his own bus so it will be just you and me."

"I don't know what I have going on," I said, trying to avoid the question.

Mike piped up and said, "Nothing. She has nothing going on for a while, so she would love to go."

Daniel took that as a "yes" without even looking at me for an answer.

"I'll ride home with you so you can pack and I can pick out your underwear since I am the one who has to share a bed with you. I have lingerie standards."

I shook my head knowing it was a lost cause arguing with Daniel. Anyway, what could it hurt to spend a week with my sweet Daniel?

Mike climbed into the driver's seat as Daniel jumped on the passenger side, forcing me to sit in the back. To make things much worse, the other two bandmates and Collin wanted to ride along, as well.

As he stood directly behind me, Collin put his hand on my hip and said, "You're small so you can climb in the very back."

Great, I thought, climbing into the backseat gave him a direct view of my ass. Trying to fit my legs in front of me in a tiny seat proved to be harder than I thought it would be, especially when Collin climbed in and sat next to me. *Even better*, I mumbled to myself, wanting more distance between us.

"Mike, please turn on the heat back here because I'm freezing," I said, rubbing my hands together.

Without looking at me, Collin reached over and grabbed my hands to try and warm them up. His hands were hot, and I wondered how he was warm when he had on less of a coat then I did. I didn't yank my hands back as he pulled them up to his mouth and blew his warm breath over them. He glanced at me and noticed I was watching him. He began to kiss my fingers slowly. *God, what this man did to me.*

On the ride to my house, we were sitting closer together by the minute when he put his hand on my thigh, perhaps a little too far north. *Why is he doing this?* I wondered while removing his hand. Very casually he put his hand back on my thigh, still keeping hold of my left hand. I knew going with Daniel for a week was going to be a huge mistake. *Once we get to the house, I have to tell him I can't go,* I reasoned. It felt like Collin was taunting me and this was all a game to him.

Trying not to concentrate on the location of his hand, I gazed out the window. I felt his hand slide up my leg further, exactly where it was off limits to him. Unfortunately, this amazing feeling surged through me as I tried with every fiber of my being not to make a sound. I closed my eyes and attempted to think about something unpleasant, not wanting to give him the satisfaction of seeing how he affected me. The way I could feel him staring at me, I knew he was enjoying watching me struggle. Slowly, I reached down and pushed his hand off of me again. He apparently had had enough of making me uncomfortable and finally left me alone the rest of the way to my house.

Upon arrival, I quickly went up to my room. Trying to regain some of my composure, I leaned against the counter in my bathroom and took deep breaths. Mike came in looking at me like he already knew what was bothering me.

"Mike, I am fine; just needed a moment to think," I said while taking off my jacket.

With a smile on his face he said, "After that car ride, I think we all need a moment free from the sexual tension radiating off you two."

"You were watching, weren't you?" I asked, feeling my face turn red.

"Guilty, but I couldn't help it. Every person in that car couldn't help but notice. Danni, the way he watches you is intense," Mike said as he stood in front of me, putting his arms around my neck.

"He is getting married, remember?" I mumbled, leaning into his chest.

His expression softened as if he had forgotten about that detail. "What're you going to do then?"

I knew he was asking if I was planning on going on tour or staying home. I didn't know what to say as Daniel entered the bathroom. Mike squeezed me close to him as we hugged each other tighter, this gave me an extra minute to think.

After a long silence I said, "Daniel, I don't think it's a good idea for me to go with you."

He looked at me like I had just taken his favorite teddy bear away. It broke my heart. I walked over and hugged him, and his hands instantly went to my ass.

"I promise I'll keep Collin away from you," he said, trying to molest me further.

I couldn't help but laugh at him as I pushed his naughty hands away and said, "I am over it, and the thought of disappointing you is more than I can take. So, yes, I will go with you *if* you hold up your end of the deal."

He looked relieved and said, "That won't be a problem. On my honor, I will avenge and protect my dirty girl, who apparently isn't wearing underwear. Commando, I want to play, too."

"Seriously, Daniel, is sex all you think about?" Mike asked, rolling his eyes at him.

"I speak three languages, Mike: English, Sarcasm, and my favorite, Dirty. I can teach you Dirty if you want?" Daniel asked as I started packing my bag.

Twenty minutes later I was ready to go and not a moment too soon to get away from the ongoing argument over whether or not "Dirty" was a language. Daniel grabbed my bag and headed back downstairs. I hugged Mike goodbye and promised him I would call him the next day. He kissed me on the forehead and told me to have fun.

The ride back to the bus was much easier because I was the one driving this time. I was the only one who knew how to get to the schoolhouse where they had parked their buses. Daniel jumped in front again, so Collin was stuck in the back by himself and I was all right with that. At the schoolhouse, I only saw one bus and glanced at Daniel.

"Relax! The rest of the buses are at the truck stop fueling up. Short ride with them," Daniel said, motioning to Collin, Rick, and Jake in the backseat.

I parked by the bus to leave my car out of the way of all the construction workers that were there every day. I wished they would finish already. I loved it out here in the country. It was quiet with no neighbors for ten miles in any direction. The only thing that bothered me was the massive fence Dad was putting in by the road so people couldn't enter the property. He assured me that eventually people would start trying, especially if Collin and Daniel kept hanging around.

⊷╬ ╬⊶

Daniel grabbed my bag and said with his typical dose of sarcasm intact, "Come on. I'll show you to the bedroom."

He had a way of making *everything* dirty, but it was hilarious. I followed Daniel to the back of the bus where he put my bag down and joked that this was home for the next week. It was a nice bus, but nothing like my dad's. It could comfortably hold five or six people if only two planned on sleeping at a time. I made fun of him for how clean it was and he just mumbled that it was because of Collin and his obsession with cleanliness.

Collin and the others stayed toward the front as I questioned Daniel about how far it was to the truck stop. He thought only about an hour or so. He knew what I was getting at and patted my hand, trying to get me to relax. He started telling me about his schedule and what towns we would be stopping in and what they had to do at each one. It was interesting to hear about their work schedule. Now I could understand why it would get a little annoying after a while of being on tour. We lay on the bed talking when I felt the bus slowing down, and he sat up grumbling that it was time for them to go. The rest of the band had been playing video games and yelling loudly at each other for the last hour.

It was four in the morning by the time everyone got on their bus and back out on the road. Daniel was exhausted and fell onto the bed as I started getting up to sleep on the couch.

"Danni, I am okay sharing the bed if you are. You're not my type. I can control myself when boobs are not involved."

I started laughing and said, "I can share a bed with you because it would be too weird to date you. You are such a child. Daniel, grow up." He threw a pillow at me and then tackled me on the bed.

I didn't even question Daniel or his intentions because I just believed him. It was hard for me to trust many people, but Daniel was quickly becoming a comfort zone that I needed very much.

I had a hard time sleeping. Between Daniel snoring like a freight train and the movement of the bus, it was a lost cause. I finally managed to fall asleep about two hours after Daniel had.

I woke up and could tell we weren't moving anymore. Reaching my hand out, I soon discovered Daniel was gone. I wondered where he was as I got up and walked to the front of the bus. I was the only one on the bus and thankfully the door was locked. I knew he was busy with all his press and meet and greets with fans and would be back when he could. I glanced at the clock and saw it was five in the afternoon. I wondered how I had managed to sleep that long without nightmares creeping in. I decided to take a quick shower.

When I turned off the water, I heard people talking and wondered how I was going to get to the bedroom in just a towel. Being naked in front of people still freaked me out. The five scars across my chest and stomach still made Mike look at me with pity on his face, so it was not a welcome reality to have other people see them.

I peeked my head out and saw Daniel on the couch talking to someone. He glanced over at me and shot me a huge smile.

"Need some help getting to the bedroom? Or, if you want to get dressed out here, I'm cool with that." I gave him an annoyed look, and he looked toward the opposite couch and said, "Excuse me, my girl is shy."

Daniel held up a blanket so I would not be seen as I made a mad dash to the bedroom, knowing I wouldn't forget to bring clothes with me next time. Getting dressed in old torn jeans and a football shirt, I put on some sparse make-up and decided I had no desire to do my hair. It was down to the middle of my back and super curly thanks to not having it cut or colored in the past year. I used to love going to the spa and getting pampered, but since the assault, I had avoided it.

I grabbed my baseball cap again and tucked my hair up, calling it good. After seeing all the girls who usually attended concerts, I had very little confidence in myself. At 5'5", and a little over 130 pounds, I wasn't bad to look at. But, the last year had taken its toll with the new physical and mental scars I now carried. I had been told many times I was sexy in a dark way. Mike had assured me that that was a good thing. He referred to it as "exotic beauty." I had naturally tan skin, thanks to my mother being Spanish, but I was told I looked like my father and had inherited his aqua blue eyes. They stood out against my skin tone, and Mike said they easily drew attention.

I walked out to where Daniel was and this time he was alone looking at his phone. I sat beside him and asked who had been here, and he said it was just an interview he had had to do. He joked that I had timed my shower departure just right and not to be surprised if I saw on the internet or in a magazine that I was his new girlfriend.

"I'll be your pretend girlfriend if you want me," I said, throwing my arms around him making him drop his phone.

"No, thank you. That might hurt my chances of hooking up with girls with boobs," he said, grabbing my hat and pulling it off.

We fell to the floor wrestling over the hat when the door opened, and Collin and Rick walked up.

"Don't you ever knock, asshole?" Daniel shouted as he held me down and waved my hat out of my reach.

Collin laughed and sat down on the couch across from us. "And miss this? Never. Give me her damn hat and I will burn it."

Doesn't anyone like my hat? I wondered as I got it back from Daniel when he wasn't looking. He quickly held me down and climbed on my stomach again, taking the hat again. Once again, he asked "who the king is" as Collin and Rick laughed at us. After finally answering him, he let me up and gave me back my hat.

He looked at me and asked, "Why do you always wear a hat?"

"I don't know why. Just easy I guess. Why?" I asked, tucking my hair back up.

"You shouldn't wear it. You look pretty with your hair down."

"Are you feeling okay?" I asked as he pried the hat off once more.

He seemed serious that he wasn't going to give it back as he went to the back to hide it. *Dammit,* that was the only hat I brought with me, so I made a mental note to scour the bus for it later. I didn't even have a hair clip with me, so I had no choice but to let my hair down and it drove me nuts all around my face.

They started talking about band stuff, so I grabbed my laptop and tried to let them do their thing. I surfed the internet, looking at the favorite songs and videos of the week. Seeing a clip of the video with me in it, I covered my mouth and was thankful the sound wasn't turned on. I started reading what people were saying about the video and was surprised. Some comments were a little offensive and one at the bottom just floored me. It asked who the model was and how to reach her agent.

I burst out laughing as Daniel grabbed my laptop from me. He started reading them out loud, especially the dirty ones. I got up to get my phone, still laughing to myself, *agent? You have got to be kidding.* I was texting Mike when I realized they were all looking at my laptop very intently.

"What are you guys looking at? Better not be porn on my computer!" I said, walking over to them.

"You, in Mexico, wearing an itty bitty red bikini. *Brrrraaaavvvvvoooooo,* Danni! I could bounce a quarter off that ass," Daniel said as Collin ripped my laptop out of his hands and took it to the other couch away from him and Rick.

I grabbed my laptop from Collin and snapped it shut, not before he managed to send an email. I was sure he sent those pictures of me to himself as he grinned at me.

"Don't you guys have a show or something to do?" I asked, annoyed.

They looked at each other, and Rick said, "I'm staying on this bus tonight hoping the bikini will make an appearance."

Collin offered to pay Daniel to let him remain on the bus as Daniel just sat and laughed at them. I figured from then on I was probably going to be the one everyone made fun of for the rest of the trip, and I was.

⚊⫻ ⫻⚊

By the third day Daniel and I had a good system worked out so, I could sleep. My sweet Daniel. His bus was always busy with people hanging around, especially Collin and Rick. One evening after one of their amazing shows, I asked him about that, and he mentioned that generally everyone spent time on Rick's bus, where the naked girls and parties usually were. He joked that he liked having me around so people would hang out on his bus for a change.

The next couple days I noticed everyone stayed away, and I wondered why. I soon answered my question when I saw that the girlfriends had arrived. Seeing Collin's fiancée just got under my skin and I tried to avoid her. One night while the guys were on stage, she sat down beside me, and I cringed.

"I know you don't like me, but I'm Steph, Collin's fiancée," she said in her whiny voice. Daniel had imitated her pretty well. I tried not to laugh.

Ugh, I just wanted to hit her. I had only seen her from a distance and up close she was as fake as they came. Fake bottle blond hair, fake tan, too white teeth, way too much makeup spackled on her face, and clothes three sizes too small for her short, round shape.

I looked at her and replied nicely, "I don't hate you, Steph. I have never even been introduced to you, so don't assume things about me."

"Oh, sorry, it's just I have been to your bar a few times and Collin said to stay away from you because you don't like me," she mumbled while playing with the giant rock on her finger.

"Oh, he said that, did he?" I asked, my words dripping with acid.

She took this as a girls' bonding moment and went on about how much fun she had at our bar and how much she liked to watch us play. She added that she was glad when Collin told her that he was going to use me in his video because she knew she could trust him with me since we were just friends. *Am I hearing all this crap right?*

"Who told you we were friends? Honestly, Steph, I hate Collin. I want nothing to do with him. He's an asshole," I said, looking directly at her.

"Well, he did. He said he thinks of you as one of his closest friends and hopes to work more with you." She seemed more confused by the minute.

"I am friends with Daniel. The rest of them just come with being around Daniel," I said, it felt great to be a little mean to her. "No offense, Steph, but I think Collin is a jackass. I hope you think long and hard before you marry him."

She grumbled, "Yeah, he is with his quick temper."

I wanted to burst out laughing at how gullible she was but didn't think that would be best. I couldn't help myself and let her ramble on about how he was never around, and if she didn't tell him what to do, he was just annoying. As soon as she started talking about their sex life, I stood up and put my hands up.

"Whoa, Steph, some details I don't want to know."

She stood up and asked, "You want to get a beer with me?"

This girl can't take a hint, I thought. I just wanted to get away from her. Although, seeing us together might scare the crap out of Collin, which could be fun. We had a beer and talked more, and, as it turned out, I didn't mind her as much as I thought I would, other than the fact that perhaps she did like Collin's money more than Collin.

She followed me back to the bus, and I told her I was going to get some sleep. She asked if they could ride with us to the next town to maybe have drinks and play cards or something. I could tell she wasn't real bright and told her it wasn't my bus, so I didn't have any say in the matter. She rambled excitedly that she would talk to Daniel after the show and then hugged me. *Freaking hugged me!*

As she was skipping away, I wondered if I was on one of those blooper shows or something. This couldn't have possibly really happened. I got on the bus and prayed Daniel would come up with some excuse for us.

I put on my comfy sweatpants and a white tank top with my black bra showing underneath, along with my baseball cap because Daniel sucks at hiding things. I sat on the couch and turned on the video games when Daniel sat down next to me with sweat rolling off him.

"Dude, you stink," I said, pausing my game and leaning away from him as he tried to hug me.

"How did you find your hat?" he asked, grabbing it from my head again and throwing it.

"I will always find it. We are on a bus, pretty small space, genius."

He looked at me and said, "You should put a different shirt on."

"Why?" I asked as he had never complained before about my shirts.

"We have company coming over, *genius*," he said, mocking me this time.

It dawned on me who and I just looked at him and whined, "You didn't!"

He looked down at his hands and said, "I couldn't say no. When Steph wants something, Collin makes sure she gets it, but the look on Collin's face when she told him that you two had been hanging out was priceless."

That did make me feel a little better. "Can't you cancel or something?" I asked as he took off his shirt and walked down the hall.

"No, that would be too easy." He leaned into the bathroom and turned the shower on before turning around to look at me. As he unbuttoned his pants, he asked, "You want to join me?"

I had to admit; Daniel has a great body underneath all his goofy T-shirts. I stood up and seductively took off my shirt, walking toward him and laughing, knowing I was completely messing with him.

"Stop," he said, grabbing the remote and turning the music up full blast.

Of course, Daniel has a disco ball on his bus, I thought to myself, laughing as the light bounced off the silver ball reflecting all around us. He returned to his position by the shower and nodded at me to continue. I started walking toward him doing my little strip tease and unhooked my bra, but kept it still covering my boobs. I stood two feet away and smiled at him, taking the same position he had.

"Your turn, dirty boy," I said as seductively as I could while dropping my bra by his feet.

He smiled his best sexy smile and slowly popped the button on his jeans, sliding them down his legs. I watched him, trying to read him and decide how far this was going to go. We were so competitive with each other, so this could be dangerous.

"Your turn, dirty girl," he said, kicking his jeans toward me.

I slid my sweatpants down my legs, and they hit the floor. I saw him looking me up and down, and I smiled at him and nodded that it was his turn. He only had on his boxers now, and I only had on my boy shorts.

"You're not playing fair by keeping your arm over your boobs," he said, smiling at me almost like he was daring me to show him mine.

I lowered my arm and gave him a full view of my breasts as I just smiled at him. It took a minute for him to take his eyes away from my chest. Finally, he shook his head and walked toward me.

"You need a very cold shower, dirty girl," he said, grabbing my hand and pulling me to the bathroom. I kept laughing trying to pull away from him as he turned the water to cold.

"Stop it, Daniel! I don't need a cold shower. You're the one pitching a tent, not me," I said through my giggles.

He started pushing me in, and I pulled him in with me. We both screamed as the cold water sprayed down on us because neither one of us was letting the other go. We both started trying to get out while keeping the other one in. He was laughing as hard as I was.

"Danni, don't you dare grab me there unless you are going to finish me off," he yelled, laughing as I tried to rip his boxers away.

"Dammit, Daniel, they are both the same size, stop touching them, you little pervert," I yelled, prying his hand off my boobs as he acted like he was surprised he was touching them.

This was very typical behavior for us, even though it was the first time we had seen each other naked. Carrying on laughing and groping each other, the music suddenly stopped. The lights came back on, and we just looked at each other with shock on our faces.

Daniel looked at me and without trying to be quiet said, "Stay here, I think we have company."

"Where else would I go, you idiot," I said, laughing.

"Who's there?" Daniel asked, looking at me while finally turning off the water. We couldn't help ourselves and kept laughing and then it was a fight to see who could stay in the shower and not get out.

Collin ripped open the shower door and yelled, "Is it possible you two could fucking try to act like adults for once!" His voice trailed off when he saw us both wearing nothing but our underwear.

To make it much worse, Daniel's arm was wrapped around my chest, the only reason my boobs were covered up. Judging by the look on Collin's face, I knew he was extremely pissed off. I could practically see the fire in his eyes as he directed his glare toward me.

Daniel let go of me and pushed me out, saying, "Quit screwing around so I can take a shower."

I was suddenly standing in front of Collin, dripping wet in just my underwear. This was a little awkward, to say the least. After a brief pause, I stepped around him when he made no move to get out of my way. I grabbed my sweatpants off the floor and my bra that was by his foot. While trying to cover my chest and hold my clothes, I passed him again to get to the bedroom. He only glared at me, and I could feel Steph's eyes on us even though Collin had apparently forgotten that she was there. After backing into the bedroom, I shut the door and started laughing with my heart practically beating out of my chest.

I found a towel and started drying off when Daniel walked in wearing nothing but a towel. He looked utterly amused and asked, "How much trouble do you think we're in?"

"He can't say much considering he's out there with her," I mumbled, pulling a new shirt on.

"You can take her, Danni, I have faith in you," he said, while pulling on sweats, as well.

I threw a pillow at him while laughing at how nothing was serious to him.

"Nice shirt," he said as I glanced down at the band shirt of his I was wearing.

"I'm running out of clean clothes," I said as I finished getting dressed.

"Get out so I can finish getting dressed, you dirty girl. I know this rocking body does something for you, but we are in enough trouble." I left the room before he could grab me again.

I walked out hoping they had left. Instead, I saw them sitting on the couch together. Collin didn't look at me. I knew he was mad and figured I should just leave him alone. I noticed they both had a beer, and I grabbed one out of the cooler. Sitting down across from them was extremely uncomfortable, except Steph seemed clueless.

"You and Daniel seem to have a lot of fun together," Steph said a little too perky.

"Yes, we do. He is that naughty, annoying little brother I never had."

"And you are that annoying, bossy big sister with no hot friends," Daniel said, sitting down beside me and taking my beer.

Collin chimed in without looking at either one of us and said, "I don't know too many brothers and sisters that play around naked in the shower together."

Daniel and I just looked at each other and told the other to "grow up" at the same time before we started fighting over my beer. Little bastard always steals whatever I'm drinking.

Apparently, Daniel thought he should have some more fun with Collin and started trying to push his buttons.

Steph asked, "Are you two any more than just friends?"

Daniel answered, "Nothing more than friends that fuck as long as she keeps her face covered."

"Oh, don't even get me started on Daniel farting during sex. He is such a pig," I said through my laughter as he tackled me to shut me up. I looked at Daniel and said "You know that thing you did with your tongue last night was awesome. I've meant to tell you all day."

He responded, "The way you arched your back and moaned was hot as hell, baby."

We were trying so hard not to laugh and just play along because Steph believed all of it. After ten minutes of us going on and on, Collin finally hit the end of his limit.

"Pull over at the next stop so we can get off this fucking bus," Collin snapped at the bus driver.

Daniel still had one trick left to play and asked, "Steph, has Collin shown you the new video yet?"

If looks could kill, Daniel would be dead by the daggers Collin was sending him.

"No, he said it wasn't ready yet," Steph said, putting her empty beer can in the trash.

Daniel took out my laptop and pulled up the video. Then he handed it to her and said, "It just came out two days ago, you should see it. Our fans love it."

I wondered if perhaps we had gone too far as she watched the video. Then her eyes got huge, and her lips pressed together firmly. *Oh boy, was she pissed.*

"Wow. That is some video, *Collin*," Steph snapped, handing the laptop back to Daniel.

She turned toward Collin and said, "You never told me that was why you were using *her* in the video." Now she was pointing and glaring at me.

Collin rolled his eyes with his back toward Steph and mumbled, "When it comes to my music and videos I don't need to explain or ask permission from you, so don't even start your bitching."

But, of course, she did until we were able to pull over and let them off.

CHAPTER 20
SO FRUSTRATED

After staying on Daniel's bus for a week, I finally walked into my house. Dropping my bag in the hall, I bowed my head in frustration as I took in the wedding crap everywhere. *Why me, Lord? Why do I have to endure this?* I maneuvered through the decorations and piles of brightly colored stacks of card stock. *They are going all out for this,* I thought, seeing a business card for a wedding planner. I couldn't wait for my schoolhouse to be done so I wouldn't have to live with all this.

Three days later I was working at the schoolhouse trying to clean up the landscaping when I saw Dad's tour bus pull into the refurbished bus barn. I didn't give it much thought as I had my headphones turned up high, trying to drown out the tractor I was riding. I only had a couple of months to go before I could move in and the landscapers were coming tomorrow to start working on the grounds. I turned around to make one last pass when I noticed a group of guys standing by the barn talking to Dad and Uncle Tony. I was curious who he had brought home now.

Dad started waving for me to come over when I parked the tractor and shut off the engine. I was wearing a sheer white tank top with a bikini top underneath and shorts as I was attempting to get some sun, I didn't want to meet people this way. I guess I was out of luck since they all started walking in my direction. I climbed down from the tractor and finally waved back at my dad.

While Dad made introductions, I half listened until he finally noticed I was practically standing behind them. The group made me uncomfortable. Uncle Tony moved up behind me. Sensing my uneasiness, he pulled me toward him and put his arm around me. He always made me feel safe as he and Dad were in the habit of blocking unworthy men from getting to me.

"Relax, Lil, I will keep you safe," Uncle Tony whispered in my ear. I hated that nickname.

It was some up-and-coming band that had asked to work with Dad and Uncle Tony. He had invited them here to the school-house to work in the new studio, considering that it had been completed for a month now. Dad made sure that was the first thing finished, and he quickly put it to use.

They looked like typical rock stars with their crazy hair, tattoos, and torn-up clothes. I started to excuse myself when Dad questioned if I was playing tonight, I nodded yes. He told me that they would come down and watch the show.

⊰⊱

I got to the bar ten minutes late, as usual, and just as they always did, everyone started yelling at me for being late. Tardiness was my thing. Dad was convinced that this was my way of doing the opposite of what everyone told me to do. I knew he was right, but it was fun how worked up Mike would get waiting for me.

After a successful set, I was trying to make my way to the bar when I ran into one of the guys I had met with my dad earlier. He towered over me, smiled, and grabbed my arm when I tried to sidestep him.

"Let me buy you a drink, Danni," he said, leaning close to my ear to be heard over the DJ.

I knew that this guy had probably been drinking all day judging by the alcohol radiating off his breath and the slur in his voice.

"Sorry, I am at work. I can't drink while I'm working," I said, giving him a friendly smile.

In response, he grabbed me around the waist and crushed his body into mine. I cringed, trying to hold back the urge to throw up on him. He smelled like he hadn't showered in days. I tried to push him off, but he wouldn't let go of me.

"I saw you in Collin's video. You looked hot. I'm good friends with him."

"What exactly is your point here?" I asked, still trying to obtain some distance between us.

"Collin told me that you fuck like a champ. I'm up for anything if you want to have a little fun with me," he slurred before he licked my neck and I gagged.

His hands gripped my ass as he tried to pull me up. I pushed back while attempting to get Chuck's attention.

"Collin told me you like it rough. I am all for you playing hard to get."

Instantly I froze and felt like I couldn't catch my breath. *Why would Collin say something so horrible and what on Earth would make this idiot think it was okay to talk to me like this?* As rage filled me, I shoved him hard enough that he stumbled backward, all while smiling at me like he thought this was foreplay.

"So, asshole, you think I like it rough?" I said as he lurched closer to me.

"I am going to have so much fun with you," he said when I took another step back, running into an older guy behind me.

I had had enough of this. My vision was blurred with rage, and I suddenly wanted to kill him. Without thinking out my plan of action, I punched him as hard as I could. He tried to step closer yet again.

Fuck, that hurt! My hand instantly started throbbing. Then I saw the blood start pouring out of his nose as he looked at me completely stunned.

"You fucking bitch!" he yelled. Before I knew what he was doing, he punched me back. The world went dark.

I opened my eyes seeing stars and the rafters of the bar. *What the hell? Oh, now I really am going to kill him.*

"Stop it, Danni. You are bleeding all over. Hold still," Mike said, kneeling over me and taking a towel from Chuck.

"You okay, boss?" Chuck asked, leaning down to help me sit up. "I threw that asshole out and may or may not have punched him a few times for you."

I saw double, and my nose throbbed as Mike held the towel under it. Chuck took a bag of ice from Jackie and placed it on the bridge of my nose. *This shit hurts. Note to self: never get punched in the nose again.*

"You okay?" Mike asked, looking down at me while holding the towel.

"I think he broke my nose."

Mike and Chuck both laughed, and Mike said, "Yeah Danni, I think he did. But, if it makes you feel better, I think you broke his nose first."

Fifteen minutes later I started to feel extremely light-headed. My nose was still gushing blood as I sat in my office chair.

"Mike, how much blood can I lose without passing out?" I asked as he decided it was time to go to the hospital. *That might be a good idea.*

Apparently I answered my question since I woke up in the passenger seat of my SUV a couple of minutes later.

"Danni, welcome back. Stay awake for me, okay? We are almost to the hospital," Mike said, driving like a crazy person.

Nausea started rolling over me. Unfortunately, I was one of those people who threw up from intense pain. It was an awful trait that I'd had, and hated, all my life. *Oh, my night just keeps getting better and better,* I thought.

We made it to the hospital after pulling over for me to throw up. Mark met us at the doors.

"You called him?" I mumbled as Mark opened my door and started looking me over.

"Yes, Danni, *Mike called me.* I am a Registered Nurse so I'm going to help you and you're going to let me. Oh, and no bitching about it either," Mark commanded as he pulled me out of the SUV.

A couple of minutes later in a private room, Mark stuffed cotton up my nose as another nurse opened packages of gauze. It's pretty hard to lie still when you want to throw up, and thankfully Mark realized my dilemma just in time to put a trash can in front of me. I threw up yet again, and it didn't even rattle Mark. He just kept working around me.

When the doctor finally came in after a round of X-rays, Mark filled him in on what had happened. The doctor said something about resetting the bone. I didn't want to stay here any longer than I had to.

"Mark, where is Mike? I want to go home," I said trying to push myself up into a sitting position.

"He is in the hall yelling at someone on his phone."

I wondered who he could be yelling at. Mark pushed me back down and motioned to another nurse to hand over the clipboard she was holding.

"Okay, Danni, here it is. We are going to knock you out and reset your nose. If we don't, it won't heal right, and you could have breathing problems. So, please sign here because we can get you in surgery in less than twenty minutes."

"I don't want surgery, Mark! I am fine. Just tell Mike I'm ready to go home," I said, pushing his clipboard away.

The next morning after losing that argument, I started coming out of the anesthesia. At first, I didn't want to open my eyes because it felt *so* good to sleep, but my nose and head were throbbing. I tried to bring my hands up to my face when I felt restraints on my wrists.

I heard Mike say, "It's okay, Danni, surgery is over. You should heal up just fine. How much pain are you in?"

I groaned, "What's going on? My nose and head hurt! Can I go home?"

I could hear Mike laugh and then say, "They fixed your nose. The doctor wants you to wake up more before they give you any more pain medicine, and yes, hopefully later today you can go home."

Then I heard someone else say, "You have had a pretty rough night, young lady. How are you feeling?"

I opened my eyes and tried to blink away the blurriness when I saw an older man in a white coat looking down at me. He introduced himself as "Doctor Todd" and explained the surgery and what I should expect to feel like for the next couple days. Next, he changed the cotton stuffed up my nose and indicated that all was looking fine.

The doctor said, "We are going to help you sit up on the count of three. Ready?"

I nodded, and he continued, "Your sense of balance might be off for a while, so you have to take it slow."

I am not helpless. I just broke my nose, it's not like a head injury or anything. The doctor counted to three, and I was pulled upright by Mike and Mark, or so I assumed. *See? I'm fine. My sense of balance is just fine.* It was at that moment that whoever was on my left pushed me back over.

"Why am I leaning over? This is not comfortable," I said, trying to move back.

I heard a huge laugh and instantly recognized it.

"Sweet Daniel, is that you?" I asked with a huge smile on my face.

Daniel whispered in my ear, "Hi, dirty girl. Didn't stay out of trouble long, did you? And, you can't make fun of my snoring anymore because you have done it all night and it's annoying and not sexy at all."

I tried to laugh and instead felt my nose start throbbing more because of my sudden movement.

"Where are you going?" Daniel asked, pushing me back up.

I felt extremely lightheaded, but the doctor assured me that this would improve soon. He held a pen in front of me and asked me to try to touch it. I could see it, but when I reached out, it wasn't there. Daniel started laughing, and someone reached behind me and hit him.

"Can I please go home?" I asked, frustrated that someone had yet again pushed me back up.

The doctor chuckled and said, "I doubt you could find your way out right now."

When I felt the person on my other side push me back up I said, "Now this is getting dumb."

I heard another familiar laugh and couldn't decide who it belonged to. I figured it must be Mark. I felt like I could finally breathe when he removed some more cotton from my nose.

"How bad?" I asked, looking at the doctor.

Daniel laughed and said, "It actually helped you in the looks department."

I could tell the person on my left had hit him again, and I said, "Thanks, but next time, aim lower."

When they let me lie back down, I heard my dad thank the doctor and felt him touch my leg. He was my comfort and safety net, so I gave into the drowsiness and closed my eyes.

When I woke up, I realized there was someone behind me and in front of me. *Well, this is weird,* I thought. It was quiet as I opened my eyes and I could now see a lot better. Things weren't quite as fuzzy as I looked to see who was in front of me. I smiled seeing Daniel sleeping. I slapped him lightly on the cheek and woke him up.

Opening his eyes with a smile growing across his face, he said, "You can see me now, can't you?"

I giggled and nodded as he pulled me closer to his chest and nuzzled my neck. The person behind me started moving, too.

"You okay? Do you hurt?" Collin's rushed voice asked behind me.

I rolled onto my back and looked at Collin with his just-woke-up look of tussled hair and stubble along his jaw, along with sadness in his eyes.

"You're here?" I asked, reaching up and touching his jaw.

He smiled his sly smile at me and said, "You look beautiful when you wake up next to me."

Daniel burst out laughing and said, "Well, I guess, if her swollen nose and black eyes do something for you."

"You can leave, Daniel, or I can throw you out the window, your choice," Collin said, as though it were a matter of fact.

"Fine, I can find a hot nurse and maybe see if she would like to examine my nuts for me," Daniel said as he got up.

After Daniel had left, I rolled over to face Collin as he ran his fingertips down my cheek.

"You okay?" He asked softly, and I nodded at him.

"You're here," I said, feeling elated even though I kept telling myself I wanted nothing to do with him. I was so in lovewith him, it was stupid.

"Danni, I need to be here with you. I am so sorry Jerry did this to you. He's an asshole," he said, leaning down and kissing my shoulder.

I started crying and said, "He said you told him."

Collin stopped me and held onto me. "He is a liar, whatever he said. I have talked to him once in my life, and that was two years ago, and it wasn't about you. God, Danni, you just mean so much . . ."

I wiped my cheek just as an older nurse came in asking if she could examine me. She motioned for Collin to get off the bed.

An hour later the doctor came in and signed me out, and this time, I passed all his tests. I was thrilled. Collin got a bag of clothes off the chair and mentioned that Mike had dropped them off earlier. I started pulling things from my bag, seeing my favorite pair of red sweats and a football T-shirt. *Mike knows me so well, but where is he?*

"Collin, where are Mike and Mark?" I asked, standing up to walk to the bathroom. I started to sway a little bit as Collin's arms reached out and steadied me.

He said, "Mark's dad died last night so Daniel and I assured them that we could take care of you."

"Are they going to Colorado?" I asked, sitting back down on the bed and feeling awful for Mark as I realized I cared for the guy now. Daniel reentered the room looking bored. The nurse asked if she could take my IV out first so getting dressed would be easier, and I nodded yes. As she started pulling it out, I watched Daniel's face go white right before he passed out.

"Oh my God, Daniel!" I yelled, trying to get up and go to him when Collin beat me to him with another nurse.

"Dipshit! Wake up, you little drama queen," Collin said as he slapped Daniel's cheek. He finally started to come around.

"Screw you, Collin, you drama king," Daniel said, sitting up as a nurse helped him lean against the chair.

Collin and Daniel both grinned at each other, and that was when I noticed the connection between the two. They might claim to hate each other, but there was no denying they needed each other in some way.

The nurse asked me, "Do you need some help getting dressed?"

Before I could even answer, Collin said, "I can take care of her."

What? She nodded toward him and then walked out with Daniel and the other nurses to get him some juice. He was milking his fainting spell for attention, especially, with the younger, cute nurse.

Collin and I sat alone for a couple of moments as he rubbed my hand with his.

"You okay?" I asked.

He looked at me and quietly said, "I am so sorry I have been an asshole to you. I just don't understand any of this yet." With his free hand, he motioned back-and-forth between us.

I pulled myself together, feeling uncomfortable with him acknowledging there was something between us. Obviously, neither of us knew what to do with it. With feelings of jealousy, love, and passion running through me, I did what I always do when I'm uncomfortable. I changed the subject.

"Can I go home?" I asked, picking up my sweatpants off the bed where he had placed them.

He nodded and stood up while he started pulling off the hospital gown around my shoulders. I was clueless as to what to say as he touched me, so I only sat there and let him take off the gown. Next, he helped me pull a T-shirt on, without a bra. Then he squatted down in front of me and pulled my underwear and sweatpants on. When he touched my bare skin, I felt a hot tingling sensation where his fingers had been. I craved more of his touch, and he must have as well since his hands ran up my thighs when he helped me stand up. I pulled them the rest of the way up with shaking hands. I wanted his hands everywhere on me.

Standing in front of him, I held onto his shoulders as I put on my flip flops. He whispered, "You have the most beautiful blue eyes. I have never seen eyes that color before."

I thought the same thing about his as I wanted to lean up on my tiptoes and kiss him. He pulled away and said, "Come on, let's get you home."

⟛⟚

When we got home, Daniel went to lie down. He felt slightly sick from fainting and Collin assured me that this was normal for Daniel. After sitting down and eating the tacos we had picked up on the way home, he disappeared as well after his phone rang for the sixth time in an hour.

Standing in the bathroom looking at my black and blue face, I heard, "What are you doing?"

I explained I was going to take a shower because I felt gross and he laughed and asked how I planned to do that. I still felt a little lightheaded, but I didn't intend on admitting that to him. He already seemed to know, I guessed, by the way, I was holding onto the counter to stop from swaying.

I looked at him as he walked closer and I said, "I can be creative when I need to be."

I walked farther into the bathroom and over to the shower, turning on the water as hot as I could stand it before I started taking my clothes off. I could feel him watching me as I threw them toward the laundry basket in the corner.

He asked, "You do realize you are completely missing the hamper, right?"

As I then took off my underwear and kicked them off, I wondered if he was getting a good look at me standing there naked. I knew taunting him was mean, but he never looked away. I leaned in and touched the water, making sure it was hot enough before I stepped in and let the water run down my body. I put my head back into the stream and wondered if Collin had left since I hadn't heard the door close. Placing my hands on the shower wall, I let the water hit my shoulders as I tried to relax and take in the last week. I suddenly felt his hands on my shoulders. I flinched as Collin started massaging my shoulders.

"Is this okay, Danni?" he asked just loud enough to hear over the water.

My heart was hammering in my chest, and I had butterflies in my stomach. Then he started washing me as I desperately tried to control myself from jumping into his arms and kissing him.

After washing my hair and rinsing it, he whispered close to my ear, "Turn around, baby."

I slowly turned to him and realized he didn't have any clothes on. I reached up and ran my fingers over his chest as he sucked in a quick breath of air. Goosebumps formed on his arms. I found myself closer and closer to him until there was no space between us. I was so turned on and desperately wanted to kiss him, but fortunately for me, a broken nose doesn't make that possible.

He asked, "What are you thinking about?"

"You don't want to know, Collin," I replied, frustrated that we couldn't go any further than this.

"It is probably the same thing I am thinking," he said, pulling my wet hair back into a ponytail.

I said, "I don't think so."

He replied, "Okay, I will go first. I was thinking about the day of the video shoot and how I didn't want to stop. I wish we hadn't had an audience so I could have touched you more."

I mumbled, "You laughed at me."

He started laughing and said, "Did you really have an orgasm?"

"Shut up, Collin," I said, trying to hide my face in his chest as I felt my cheeks turn bright red.

I could tell he was laughing at me. "It had been a while," I said as he quit laughing.

"What were you thinking about?" he asked, circling his arms around my shoulders as our naked bodies pressed against each other.

"You, Collin. I always think about you."

"What do you mean?" he asked.

"Things I shouldn't think about," I said, letting my hands explore his back.

"I was furious seeing you and Daniel in the shower together, practically naked," he whispered, tipping my chin up so we could look at each other.

"I guessed that. You know I adore Daniel like a brother, right?" I asked.

"After you came home, Daniel talked to me about that and said it wasn't like that between you. So now I am trying to understand that."

"Daniel means the world to me, but I don't have the same feelings for him I seem to have for you," I answered as he shut the water off that was turning cold.

We dried off in silence, both processing the conversation we had just had. I went to my closet to grab something to sleep in. As I pulled open a drawer, I felt him step up behind me. I closed my eyes, feeling his warmth when he leaned down and kissed my bare shoulder. Just as he had the last time he saw me naked, he touched my scars on my chest and stomach.

"Do they hurt anymore?" he asked, running his fingers over them again.

"No," I whispered, standing in front of him.

After touching me in silence for a couple of minutes, I groaned, "I am so frustrated."

He couldn't stand it and started laughing at me. "What kind of frustrated?"

I could feel his breath on my neck and said, "You're making it worse. And, by the way, your stunt in the back of the car didn't help either."

"But I got your attention, didn't I?"

"Collin, you always have my attention. I won't deny that." I said, reaching back and touching his jean-covered thighs. *Dammit, he got dressed.*

"And you always have mine," he whispered as he pulled the blue T-shirt he had given me out of my dresser drawer. "Wear this for me."

After getting dressed, I crawled into bed, and he slid in behind me. We were playing a very dangerous game and we both knew it. I like to win, so I pulled off my shirt and rolled over so I was facing away from him, kicking off the covers. We lay there for a little bit before he propped himself up and was leaning over me. I turned back not knowing what else to do when he ran his hand down my side, over my hip and thigh.

"What are you doing?" I asked in a sad voice I couldn't stop.

"Do you know how badly I want to touch you every time I see you? That day rolling around on that bed was a pretty spectacular day for me. I was selfish when I asked you to do that. I just wanted to touch you, and when you kissed me, it was the best moment for me in a very long time."

Without realizing what I was saying I said, "When you touch me, I feel like my skin is on fire. I have never felt that before."

He looked me in the eye as his lips parted and he slowly started touching me again. I had to take a deep breath to contain myself when he put his mouth on my shoulder. *Why did he kiss my bare shoulders whenever he could?*

He whispered, "I like the way I can change your breathing with a simple touch or kiss. At the video shoot when you arched your back and moaned, I almost lost control. I have never wanted someone as much as I want you."

"I have no control around you, Collin," I whispered as he nodded at me.

"I figured that out, too. When we bailed you out of jail, I planned on taking you back to the schoolhouse. I wanted to make love to you, but I got mad at myself when you told me how you felt about me. I don't want to hurt you," he said, pushing me over on my back as he moved on top of me.

"I meant what I said to you. It scares the hell out of me, but I love you," I said wrapping my legs around his waist.

"I have known that all along, Danni. The way you look at me gives it away."

I put my hand on his face and said, "I wish I could kiss you right now."

He leaned toward me and said, "I can kiss you." He began at my shoulder and then moved up my neck. I moaned feeling his warm lips on my skin.

I raised my arms above my head as we had done for the video shoot.

"Relax, baby. I want to hear your breathing as I touch you," Collin whispered in between kisses.

I felt like I was going to burst into flames. I still wanted every part of him even though I knew I shouldn't. His hands moved lower, and I wanted to scream because it felt so good. I was afraid that at any moment, he would stop and realize how wrong this was.

Fortunately, he didn't stop and two orgasms later from his touch, I wasn't so frustrated anymore. He wouldn't let me touch him back or return the favor. He pulled the covers over us, and we both quickly fell asleep.

CHAPTER 21
ABSOLUTELY NOT

When I woke up the next day, Collin was gone, and I hoped that the previous night hadn't been a dream. I was happy for the first time in quite a while, and I knew it had everything to do with Collin.

I crossed my fingers that there was coffee when I walked into the kitchen and saw Rosa standing there making breakfast.

"He estado muy preocupada por ti (*I have been so worried about you*)." Rosa pulled me into her arms for a big hug.

"Estoy bien. Gracias por estar aqui (*I am fine. Thank you for being here*)," I said as we pulled away from each other. She nodded at me and then held her wooden spoon up toward me.

"No más peleas. Voy a golpear a usted! (*No more fighting. I will spank you*).

I laughed and said, "Voy a estar en mi mejor comportamiento. (*I will be on my best behavior*).

I loved her for always taking care of me, no matter how many times she raised her wooden spoon at me and threatened to spank me. Mike and I were very familiar with her wooden spoons. They hurt like a son-of-a-bitch, but they got our attention.

She pointed to the table and asked, "¿Quiénes son? (*Who are they?*)

I glanced over at Collin and Daniel eating the breakfast Rosa had made and smiled. "Son Collin y Daniel, mis buenos amigos (*Collin and Daniel, my best friends*)."

She handed me coffee and pointed at the table, indicating that I should eat. I went and sat down by them and made my plate.

"I take it you speak Spanish," Collin said, smiling at me as he pushed his plate away.

"Yes, Rosa taught me when I was six. By the way, that's Rosa. She's Mike's mom and pretty much my mom, too. Be nice to her and she will take very good care of you. Oh, and Mike might kill you if you piss her off. She likes using that wooden spoon as a weapon," I said as Daniel finally looked up from his plate, as well.

Collin was looking at me with his sly smile and Daniel laughed and said, "Loverboy there gets all hot and bothered hearing you speak Spanish. I bet he is pitching a tent right now."

I burst out laughing when Collin jumped up and yanked Daniel out of his chair and tackled him to the ground. They were both laughing and calling each other names. Daniel was quick, but Collin always seemed one step ahead of him.

⊷╌╌⊷

After breakfast, I sat in my office looking through emails as the two guys sat across from me on the couch. Daniel kept looking at me with complete confusion on his face while Collin had a faint grin. I tried to avoid eye contact with both of them so as not to give away what Collin and I had done last night.

As I looked through my unread email, I found something I didn't like. It was from my dad's attorney. *Well, this could be interesting,* I thought as I dialed the all-too-familiar number. I put the phone on speaker and told the receptionist who I was, she put me right through. Ralph, our attorney, was not a likable guy. Over the years, he and I had had many disagreements. He was old and wanted to retire, so he always took the easy way out of every case. Dad had noticed this and mentioned trying to find a new attorney, and I wish he would already.

"Hi, Danni, happy to see you can keep things stirred up."

I lit right back into him and said, "What the hell, Ralph! What is going on?"

"Well, Danni, judging from the video sent to me from the plaintiff, you assaulted him and caused bodily injury. Now he is suing you for medical expenses and pain and suffering. Oh, fun fact, you're still on probation from the last mess, so the judge wants to see you tomorrow at ten."

"I am going to guess he wants to settle with me for a little cash," I said, practically yelling into the phone.

Collin and Daniel were sitting on the edge of the couch staring at me by now as they listened to my humiliation.

"How much does he want?" I asked.

"A million."

Collin jumped off the couch and grabbed my phone and said, "This is Collin Tabert, and I am obtaining different legal representation for Danni. My attorney will be in contact shortly, and you can send him all the paperwork."

"Danni, is this what you want?" Ralph asked, sounding relieved.

"God, yes, Ralph, you suck as an attorney," I said. Collin took my phone off speaker and left the office to finish the conversation.

"That went well," I mumbled and Daniel laughed and said, "Don't worry. Collin is the master of making bad things go away."

I looked at Collin after he finally came back. "I don't want to go to jail."

"I will personally make sure that doesn't happen," Collin replied, bending over my desk to reach me. I leaned into him as we both wrapped our arms around each other.

Daniel asked with a playful grin on his face, "Dirty girl, is there anything I can do to relieve your frustration?"

Then he winked at me, and I knew he had figured out what was up, or Collin had come clean and told him. I had complained to Daniel enough that I was lonely and frustrated every time he'd tell me about his latest hookup.

I stood up, took off my hat, and walked toward Daniel. In my best sexy voice, I whispered, "What exactly do you have in mind, dirty boy?"

I was wondering how long Collin would let this go as Daniel said, "Perhaps we should turn on some music and take off our clothes." He took off his shirt.

Not wanting to be outdone, I started taking mine off, too, when Collin grabbed me and said, "I don't think so! What is it about the two of you and not being able to leave your clothes on?"

We both started laughing, and Collin said, "I don't think either one of you will ever grow up."

We started making fun of Daniel for passing out when his phone rang, and he left the room. Collin pulled me into his lap, and I quickly settled against him and put my arms around his shoulders. We fit so well together. It was easy to forget he was getting married.

"Danni, promise me something?" he asked, running his nose along my jaw softly.

"What?" I whispered as he pressed his warm lips against my ear.

"That you start keeping your clothes on around Daniel."

I laughed and said, "That might be hard to do."

Collin silently laughed before saying, "I think maybe I should be the only one who can see you naked."

What would your fiancée feel about that? I wondered. But I was enjoying him too much right now to ask questions.

⊷⊷⊷

Late in the afternoon, Collin drove us out to the schoolhouse after they both begged me to show them the recent renovations. We walked in, and it looked amazing, nothing like the decrepit school it had looked like two months ago.

I walked them around and explained my vision to them in great detail. Next, I showed them the extra room adjacent to mine. Daniel claimed it as his. We walked into my soon-to-be-bedroom, and I saw that the fireplace was done, the closet had been put in, and the construction company had managed to save the three old floor-to-ceiling windows that revealed a perfect view of the hills behind the school. I went to look at the bathroom, and it was perfect, too. I opened the shower door, and Collin pushed me inside with him.

"I can't wait to take a shower with you in here," he said as we hugged each other and stole a few kisses before Daniel walked in.

"We can easily fit ten or so in here. This shower is excellent, Danni. Is that four showerheads I see?" Daniel asked, taking in all the details.

Collin said, "No more showers together. No more naked together. I will hurt you if you do."

Daniel walked out and mumbled, "You take the fun out of everything."

I started to walk out when Collin asked, "Are we still on for a shower later tonight?"

I knew I should say no and stop this before it got out of hand, but I just couldn't. I was enjoying him way too much. I assured him we would by kissing him again.

We had walked downstairs and were heading toward the gym when Daniel stopped suddenly and asked, "What is this?" He ducked into the studio and turned on the lights.

I followed him and said, "This is the studio, my favorite room in the whole house."

Collin walked past me and said, "This is great." He looked at me and asked, "Why have you never mentioned it?"

"I don't know. You never really asked, I guess," I said, flipping on the mixing board. I started playing the latest piece Dad had been working on.

"Anyone use it yet?" Collin asked as he examined the high-tech equipment Dad had insisted on.

I answered, "Sometimes the house band rehearses here, but mostly Dad and I write here."

"This is the perfect place to write and record, Danni. I would love to work with you," Collin stated as he sat down and looked at the notepads lying around.

"Collin, is that your way of asking me to write with you?" I asked, sitting down beside him with my curiosity piqued.

"Yeah, I guess I am. You have written some great songs, and I liked the soundtrack you did last year," he said as I laughed, knowing the movie he was referring to was a total flop at the box office. I loved writing and creating music and had only just started working at scoring movies as well.

"I got into scoring last year by accident and the movie was awful. So I probably won't be asked to do another," I said as Daniel began beating on the drums.

Collin got up and started walking around looking at the autographed guitars hanging on the walls. Daniel finally quit playing and joined Collin.

"Where did you get all of these?" Collin asked right before he stopped Daniel from touching one of them.

"I started collecting them when I began playing. I was around ten, I think," I said, walking over to the one they were inspecting.

I wondered why they were so fascinated with them. I was sure they had plenty of instruments. They were, after all, currently one of the most popular rock bands.

Collin looked at Daniel and said, "You know what we need to do, don't you?"

Daniel said, "Yeah, but which one are we going to take down to make room?"

Collin answered, "We will figure that out later. We have to represent our band here with all the great ones."

I laughed and took off for the gym. The first thing I always looked at was the stage, hoping to see the bed there again. I shook my head and looked up at the old scoreboard I was trying to save. I walked over and started messing with the switches, but once again, it never came on.

I heard Daniel behind me as he asked, "You found one yet?"

We had talked about the scoreboard in detail, and he had even taken to trying to help me find someone to fix it or replace it, we both were at a loss.

"No, I think it's a lost cause," I said with a little sadness in my voice.

Daniel and I turned around when we realized Collin was playing basketball at the other end of the full-size gym. We looked at each other and knew what we wanted to do. As we walked toward Collin, we began discussing the rules.

Collin looked at us and said, "Absolutely not!"

Daniel laughed and said, "You don't even know what we're talking about."

"Let me guess. You two are coming up with some clever game that involves taking your clothes off."

CHAPTER 22

SUCH CHEMISTRY

A few weeks later, my new attorney, Nick, managed to keep me out of jail by convincing the judge that I was only protecting myself. The video posted on the internet also helped to prove that fact, as well.

I was thrilled about Nick's determination to win his cases. I liked him so much, in fact, I asked him to handle all of my affairs. He gladly accepted and warned me that I needed to control my temper. I said I would try to make sure that it didn't happen again. He stayed couple extra days to go through all of my papers.

Mike had come back, as well, to help with the business side of the meetings. He liked Nick, too, and quickly decided to hire him, as well. I was surprised by all the details in my life that I had ignored. I think Nick was a little overwhelmed, but he was smart, and I had a feeling he could handle it.

Three days later he left, assuring us that he would be in contact when everything was ready for us to sign. Before he left, he gave me another warning about my temper and Mike promised him that I would behave.

Collin and Daniel had gone back to Seattle a week after I got out of the hospital. They needed to get ready for some award show they were performing at in a couple of weeks. Daniel tried to get me to go with him, but I quickly shut that down. My face was still pretty black and blue, and the tabloids were *still* talking about my run-in with Jerry. I had even seen a few photographers around town trying to get shots of me. Funny how getting in trouble could bring paparazzi to a small town in South Dakota. They were lucky to get a few pictures of Collin, Daniel, Mike, and me around town.

I had loved having Collin around and getting his complete attention. Perhaps I had let things happen that I shouldn't have, but I just couldn't say no to him. I was stupidly in love with him and wasn't thinking clearly at all.

Unfortunately, Steph had started calling him nonstop once the pictures of us together were posted online. I overheard him once telling her that the band was here writing with my Dad, it was entirely innocent, he claimed. I knew I was going to get hurt over my feelings for him.

The bed felt empty without him. He had slept in my bed the whole week he had been here. We had fallen into the pattern of a typical couple, touching, kissing, handholding, and constantly laughing and playing around in bed. Short of actually having sex, we had managed to become very intimate and familiar with each other's body. I was still confused by his obsessive need to kiss my bare shoulders every time he saw them and the way he would run his fingers over my scars.

I started thinking about everything that had happened between us and wondered how much he has told his fiancée, or if he would continue to act like nothing happened. I thought it was odd how Collin never crossed the line. Daniel was the only one I talked to about it. He teased me and was very seldom serious, but he never judged me or told me what I was doing was wrong. We shared some pretty deep talks, and he just hoped I wasn't being set up to be hurt again. Daniel even mentioned that he didn't think Collin had any intentions of leaving Steph. He wondered if not sleeping together was Collin's way of avoiding guilt. I knew he was probably right, but I did what I was good at, I ignored my hurt feelings. Daniel knew I was doing it, as well, but never badgered me to talk about it the way Mike would.

A couple more weeks passed as I sat across a table from Nick as Mike and I signed the new paperwork regarding the bar. I was getting lost in thought, and Mike grabbed my hand after I had started tapping it on the desk. He hated this tick of mine with a passion and I tried not to do it, but sometimes I just couldn't help it. Mike brought my mind back to the conversation as Nick explained contracts for the bar. Because Mike was in the midst of all his wedding planning, I didn't want to bring him down with my train wreck of a dating life, so I went into business mode and tried to listen.

I was suddenly a little distracted by how beautiful Nick was, and I found myself having trouble listening to him talk about vendor contracts. Nick was tall and muscular, with dark hair and dark eyes, best of all were his tattoos that appeared behind his cuffs and collar when he moved in certain ways. He was the guy who I would go for in the past. The likely bad boy. I was a little frustrated in the sex department, and that had me thinking all kinds of naughty things I could do with Nick. It was then that I noticed he wasn't wearing a wedding ring, and I wondered what his deal was.

"Danni?" Mike said, nudging my shoulder. "Maybe you could pay attention to what is going on, so we don't keep Nick here all day."

I knew by his smile that Mike could tell what I was thinking, and I felt myself turning red. I suffered through the next hour of signing papers and listening to Nick. Mike kicked me under the table, and I realized I was staring at Nick again, but he was smiling at me, too.

Nick shook our hands and mentioned that he hoped to see us again. I wanted to more than just see him again. Mike just laughed as he pulled his phone out of his pocket. Walking out of the office, I turned around when I heard Nick call my name.

"Do you know of a good place to eat in town?" Nick asked, walking closer to me as my mouth went dry.

Mike smiled widely at me and motioned he would be in the SUV. I turned around and gave Nick my attention again.

"Well, Nick, you're in luck. We have a restaurant by the bar if you want to try it."

He smiled and asked, "Are you playing tonight? Or could you join me for dinner?"

I answered him, "I'm not playing tonight, and I will be at the bar if you want to pick me up for dinner."

Looking down briefly, he smiled and said, "Only if you buy me a drink before dinner."

I laughed and said, "I can handle that as long as you buy dinner."

He nodded as I turned and walked out, feeling him stare at my ass.

When I got in the car, Mike was on the phone with someone laughing hysterically and talking about me. He told the person on the other line to hold on a minute and handed the phone to me.

"Hello," I said and instantly heard Daniel laughing just as heartily as Mike. "What is so damn funny?" I asked, irritated.

"Dirty girl, I am thrilled that someone has sparked your interest. Mike said you two would have probably fucked on the table if he hadn't been there," Daniel said.

"And fuck you very much, Daniel," I snapped.

"Hey now, dirty girl, no need to get pissed. It's a good thing for you to start dating again. Maybe I won't hear about Collin anymore," Daniel responded with his normal bit of sarcasm.

I wondered if he was right: *maybe I should move on from Collin.* Daniel quit laughing long enough to tell me about the award show that I needed to watch because they were performing their latest song with my dad. I said I would watch and asked him to text me before they went on. I could hear people in the background when Daniel complained that all the girlfriends had crashed his dressing room to get ready.

I couldn't help myself. "Is Steph there?"

After a moment of silence he answered quietly, "Yes, Danni, she's here. Sorry."

I hung up the phone trying not to let my tears fall as I put the phone in the console. Mike grabbed my hand and asked if I was okay. I tried to smile and say I was, but he knew better.

To change the subject I asked about my dress for the wedding and he launched into great detail about everything they had planned. He surprised me when he asked if I had started working on my best man speech. I had forgotten all about it, but I told him I was working on it so he wouldn't get mad at me. I didn't mind being on stage with a guitar, but this wedding would be different, and it terrified me. Getting all dressed up to stand up in front of three hundred people and talk about Mike and Mark had me completely blocked. *What do I know about love?* I wondered if it was too late to get out of it somehow, but quickly decided it was something I had to do for Mike.

Before heading to the bar, Mike and I turned on the television to the interviews with Daniel and the band. Knowing Daniel's dirty mind, I guessed this could be kind of interesting. I found the channel just as the host welcomed them on stage. The four of them walked out on stage and waved to the audience. The host started asking about the video they had just shown.

Mike said, "Shit, we missed it," while smiling at me. I knew he liked it because it embarrassed me.

The host continued saying, "In the past you have always gone the same direction with your videos. So tell us why you did something we have never seen you do before with this video."

Daniel, Jake, and Rick all looked at Collin to answer, and I couldn't wait to hear his response.

"Well, we met this great girl who has been a victim of sexual assault and we wanted to show the world that she is still beautiful. Also, we wanted to help bring attention to the problems of sexual assault in the world today. We are donating some of the record proceeds to charities that help sexual assault victims get the help they need."

My heart sank, and my lunch threatened to come back up.

Mike and I just looked at each other knowing we were both pissed. The host then asked, "Who is the woman in the video?"

Daniel jumped on that and answered, "We are not going to name names so she can have some peace in her life, but I will say she is one of the greatest, most talented women I have ever met. I am thankful to have her as a friend."

"Wow," I said, surprised. "He can be so sweet when he isn't making everything so dirty." Mike quickly agreed.

The host then turned his attention back to Collin and said, "I understand you are getting married this summer. Are you excited about that?"

Collin responded with a smile, "I am very excited. Steph is a great woman, and I am excited about what the future holds for us."

The host went on to say, "Collin, in the video you are in bed with this beautiful woman. It looks pretty steamy between the two of you. Is it hard for your fiancée to see you do that?"

Collin thought for a minute and replied, "Honestly, she wasn't thrilled about it, but we both looked at it as me playing a character. We are bringing to light a subject that should be more recognized. She is stunning and just because something hideous happened to her, doesn't change who she is or take away her beauty."

The host chuckled and said, "Well, you played the character very well. I could see a lot of chemistry between the two of you."

Collin started laughing, and I noticed Daniel was not looking pleased. Then they went to a commercial break, and Mike turned the television off, obviously upset, as well. I sat back on the couch with all these thoughts going through my head. I finally whispered, "He only sees me as a victim."

Mike and I sat there trying to figure out what had just happened. Mike jumped as his phone started ringing. After picking it up off the end table, he answered it without any enthusiasm in his voice. He listened for a minute and then he said, "Yes, we saw it. I will tell her."

After putting the phone down, Mike said, "That was Daniel. He was hoping you missed the interview. The things Collin said were news to him, too. He didn't know Collin was going in that direction. He asked me to tell you that he and Jake are very sorry."

I knew Daniel had nothing to do with it, but Jake apologizing, as well, surprised me. He was always so quiet around me, and I assumed he didn't like me. I sat there staring at the ceiling, not able to pinpoint a single thought, even though I had a million of them going through my head. The only thing that stood out was Collin. *He simply thinks of me as a victim.*

Mike stood up and mentioned that we needed to get ready for work. He headed downstairs to shower knowing I needed a couple of minutes to take it all in.

I got ready in time to go to work as neither Mike nor I brought up anything about the interview on the way to the bar. Once we got there, he started organizing our office. This was something he did since we were little. When he was extremely upset, he organized instead of reacting. I thought maybe he was more upset than I was when he started cleaning out *my* desk after thoroughly organizing his.

I accomplished a lot over the next two hours. I finished payroll, paid our vendors, approved vacation time, and got some supplies ordered. *Why can't I get this much work done all the time?* I knew exactly why, I had left my phone on the counter at home.

I knew I would miss Daniel's call, and he would be concerned. Then a knock at my door scared the crap out of me, and I spilled my cup of tea on my desk.

"Sorry, Danni, I didn't mean to scare you," Nick said as I jumped up to avoid the river of tea running toward me. After cleaning up my mess, Nick and I decided to walk to the restaurant to have dinner instead of drinks. It was only two blocks away, and it gave us a chance to talk. As we talked, we discovered that we were both runners, and we compared our times. He told me that he liked to run marathons and if I wanted to, he would help me prepare for the upcoming one. I said I would have to think about it, knowing I may not be dedicated enough to do it.

Nick and I ended up having a lot in common. He told me all about his family and how his dad was the founding partner of his firm with offices all around the country. It was apparent by the way Nick talked about it that he liked his job.

We discussed how I had grown up with a famous dad and the ways I had managed to keep myself out of the spotlight until recently. He briefly mentioned he was sorry to hear about the events that had happened to me in the last year and a half. He genuinely hoped things would get better. *Wow, this guy is actually charming and smart.*

He reached over and held my hand, and I was enjoying it until I realized it was time to leave. We made our way out of the restaurant, and I was surprised when I looked at my watch and realized I had just had a three-hour dinner date with Nick. He held my hand as we walked back to the bar.

I was a little giggly when he asked, "Why do you seem so nervous?"

I laughed and said, "It has been a very long time since I had a regular date. This is strange for me."

"I hope it's a *good* strange," he said, stopping in front of the bar and turning to face me.

"Nick, this is a *very* good strange," I said as we both stepped closer together.

My mind went blank as he slowly leaned in and kissed me. He was an excellent kisser, but my mind flew instantly to Collin and his passionate kisses. I tried not to let that thought ruin the moment when Nick pulled back.

"I had a great evening with you," he said, still standing close to me. "I hope we can do this again very soon."

"I would like that, Nick, very much." This time, I leaned up and kissed him.

After he had walked down the street to his car, I stood there for a moment trying to gather my thoughts. I wondered what exactly I was doing.

As I walked into the bar, Mike was smiling and said, "That looked like some kiss."

I couldn't help but laugh as I kept heading to my office with Mike following me.

He leaned on my desk and said, "Details please."

We had always talked about the intimate details of our lives, nothing was off limits. Since the assault, I was more guarded with him. I hadn't told anyone about so many details from the night of the assault, and it made me feel guilty to think I was keeping things from my best friend. So, I thought I could try to tell him about the date.

"Nick is a great guy and sexy as hell."

Mike stopped me and said, "Why do I hear you dragging your feet then?"

Sometimes Mike knowing me so well worked against me. I answered, "I'm not, Mike."

"Yes, Danni, you are. What is the problem?" he asked as he leaned on my desk in front of me and I sat down.

"I don't know what I want, Mike. This whole Collin mess has just got my mind going in so many different directions. I don't know how or what I feel."

Mike quietly said, "It's not like you have to marry the guy. Just try dating him and see what happens. No expectations."

"I don't want to do to him what Collin is doing to me by stringing me along. All this time I thought maybe he felt something for me, but he just sees me as a victim. He only felt sorry for me," I said, realizing I sounded like a victim, too.

Mike stood up and yelled, "I am so glad Collin is a thousand miles away, or I would kick his ass."

I laughed at the thought of Mike hurting anyone. As many things as I tried to hide from him, I knew he was onto all of them. After he had taken a few calming breaths, he continued, "I told Daniel you would call him later no matter how late it is. He is upset and wants to make sure you're okay."

"I'll call him when I get home. By the way, you didn't tell him I was out with Nick did you?"

He grinned before leaning down and kissing the top of my head.

It was two in the morning when we got home. I decided it was too late to call Daniel back. I lay in bed looking through my missed calls and text messages. Daniel texted me insisting I call him back, or he would keep calling, and that was only twenty minutes ago. Nick had left a nice voicemail saying again he had a great evening and was looking forward to seeing me again. One last text that stood out from the others was from Collin with one simple word.

Collin: Sorry

Mike was lying beside me at this point and said, "I would be happy to respond to that message if you want me to."

I hit delete and decided I was going to put it out of my mind and go ahead and give Nick a chance. Mike was glad to hear that. My phone rang, and I saw it was Daniel. I debated answering but, knowing Daniel, he would keep calling unless I picked up.

"Hey, Daniel," I answered, trying not to yawn.

"Did I wake you up?" he asked, sounding just as tired as I was.

"No. We just got home a little bit ago."

Of course, he had to make it dirty by asking, "So, did Nick wear you out?"

I laughed and said, "Shut up, Daniel. Nothing happened but a goodnight kiss. He is a gentleman. This is how adults date."

He laughed and said, "I like how I date better. I want a good-night blowjob, not a goodnight kiss. *Pffft* that is lame."

After laughing at each other, we talked about him heading back home. With a lot of irritation in his voice, he explained that Collin's bus had broken down. They had only taken two buses to the show, so now the whole band and the girlfriends were on his bus. I was hoping Collin wasn't listening to our conversation.

I tried not to talk about Nick as Daniel asked me more about him, so I had a feeling Collin was, in fact, listening in. I mentioned I didn't want to talk about Nick, but Daniel kept going on. I started laughing when he asked if Nick looked as good naked as he does. I knew exactly why he said that as he went on to have a five-minute pretend conversation with me about it. He was trying to piss off Collin, and I loved him a little more for that. We had talked about little things for the next hour before I told him I needed some sleep. He laughed and made a joke about how having hot sex for hours can make you tired.

Mike had taken off the following weekend to work on wedding stuff with Mark, so that meant I had to cover at the bar. I liked anything that would keep my mind busy, but instead, it turned out to be a quiet weekend with not much happening.

I had even taken the time to go to the spa and do all the things they managed to do to me at the video shoot. It did make me feel a little better about myself.

I had talked to Nick multiple times, and I was starting to like him. As I drove home from the spa, he called saying he had good news for me and a personal question, as well.

"I'll start with the good news first. I got your probation lifted on account of the judge not offering you diversion classes, he was obligated to since you're a first-time offender."

"Really?" I asked, shocked. "It's over just like that?"

He laughed and said, "Yes, your record is clean once again, so stay out of trouble."

He went on to tell me, "We settled the case with Jerry."

In-depth Nick explained that instead of me settling with him, Jerry was settling with *me*. He finished by saying that his band was on the rise and hitting a girl was not something his record label would want the world knowing. So, he was paying me as long as I signed a non-disclosure agreement preventing either of us from talking about the incident.

I was so grateful to have the whole incident behind me and thanked Nick for that.

He said, "Now, I have two personal questions for you. Would you be interested in being my date next weekend for two reasons? One is for a benefit dinner, and two is because Collin is throwing a surprise birthday party for Daniel. He asked if I would let you know."

This upset me. *Couldn't Collin even call me himself? What an ass.*

"Nick, I don't know about the dinner thing . . ." I said, discouraged at the idea of a stuffy dinner function with people I didn't know.

"Come on, Danni. You can put on a nice dress and look beautiful for me."

"Do you know how hard it is for me to keep something from Daniel?" I mumbled.

"Collin mentioned that to me, as well, so I can't give you too many details," Nick said, almost laughing.

I knew I couldn't skip it. I had to be there for Daniel, so I agreed to both dates with Nick. He was thrilled and excited to see me.

The next day Mike was happy to take me shopping for a dress to wear to the benefit. It was a black tie dinner, and I thought maybe I had bitten off more than I could chew. I sat in the chair of the changing room playing on my phone, waiting to see what Mike had found.

He held up a black satin number with the straps covered in crystals that ran all the way down the sides of the backless dress.

I started laughing at him and called him a dumbass. He looked confused by my reaction.

I said, "I will practically be naked in that. Remember, I have a scar on my back? I want to cover it up, so look for something else."

He glared at me in frustration and said, "If you don't at least try it on, I will call Daniel and tell him all about the party."

I knew he would, and I didn't want that, so I took the dress from him. It irritated me more when I realized it was a dress with which you couldn't wear a bra. I slid it over my head and tried to figure out the straps. Hearing me cussing to myself, Mike barged in. He helped me put the straps on the right way and stood back looking proud of himself.

"I wish I had picked this dress for the wedding. You look gorgeous in it," Mike said smugly.

"You don't want me to look better then you on your wedding, do you?"

He started laughing at me and then said, "No. I want Mark to marry me. Not you."

I had to admit the dress fit perfectly, but it made me nervous how much skin it showed. Also, both scars on my back showed clearly.

I asked the sales lady, "How do you move in this and not show everything?"

She said, "Double-stick tape, honey. It holds everything in place."

"Won't that hurt to remove?" I grumbled, not liking her idea.

"I think someone will have a lot of fun removing it," Mike said, laughing.

CHAPTER 23
SURPRISE

As the plane touched down in Seattle, I couldn't wait to see Daniel. It had been a month and a half since I had seen him last. I wasn't black and blue anymore so that he couldn't make fun of me for that, at least. Nick was waiting for us when we got to the baggage claim. He pulled me into his arms as we hugged and kissed. I was glad to see him, too. Mike introduced Mark to Nick after I realized from Mike's dirty glare that I had overlooked it. I wasn't trying to leave Mark out, but I was anxious, and we both knew it had everything to do with Collin. I spotted my bag and grabbed it, pulling myself back into the present.

We got to our hotel, where the party was taking place and got checked in. I decided not to share a room with Mike and Mark. After a couple of drinks, they always got a little touchy with each other, and I didn't want to witness it. Daniel's party was tonight, and the benefit dinner was tomorrow night. Two seconds later my phone rang, and it was Daniel. It had been so hard not telling him I was coming to see him.

"Hello, dirty boy," I said sitting down on my bed.

"What are you doing, dirty girl? Are you naked in the tub?" he asked, sounding hopeful.

I realized he had never once let on that it was his birthday. I wondered why he had never said anything before. Probably the same reason why I hadn't mentioned mine that year. I had never liked a big deal made of my birthday. It was simply another day.

We talked for a little bit about the bar and the schoolhouse. He sounded off, almost like he was upset about something. Soon he answered my assumption.

"Collin is a dick. He said I was grounded and needed to stay close to him because of some stupid party or something tonight. I don't know. I wasn't listening to him much. He irritates the shit out of me most days."

Being mischievous I said, "If you're not doing anything tonight, you could watch us play at the bar."

He laughed and said, "I have other ideas that involve naked, hot women. Sorry, you're on your own, dirty girl."

I laughed and said, "Well, have fun with that and use a condom."

He laughed loudly and said, "I always wrap it. Don't want any little Daniel's running around. That could be dangerous. I will send you videos later, but send me one back this time."

I laughed as I hung up, knowing he would send something. I loved Daniel, but I didn't need to see him naked *again*.

Nick went back to his office to finish a few things after he told me he was glad I was there. He gave me a pretty passionate kiss before he shut the door behind him. I liked Nick, but the realization was setting in that I didn't feel much more than that for him.

I took a shower to try and calm my nerves. The thought of seeing Collin made me a little sick. I started thinking back to that stupid interview on the talk show. His words still hurt just like they did when I heard them come out of his mouth. I told myself that tonight was about Daniel. I wouldn't let Collin ruin that, and I would avoid him at all costs and make the best of it.

I had been racking my brain for gift ideas ever since I had found out Daniel's birthday was coming up. Neither one of us was the regular gift-giver, so I decided that keeping our competitive streak going would be fun. I would try to talk him into doing something neither one of us had ever done, but something I had always wanted to do. Knowing Daniel and his aversion to blood, I thought I could win this one, considering he had passed out at the hospital the last time he saw blood. Nick had helped me arrange the whole thing last week, and I was so excited about it. I looked at the red envelope that enclosed the details and got super excited. Mike knew what I was up to and had even mentioned he had thought about it one time, and maybe he would do it, too.

I got dressed in the clothes Mike had picked out for me. Once again, knowing I would have worn jeans and a T-shirt, he had packed me a short black skirt and a red tank top that had part of the back cut out. Of course, my outfit included those stupid, black strappy heels. I tried to throw them away a couple of different times, but they always came back. After getting dressed and putting my hair in a messy knot off to one side, I was ready. Mike

decided to put a red flower thing in my hair, saying it comple-
mented the outfit; Mark agreed.

When Nick showed up, we were all finally ready to go to the
party. They had all cleaned up nice too, though I pointed out
how unfair it was that they got to wear jeans and I couldn't. Mike
fired back at me saying this was because I was a girl and had lovely
legs. I stuck my tongue out, and he rolled his eyes in frustration.

Walking downstairs to the party, Nick reminded us that
Daniel still didn't know we were in town or what was going on.
Then he explained that they had told Daniel the record company was having a party for them in honor of the success of the
video, so Daniel was under the impression that it was something
work-related. I was so excited.

We went in through the staff entrance and were taken to a
room with lots of other people already waiting.

We were standing around talking when I caught a glimpse of
Steph pointing at me and talking to an older woman. *Great, this
can't be good.* The older woman started walking toward me. *Shit!
She's probably coming over to yell at me on Steph's behalf.* I tried to move
behind Mike as he looked at me like I was crazy. Mike moved after he noticed her and she stopped in front of me, smiling.

"Are you Danni?" she asked, starting to smile at me.

I responded hesitantly, "Yes."

Before I knew what she was doing, she had her arms around
me in a tight hug. *Okay, maybe she wasn't going to yell at me.*

"I am so glad to meet you finally. I have heard so much about you," she said, pulling away to look at me.

I was dumbfounded about who this woman was. Mike and Mark looked at me with puzzled looks on their faces. She finally let go of me when she noticed I was confused.

"I'm sorry to overwhelm you. I'm just happy to meet you. I am Paige."

It dawned on me finally. She was Daniel's mom. He had mentioned her before, specifically how they were very close.

"It's nice to meet you too, Paige. Daniel talks about you a lot," I said before she hugged me again. She seemed very happy to meet me, and this confused me even more.

"I am so glad you came. Daniel will be thrilled you're here. He adores you," she said as she let go of me again.

I saw Collin watching us out of the corner of my eye with Steph draped on his arm. I glanced away, trying to give Paige my full attention. She was a breath of fresh air and a joy to talk to. After I examined her, I could see that Daniel looked a lot like her. I was surprised how much she and Daniel even carried on a conversation the same way. Nothing was off limits when she mentioned she thought my nose had healed nicely. I was surprised he would mention me getting into trouble, but she assured me that he has always told her everything.

After we had talked for twenty minutes and I introduced her to Mike and Mark, she excused herself to help with the party.

She walked toward Collin, and I looked somewhere else, finally noticing Nick was nowhere around. Soon they ushered us into the main room, saying Daniel was in the lobby. I grabbed onto Mike out of habit, as he wrapped his hand around mine. He was my comfort and safety net tonight, and even Mark put his hand on my back protectively.

I heard someone say, "On the count of three," and then everyone erupted into "*HAPPY BIRTHDAY, DANIEL!*" I could hear his laughter but still couldn't see him. I heard lots of people wishing him a happy birthday. With all these people I would have to wait forever for my turn to see him. I heard him joking about hating his birthday when someone bumped into me. *What a jerk*, I thought to myself as I looked around and saw that it was Collin making his way to Daniel.

I wasn't sure where Nick had gone, then felt two hands wrap around my waist. I smiled knowing Nick had found me. He kissed my cheek and asked, "Have you seen Daniel yet?"

"Not yet," I said, wrapping my arms around his neck.

He whispered in my ear, "I could help you pass the time if you want?"

I giggled a little devilishly and started to kiss him when I heard someone clear their throat.

"Hey, it's my birthday, and I want my present," Daniel said, pouting, as I pulled away from Nick.

I jumped into Daniel's arms as I felt his arms around me. He said, "You have just made my list of all-time best birthdays."

I laughed and said, "But I haven't slept with you yet, dirty boy."

He laughed too when I heard Collin say, "They will never grow up."

Daniel finally released me, and I said, "Happy birthday, sweet Daniel."

He looked at me with his playful grin and said, "All the other cute girls have given me a birthday kiss, so I am waiting for yours. Make it dirty."

I quickly planted a big one right on his lips and in typical Daniel style he wouldn't let me go as he tried to french me. Someone elbowed me in the ribs, and I couldn't help but grunt in the pain. Daniel felt it too and let me go.

"That was meant for me," he said as he started rubbing my ribs.

I looked up and saw that it had come from Collin. Then Daniel pulled me along to meet his mom, even though I explained that I already had. I looked at Nick, and he laughed, motioning me to go play. Of course, Collin gave me a pissed-off look as Steph hung off of him in her super tight red dress that barely covered her ass.

Daniel and I talked to his mom for quite a while. The more we talked, the more I liked her. I had just taken a sip of my drink when I heard Daniel's mom say, "What is wrong with your brother tonight? He has been upset all day. Are you fighting *again?*"

Instantly I started choking on my drink, spilling half of it down my shirt. I quickly had all their attention and Daniel looked nervous.

Paige asked, "Honey, you okay?"

I nodded that I needed a moment to learn to breathe again. Daniel started handing me napkins to dry myself off. I thought to myself: *wait a huge minute, did I hear that right?*

I looked at Paige while trying to control my coughing and said, "Excuse me, did you say '*brother*'?"

She looked at me with a confused frown and asked, "Didn't they tell you that they are brothers?"

The look on my face explained it to her as my coughing left me unable to speak. The look on Daniel's face was completely serious for the first time since we had met.

"Daniel, could I have a moment alone with you?" I asked before slamming back the rest of my drink.

He grabbed my hand and pulled me out into the hallway with him. I had to stop to take my shoe off and attempt to dry it off. I had red streaks from the cranberry juice staining my leg and shoe.

"Daniel, you have some explaining to do," I said trying to make a joke, and he started smiling at me. He took a handful of napkins and squatted down in front of me, wiping off my leg.

"You have your drink all down your legs, you klutz." His hand was getting too far north. I tried to stop him, but I was laughing hysterically when a voice yelled, "Knock it off Daniel, *now.*"

Daniel and I looked at each other and laughed harder. We knew who it was, and that made it even funnier.

Laughing, Daniel said, "Quick, turn around, and I will get the back, too."

Collin's voice was ice cold when he muttered, "Daniel, stand up, you're making a scene."

Daniel stood up as neither one of us could quit laughing. "I missed you," I said, jumping into Daniel's arms. He hugged me and said, "I'm thrilled you're here, too."

While I stayed in his arms, Collin stared at us.

"Danni, I would like you to meet my brother, Collin," Daniel said.

I whispered in his ear, "It doesn't matter to me, as long as you are my friend, Sweet Daniel."

He added, "Best."

We let go of each other, and I excused myself to go clean up and give them a chance to talk.

I took ten minutes to tidy up and get my shoes clean before I headed back into the party. The music had been turned up now, and everyone was dancing. The crowd had thinned some as I saw Mike and Mark sitting at a table with Jake and his date. I went to talk to them and told them the big news. They were as shocked as I was. Jake mumbled that they were both idiots. Mark wondered if Collin was still an ass and I nodded that he was. Mike looked at me and then pointed to the dance floor. I saw Daniel out there with some girl, who was hardly wearing any clothes. We both laughed.

Soon Nick had found us as well, and sat beside me. I was on my fifth drink, so Nick was becoming much more appealing. A slower song came on, and Nick led me to the dance floor. He grabbed my waist and pulled me close to him as we started moving to the music. He definitely had rhythm.

Daniel bumped into us on purpose and grabbed my ass, and I started laughing. Nick tried to turn me away from Daniel so that he could have my attention to himself. I noticed I had Collin's attention, as well. He was standing at the bar watching as someone was talking to him, but he wasn't paying notice to anyone but me. I locked eyes with him, and he toasted me before taking a shot.

The song ended, and a more upbeat song came on as Nick pulled me closer to him, putting his hands on my hips and grinding against me. He was starting to turn me on. I put my arms around his neck and let him lead when he turned me around, so my back was to his front. I could feel his breath on my neck and went along with the sensations as I closed my eyes and leaned my head back on his shoulder. He started kissing my neck slowly. It felt amazing as we got lost in our little world.

After a few more dances, Nick excused himself to use the bathroom, and I started walking back to my seat. Daniel grabbed me and pulled me back to the dance floor.

As we slow danced he said, "That was quite a show."

I laughed and said, "You should have been in my shoes."

He laughed and said, "Your shoes are sticky, but on the plus side you don't seem so frustrated."

I started laughing with him when I got elbowed in the ribs once again. *I am going to hit someone hard if that happens again*, I mumbled to myself. Daniel whispered in my ear, "Again, that was meant for me."

This time, we both started laughing. I left Daniel so he could dance with a blonde and then found Nick sitting with Collin, Steph, Rick, and his wife. I sat down next to Nick, and he turned to me and pulled me closer to him, putting his arm around me as I rested my hand on his leg. I felt this burning stare and knew Collin was watching us.

Nick was talking to Collin and Rick about someone else they all knew, which gave me a chance to take fully in my surroundings. Most of the guests still in the room were a younger crowd, drinking heavily and trying to get the band's attention. I lost track of how many times Collin's conversations had been interrupted.

I noticed Daniel dancing with Steph and instantly liked him less for that. Nick leaned over trying to get my attention and started kissing my neck. I couldn't help myself and let out a little moan as I closed my eyes.

He whispered in my ear, "I like that sound."

I turned toward him as he kissed me softly. Soon I found myself sliding my hands under his shirt and jacket to feel his bare skin. I wondered if I was going too far when I felt his hand slide a little farther down my back. I was ready to start taking his clothes off when the song ended, and others sat back down beside us.

I indicated I would be back after deciding it was time to put out my fire before I did something I would strongly regret later. Standing at the bar, I ordered two shots of whiskey. The bartender flirted with me as I ignored him and quickly downed the shots. When I ordered another one, Collin was next to me ordering drinks, as well.

Without looking at me he said, "You know that won't help, right?"

"It always has in the past," I mumbled before downing the second shot.

When I turned to walk away, he stepped in front of me, blocking my path. In a very firm, cold voice, he looked into my eyes and said, "You should stop being everyone's whore." Then he stepped aside.

Instantly, tears filled my eyes as I looked down, not wanting him to see how his words affected me. I headed outside to get some fresh air.

Alone now, I wiped away my tears. That was the meanest thing he had ever said to me. I couldn't believe he could be that cruel. I had learned long ago not to listen to the painful things people said because of the business I was in. I was constantly a target in the media because of my dad and the assault. But Collin could get to me faster than anyone ever had.

"Hey, dirty girl, what are you doing out here?" Daniel asked, approaching me from behind.

I wiped my eyes before turning back to him and said, "Hey, birthday boy. I think I'm going to call it a night. I am really tired."

I knew he was aware that something was wrong as he ran his finger under my eye to wipe away my mascara.

"What is wrong, Danni?" he asked sweetly.

I answered, "I am fine really, just tired."

"Then why are you crying? You are not fine," he said, wrapping me in a hug.

I tried to hide my crying, but Daniel could tell I was upset when he asked, "What did he say to you?" There was anger in his words as he let go of me and looked at me.

"Nothing, Daniel, everything is fine. Enjoy your party and I will catch up with you tomorrow, okay?" I said, trying to forget Collin ever existed.

"I am going to fucking kill him!" he snapped as he let go of me and headed back inside on a mission.

Lying in my hotel bed with the lights out, I cried as I thought about how cruel Collin was and how hearing him say that had cut me to the core. No one had ever called me a whore before. I now knew why girls didn't like to hear it. Nick understood that

I wanted to be alone. I could tell he was disappointed that we didn't take a step further in our relationship that night. I knew I was fooling myself with him.

A knock on my door brought me out of my deep thoughts. It was probably Mike checking on me. I had told him everything before I left and he swore the next time he saw Collin, he would punch him for me.

"Who is it?" I asked as I climbed out of bed.

I heard Daniel say, "Me. Open the door."

I opened the door and stepped aside as he came in looking disheveled.

"I'm sorry. I hope I didn't ruin your party," I said, closing the door as he sat on my bed.

"You didn't. Collin has a way of ruining everything," he said, taking off his torn jacket.

"Why didn't you tell me you were brothers?" I asked, sitting down by him.

"Well, Collin is not easy to like. He has a hot temper, and he can tear you down so quickly you don't see it happen. Danni, Collin is in such a fucked up predicament with Steph, he is just mad at everyone, especially you."

"What did I do?" I asked, even more frustrated.

"Don't you get it, Danni? He is so madly in love with you that he tries to piss you off so you will just hate him. But, instead, you ignore him, and that pisses him off even more. Collin is very controlling, and he realizes he can't control you. And believe me, you are the one person that he wants to control." Daniel stood up and handed me a pair of jeans and a T-shirt.

Looking down at my hands I said, "I want to hate him, ignore him, strangle him sometimes, but he is all I think about. Is that love?"

"No, Danni. That is the both of you fighting against your destiny to be together," Daniel said, throwing the clothes at me. "Now get dressed. My real birthday party is about to get started without me."

CHAPTER 24
IDIOTS

Daniel lived in a gated community. The house, sitting back among the trees, had a rounded brick driveway. Pulling up in front of his house, I realized how well he must do for himself. The house was comparable in size to my schoolhouse, but this was much more elegant. It had more of a refined cabin look to the outside. Lanterns hung from the porch all the way around the front. Instantly it felt like home.

As I made my way up the porch, I said, "Your house is beautiful, Daniel."

Smiling, he unlocked the door and said, "It isn't mine. It's my mom's. She just lets me live here."

Then I remembered him saying a while back that he couldn't live without his mom, so he just made her live with him. He was the sweetest person I knew.

The inside of the house was just as beautiful as it was on the outside. Hardwood floors as far as I could see, a large kitchen to the right, a dining room and office to the left, and my favorite, an older style wooden staircase leading upstairs.

"Mom!" Daniel yelled, scaring me out of my house-envying stupor.

"Kitchen!" Paige yelled back, and I laughed at their one-word responses.

Heading into the kitchen, I saw Paige in sweatpants and a baggy T-shirt. She stepped toward me and said, "I am so glad you are here. Are you hungry?"

"Hi, Paige. Sorry to barge in so late, but Daniel wouldn't let me go to bed. Thank you, but I'm not hungry," I said, sagging down on the leather stool in front of the island.

She watched me for a minute and then stepped around the island and put her hand on my cheek. "What's wrong?"

Now I understood where Daniel got his ability to read people so well.

"I am fine, just tired."

"Why do you look like you have been crying then?" Paige asked.

While looking in the fridge, Daniel said, "Jackass called her a whore. Beat his ass, Mom."

"You're kidding?" she asked, with a mix of anger and frustration.

I wondered how he had found out. I hoped I hadn't ruined his birthday. Daniel started putting food and drinks on the island as if on a mission. Then Paige gathered it all up and put it in two bags for him like she already knew what he was doing. Daniel smiled and kissed her cheek. Their undeniable bond made me think of my mom and all the things I had missed out on with her.

Paige looked at me and said, "Collin can be cruel when he is hurt. I'm sorry he said that to you."

"Thanks, Paige, but please don't apologize for him. He is an adult so he can do that himself."

"Really? You're friends with him?" Paige said, pointing to Daniel.

"Hey, Mom, that wasn't nice. I'm your baby, love me and hug me and tell me I'm pretty," Daniel said, half laughing as he tried to hug her playfully.

Paige laughed, untangling herself from him, "I love you, son, but I am surprised a smart woman like Danni is friends with you. Usually, you pick the ones with not much going on up here," she said, tapping his forehead.

I burst out laughing, knowing she was right, and Daniel made a sad face at her, playing for sympathy. He got it when she hugged him tightly, almost protectively. Daniel turned to me and stuck his tongue out in victory.

Down the hall behind a set of double doors, I said, "Wow, Daniel this place is huge."

He laughed and said, "Thanks, but you haven't seen it all yet."

He explained that this was his corner of the house. It was a huge room with tons of arcade games, a pool table, a stripper pole, a full-size bar, and a pool.

"Wow, you don't ever need to leave this room. It has everything," I said as I noticed the full kitchen behind the bar and two more closed doors. I assumed they were bedrooms.

He walked over to the bar and asked if I wanted to play a game as he put shot glasses out. I thought, *what the hell,* and took off my coat, making myself comfortable on a stool across from him. He laughed when he saw my T-shirt was one from his band. After turning a stereo on, he explained that we weren't doing bad shots like the game we had played at my bar. Instead, we would be doing straight shots, and he wanted to make it interesting. Then he explained the basic game he insisted was a classic, Truth or Dare or Drink. I knew the game, just not his version of it. Answer a question truthfully or take something off, dare someone to take off a piece of clothing, or drink. I liked his way of thinking. It was always about getting someone naked.

His phone suddenly rang, and he had a brief conversation that amounted to, "Use the side door." Then he asked if I minded adding a few people to the party and I nodded that it was okay. About ten minutes later, all of these people started coming in through a door by the pool. I saw Rick walk in with his arm around some woman I knew wasn't his wife. I noticed Jake and his date from earlier come in and sit down on one of the brown leather couches. Most of the people I didn't recognize and I wasn't surprised at all by the girls who barely had any clothes on.

Daniel went first after roughly seven others joined our game, and he had explained it to them. Of course, he picked me to start, and I chose to drink. The next guy dared his date to take off her shirt, and she did with no embarrassment at all. This went on for an hour, and I was the one with the most clothes on, but I was also well on my way to being drunk.

I noticed Daniel kept looking over at something, and I figured it was some girl he liked. He looked back at me and said, "I dare you to kiss her."

I strongly regretted telling him about my bisexuality. He had never brought it up until now, *in front of people.*

"Fine," I said, standing up and walking over to the blond he had his arm around.

She was pretty enough and had a huge pair of fake boobs, but she was a little too showy for me. She had it all on display for anyone to see as she stood there in her bra and underwear. When it comes to women, I preferred more conservative women, but give me a bad boy any day.

I stepped in front of the now-smiling blond when Daniel said, "No, no, no, right here." He pointed behind the bar so he and his little friends could watch. "And it has to be for at least a minute."

She walked behind the bar with me, and I mumbled, "Let's just get this over with."

She launched herself at me a little too eagerly. I backed into the wall to stop us from falling over as she kissed me with enthusiasm. She was a great kisser, and I slowly remembered why I played for both teams. Of course, Daniel had to count it down for us, and we even went past the one-minute allotment before I could loosen her grip on me. I finally managed to pull back from her, and that's when I realized that perhaps she knew me.

"I can't believe I just kissed Danni Brisco. Can I take a picture of us to show my friends?" she asked in a high-pitched screech. Just like that, she had lost her appeal, and I went to sit back down.

I played the game and continued drinking. At one point I thought I saw Collin and wondered if I had had too much to drink. I looked more carefully and, sure enough, it was Collin and Steph. She appeared to be yelling at him with her finger in his face. Collin glanced at me as I watched their fight progress. I toasted him with my shot of whiskey, just like he had done earlier when Steph grabbed his face and made him look at her. Their argument was drawing quite a large crowd. Then, over the crowd, I watched Collin yank her out of the room by her arm. She looked fuming mad.

Daniel pounded his hand on the bar and told me to pay attention. He then caught sight of Collin, rolled his eyes, and mouthed, "Sorry." I shrugged it off, and we went back to playing our game.

A few too many shots later, I asked, "What am I doing?"

Daniel pointed at me and said, "Your turn on the pole, dirty girl."

We had already witnessed three drunk girls pole dance, and one was pretty good, but I wasn't drunk enough to do it. I was the only one still fully dressed in our little game. In no way was I going to show anyone my naked body.

"What else you got, dirty boy?" I asked, Daniel already knew I wouldn't do it.

"How about a private lap dance?" Collin asked from behind me. I could feel his warm breath on my neck.

Daniel looked at Collin and said, "Both of you need to cool off, game's over."

I laughed and said, "I am pretty sure I can handle it because I am a *whore*."

Collin was the absolute last person I was going to back down from. He started this war, and I was ending it.

"Come on guys, let it go," Daniel said, frustrated.

Collin said, "No Daniel, let the *whore* work."

Daniel put his hands up and said, "This is not a good idea. But, do whatever the fuck you two idiots want to do." Then he walked back to his blond, and the two disappeared down the hall.

Collin pulled me down the hall to another room and, after knocking and finding it empty, we went in. *Alone.* He flipped on a small light, pulled a chair over, and then sat down.

"Okay, *whore*. Strip and let's see what you got," Collin said, placing his drink on an end table.

Hearing the word "whore," *again* just made me even more determined to get the better of him. I would show him exactly what I could do. Collin pushed a button on the remote he was holding, and music started. Surprise, it was one of his slower sexy songs. I looked at him watching me as I started taking off my clothes. It was funny how watching him see me naked turned me on. My scars didn't even register in my mind when I was with him.

I straddled his lap and put my arms on his shoulders so that he could see my breasts. I would give him the best lap dance anyone could ever receive. I started grinding on his lap, remembering how he had said he liked that when I had moaned that day during the video shoot. I ran my finger down his chest as I leaned into his neck and moaned in his ear. I was trying to get him to give up, but he only leaned further back. *Okay, what next?* I wondered. I pulled his shirt over his head, and he didn't hesitate to lean forward so I could pull it off. I ran my fingers through his hair as I circled my hips against his lap. Finally, I heard him groan as his hands gripped my hips. *Maybe I'm on the right track.*

Slowly I put my hands in my hair and continued moving my hips back and forth when he suddenly stood up with me attached to him. Pushing me up against the wall, he started kissing me like he never had before. It was pure need on both of our parts as we gripped ahold of each other, each trying to control the kiss.

After moving away from the wall, we fell on a bed as I was trying to unbutton his pants. The way his body felt was something I had never experienced until this moment. He was so passionate about the way he touched me. All I could think was, *wow, he's beautiful!* The heat coming off of my skin felt like fire as he sat up and pulled off my underwear. I prayed this was real and that

I wasn't dreaming. When he stood up and took off the rest of his clothes, it was clear that this was not a dream. I've had so many fantasies but never thought I would see something like this come true.

As he lay down on top of me, both of us were now completely naked, and I couldn't help but wonder if this was the biggest mistake of my life. That thought didn't last long, due to his returning kisses and the feeling of our naked bodies pressed against each other. I wrapped my legs around him with my hands in his hair as he made that sexy-sounding groan again.

Finally, he did the one thing I most desired from him as he entered me in one fluid lunge forward. It was better than I could ever imagine. Even though he kept rocking against me and moaning, I just wanted more of him. The way he kissed me, touched me, put his mouth on me, it was the most incredible moment of my life, and I didn't want it to end.

"Oh, fuck, Danni, you feel so fucking good," he groaned in my ear as the first orgasm ripped through me. Soon he followed me with his.

Time stood still as we both had another orgasm and the kisses, touching, and breathing grew more frantic.

He rolled off of me as we laid there trying to catch our breath. After a couple of moments of not speaking, he sat up and grabbed his pants. He couldn't get off the bed fast enough as he started putting his clothes back on. Then, without looking at me or saying a word, he left, slamming the door behind him.

I lay there trying to process everything that had just happened and as much as it was everything I could have imagined with him, the way he left hurt tremendously. I couldn't help myself as I started crying, questioning what the hell I had just done.

⊷ ⊶

The following afternoon I sat in a chair getting my hair done for the benefit that evening. I couldn't help going over everything in my head for the millionth time. Again, I touched my lips as they were sore from the way Collin had kissed me.

"Hello, hello," Mike said, trying to get my attention. I glanced at him, and I knew he could tell I had something on my mind, but I hadn't mentioned last night with Collin and me. More than likely he assumed I had taken things a step further with Nick. *Oh God, Nick was going to hate me.* I groaned, still trying to get my head around the whole thing. I hadn't even told Daniel, because when I left his place this morning, he was still sleeping next to a very naked blond.

I just wanted to get this benefit behind me and go home. After sitting through hair and makeup and listening to Mike and Mark go on about the bar they had gone to last night, I finally got dressed. I couldn't focus on anything as I fought with the stupid straps on my dress. Mike was starting to get mad at me for not listening to him. I tried to pay better attention to what he had been talking about, and I nodded, acting as I was listening.

I hadn't told Daniel about the benefit and figured I would just call him when I got home. Otherwise, he would want to be my date, and I was already feeling guilty enough.

Finally, Nick kissed me on the cheek and smiled, whispering in my ear that I looked stunning. *I am such a bad person.* I chanted in my head over and over again. I didn't have the heart to tell him what I had done, so I smiled back and returned the compliment.

Inside the grand hotel, we found our table and sat down. I quickly ordered a drink, and Mike elbowed me, saying that this was a benefit, not a bar. I rolled my eyes at him as Mark started laughing while handing me a glass of champagne.

Nick leaned over and asked, "Is everything okay? You seem distracted."

I smiled at him with tears in my eyes and said, "Just having a bad day."

After a wonderful dinner of steak and shrimp and little conversation on my end, I was asked to pose for pictures. I didn't mind donating to the music programs, but I didn't do it for the recognition and preferred to remain in the background. I usually let my dad handle this stuff because he didn't mind the attention.

Mike and Mark posed for pictures with me. I had never felt prouder of the two of them in my life as they didn't hesitate to mention their upcoming wedding to the line of reporters. I posed by myself as reporters shouted questions at me regarding the assault, new songs coming out, and the most hated question they always asked, "Who are you dating?" I answered a few about my work and a movie I was working on, but I wouldn't look at the reporters who asked the other questions.

All of a sudden, I heard someone ask, "Can I be in the pictures with you?" I turned around and saw Daniel in a tux, reaching out for me.

"What are you doing here?" I asked, hugging him.

"Jim insists we attend this benefit every year to support the community. It's cool. The kids are fun to work with," Daniel said, smiling at me as Collin, Rick, and Jake walked up next to us. *Wow, all of them in tuxes: doesn't get much hotter than that*, I thought.

I posed for pictures with Daniel and Collin at my side as flashes went off like crazy. I felt my heart beating hard as Collin's hand wrapped around my waist and pulled me closer to him. I couldn't understand any of the reporters as they grew loud trying to talk over one another. After pictures, Collin stepped closer to them and started calmly answering questions.

I sat back down with Mike and Mark, looking around and wondering where Nick had disappeared to. Talking to the press was not my thing, and I had pretty much abandoned Daniel as he tried to get me involved with the reporters.

For the closing performance of the night, Daniel, Collin, Rick, and Jake were going to do a song Daniel had written. It was his first attempt at writing, and I had helped him a little as he put it together. He was good at it when he paid attention and didn't try to make it dirty.

I watched them all take their place as the lights dimmed and Mike stopped my hand from tapping on the table. It was a slow song about healing and finding the strength to keep going; it was beautiful. Collin's voice was amazing as he closed his eyes and sang. I could see a softer side to him as he moved his hands to the words, almost like he could feel it, too.

There was an enormous standing ovation at the end as they all came to the front of the stage and bowed. Daniel was handed a mic and asked me to come to the stage. I wanted to crawl under the table, but the spotlight found me first. Mike laughed and stood up to help me not fall over as I cussed under my breath. I was going to kill Daniel for this.

I walked up on stage and stood beside Daniel. He grabbed my hand and said, "This is my inspiration for writing this song. Danni has endured more than anyone should have to, but through it all, she has kept moving forward. I admire her strength and I am glad I was lucky enough to meet her and have her become my best friend."

I was frozen to his side as Daniel handed the mic to Collin and he talked briefly about how the proceeds from the song were going to the music organization to help others keep moving forward. I could tell he had prepared for this as he sounded knowledgeable regarding the organization.

After all of that was over, I finally relaxed, feeling the effects of the drinks Daniel and I had ordered. The music started, and couples headed for the dance floor. I smiled seeing Mike and Mark dancing together, looking completely enamored with each other.

"Where did you go this morning?" Daniel asked, looking more at his drink than at me.

"You were asleep with the blond, so I thought I would let you be."

"Now, dirty girl, you know what I'm asking. What happened between Collin and you?" Daniel asked, now grinning at me.

I sighed and said, "I. . ."

We both nursed our drinks and looked around at the growing crowd on the dance floor as the music sped up.

"I think your date is hitting on someone else," Daniel said as he pointed at Nick exchanging numbers with some girl.

I laughed and said, "It wasn't going anywhere anyway."

He chuckled and said, "Yeah, we already guessed that."

The rest of the night was fun, as we danced and visited with others. I was ready to go back to the room and get some sleep since we had an early flight the next morning. Daniel insisted on staying with me, and I was grateful.

We got back to the hotel room laughing like little kids as he was helping me pull off the double stick tape. It hurt like hell to rip off, but Daniel said it would hurt less to get it off fast. I think he liked pulling it off as I screamed a little with each tug. There was a knock at the door, and I told him to answer it so I could finish.

Through the bathroom door, I heard Daniel talking to someone and then I heard him say that he would be back in a little bit. I was too late asking where he was going when I heard the door shut.

"Daniel?" I asked.

"No, it's me," Collin said as my heart sank to the bottom of my stomach.

"What do you want?" I asked without opening the door, thinking a closed door would make the awkwardness go away.

"Come out here and talk to me," he asked more than said.

I gave one more good pull and finally got the bra unstuck, mumbling a few choice words. I pulled the straps of my dress back up, took a deep breath, and opened the door. I walked out and saw Collin sitting on the bed looking nervous. I had never seen him nervous before, it was touching.

"What are you doing here?" I asked as I took off my shoes.

"I'm not sure."

I threw my shoes over by my bag, and finding another piece of tape I had missed. I cursed to myself.

"What's wrong?" he asked as I started to tug on the tape running around my ribs.

"I found more tape."

He stood up, moved behind me, and said, "On the count of three. Ready? One, two, three."

Then I felt the sting of the tape being ripped off, and he quickly started rubbing my side where he had pulled it, it helped. I tried to pull away from him, and he didn't let go of me. I froze not knowing what to do. He slowly slid the straps of my dress off my shoulders and it fell to the ground.

"Turn around," he whispered, leaning into my neck.

I turned, knowing it was the worst thing I could do for myself at that moment. He leaned down and kissed me slowly, but then the fire started, and we both grew passionate, fighting for control of the kiss. I found myself in the same moment like last night. I wanted him and wouldn't stop him. It grew very intense very quickly, and I found myself undressing him. He was kissing me all over like he had done last night. My body was once again on fire as I watched him push his slacks and boxers down before sitting on the bed and pulling me onto his lap. I crawled on top of him eagerly as our kissing grew heated again. I slowly pushed him back and he lay back and watched me. I ran my hand over his muscled chest and stomach. He closed his eyes as he took a quick breath. Leaning forward I planted kisses on his stomach before I slowly licked my way further down. He groaned, and I looked up at him as I took him in my mouth and finally tasted him. He was perfect. His eyes slowly opened as he weaved his fingers into my hair. He didn't let me continue much longer before he sat up and rolled me over. I wrapped my legs around him as he kissed me again. We locked eyes as he pulled back and slammed into me. I moaned as my eyes closed feeling such intense pleasure. He started thrusting into me while kissing my neck. It was unbeliev-able, and we couldn't get enough of each other. All I could do was feel him. My mind shut off as we fucked each other. It wasn't romantic or special. It was letting our needs control us. He was my need, and I was finally accepting it.

He lay on top of me for a moment while we both tried to catch our breath. I started running my fingers through his hair when he suddenly sat up and, once again, practically jumped out of bed. He started getting dressed, again saying nothing. Instantly I was mad at myself for letting this happen, *again*.

He left without saying anything, and I didn't stop him. I had no idea what to say to him either. I rolled over and pulled the sheet up and just started crying. After a couple of moments, there was a knock at the door, and I jumped up thinking maybe he had come back. I looked out and saw Daniel and opened the door to let him in. I knew he knew exactly what had just happened as more tears streamed down my face. He hugged me, and neither one of us said a word.

I hated myself more that I hated Collin at that moment.

CHAPTER 25
HIDE AND SEEK

I woke up and realized Daniel was no longer next to me. I heard someone whispering when I looked around and saw Daniel talking to Mike very quietly. I wondered what they were whispering about when they saw I was awake.

Mike came over and sat beside me on the bed and said, "Good morning."

I yawned and asked, "What time is it? We need to be at the airport soon."

"Relax, Danni," Mike said, grinning at me. "Against my better judgment I gave Daniel permission to keep you for a few more days."

I looked at Mike and then pulled the cover over my head and said, "I think I need to get as far from here as possible."

They both started laughing at me. Daniel said, "Dirty girl, I will take great care of you and keep the evil man with the candy you want away from you."

I couldn't help but laugh and said, "That is what you said the other night and look how well that turned out."

Pulling my covers away, Daniel said, "Yeah, sorry about that, but I promise I will this time."

Mike looked at him, and in a stern voice said, "You better or I will kick your ass."

Mike mentioned they needed to get to the airport and kissed me on the forehead.

I asked, "Mike, is it a good idea to leave us alone?"

"When it comes to the two of you, nothing is a good idea. Stay out of trouble, but you both have Nick's number if you need to be bailed out of jail," Mike said as we all started laughing.

After Mike and Mark had left and I took a shower and got ready, Daniel sat on my bed, deep in thought.

"We have to come up with a new game to piss off my brother, and I know the perfect thing," Daniel said, smiling devilishly.

"What's that?" I asked, nervous what he was up to.

"We are playing 'keep away from Collin.'" I had to laugh when he went on saying, "This is as much for his sake as it is yours. Besides, *I love to piss him off.* His face gets all red and shit."

I thought it would be fun to push Collin's buttons, but this time, we would be doing it from a distance.

After I had got everything packed up, I asked, "Where are we going to stay?"

"My house, of course."

I laughed at his answer and said, "That is the first place he will look, you idiot."

Daniel raised his finger and said, "No, he will think that is the last place *you* will go. Want to test that theory right now?"

My mind was screaming at me about how bad of an idea this was as Daniel sent Collin a text telling him he would be unavailable because I needed particular attention after a horrifying event. I had to laugh at that one. Daniel could be so vague about things, but at the same time, he made you want to know more.

He grabbed one of my bags and said, "Let's go. We have an appointment."

"I'm scared, Daniel. What are you up to?" I asked, following him with my other bag. He just smiled and kept walking.

We got in Daniel's car, and he pulled out his phone after it dinged. "We just got our first text." He read it and started laughing.

"What does it say?" I asked as he handed me the phone.

Collin: Where you at? Can I help out little brother?

"That is Collin's way of trying to get to you," Daniel said as he drove out of the parking lot. "Let the games begin."

We had been driving for about twenty minutes when he reached in the console and pulled out the red envelope that I had given him for his birthday.

"You got it," I said, laughing.

"I found it yesterday. It's my favorite present," he said, holding it out to me.

I responded and said, "You're a chicken. You will never do it."

He turned and grinned at me, "Well then why did I call and make the appointments?"

"Appointments?" I questioned. He pulled off his sunglasses and said, "You didn't think I would do it without *you*, did you?"

We both started laughing and arguing over who wouldn't do it.

⟞⟤ ⟞⟤

We sat in the tattoo shop filling out our forms giving permission for the tattoos, and I started second guessing this decision. Daniel saw the look on my face and began making chicken sounds, and that is when I knew I could do this. They had closed the shop for us because apparently Daniel was a big deal in Seattle. I had to give him crap for that as well, and he shot back that I was just jealous.

We made it more interesting by letting the other one pick out the tattoo that we would be getting. I decided on the bar logo, and after the artist had told me the ribs were pretty painful, I indicated that that was perfect. Neither one of us could see what the other had chosen until it was over. I wasn't too scared. Daniel would never hurt me by putting Collin's name or something like that on me.

I walked into the room, and Daniel was sending another text. He hit send and then handed me his phone. His fan site was pulled up, and he was posting messages on it. I rolled my eyes and gave his phone back as he blew me a kiss. *Idiot!*

DanielDrums: I am taking a huge leap of faith with my best friend. Wish us luck.

The two artists asked if we were ready and I suddenly had butterflies in my stomach.

"Daniel, are you sure you won't pass out?" I asked, teasing him in front of the tattoo artists.

"Shut up and take off your shirt!" he responded, acting all big and tough. I knew better.

"Where exactly is this going?" I asked, pulling my shirt off. *Very thankful I wore a bra today.*

"Same place mine is going, dirty girl," Daniel said, mocking me.

I wondered if I was tough enough for this. *After being stabbed and punched by a guy, this couldn't be that bad, right?*

Daniel started laughing hysterically and handed me his phone to see the comments fans were posting. A few said "congratulations" and a few asked for "details." I started laughing too. That was sure to get Collin all worked up.

We both hopped on our respective tables after they had said they were ready to start.

Daniel said, "Well, hopefully, she won't start crying *again*."

A few others laughed at us when I threw a magazine at him, calling him an ass.

I was so wrong. It was the worst hour of my life as the tattoo gun was dragged over my ribs countless times. I had to have him stop once so that I could relax my stomach muscles. They were starting to hurt from tensing up so much. Daniel was in no better shape as he had to get up and walk around once after complaining he felt lightheaded. That made it even better.

Two hours later Daniel was done before I was as he sat up looking dizzy. I looked over the artist's shoulder and said, "It looks pretty awesome, Daniel. It would be hot if it were on someone more attractive." Everyone started laughing as Daniel gave me a devilish grin.

He got out his phone and said, "We have four more congratulations and Collin has left three messages wanting to know where we are. Okay, let's give him a hint and see if we can't get him in the maze."

Daniel took a picture of my tattoo when I was finished. Posting to his fan site again, he wrote: *Better than any ring.*

I wanted to see the picture so that I could see the tattoo as he pulled the phone away from me.

"Don't worry, Danni, I left your face out, but I did keep your mini boobs in the picture."

The tattoo artist had to stop applying the temporary bandage to my ribs because he was laughing, along with everyone else, as I caught one of them trying to see my chest.

Finally, I was done and could get up. After waiting to see his tattoo finished, we both walked over to the mirror. I hoped for the best. After counting to three, we both looked.

I was thrilled at what he had picked for me, seeing the bar logo I had designed just recently. I loved old-fashioned pin-up girls and used one with the bar logo wrapped around her. It turned out very bright and colorful, I thought, hearing Daniel say "awesome." It was funny how we both picked the same tattoo for the other one.

Daniel finally pointed at me and said, "Just so we are clear, you don't own me."

I laughed and looked at his tattoo. It was as colorful as mine and fit Daniel's ribs perfectly.

"Come on, we have a picture to take," Daniel said, handing his phone to one of the artists.

Daniel told me to turn around so my back was to him and I stopped him and said, "You know what would be better?"

He laughed and said, "Now you get the game we are playing."

I took off my bra and pushed my back up against his chest. I put my arms up around his neck, and he put his arm around my chest to hide my boobs. The guy taking the picture asked if they could take some pictures for their shop as well and Daniel made sure I didn't mind, then said it was all right.

After hunting down my bra he thought would be fun to hide, I got dressed, and we thanked them and went back to the car. Daniel pulled out his phone and listened to the voicemail Collin had left.

Daniel laughed loudly before saying, "He's demanding to know where we are. He sounds pissed, and that just made it so much better."

After eating at a greasy burger joint, Daniel showed me around Seattle. We went so many places. He showed me where he had gone to school, the house he grew up in, where they got to play live for the first time, and of course, where he had lost his virginity. It was an old roller skating rink. We both laughed when I told him mine was in college in a bar bathroom. We spent the afternoon laughing about all the stupid little things in our lives as he showed me famous sites around town. It was a beautiful place, but it had rained two out of the three days I had been there so far, and I wasn't sure I liked that.

After he had called his mom to make sure Collin wasn't there, we went to his house to clean up. When we got there, his mom asked what we were up to, and Daniel pulled up his shirt. Paige said she liked it and requested to see mine. I showed her, and she joked that she liked mine better to tease Daniel.

She went on to say, "Collin has been calling all day and stopped by twice, wanting to know what you two are doing."

Daniel explained our game to her and how it was revenge for Collin being an ass to me. She laughed and decided not to tell him either because he deserved it.

We grabbed my bags and headed to Daniel's side of the house to get ready to go out. When we walked into his room, I just put my hand over my mouth, and he looked at me, slightly irritated.

"Oh, hell no. Please tell me this isn't where you two did the deed," Daniel said, dropping my bag.

I nodded at him, and he pointed at me and said, "You owe me a new bed."

I couldn't help but laugh at him. My phone rang at that point, and it was Mike. He told me that they were home and asked what we were up to because Collin had been texting him nonstop, asking if he knew what Daniel and I were doing.

Daniel soon pried the phone out of my hand and said, "Mike, here is what I want you to do."

I went to the bathroom to clean up. I knew Daniel would come up with something clever with Mike. I changed my clothes and decided to wear a black tank top that I had brought to sleep in and white jeans. I left my hair down with its natural curl, so I wouldn't have to fight with Daniel over my hat. He changed into dark jeans and a V-neck T-shirt that showed off his arms. I had to admit it, he was definitely sexy.

There was a car out front, and the driver opened the door for me as we climbed in. Daniel pulled out his phone and mentioned that Collin was fuming at this point, wanting to know where we were. *Why does he care anyway? He's getting married in two months.*

Daniel looked at me and asked, "Should we give him a hint?"

"No, Daniel. I want to have a fun night, not a drama-filled evening," I groaned in frustration. Daniel could outlast anyone in a game, I thought. He went on and posted anyway.

DanielDrums: I am thrilled about my new adventure in life. Now it is time to sign on the dotted line.

I laughed at how he could say something, and it could be taken a million different ways.

⇌ ⇌

After spending a chunk of money at the bar, many lap dances, and many more drinks, we decided to call it a night. On the way back to his house, we looked through his phone and Collin hadn't texted or called anymore. I thought maybe he finally had given up, or Steph was with him. Daniel assured me that he didn't give up that easily and grumbled that he was up to something, he just needed to figure out what it was. He tapped his phone against his chin, deep in thought.

"I got it," he said while dialing Steph. I rolled my eyes not wanting to hear anything she had to say. Holding the phone out after putting it on speaker, Daniel asked, "Steph, where is Collin? I'm having trouble getting a hold of him."

"I don't know. Do you know why he is in such a bad mood?" Steph asked in a not-so-nice tone. I knew that she and Daniel weren't exactly fans of each other, but she was a downright bitch.

Daniel couldn't help it and started laughing, "No, you stupid slut." Then he hung up on her.

"Why did you call her?" I said, frustrated.

"Because she will call him and make him go home," Daniel said, putting his phone back in his pocket.

"He jumps and runs for her, doesn't he?" I asked more to myself than to Daniel.

Daniel nodded and mumbled, "He sure does."

A couple of minutes later Daniel called his mom and asked if Collin was there. Paige told him that he had just left because Steph had called him telling him to come home.

Daniel got serious and asked, "Do you want to see where he lives?"

I wanted to as much as I didn't want to. *Why did I keep doing this to myself? Oh, yeah, because I was stupidly in love with him. Bright, Danni, real bright.* After Daniel had decided for me, the driver took us to Collin's house, parking about half a block away with the headlights off.

His house was twice the size of Daniel's, and I asked, "Who needs a house that big?"

"Steph does," Daniel mumbled.

I watched Collin pull into the garage and walk to the house. Steph opened the door in a short robe displaying her near-nakedness to the neighbors. She quickly put her arms around him and started kissing him. I instantly looked down, trying to fight back tears. I felt my heart breaking further.

Daniel asked the driver to take us home.

CHAPTER 26
KNOCK YOURSELF OUT

I t was a month later, after a grueling three hours playing in the house band and bartending, I was finally done. I couldn't quit yawning and just wanted to sleep. I had been spending most of my time at the schoolhouse finishing little projects and working in the studio. I was always running on fumes, but thankfully Mike and Mark were doing all they could to help.

A week later I got the best news of my life, the schoolhouse was finished. The moving truck would be at my house in two days. I didn't have much, as most of the furniture, I let Mike and Mark keep. Mark had already moved in, and I was more than happy to go.

Mike was smart and hired an interior designer to manage the inside of the schoolhouse. I wasn't a horrible decorator; I just hated doing it. It was such a great feeling to have my own home, and yet I felt sad leaving Mike. This would be the first time since we were six years old that we wouldn't be living together. We had both cried over it. He assured me it wouldn't change anything. I was nervous because I had never lived alone, but then I remembered Dad had already moved into his house on the property two weeks earlier.

I was going through my stuff, trying to decide what to keep and what to get rid of when Mike walked in. He was holding my dress for his wedding that was now only two weeks away. I also knew that meant Collin's was just next month, and I couldn't help but feel a little sorry for myself.

"It's a beautiful dress," I said, trying to sound excited.

"You okay?" he asked with a sad look on his face. I had given him all the details of what had happened in Seattle and neither he nor Mark were surprised.

"I am perfect," I responded so I didn't take the focus off his wedding.

"Liar!" he said as he hung the dress in my closet.

After he had left to go to work, I knew I needed to get going on the packing. I was dragging it out, so I decided to get my headphones to make myself work faster. After a twenty-minute search through the whole house, I couldn't find them. I wondered what I could have done with them. Dialing my phone, I wondered if I had left them at Daniel's?

"Oh, baby, I was just thinking how badly I wanted to ram it in your hot . . ." Daniel stated before I abruptly cut him off.

"Stop it, you dirty little pervert. Gross! Hey, I can't find my headphones. Did I leave them at your place?"

He laughed for a moment and mumbled something about me being no fun before he finally responded to me.

"I don't know. We're on the road. Remember, dirty girl? You can join me and let me finish my dirty talk."

I laughed and said, "No. *Remember,* I am moving tomorrow. Why don't you help *me?*"

"Is my room ready? Did they deliver my stuff?" he asked, more serious now.

Yes, I had caved and let him claim the room across the hall from mine. He had it painted and decorated the way he wanted, although I put my foot down when a contractor tried to install a sex swing in the middle of the room.

"Whenever you get here, it will be ready. Yes, they delivered your furniture," I said, rolling my eyes. He was persistent with decorating questions since I let him have it.

"Seriously, Daniel, have you seen them?" I asked, more frustrated after dumping my cosmetics bag upside down and not finding them there either.

I could hear someone else talking to him, and then he said, "Wait a minute, Collin is trying to talk to me."

My heartbeat sped up just thinking about him and now, even more so, faintly hearing his voice in the background. Daniel came back on and said in a weird tone, "Danni, have you looked in the side pocket of your red suitcase?"

"I never put them there," I insisted as I walked to my closet to find the suitcase.

"You might want to check," he said, more annoyed than anything.

I stopped and asked, "Daniel, you okay?"

"I'm not sure. It strongly depends on what someone is up to, or if I have to kick his ass," Daniel said, I wondered if he was talking about Collin now.

"Just a minute, Daniel," I said, putting my phone on the dresser in the closet as I pulled out my suitcase. I placed the bag on the bed and picked up my phone again.

"I knew they wouldn't be there . . ." I said when I found the headphones and started pulling them out. "Hey, I found them . . ." I said as I trailed off when I saw an envelope fall on the floor. "Daniel, let me call you back."

"What is going on?" he asked in a demanding voice.

"I'm not sure. I will call you back," I said, hanging up and throwing my phone on the bed.

I sat down and grabbed the envelope with my heart going a hundred miles an hour. There was nothing on the outside of the plain white envelope, and I wondered if I should just leave it sealed. I just knew it had to be from Collin, and I wasn't sure I wanted to see what he had to say. I sat there holding it in my hands for a good twenty minutes before I decided to open it. I hit ignore on my phone before muting it as Daniel kept calling.

I pulled out the piece of paper in the envelope, unfolded it, and looked at the letter. It simply had three words on it:

I am sorry

What the hell? Is that all he has to say to me? I crumpled it up and threw it across the room as Daniel called again.

"WHAT?" I yelled in a not-so-nice tone.

Daniel asked, "What is it?

I just said mockingly, "*I am sorry.*"

"Is that fucking all?" Daniel snapped.

I repeated it again, and he could tell by my tone of voice that it made me mad.

He calmly asked, "Do I have permission to kick his ass *now?*"

"Knock yourself out."

What an ass, I kept thinking. *Just when I am putting some distance between us, he does this.* Ugh, I just wanted to forget Seattle ever happened.

I put my headphones on, turned the music loud, and decided to pack instead of calling Collin to yell at him.

It is amazing what you can do with the right music and no phone. I was finally done with my room when I noticed my phone vibrating. Wanting to make sure Daniel wasn't hurt, I picked up my phone. I didn't recognize the number, so I let it go to voice-mail to see if they would leave a message. Sure enough, they did. I listened to the message and had to play it three more times before I heard it right. *No way!* It was from a popular music magazine, asking to talk to me about doing an interview and a photo shoot.

Instantly, I called my dad. He would know how to deal with it. We talked for a while about what he thought it could do for my writing career. I was for that, but I never wanted to have pictures taken. He reminded me of the music video, and I cringed. I didn't know what to do.

Thirty minutes later he brought up Seattle.

"What does Daniel think? Or did you two talk more about a particular older brother?" Dad asked. I knew he was digging for details.

"I haven't called him yet. Daniel is kicking his brother's ass right now, so he is busy," I said, trying to hide my smile.

"Ah, yes, he called me about that a little bit ago. What exactly happened on your trip?" he asked while laughing.

Sitting down on the bathroom floor, I caved. I laid it all out for my dad, bad decisions and all. It felt right to tell him and get his take on the whole situation.

"Baby girl, I'm not surprised. What is it between you and Collin that you two can't stay away from each other?"

I laughed and said, "I don't know, but I need to figure out how to stay *away from him.*"

He laughed and said, "I don't know if either of you could do that."

"Thanks for the vote of confidence, Dad."

I made it through the move the next day, barely. With movers, Mike, Mark, Rosa, Dad, Kendrick, and Chuck, we finished shortly before we all needed to get to the bar. The house band was playing that night and Rosa assured me she had it all under control, insisting that when I got back later, everything would be done.

While playing that night and doing the standard bar thing, I couldn't shake the whole magazine thing and still wondered what to do. I didn't tell Mike or Daniel about it, knowing they would try to make the decision for me.

Taking our final break, two guys in suits walked over to me as my heart started hammering in my chest. If these two were cops, I was going to freak the fuck out. I was sick to death of being questioned about my memory of the assault. *Hell yes, I remembered much more now, but I wasn't about to tell any of them. Ever!*

One of them handed me a business card and asked if they could speak to me. I read it and sighed in relief, realizing they were from the magazine. I showed them to my office and told them to have a seat.

"What do you want with me? I'm not a model and have no plans to become one," I stated, a matter of fact.

The younger one said, "Exactly! You are a musician and a pretty good one from what we just saw. I won't lie either. You are beautiful, and we would love for you to model for us."

The older one asked, "Did your father teach you how to play?"

I laughed and asked, "Are you trying to interview me now?" I knew too many reporters who tried to get people to say the wrong thing so they could completely blow it out of context and use it against them later. I wasn't about to let that happen now.

The older one smiled, looking amused, "Good point. Let me tell you our idea first."

The younger one leaned forward and said, "We heard about the benefit and saw the pictures with your friends in the band 'Dark Pieces.' We have done our research on you and learned that you are the woman who stars in their popular video. We would simply like to talk to you about music, writing, growing up with your dad, your relationship with Daniel and Collin Tabert, and perhaps have you pose for us. You don't have to talk about anything you're uncomfortable with. And, if you don't mind, we'd love a side-by-side layout with the band."

I sat back in my chair and thought about it for a little bit. *Why did I do that stupid video? So far it was way more trouble than it had been fun.*

The older man added, "If you do it, the magazine will make a large donation to the charity that hosted the benefit you attended with the band."

Well, I'm a sucker for donating to good causes, so I said, "Fine, I will do it, but here are my demands: I don't want Daniel and his band to know I am doing it until after my part is done. You can do theirs separately. Otherwise, no pretty pictures of me."

"We can handle that," the younger one said as he jotted something down on the piece of paper he had been taking notes on.

They asked if they could stay and take pictures of us playing for the article and I agreed, but only if I got to pick the ones, they used in the article.

◄═╬ ╬═►

Out of habit that night, I headed to Mike's house, before I realized it and had to turn around. I wondered how long it would take me to get used to going to the schoolhouse. I got home and pulled into the three-car garage, finding myself scared to be alone, but this was a new beginning, and I was somehow ready for it.

I went inside and flipped on the lights, walking up the stairs and seeing that Rosa had been true to her word. It didn't look like someone was moving in. Instead, it looked like someone had lived there for years. I put my stuff on the kitchen island and walked to my bedroom. It was the exact vision I had had for it when we first looked at the place. It had the exposed red brick walls with an enormous king-size bed and a red couch in front of the fireplace. I couldn't help myself and walked over and turned it on. I watched the fire for a couple of minutes, reeling at how cozy this felt to me.

I decided I needed a shower and took off my clothes, looking for the laundry hamper, before I found it in the bathroom.

I eyed the shower and remembered when Collin had walked into it saying he was looking forward to showering with me. I hated that I wanted to do that with him, but I did more than anything. I stepped in and turned on the water as hot as I could take it. I took the longest shower I think I had ever taken.

Slipping on only underwear and a t-shirt, I thought it was weird that I didn't have to cover up. I could get used to this. I couldn't help myself and picked up my phone to call Daniel as I walked back to the kitchen.

"Hey, dirty girl, are you naked?" he asked, sounding like I had woken him up.

"Sorry, I'll just call you back tomorrow. Sorry to wake you up," I said in a quieter voice, thinking that was going to help.

"Don't you dare hang up on me! What are you doing?" he asked before yawning.

I had walked downstairs and, trying to be a little mischievous, I asked, "How sexy would it be to see a half-naked woman walking down a newly renovated schoolhouse while running her finger over the lockers in the dark?"

He groaned and said, "Stop it. You're waking up more than just my mind, but please continue if there is a chance you will tell me how naked you are. OUCH!"

Sounding like someone hit him, I asked, "Who is that?" I had an idea who it was but hoped I was wrong.

He laughed loudly sounding like he was wrestling with someone and said, "A tall blond with big boobs. Do you want to join us? I could put it on speaker. OUCH, FUCK, COLLIN, THAT FUCKING HURTS!"

After a long wrestling match with both of them cussing, he asked, "Are you in the gym yet?"

"I just walked in. Why?" I asked, flipping on lights.

"Tell me the score," he said sweetly.

"What are you talking about?" I asked, looking around, confused.

"Look up, Danni."

I gasped, seeing the brand new scoreboard. It was incredible as I flipped on more lights.

"Daniel, it's perfect! Why did you do this? It's too much," I said through my tears of joy.

"Danni, I didn't do it. Collin did. He hopes you like it."

Instead of displaying "Home Team," it was their band name. The board was beautiful, and I said in a broken voice, "You have to see this, Daniel. It is so cool."

He asked, "Are you happy with it?"

All I could say was, "Wow!"

"I will take that as a yes. Now, if you don't mind, I need to get back to the blond being that you got me all worked up. I will see you next week," Daniel said, amused with himself.

After I had hung up with Daniel, I looked at the new score-board in awe for twenty minutes. *Why did Collin do something so wonderful for me?*

I slept well past my alarm the next morning. Trying to make myself get out of bed after another hour, I finally managed. It was so quiet and easy to sleep without anyone there to wake me up. This newfound freedom of living alone was heaven, and I kept telling myself that this was the perfect way to live.

In town at our local gym, I started by running five miles, before asking for a trainer. I needed to tone my body if I was going to pose for pictures. The more I thought about them, the more I wanted to do them. The trainer who met me in the gym was male perfection. Tall, all muscle, with a gorgeous face and smile. "Wow," was all I could seem to get out after he introduced him-self. I didn't even catch his name. I was so embarrassed when my brain started working again. It had been a little over a month since I had slept with Collin. He must have woken something in-side of me that I had ignored for a while. Now it was in the front of my mind and all I could think about with this trainer now smirking at me.

After a very intense workout, I left the gym in sad shape. I was sore from head to toe, not to mention a little sexually frustrated. I did the only thing that I could think of and called Daniel. He picked up on the first ring.

"Talk dirty to me," I groaned as I drove home.

He did and sounded so sexy while he was doing it. I almost pulled over on the country road to relieve the needy ache.

"FUCK, COLLIN, I AM GOING TO KILL YOU! YOU BETTER RUN!" Daniel shouted before coming back on and calmly saying to me, "What's going on?"

I told him about the gym and the trainer and my sudden need to get laid as he laughed at me.

"Danni, being that I am such a good friend, I would take one for the team and fuck you. Maybe with a bag over your head or something."

I burst out laughing, and he mumbled something about calling me back.

Lying in bed that night I couldn't stop thinking about sex. My night with Collin in the hotel was stuck on repeat in my head. I had already taken care of the itch twice since I had gotten home, but I wanted more. *Had Collin restored my need for sex? Or, was it just Collin that I needed?*

The next couple days I ran with Mike, trying to control my desire and think about anything else. But, it always ended the same way. I would go to the gym and come home and take a long shower while using my new waterproof vibrator Daniel had sent me. I knew it was funny to him, but damn, it did help ease my sex drive.

I was standing in the kitchen talking to Mike after our run one day when someone rang the doorbell. Mike went to see who it was as I was looking for something to eat. I had located some licorice. Unable to find an expiration date, I started eating it anyway. I hated black licorice, but I was starving, and I ate three pieces at a time. Mike walked up the stairs holding a box and set it on the table.

"You order something?" Mike asked as I handed him some scissors and stuffed more licorice in my face. "You really shouldn't eat crap like that before a photo shoot *tomorrow*," Mike said as I stuck my tongue out at him.

He opened the box and started digging through the packing material when he looked at something and said, "Oh my God. Only Daniel would do this!" He pulled an assortment of sex toys out of the box.

I wanted to die and felt myself turn beet red. Mike kept pulling things out and setting them on the table while reading the names off their boxes. At this point, Mike had Daniel on the phone laughing while he read off more names of the products. I just kept eating licorice, trying not to make eye contact with him. I heard my name a couple more times as I threw my wrapper in the trash and went back to the fridge looking for something else.

Mike told Daniel, "She is eating anything she can find. Yesterday I caught her eating cotton candy and marshmallows. She hates that stuff." I was trying to avoid the toys on the table and the conversation when I found peanut butter and got a spoon.

Mike looked at me and said in a frustrated tone, *"Really, Danni? Really?"*

"What? It's protein," I said as I could tell they were both laughing at me.

They talked a little more, and I heard Mike say "really" and "great" and "I will see you then" before hanging up.

"What was that about?" I asked. He took my spoon and put the peanut butter away.

"Just wedding stuff. I think you're working out too much. The last couple days I swear I have seen you eat anything you can get your hands on," Mike said while he put the sex toys back in the box before taking it to my room.

He was right. I was eating a lot, but I was nervous as hell, and I was pretty sure I was eating my feelings.

⊱ ⊰

The next morning Mike and I ran again, and my stomach was doing flips. I motioned to Mike to stop for a minute. I leaned over the side of the trail as I put my hands on my knees and threw up.

"You okay?" Mike asked while he started rubbing my back.

"Yeah, I think I am way too nervous about this photo shoot and interview," I said before throwing up again.

"You think?" He mocked me, being a complete smartass.

After a short break, so I could empty my stomach entirely, we walked the rest of the way back to my house. He talked about wedding plans and how it was only two days away and then the honeymoon to Mexico. I was glad to see him so happy with Mark, although, it was funny how Mike was spending a lot of time at my house whenever Mark was at work.

I got home and ran through the shower, not bothering to put any make-up on or do anything with my hair. Today was the day of the photo shoot and interview, so I knew they would do it there. We had agreed to do the photo shoot at the bar.

"I can't believe I am doing this at ten in the morning," I grumbled as the girl in the drive-thru window handed me ice cream and a corn dog. I couldn't wait to eat it, but decided that after this one, I had to get back to eating right.

On the way to the bar, I scarfed down the corndog before I parked in the back garage. I grabbed the door handle, and it wouldn't open, it was locked from the inside. Mike and I both bitched numerous times that we needed to get the lock fixed, but neither of us ever did it.

I was trying to juggle my laptop, purse, phone, clothes, and ice cream as I walked to the front while trying to get my keys out. I put the ice cream cup up to my mouth, holding onto it with my teeth while trying to keep hold of everything else. I opened the door and pushed it open, stepping inside to the surprise of my life.

I dropped my laptop, clothes, but not my ice cream when I saw Daniel, Collin, Rick, and Jake sitting around the bar staring at me.

Before anyone said anything, I held my finger up. I threw my ice cream on the ground as I put my hand over my mouth and went running for the bathroom. I was going to be sick again.

CHAPTER 27
I CAN'T STAY AWAY

"Surprise! We're doing the article together," I heard Daniel say as I fell to my knees in front of the toilet.

After emptying the contents of my stomach yet again that day, I started pulling myself back together. I rinsed out my mouth the best I could, trying not to throw up again. I glanced back at Daniel as he winced and stepped farther back. I didn't understand why he couldn't wait until I came out of the bathroom. Sweet Daniel just stood there quietly watching me, knowing I was pissed.

"One: tell me why on Earth you just watched me puke my guts out in the women's bathroom? And two: what the fuck are you guys doing here?" I practically yelled at him.

Daniel gave his sad puppy dog face and said, "I wanted to surprise you."

"Well, you did, Daniel, and not in a good way," I said as he followed me back to the bar.

We all said our casual hellos as I tried to lift the bar top, but it wouldn't open. I had to crawl under it, and I hit my head on the way up and yelled a choice word as everyone turned to look at me. I was mad that they were here and furious with Daniel for not telling me. Hitting my head just made it worse. I walked to the end of the bar and started cleaning up the ice cream that was now melting all over the bar top and floor.

"Can I help you clean that up?" Daniel asked me, trying to be sweet.

I couldn't stay mad at him no matter how hard I tried, and I nodded while taking a deep breath. Collin, Rick, and Jake were watching us as we quietly cleaned up.

"When did you start eating ice cream this early in the morning?" Daniel asked, throwing the cup and spoon in the trash.

I smiled, looked at him, and said, "Since the box you sent me isn't working anymore." They all burst out laughing as Daniel hugged me.

I wanted something. I wasn't sure if it was to tear Collin's clothes off, or tear open the bags of chips hanging on the rack. I grabbed the chips and started eating them instead of Collin. Daniel just kept looking at me with a puzzled look on his face.

"What?" I asked as I poured more salt on the chip I was trying to eat.

"Is everything okay? And what the hell are you doing? Salt on already salted chips? Are you trying to have a heart attack or something?" Daniel said, taking the salt shaker from me.

An hour later I was in a pair of barely-there ripped up jeans, a bar T-shirt, and six-inch black heels. The photographer first took some shots of me with my guitar on stage as I played around. Collin stood in front, watching me closely, making it worse. My stomach was already doing flips, and he was not helping me stay focused.

Twenty minutes later I was ready for the bar shots, and I was regretting taking Mike's advice. "Do it, Danni. You're gorgeous and have a killer body, show it off," I could still hear Mike telling me. *It was now or never,* I thought to myself as I walked over to the bar with my guitar.

Daniel and Collin watched me carefully as they sat against the brick wall talking quietly. Taking the photographer's directions, I hopped up on the bar as his assistant held my guitar. My heart was ready to beat out of my chest as I pulled off my shirt and bra. I tried to cover my boobs the best I could when I lay back on the top of the bar. The assistant positioned the guitar for me as I felt a million eyes on me. I listened to the photographer's instructions and arched my back, closing my eyes as the assistant put the guitar carefully over my chest so I would kind of be covered up. He started shooting and telling me to move this way or that way. It wasn't too bad with my eyes closed.

"Last shot, Danni, go ahead and slip off the rest of your clothes, but keep the shoes on," the photographer said as I felt myself turn bright red.

I had never felt so many people stare at me before. I could play on stage, but posing for a picture was entirely a foreign idea to me, especially while naked. Mike was such a dumbass for talking me into this.

I knew I should be feeling pretty good about my body, considering I had been working out a lot lately. I undressed while the assistant held up a robe, trying to help me keep some of my dignity. I sat up on the bar and put my feet on the bar stools in front of me as they handed me the guitar. I placed it on the stools, so it covered my nakedness and my arm covered my one boob as the neck of the guitar covered the other. Carefully listening to the directions, I arched my chest out and gave the camera a" sexy, come-get-me smile." per the photographer.

"Perfect, Danni, tilt your head to the side, open your lips a little, lean forward, and one more, perfect. Got it, you're done. Thank you, that was great."

After getting dressed and wiping some of the make-up off, I walked back out to the bar. Collin, Rick, Jake, and Daniel were in their serious poses in a corner booth as they had their pictures taken. I stuck my tongue out at Daniel, and he started laughing.

"What's with the shirt, Daniel?" I asked, mocking him.

"Oh, don't you worry, dirty girl, no one will be looking at the magazine for me," Daniel said as he gave me a dirty smile and they all laughed.

I walked over to the bar and hopped up again to watch them. It was a funny scene to witness because they all acted so serious and I couldn't help but laugh at them. I grabbed a jar of cherries and started eating them before I grabbed the olives and mixed them together. I wondered if Mike would get mad at me for eating everything. I was starving.

They were finally done, and Daniel came over to me and hopped on the bar beside me. "Have you had enough to eat yet? That is just wrong." He took the olive-cherry mix away from me.

I looked at him and said, "There are more over there, you know, and I have the key."

We both grinned at each other as we grabbed onto each other. Each of us trying to get down first, we fell off the bar, and I landed on top of him. I heard Collin tell someone to come over as Daniel was trying to push me off of him. I managed to get over him and get a good lead away from him as he grabbed the bottom of my jeans and asked, "Where are you going?"

I started laughing hysterically saying, "You're pulling my pants down."

"Good!" he said, pulling me closer to him.

Trying to keep my pants on, I grabbed his shirt as he attempted to get by me. I heard it rip, and everyone began laughing at us. He continued pulling my pants down, and he teased, "Rip my shirt, will you."

He made the hole in my jeans a lot bigger, and I kept laughing. Daniel finally managed to pull me back to him and as he swung around his elbow, getting me in the nose, and I instantly saw stars. His eyes got huge, and he started getting off of me to try and help me. I could tell my nose was bleeding, and he began pulling me up as I kept my hand over my nose. Collin was right behind me, holding me close to him and trying to help me not fall.

"It's just a bloody nose. I'm all right," I said, taking my hand away from my face as Collin pressed a towel to my nose.

Daniel looked at me and said, "You fight like a girl," as he started walking away from me.

I tried to take off after him when Collin's arm went around me, "Perhaps you've had enough messing around with my little brother today."

There were so many people laughing at us at that point. I didn't pay much attention to them. Daniel shoved some Kleenex at me as Collin told me to tilt my head back. I closed my eyes and tried to think about anything but him as he had a way of touching me that set my skin on fire. I moved away from him when his fingertips brushed the side of my boob.

I went to my office and lay down on the couch to try and get my bloody nose to stop. I looked up to see Collin sit in my chair, and Daniel settle on the couch by my feet.

"I'm fine, no big deal," I said, closing my eyes and feeling slightly nauseous again.

Collin laughed and asked, "Will you two *ever* act like adults?"

"No," I stated matter-of-factly. Daniel agreed and said, "I think that's a little out of our grasp."

Opening my eyes, I looked toward the door hearing Mike walk in at that moment asking, "What happened?" He stood over me with a concerned look on his face and then glanced at Daniel and shook his head. Yeah, of course, he knew it involved Daniel.

I could smell food and asked, "What did you bring me?"

"Tacos and cinnamon chips. Like you requested in your ten texts begging me to bring you food," Mike said, rolling his eyes as he set the bag down on my chest.

I removed the Kleenex and asked Daniel if the bleeding had stopped and he nodded yes. I slowly sat up, hoping it wouldn't start again. I set the bag of food on the coffee table and reached in to pull out a taco. I started eating it as I was famished. They were excellent, good and greasy, my favorite. I was on my fourth taco when I realized they were all staring at me.

"What?" I asked with a mouthful.

Daniel asked, "Really, you okay?"

I asked, "Why does everyone keep asking me that?"

Collin didn't hesitate to sit down beside me and help himself to a taco, as well, before Daniel took the rest of them. Between the three of us, we managed to finish it all off, and we definitely could have had more. Collin loved the cinnamon chips and started questioning Mike about where he could get more. I grabbed Collin's water and took a drink before he took it back and finished it. Apparently sharing food and drink with me didn't bother him, but he wouldn't touch anything from Daniel. I noticed he was kind of a germaphobe with most people, but not with me.

"What time is it?" I had asked before I jumped up. *Crap, I forgot about rehearsal.*

"Almost three. I bet you forgot you had practice today, didn't you?" Mike said, not looking surprised.

I was late and needed to get home. I started looking for my stuff and gave up, deciding I would just come back and get it later.

Daniel asked, "Can I go with you?"

"I figured you would," I said as Collin stood up and took my bag Mike was holding up for me. Seriously, Mike was the only reason I ever kept track of my stuff.

We started walking to the garage, and I stopped as a wave of nausea came over me again. I put my hand on the wall and closed my eyes, wondering if perhaps I had a touch of the flu or something. I felt a hand on my back as someone took my keys from me. I stood there for a minute taking deep breaths until it passed. This was starting to get old. I was never sick. I was usually the lucky person the flu would miss, but lately, sickness kept finding me.

Daniel held the door open to the garage when I realized it was Collin with his hand on my back. I started walking forward again, and his hand stayed there until we got to the car. Collin opened the passenger-side door for me as I climbed in. He walked to the driver's side after taking the keys from Daniel, saying he knew how to get to the schoolhouse. Daniel didn't argue with him and got in the back.

I was feeling better as we got closer to my house until I had to roll my window down for some fresh air. I thought to myself, *yep, I have the flu and Mike's wedding is in two days. Perfect timing.*

Collin pulled into the garage and said, "Go ahead, baby, I'll take your stuff upstairs for you."

God, his sexy voice and him calling me "baby" made my body tingle with need. He was quickly becoming a drug I needed. That couldn't be a good thing for either of us.

We only practiced for an hour because Kendrick didn't feel right either, so I figured I *did* have the flu after all. I walked upstairs to the sounds of laughter. They were sitting at the kitchen island playing with all the stuff Daniel had sent me. I was instantly embarrassed, and I opened the refrigerator.

"There is nothing to eat in my house," I said searching the full shelves of healthy food. I wanted grease and sugar. "Oooh, pancakes," I moaned seeing the batter mix I was sure Rosa had left for the following morning.

Ten minutes later I had made two and started on another since Daniel was eating them, too. I grabbed the syrup from the fridge and set it on the counter before flipping another pancake. Getting the syrup and a spoon, I decided that sounded pretty good, too. I started eating the syrup on its own before I put the pancakes on my plate and smothered them in it, as well. I looked up to see Daniel and Collin staring at me with their mouths open.

"What?" I snapped, frustrated that everyone seemed to be making comments on my eating habits lately.

"No judgments," Daniel said as Collin just held his hands up, obviously knowing when to keep his mouth shut.

I ate my pancakes, and they were the best pancakes I had ever made.

After I had eaten, we walked around the school, and I showed them how everything had turned out. We ended up in the gym admiring the scoreboard.

After a while, I asked, "You guys need a ride or something?"

Daniel laughed and said, "A ride? Where are we going?"

"Back to your bus or something, dumbass," I said, not sure what their plans were.

He laughed and said, "No, the bus is already parked in the bus barn. We're here for the wedding, remember?"

I didn't realize they were staying. I assumed they would only be in for the wedding day and then leave.

Daniel said, "I will sleep in my room and Collin can sleep on the bus."

Collin glanced at me, and I immediately felt bad. So I said, "No, you can sleep in the apartment if you want."

Collin gave me a grin and said, "Thanks. I appreciate getting off the bus for a couple of days."

I was already planning on locking my bedroom door as I nodded at him.

We had all been in bed for about three hours when I decided I was too thirsty to stay locked in my room. I passed by Daniel's room, and I could hear him snoring loudly. I figured he was tired and needed a good night's sleep. I turned on the small light over the sink so I wouldn't wake him up.

I grabbed a glass when I heard someone ask, "What are you doing?"

I dropped the glass, and it shattered all over the floor around me. I closed my eyes, praying I hadn't woken Daniel up. After a few seconds, I heard him start snoring again.

"You scared me," I whispered, taking in the sight of Collin in nothing but loose shorts.

"Don't move. Where's your broom?" he asked, pointing at all the broken glass on the floor.

As I stood there, barefoot in my underwear and a T-shirt, I pointed to the pantry. He grabbed the broom and dustpan and started sweeping around me. After throwing the collection of glass in the trash, he said, "I think I got it all."

Stepping away from the sink, I painfully realized that he hadn't gotten all of it after all. "Ouch," I winced.

I knew I had a piece of glass in my foot. It burned as Collin came around the island and grabbed me. He helped me hop up on the counter and went and got the broom again. I stared at his bare chest as he cleaned up the rest of the glass.

When he was done, he asked, "Can I see your foot?"

Words failed me as he pulled my foot up so he could see the sole. His touch rendered me too stupid to think when he pulled out a little sliver of glass, Goddamn, it hurt. He washed his hands and got a wet paper towel to clean up my foot. Neither one of us said anything when my dad's question popped into my head: "Why can't you two stay away from each other?" *Truth be told, I didn't want to stay away from him.*

Collin washed his hands again and leaned against the sink. "Danni, I am sorry for everything I did to you when you were in Seattle," he whispered.

I thought for a moment before saying quietly, "It wasn't *entirely* your fault. I was a willing participant."

He grinned and said, "Yes, you definitely were."

I slid off the counter and walked over to the refrigerator, grabbing a bottle of water. Collin pulled me to him, and I couldn't stop myself, or him. He leaned down and gently kissed me as I wrapped my arms around his neck. I kissed him back when I felt his hands inside of my shirt as he backed me up against the island. The kissing became frantic and intense as he picked me up and sat me up on the island.

I wrapped my legs around him as he kissed my neck and I whispered in his ear, "Why can't I stay away from you?"

"I can't stay away from you, either," he said in between kisses along my jaw and neck.

We started kissing again as he lifted me up and started walking down the hall with me wrapped around him. We made it to my room while trying to be quiet as he shut the door with his foot before pushing me up against it. I locked it, and he moved us to my bed, falling on top of me.

He was kissing me just as passionately as he had last time and I let out a groan, "Why are we doing this?"

"I don't know, but I *really* want you," he mumbled in between all the kissing and touching as we fell on the bed.

He pulled off my shirt as I pushed down his shorts and I watched him kick them off. He sat up and pulled off my underwear before he came back to my mouth and my neck. I let out a moan, and he whispered, "We have to be quiet. Daniel is across the hall."

He rolled me over, so I was on top of him as I began kissing his chest and neck. He moaned as his hands ran down my back. I whispered in his ear, "What happened to being quiet?"

He rolled me back over and said, "It's impossible with you."

We made love on my bed, the couch, and on the floor in front of the fire before we made our way back to the bed.

Trying to catch my breath, I quietly asked, "Are you leaving?"

"Only if you want me to leave," he said as he kissed me again and put his arms around me. I was getting exactly what I wanted. Collin wrapped around me all night. I felt utterly safe and relaxed. For the first time since the assault, I felt hope.

CHAPTER 28

PARTNERS?

My alarm went off at nine a.m., and I reached over Collin to turn it off. He grabbed me and mumbled, "You aren't leaving this bed." He rolled over onto me as I felt him moving my legs apart with his knee. I knew at this point I couldn't stop him, nor did I want to.

Later, after prying myself out of bed, I was getting my running clothes on as I admired him lying there with nothing but a sheet on, watching me. I sat down to put my shoes on as I heard Mike knock on my door asking if I was ready. I yelled back that I would be right out. Collin sat up and started kissing my shoulder while running his fingertips over my ass.

"Behave. I have no willpower when it comes to you, Collin," I said, looking at him as he grinned.

"I know how you feel, baby. My self-control is nonexistent around you," he said before he playfully pulled me back down on the bed.

I let out a laugh, and he laughed too and kissed me again. I was falling in love with this new, playful side of Collin quickly.

I pushed him away and said, "I have to go, or Mike will know something is up."

"Okay, how about I wait here for you?" he whispered seductively in my ear as his hand slid in my shorts and I groaned.

After Mike knocked again and tried to open the door, I whispered, "I will lock the door, so if you're still here, you could shower with me when I get back. I mean, if you want to."

"Oh, baby, I want to. You're sexy as hell all sweaty and I like making you sweaty," he said, giving me his sly smile.

God, what this man does to me. My body begged for him as I leaned up and kissed him again.

I closed the door behind me and walked right into Mike as he asked, "Who is in there?" He had a huge smile on his face. I could feel myself turning bright red. I grabbed him by the arm and said, "Let's go."

"Oh, come on, just tell me," Mike begged as I dragged him outside and headed to the trail.

I heard Daniel still snoring when we left and was thankful Collin, and I hadn't woken him. Collin was not quiet during sex, *bossy as hell, but definitely not silent. I loved it.* He made me do things and say things I would never have done. I had always been quiet and shy in the bedroom. But with him, I felt sexy and powerful.

He was an animal in bed and held nothing back. Was this the type of sex people were always calling "mind-blowing" or "the best sex of their life?" This was new to me, and it scared the hell out of me.

Sure enough, Mike got all the details out of me as we ran the six-mile trail around my property.

Mike asked, "Danni, do you know what you're doing with him?"

"I have no idea what I'm doing. But, it just feels right, I guess. Does that make any sense at all?" I answered, trying to keep pace with him.

"Does love ever make sense? All I'm going to say is I love you, but I think you're going to get hurt in the long run. Remember he *is* getting married in a month."

I hated hearing those words. It was gut-wrenching, but I knew I didn't want to stop sleeping with him, even if he was getting married. It wasn't like I was the type of girl someone would want to settle down with. I didn't have the mommy vibe and sure as hell didn't have the bride vibe. I was enjoying living alone, and truth be told, I was a bit selfish with my alone time.

Pulling me out of my thoughts Mike said, "I hate to tear you away from Collin, but we have a couple of interviews for waitresses, and our realtor Robert is coming by to talk to us."

I laughed, and Mike said, "Are you trying to decide if you can get out of it and stay in bed all day?" I grinned at him, and he said, "No, you're coming to work. I need your help if I'm going to leave you for two weeks so I can go on my honeymoon."

Mike left after telling me he would meet me at the bar at noon, and I nodded before waving goodbye.

I walked up the stairs as my heart pounded. I was wondering if Collin was still in my room, scared that he had disappeared like he had done in the past. I walked down the hall and heard Daniel snoring and wondered how late he usually slept. I tried the door knob to my room, praying it was still locked, and it was. I instantly felt a huge sense of relief. I opened the door with my key and stepped inside. Collin was still in my bed with nothing on but a sheet. I was thrilled.

I tried to be quiet and let him sleep as I went to the bathroom and turned on the shower. I kicked my shoes off and got undressed before stepping into the shower. I realized I felt better today than I had the last couple days. I told myself: *no more magazine interviews; they make me way too nervous.* I started shampooing my hair and tilted my head back to rinse when I felt a pair of hands touch my hips.

Collin whispered, "You came back."

I whispered back, "You stayed," with a huge smile on my face. His hands started exploring my body, and it felt wonderful.

I finally opened my eyes and looked at him, he was happy. I tried to remember when the last time was that I saw him this happy. I really couldn't remember as I gave up and he kissed my neck. All thoughts left my mind as we decided to do other things in the shower that involved both of us on our knees.

We made our way to the bed and passionately made love again, dripping wet. This time, perhaps I was a little too loud when I was in the middle of a mind-blowing orgasm as I rode Collin. He groaned and held my hips down against him when I heard a knock at the door.

"You okay in there, Danni?" Daniel asked with sarcasm in his voice. I couldn't stop it at that point as Collin was enjoying his release, too, and bucking against me.

I came back to Earth while I was still on top of Collin and I noticed he was laughing hysterically. Daniel knocked again and in a broken voice, I answered, "I'm good, Daniel. I'll be out in a minute."

"Are you sure? It doesn't sound like you have any reason to be frustrated after that orgasm. You must be that good with your hands," Daniel said through his laughter.

"I'm fine. Go away!" I said as Collin continued laughing.

I wanted to die, or better yet, get some revenge for Collin laughing at me. I leaned over Collin, so my boobs were in his face as he suddenly got more serious and reached up to touch me.

"Collin, do you want to play a game with me today?" I asked as I leaned down and kissed his neck.

He groaned, rocking his hips against me, "I would love to play a game with you, baby."

"Okay, the first one to cave into the other's desires gets a lap dance from the other one," I said, sitting up straight as I felt him growing inside me again.

"You are going to lose, baby, but I so look forward to the lap dance," Collin groaned as I started riding him again before he flipped me over and kissed me.

Half an hour later we finally emerged from my bedroom. Daniel was still in the kitchen sitting at the island reading something on his laptop. He looked up and didn't seem surprised to see his brother with me. Collin went downstairs to the apartment to change his clothes. I went to my office with my breakfast and a cup of coffee, hoping to avoid Daniel's comments.

I flipped open my laptop and read the news when Daniel finally came walking in, he grabbed my coffee and started drinking it.

"That was mine," I said, frustrated that he always took my coffee.

"I know, but you should be nice and get me a cup because I am a guest, and you didn't offer me a morning treat like you did my brother."

"Fine," I said and walked back to the kitchen to pour him a cup.

"Look at you, see, you can look sexy if you try hard enough," Daniel said, taking the new cup of coffee I held out for him. I hit him in the shoulder before I took my cup back from him.

Collin was walking up the stairs as we made our way into the kitchen as Daniel rubbed his arm, complaining that I hit like a girl.

Collin said, "Good, she finally hit you."

We all read the news and kind of did our own thing for a while. My thing was watching Collin, he had put on a black button-up shirt, keeping it untucked with a dark pair of nice-fitting jeans. I noticed he was glancing my way and smiling when my dad walked in.

He shook Daniel and Collin's hands, and they talked about the success of the song and video. Dad asked if they wanted to do another and of course, they said yes as I stood up and gathered my stuff together, wanting no part of the conversation. Dad asked if he could get ready at the house the next day because Mark's family was taking over his house and I nodded that that was okay. He then mentioned he would just stay in the apartment tonight, and I wondered where Collin was supposed to sleep.

Daniel grabbed Collin and put his head on his shoulder, "If you spoon with me tonight, you can sleep with me."

I burst out laughing as Dad looked at me and pointed to Daniel, "He really is a child."

Collin managed to get away from Daniel and said to my dad, "You have no idea how immature he can be. He's a pain in my ass all the damn time."

Dad offered to babysit them so I could go to the bar and they were fine with it. Collin seemed to enjoy being around my dad, which concerned me. I hoped Dad wouldn't tell him details about the assault or the problems surrounding the investigation. Lately, it had been one problem after another and I was always fielding calls from the investigators and Nick, my attorney, who was already dating someone else. He mentioned a few times that I needed to cooperate more and reminded me that I had again skipped another appointment with a therapist. Mike was trying to help me, Dad was, too, but they didn't understand. I was not about to talk about it to anyone. Not even the state prosecutors.

Mike pounced on me as soon as I walked into the office and said, "Our interview has been waiting for ten minutes, Danni."

"Sorry, I got distracted," I mumbled, trying to hide my smile.

He laughed and said, "You need a little distracting right now. Is he good in bed? Please tell me he is as good as I imagine he is?" He hadn't asked for details after the Seattle disaster.

Mike had had a crush on Collin since we first saw his band in concert. I hit him in the ribs and laughed as he said, "I knew it! He is AWESOME in bed, isn't he?"

The good thing about the bar interviews is that they were something Mike had always taken control of, he just insisted I be there. The guy left, and Mike looked at me and said, "Absolutely not. He stared at your boobs the whole time." I laughed because I had noticed it, too.

The next interview started, and I was surprised as a scorching hot woman walked in. I paid more attention to this conversation than I probably ever had before. It was fun to watch Mike sound professional.

Her name was Beth, and she went on to say that she had been bartending for the last four years and was currently in law school. She was a beautiful girl with long dark hair, smaller boobs like mine, and she seemed intelligent. I liked her determination right away, and I looked over at Mike and nodded. He hired her on the spot. She wanted to start that night, which was perfect with the wedding tomorrow. She said she would be back at seven and Mike asked if I could show her the ropes so he could go to dinner with Mark's family. I agreed. I was thankful he let me out of the rehearsal dinner and wedding crap scheduled for the night.

As I lay back on the couch, I put my feet up and yawned, realizing how tired I was after not getting much sleep the night before. Just as I dozed off, someone kicked my feet off the table. I opened my eyes and saw it was Daniel, and Collin was right behind him.

"Why are you so tired?" Daniel asked in a sarcastic voice.

I flipped him off as he sat down beside me. Collin sat in my chair and started messing with my computer when Mike walked back in and mentioned that Robert, our realtor, was here. Collin asked Mike if they should leave and he said they were fine.

After shaking hands, I asked, "What's up, Robert? I haven't seen you for a while."

He talked about the real estate market, and I found myself staring at Collin as he smiled at me, knowing I wasn't paying any attention to Robert. Mike kicked me under the table and gave me a look before we both directed our attention back to the conversation. Robert talked about when we first bought the bar and how I had mentioned back then that we would probably outgrow the space eventually. Pulling two folders from his briefcase, he handed one to Mike and one to me as I sat up. He went on to ask if we had noticed the hardware store next door had closed and we both nodded.

I started reading this proposal, standing up and making Collin get out of my chair so I could get on my computer. He went and sat where I had been and started looking at the folder in front of Mike. Robert told us that the man who owned it had passed away a couple of months back and his wife wanted to sell it, but before she put it on the market, she was offering it to us first. I thought it was a hefty sum as I read the price on the bottom of the information sheet

Mike piped up and said, "We are interested."

I couldn't stop myself, so I said, "Slow down, Mike. She's asking twice the market value and right now businesses are closing all over town. Maybe we could find a different location altogether."

Everyone looked at me, surprised. I saw in the fine print that Robert was representing the seller, as well, so this was a win-win for him and his commission. Mike knew I was analyzing the numbers and trying to play poker with Robert and his asking price.

A couple of minutes later Robert left and shut the door, giving us a moment to talk privately. I threw a red stress ball at Mike, one that he had gotten me as a gift.

"What the hell?" he asked, laughing.

"You didn't even bother to look at how much the old lady wants. That is *a lot* of money, and it also means we would be doubling the size of the bar, which means more employees, more products, more liquor, more advertising, and more work for us. I love you, Mike, and I like what we have here, but I'm struggling to keep up with my writing, not to mention the soundtrack the studio is trying to get me to finish up, and last, the country artist that will be in here in two weeks to finish up the songs I've done for him. I am stretched thin enough," I said, very frustrated.

Daniel looked at Mike and said, "When did she get so smart?"

Mike laughed and told him to shut up and then looked at me. "Okay, Danni here is my piece. You stretch yourself too thin because you are not organized. You take on too many projects and don't give yourself adequate time to finish them. I know you love writing and scoring movies, but we started this bar together, and we are equally invested in this. The biggest problem is you work to avoid unpleasant things going on. You avoid them, but that doesn't make them go away, and you are this fucking close to getting thrown in jail for not cooperating with the state prosecutors. So maybe we should think about taking on a partner or two, not to mention that personal assistant your agent has tried so desperately to hire for you. Mark would love to be part of this."

Mike crossed the fucking line. I stood up and walked out of the office, slamming the door behind me. That was too much personal information Daniel and Collin didn't need to know. The look on both of their faces was nothing but pity for me, and I was so tired of seeing that look on people's faces.

An hour later I was finishing off my bacon cheeseburger and fries at the diner six blocks from the bar when Daniel sat down beside me. He didn't say anything as he helped himself to my fries. I was thankful he didn't push issues. Mike sat across from us as Collin sat down by him.

Mike reached over and grabbed my hand, "I'm sorry, Danni. I was rude, and you didn't deserve to be called out on your issues in front of people. I should have handled it better. But, you have to help all of us so you can better help you."

I swiped my hand across my cheek, hoping they didn't see my tears. I just couldn't talk about all the pressure right now. I was terrified of all of it, and I couldn't stomach the idea of having to go to court and be face-to-face with Thom, my attacker. So, yes, I was making it difficult for everyone involved, but mostly myself.

About that time the waitress put my strawberry shake and a plate of crackers in front of me. The guys were all looking at me weird as I dipped a cracker in the shake and ate it.

"What? Haven't any of you liked a little salt in your ice cream?" I asked, looking at them.

Daniel glanced at me and said, "You are so odd lately."

We went back to my office, and I dialed Nick's phone number. I wasn't looking forward to talking to him. I just hoped he didn't bring anything up as Mike started explaining the question of buying the building next door. We decided to go through with it and make Daniel and Collin partners, as well. They were going to purchase the building, and the renovations would fall on Mike and me.

Two hours later the deal was done, and Daniel was so excited, he called his mom to tell her the news. He handed me his phone and made me talk to her, as well. I had to promise her I would come back and visit soon. She also wanted to see the bar when it was all done and, surprisingly, I hoped she would. I handed Collin the phone after she asked to talk to him and he walked out of the office with it. Mike hugged me and said he was glad we were doing this.

The three of us sat in my office checking emails and playing on our phones for a while when I noticed Collin had closed his eyes and was sleeping. I was jealous.

There was a knock at my door, and I looked over and saw Beth, the new girl. Before she could even sit down, Daniel was in front of her introducing himself and Collin had opened his eyes and was checking her out, too. I shot him a look before he started smiling at me. Daniel was laying it on pretty thick when Collin stood up and said they should get a drink or something and pulled Daniel out of the room. Thank heavens for that.

Beth sat down and asked, "Are they the two guys from that band that has been rumored to be hanging around here?"

"Yes, they are, but here we do value people's privacy, so I hope I don't see you advertising it on the internet."

"Of course not, I would never invade their privacy. I would hate to be followed around constantly by photographers and fans. It won't be a problem," she said as I finished entering her information into our system.

We got through her paperwork, and I took her out to the bar and showed her around. Another bartender offered to train Beth so I wouldn't have to do it. I found Jackie and introduced her and told Beth if she had any questions that Jackie was the boss if Mike and I were not around. Jackie was very excited to hear those words come out of my mouth.

I saw Daniel sitting at the bar watching Beth when I mentioned to Jackie to warn Beth about him, and she whispered, "Yes, he is a jerk," before she walked off. I knew exactly who Daniel had sex with in my office chair the previous night after he had disappeared before I went to bed and I couldn't help but start laughing.

Later I walked into the walk-in cooler in the garage to grab more vodka, and I made sure I had my keys this time. I could feel that Collin had followed me in and I grinned. I wanted to win our little game at all costs.

I asked, "What are you doing out here, Collin?"

"Just watching a very sexy bartender that I want to fuck right now, right here, up against that cooler," he said, leaning against my SUV and pointing to the cooler I had just walked out of.

Oh, his words made my lady parts tingle with need, but I wasn't about to give in. I started walking to the door to go back inside when I saw my keys were not where I had left them.

Collin asked in a very sexy voice, "Are you looking for something?" He then twirled my keys around his fingers.

I put the bottles down and said, "You do realize you aren't going to win this, right?"

"Oh, baby, I guarantee I will win this. I *always* win," he said as I moved in front of him.

I stood a couple of feet away from him, trying to focus when he walked toward me and circled me. He then stopped behind me and asked, "How frustrated are you? Or, has my dick relieved some of that frustration? Your tight little pussy is addictive, and I would like to be inside it right now."

No one had ever talked dirty to me before and, holy hell, it was a huge turn on. I felt his hot breath on my neck and instantly shivered. Then he walked back over to my SUV and leaned against it, crossing his arms over his chest like he had just won our game.

I thought *I can dish it out, too.* I walked over to him so I was less than an inch from his body and I put my hands on the hood on either side of him. I whispered in his ear, "What was your favorite part of last night? Was it me riding you, or when I was letting you fuck my mouth, or perhaps was it when you were fucking me from behind? My favorite was you fucking my mouth. Just imagine how easy it would be for me to drop to my knees right now and suck you off and let you come in . . ."

The door flew open, and Daniel and Rick walked toward us. They laughed, oblivious to the fact that they had just ruined a scorching moment.

Collin looked at Rick and instantly shut down and moved far away from me. That hurt more than I thought it would as I looked away. My eyes filled with tears as they all started joking with Daniel about him hitting on Beth. I grabbed the vodka and left.

Shortly after two in the morning I pulled into the garage. I was tired and had plenty of hurt feelings I didn't like or want to feel.

Collin, Daniel, and Rick left when another bartender told them about the all-nude strip club on the outskirts of town. Collin didn't say a word to me or even look at me. He was suddenly different and extremely cold to me.

After heating up leftover Chinese food, I started looking through the mail piled on the kitchen island. I mumbled to myself, "Junk, junk, a magazine I don't ever remember subscribing to, bill, bill, oh, no thank you," before crumpling up another letter from the doctor reminding me for the third time about my annual exam. Also two more letters from that attorney in Canada that handled the inheritance stuff. I already had an attorney and he was a pain in the ass. *I can't believe I liked him.*

I lay in bed playing on my tablet when I heard voices outside my room. I turned off the light from the tablet and didn't answer the quiet knock. I then heard Daniel and Collin laughing. *I was not going to simply be Collin's fuck buddy after his night of drinking and getting lap dances from strippers.* I was done playing games with him.

CHAPTER 29
VIBES

M ike was yelling at me to get dressed for the tenth time. All morning I had been distracted. I hadn't seen Daniel or Collin yet and didn't ask about them either. Mike was glowing, and I was happy for him, but I just couldn't get myself happy. Collin had dropped me like a bad habit the previous night, and it made me feel cheap, although I let him do anything he wanted to me. I had been so stupid.

I looked outside and saw all the white tents had been set up around my home. I hoped the weather would hold up, so we didn't have to move it into the gym. Mike was against that because he thought it would feel too much like prom. Mike and Mark had told me they were having their wedding at my house because it had so much space. I was the one paying for it as my present to them, so I let them do whatever they wanted.

It was ten minutes until the ceremony was supposed to start as Daniel finally made an appearance at my side. We had been chosen to walk together by Mark, against Mike's wishes. Mark knew what we were capable of doing together and he thought keeping us together was an easier way to babysit us. Luckily Dad was the one assigned to watch us, and so far he was soft and protective over me, as though he knew something was wrong. Every time Daniel moved toward me, I nestled more into Dad, and he held me tighter against him. I had no reason to be upset with Daniel, but still I just wanted to be left alone.

The wedding started as Daniel stepped on my dress when we got up to walk down the aisle. I heard a rip and Dad mentioned that it was just at the bottom, and no one would see it as he motioned us to go already. Mike had picked a red strapless satin gown for me with black accessories to match. He even told the hair stylist what to do with my hair, a low side bun. We finally made it to the altar as I let go of Daniel and went to my side. I was the only girl on Mike's side, considering I was the best man, or worst woman, according to Daniel.

Mike and Mark each came down the aisle with their moms on their arms and I looked away, not wanting to cry. I had never been so uncomfortable in my life. I felt too many people watching me, too many voices around me, and too many feelings trying to break through the surface. Kendrick leaned into me and put his hand on the small of my back.

"Danni, take a breath and calm down," he whispered close to my ear as we stood there.

"I need to leave. I can't . . ." I mumbled as I felt fingers interlock with mine. I looked up, and Mike was looking at me with compassion. He nodded and very quietly said, "Just hold my hand. I got you."

I took a deep breath and we all turned around to look at the justice of the peace as he began addressing everyone. After tuning into the words he was saying and watching Mike and Mark commit to each other, I finally relaxed, completely happy for them. It was such a beautiful wedding, and they knew exactly what to say to each other. I was so proud of Mike at that moment for picking Mark.

We made our way to the tents when I finally asked Dad, "Did they leave?"

He stopped and looked at me and quietly asked, "Baby girl, what did he do now?" I could hear the anger in his voice as he started looking around, I assumed, for Collin.

I was not going to ruin Mike and Mark's night, so I said, "Let's just enjoy tonight." Dad nodded at me, but I could tell he was angry.

Everything went as planned, even down to Mike and Mark smashing wedding cake in each other's faces. I mentioned to Dad that it was weird to see Mike with a wedding ring on as he handed me some cake.

We danced and visited with people, and I never saw Collin once. I wondered if he skipped the wedding. I stood there with my arms around Dad as we watched Mike and Mark drive off for their honeymoon.

"Mike isn't mine anymore, is he?" I asked as Dad kissed the side of my head.

"He will always be yours. Now you just have to share," Dad said as something caught his eye. "Baby girl, hang tight with Uncle Tony for a minute. I need a moment with someone."

He walked away as Daniel stepped up to my side, looking nervous. "You enjoy this evening?"

"Yes, did you?" I asked, looking everywhere but at him.

"Danni, listen, I am sorry my brother is an asshole. But please don't shut me out because of him. You're my pal, and I need you. Please tell me you don't hate me, too," Daniel said, pulling me into him for a hug.

I let out a sigh of relief as I hugged him back and said, "Daniel, I'm sorry if I gave you the impression I was mad at you. I'm not. I just don't want to address my feelings. It makes me . . . uncomfortable."

Daniel laughed and said, "Yes, we all know you get a little bitchy when feelings get involved, but if it makes you feel better, I think your bitchy side is sexy."

I finally had a good laugh with Daniel, and it was what I needed.

Half an hour later everyone was starting to leave as Daniel and I talked to people. We were saying our goodbyes when my dad walked up to us.

"Please come with me, baby girl," Dad said, taking my elbow and leading me toward my house.

After following along into my house and stopping by the hall-way lockers, I said, "Dad, you're scaring me. What's wrong?"

He put his hands on my cheeks and said, "You know I love you and would do anything for you, but I refuse to stand by and let him hurt you."

I glanced over his shoulder and saw Collin leaning up against the lockers with his head down. My dad kissed my forehead and said, "I will be right outside if you need me." Then he left us standing in the hall.

I turned toward Collin and slowly walked down to him as my heels echoed down the hall. I tried to ask casually, "Where have you been all night?" I leaned against the wall on the opposite side of the hall as him.

He just stood there for minutes upon minutes saying nothing when I finally asked, "Are you going to talk to me or what?"

He still didn't say anything and wouldn't even look at me. I turned to walk away, and he reached out and grabbed my wrist. He pulled me into his arms and hugged me tightly. Then he leaned in and kissed me softly, but not like before. I reached up to touch his face as he kissed me and he grabbed my wrists and pulled back angrily. "STOP IT!" Collin screamed.

He let go of me and stepped back. I said, "I don't understand what's happening with you."

Tears started falling down my face, and he yelled, "I am getting married in two weeks. What the fuck is wrong with *you?*"

His booming voice scared me as I jumped back. I quietly said, "You moved it up."

Very frustrated, he yelled, "I don't want to get married on your birthday!"

He stepped back as I tried to step closer to him. My dam burst, and I felt everything I had been trying to bury. "I love you. I love everything about you. You're all I think about, and I want you, every part of you, I want you."

He cut me off and yelled, "Quit saying those things. You don't mean any of them."

He was so angry. I calmly replied, "Stop it, Collin, stop being cruel."

He stepped toward me with an evil look on his face and very calmly said, "Don't you fucking get it? I *am* that cruel guy. You are nothing more than a toy to play with, and you were fucking easy. *Too easy.* You don't honestly think I gave a crap about you? All you are is damages someone left behind. Who would want someone so fucked up?"

"That is enough, Collin. Get out of this house now!" Dad shouted as he came down the hallway with Daniel close behind him.

I stood back and felt like I was in that cornfield again. Only this time it was Collin standing over me repeatedly kicking me. My knees gave out as I fell to the floor sobbing.

"SHUT THE FUCK UP, YOU STUPID BITCH!" Collin screamed standing over me.

"NOW, Collin, let's go or so help me God, I will beat the shit out of you," Daniel yelled as he pulled Collin down the hall toward the front door.

I didn't think, I just yelled, "Collin." He stopped with his back to me. Through very broken breaths I sobbed, "I never want to see you again. I don't even want to hear your name ever again. Stay the hell away from me."

"Fine!" he shouted back before he and Daniel disappeared out the front door. I lost it and started crying uncontrollably.

I cried like I never had before, sobbing like a baby as Dad kept saying, "Oh, baby girl, I am so sorry." He put his arms around me and just held me. I cried and cried. I had never felt this hurt in all my life. This moment hurt worse than being raped because I was in love with Collin. I lost the love of my life and my best friend on the same day. I couldn't see Daniel anymore, and that hurt, too. They were a package deal, so I had to let Daniel go, as well.

I woke up long enough to realize Dad was trying to put me in bed. I vaguely remember changing into sweats and crawling into bed and Dad saying it was okay to cry before I drifted to sleep.

◁+ +▷

I cried for three days before I finally managed to take a shower and eat something. I was so sick, and the thought of food made me want to throw up. All I wanted to do was sleep, but Rosa kept bugging me to get up and eat. Finally, my dad promised he wouldn't call Mike and ruin his honeymoon if I got up, ate something, and tried to move forward.

A week after the wedding, Dad and I sat on my front steps. He had his arms around me, and I assured him I was okay. He knew I wasn't, but he needed to go on the road for a couple of shows. I could tell he didn't want to leave me in my depressed funk. I wanted some time alone, and I assured him I wouldn't do anything stupid. He wanted to give me the benefit of the doubt, but he knew my history was hard to ignore. I couldn't blame him at all for that. We finally said goodbye, and I promised to check in with him every couple hours since he said he would call Mike if I didn't.

After tossing and turning in bed for two hours, I walked down to the gym in the dark. Looking up at the scoreboard, I couldn't help but start crying as I slid down the wall. I sat there for hours unable to move, just looking at that stupid scoreboard. I decided it had to come down.

Two days later, sitting on the bleachers and drinking a cup of coffee, I watched the company that put it up take it down. They kept asking if I was sure and I assured them I was, as they kept pulling parts of the scoreboard down.

I walked back upstairs and sat in my office chair, seeing the mail on my desk. That was it. I would busy myself with everything I could so I wouldn't have to think about him. I started opening and going through the mail. I saw the reminder from the doctor about my annual exam, so I made a doctor's appointment for Monday, a dentist appointment for Wednesday, a spa appointment for Thursday, and an appointment for my SUV for an oil change. It was working, was already refocusing on other things as I found more and more to occupy my mind. I was looking for anything I had been putting off so I could finish it.

I had to tend bar because Mike was still on his honeymoon. I found myself working more and now I understood why Mike organized when he was upset. The bar was extremely clean and orderly when we closed up that night. Then I turned the lights off, wanting to head home myself.

As I started backing out of the garage, I stopped. I turned the ignition off and got out. I don't know what I was doing or what made me think about it as I walked out into the middle of the parking lot that used to be a cornfield. I wasn't sure of the exact spot where I had been raped or if I wanted to know. I looked up at the moon and stars, and out loud I asked, "God, what exactly is your plan for me because so far this sucks." I stood there and talked to him for an hour before I decided he probably had had enough of me. But, I finally said things out loud I hadn't had the strength to say before and it felt like the weight of the world had been lifted off my shoulders.

I got home and felt energized as I walked into my studio. I sat down and turned on the music that was played last. It was some of Dad's recent ideas. Like lightning, a million different ideas struck me as I pulled out a notepad and pencil and started writing. My thoughts and feelings were finally easy to write down. I grabbed my guitar and plugged it in as I thought, *let's see where this takes me.*

⋯

I spent three days in that studio by myself just writing about everything. I had to take a break finally to go to my doctor's appointment. I was not looking forward to it at all. I walked in, and the nurse took me back and told me to hop on the scale. Well, that would put anyone in a bad mood. I put my purse down and stepped up. I gasped: *that can't be right.*

I asked, "Is the scale wrong? That can't be right."

The smiling older nurse assured me it was right. I had gained fifteen pounds since I was last there two years ago. *Maybe I should get off my ass and run tomorrow.* I thought to myself as she told me to get undressed and sit on the table. She started asking me routine questions about my health, and I answered them all except four questions that caught me off guard.

She asked, "How many sexual partners have you had in the last year?"

I didn't understand why they needed that piece of information, but I was honest and said, "Two."

"When was your last period?" she asked, continuing to write notes down.

I replied, "I have no idea. I have never had a regular one before."

"Are you on anything to prevent pregnancy?" she asked, finally looking up at me.

"Not since the assault. I quit taking the pill after that. I didn't think I needed it anymore." *Shit Shit Shit!*

She gave me the pity look and asked, "Could you be pregnant?"

"No," I answered a little too quickly, angry at her for even thinking it.

The nurse took my attitude in stride and said, "Well, the doctor will want to know for sure. So just to be safe, we will have you take a quick test anyway."

I rolled my eyes but followed her to the bathroom. After peeing on the stick and washing my hands, I went back to the exam room and waited for the doctor.

I hoped they would hurry up so I could get to the bar to open it for the night. The doctor and nurse finally walked in with a few tools I had never seen before.

"Danni, how have you been feeling lately?" Dr. Arthur asked as he shook my hand.

Nervously I said, "A little tired, but otherwise okay I guess."

As he listened to my lungs, he said, "You should be tired. You seem very busy at the bar these days."

I lay back and put my feet in the awful stirrups with the nurse's help. I hated this part the most. Next, he examined my breasts. I practically jumped off the table and groaned, "Ouch."

He asked, "Is that tender?"

"What do you think?" I fired back as I rubbed my boob.

He asked me to sit up for a moment and then helped make me comfortable before he sat down on a stool.

"You're making me nervous," I said, looking between him and the nurse.

He quit writing something down, set my chart on the counter, looked at me and said, "Nothing to be nervous about. Just the opposite in fact." I looked at him with a puzzled look on my face. "You're pregnant. Congratulations."

It was like someone had just told me the worst, most cruel joke I had ever heard. Everything stood still as I just stared at him dumbfounded. *No, no, not me. This has to be a joke.*

"I think you're wrong," I said as I felt like I was swaying back and forth when the nurse stepped to my side and held me still.

He said, "No, but if you want, we could do another test to confirm it for you."

I gladly took another test, waiting for it to be wrong. He showed me the stick this time, and it was definitely positive. I burst into tears.

The doctor said, "I take it this was not expected."

"Not in my lifetime," I mumbled before blowing my nose.

I tried to wrap my head around this as he finished his exam and ultrasound and explained that I was seven weeks along. I did the math in my head and knew that was the weekend of the benefit and the birthday party in Seattle. *God, what have I done?*

The doctor asked, "Would you like a picture to give to Dad to surprise him?"

I sat up and grumbled, "No. I am pretty sure he will never know."

The mood in the exam room changed from congratulatory to somber as the doctor explained that I had options. After I had got dressed, I left the brochures explaining those options on the chair. I knew that was something I could never do. I scheduled my next appointment in a month and wondered what the hell I was going to do now. If there was anybody who could royally fuck up any situation, it was me. I was the Master of fuckups!

———✦ ✦———

Later that night I was probably the worst bartender ever. Everyone kept getting mad at me as I served the wrong things, mixed the wrong drinks, and dropped stuff. I felt like I was watching a movie with everyone around me moving fast as I was stuck in slow motion.

I finally got home and went to the studio, my place of solitude. I just sat there wrapping my head around the idea of a baby. None of the mommy things ever appealed to me, but now suddenly, they did.

I started writing about how love leaves you and comes back to you in other ways. All these lyrics just flowed out of me. I could even hear the music in my head as I wrote and wrote.

At dawn the next morning, after taking a break from the studio, I sat on the front steps of my schoolhouse drinking coffee. I watched the sun come up and I thought to myself, *everything is going to change. Maybe this is what the plan for me was from the very beginning.*

⚔

That afternoon in the studio, I had my headphones on, trying to get the words right with the music when someone shut the lights off briefly. That was Dad's way of getting my attention, so he didn't scare me. I looked up and smiled at him as he came in and sat down by me.

"What are you doing, baby girl?" he asked, picking up one of my notepads.

I launched into all of it. I explained song after song and why I thought it was important to express the different sides of it all. He flipped through my full notepads with a million different ideas and he said, "Okay, how about we do this together, and you and I get back to work? We have many artists requesting new music."

"Dad, before we start, I have something to tell you. And for once you are the first to know," I said, smiling at him and practically bouncing off my chair.

He turned toward me, and I finally saw the look of pride on his face that I hadn't seen in a long time. "Spit it out then."

"Dad, I'm pregnant," I said and watched him completely melt from the inside.

It felt like forever as he just sat there and stared at me when I noticed his eyes watering. It was the first time in my life I saw him this thrilled with something I had done, in a good way. He stood up and pulled me into his chest as he hugged me.

"Really? I am going to be a grandpa?" he asked, pulling back and looking at me.

I laughed and nodded before burying my face in his chest, and he said, "Wow, you have made me the happiest person in the world."

After a few moments and us wiping away tears, we got to work. I had never seen him that excited with emotions, and it made me smile, knowing he must be who gave me my ability to bury my feelings.

I decided to take a day off because Mike and Mark would be home that day. I couldn't wait to tell Mike the big news.

As I sat in the gym with a pint of strawberry ice cream, I thought about Daniel. I missed him so much. I didn't answer any of his calls, texts, or emails. I had to let go, but the look on his face when he had left reminded me that he would understand. Collin popped in my mind, how he had called me "someone else's damages." That still hurt tremendously. I didn't have the strength to have my heart broken again, so I couldn't bear the thought of telling him about the baby.

I heard Mike calling my name, and I had to smile thinking. *Finally, he is home.* I yelled back that I was in the gym, and he came running down the hall.

After hugging each other and grinning like kids, we sat back down.

"You okay, Danni? You seem different," Mike asked as he noticed my ice cream.

"Mike, I have been dying to talk to you. So many things have changed, and I am scared," I said, clasping his hand in mine.

He looked up and asked, "Where's the scoreboard?"

I laughed, looking at the spot on the wall where it had been and said, "I burned it."

He gave me a look of confusion and through my tears I told him everything that had happened.

"That is why I got home to dozens of messages from Daniel," he said, putting his arm around me.

"I couldn't take the heartache anymore, so I had to let both of them go."

"Yes, I think that's for the best. Billy caught me before I came over and pretty much said he would kill Collin if he sees him here ever again," Mike said, trying not to laugh.

He grabbed my ice cream and asked, "Why are you eating this crap? You know it's not good for you." He threw it in the trash as I stood up.

"I have something else to tell you, Mike," I said as he looked at me with complete confusion on his face.

"Okay . . . what?" he asked cautiously.

I grabbed his hand and placed it on my stomach. He looked at his hand as it all sank in. Then he looked into my eyes and gasped as a huge smile grew across his face. I nodded to confirm his suspicions.

"Are you serious?" he asked with tears forming in his eyes.

"Yes, Mike, we are having a baby," I said, grinning like an idiot.

He grabbed me, and we both started jumping up and down when my dad said, "You told him."

Next, Mike went and hugged him and called him "Grandpa."

For being such a screwed up mess, it sure was a beautiful mess.

www.ingramcontent.com/pod-product-compliance
Lightning Source LLC
Chambersburg PA
CBHW071146250626
47159CB00001B/4